"Kennedy's wilderness is the freezing, rain-soaked Tasmanian mountains, with their blazing red fagus trees and bizarre, secretive wildlife. It's a bewildering heart of darkness. . . . [A] bracing, unsentimental, and often very funny full-length debut . . . [that follows] the spiky, uncompromising Sophie, forced to find reserves of strength and forgiveness for her two infuriatingly childlike parents." —Patrick Ness, *The Guardian* (UK)

"Written in precise and singing prose, [Cate Kennedy's] powerful first novel begins with three unlikable characters and blossoms into a work of mythic depth, lyrical description, and gripping suspense." —*Adelaide Advertiser*

"*The World Beneath* is the first novel by Cate Kennedy, often cited as Australia's queen of the short story. In the longer format Kennedy doesn't disappoint, delivering her characters with unnerving accuracy—the disdain of a teenager, the searing frustration of a man whose life has passed him by—while the Tasmanian wilderness looms as vividly as anyone else on the page." —*Time Out Sydney*

"*The World Beneath* is an intelligent, equivocal, unusual, and often amusing novel, one that comprehends the comfort of stereotypes and pushes beyond them, one that, in the words of its epigraph from Turgenev, sees that 'the heart of another is a dark forest.'"
—Peter Pierce, *Sydney Morning Herald*

"Cate Kennedy, celebrated for her short fiction, this year began her long-distance career with *The World Beneath*. To my mind, she enters the stadium a hundred meters in front of the next novice and with the best time for many years." —Peter Temple, *The Age*

"A stunning book with a heart-stopping climax."
—*Woman's Day* (Read of the Week)

Civic Center

"When the inner lives of ordinary people are made gripping and moving and enlightening, then you know you are in the hands of a great storyteller." —Lucy Clark, *Sunday Telegraph*

"Vivid and robust realism shading occasionally into satire, full of humor and drama, told through different and conflicting points of view . . . In some ways it's reminiscent of Christos Tsiolkas's *The Slap*: an unsentimental, beady-eyed look at contemporary Australian middle age and its treatment of its children."
—Kerryn Goldsworthy, *Australian Literary Review*

"Cate Kennedy is a brilliant storyteller. She possesses the power to find in ordinary lives their poetic and mythic dimensions and to remind us that vernacular speech and everyday experiences betoken the tender mysteries that lie beneath family life."
—Gail Jones, author of *Sixty Lights*

"*The World Beneath* is pitch-perfect, an exquisite story of an estranged middle-aged couple and their alluring, disenchanted daughter . . . Cate Kennedy inhabits these characters so sensually and truly, exploring souls that feel like our own. If she doesn't touch your heart, it may be you don't have one."
—David Francis, author of *Stray Dog Winter*

"Cate Kennedy's ironic humor nails out-of-touch grandparents, flailing Baby Boomers, and tech-head adolescents. *The World Beneath* is a treasure of a first novel by a prize-winning short story writer and poet. This is Australia calling. I loved it."
—Eleanor Massey, *Good Reading Magazine*
(5 Stars—"Outstanding")

"*The World Beneath* displays all the hallmarks of the short-story writer's art; acute observation and concise execution."
—Sandy McCutcheon, *Courier Mail*

"This is a thought-provoking journey into contemporary Australia; an impressive debut novel." —Jo Case, *Australian Book Review*

"*The World Beneath* is a rare combination of a well-paced, gripping plot with very real characters and spare, elegant writing. Beautifully observed, Kennedy's novel is painfully honest about the ways in which family members hurt—and heal—each other."

—*Who Magazine* (4 stars)

"The vast terrain of relationships and family ties proves to be as much uncharted territory as the Tasmanian wilderness that Cate Kennedy describes with such stunning clarity. Here, ordinary lives are caught in a compelling story that grips tight until its exhilarating end. She exposes the perilous gap between ideal and delusion, between noble aspiration and mere ambition, against a mighty landscape that remains unpredictable despite the reverence it receives. I read the final third with a sense of thrilling fear, for the characters' plights, for the hazards created by both their actual and emotional insecurity."

—Debra Adelaide, author of *The Household Guide to Dying*

"*The World Beneath* is an intelligent modern Australian novel, displaying that fine eye for unexpected humor and everyday tragedies that made Kennedy's stories so appealing."

—*Bookseller & Publisher* (4 stars)

THE WORLD BENEATH

To Rosie,
for all the hours this book has taken

THE WORLD BENEATH

CATE KENNEDY

BLACK CAT
New York
a paperback original imprint of Grove/Atlantic, Inc.

First published in Australia in 2009 by Scribe

Lyric on p.122 from "Let the Franklin Flow" © 1983 Shane Howard (Big Heart Music / Mushroom Music) reprinted by kind permission.

Published simultaneously in Canada
Printed in the United States of America

ISBN: 978-0-8021-7071-2

Black Cat
a paperback original imprint of Grove/Atlantic, Inc.
841 Broadway
New York, NY 10003

Distributed by Publishers Group West

www.groveatlantic.com

11 12 13 14 15   10 9 8 7 6 5 4 3 2 1

31232009133457

In every walk with nature one receives far more than he seeks.
John Muir

The heart of another is a dark forest.
Turgenev

One

It was the broken-resolution end of January already, and Sandy was sitting in the kitchen drinking decaffeinated coffee with her oven's green, digital-clock display panel flashing, if you could believe it, *HELP HELP HELP* instead of the time. Last night, full of the beady-eyed purpose a late-night joint always gave her, she'd stood there trying to reprogram it to bring the clock back without making the bloody oven alarm go off, pressing and fiddling and relighting the stub of her roach, until finally she'd sworn at it and given up.

So now it was signalling her for help. Her oven, for crying out loud. An appliance.

And even though she couldn't fix the timer, the clock still ran with a snickering whirr, a nasty little calibrated sound of time mouse-wheeling itself determinedly away, even if she was sitting here marooned in the long slack middle of the afternoon, picking hard candle wax off the tablecloth and waiting for the caffeine rush that would never come.

Sandy raised the mug awkwardly in her left hand and took another sip. She was right-handed but her friend Alison had made these mugs on her new pottery wheel a few years back and Sandy had loyally bought them, and there were fragments of grit embedded in a dribble of glaze on the other side, just at the point where you sipped. Just one little gravelly flake of grit, but enough to drive you nuts. It was hard enough picking the things up with the lumpy handles Alison had stuck on. Proletariat cups, Sandy would think as she washed them roughly in the sink, hoping to break one so that she could justifiably throw it out. Nothing would kill them. They were made to withstand a revolution.

She'd recognised the handwriting as soon as she'd fished the envelope out of the mailbox, felt that little twisting jump of tension. No return address, of course. And inside, just a postcard, one of those free ones you get in coffee shops, with his message scribbled on the back.

Would like to ring Sophie for her fifteenth birthday. Please let her know. I'll call around 6.30 your time. Hope life is treating you well. And a mobile number. That was all. As if he was paying by the bloody word.

Was life treating her well? Sandy frowned, lifted a splatter of candle wax with her fingernail from the batik cloth. Everybody seemed finally to have accepted resignedly that this was the state of play, she thought: you let life happen to you. In it came like a party-crasher, ignoring any plans you might have had for yourself, and treated you to whatever it had in mind.

And you just sat there and took it. Nobody ever said, for example, *how have you been treating your life?* which made you sound a bit less passive, at least. Maybe that could be the start of an article, something she could write for the community-centre newsletter, or even the local paper.

Did he really have to be so terse, even in a postcard? Not that his brusqueness surprised her — that was Richard all over, exactly as she remembered. *Hope life is treating you well* would be just what she would have expected — one of a couple of careless, studiously distant sentences as if he'd spoken to her last month instead of about five years ago.

Sandy, in uncharitable moments — and OK, these surfaced occasionally, she was the first to admit — believed that Rich did this on purpose. Whatever he was doing now, and God knows he was evasive enough about that, he made a point of being somewhere exotic around Christmas and Sophie's birthday, just so he could write things like *Greetings from Dharamsala!* or *Not sure if this will get to you, boat's not docking in Borneo till next week.*

Like this one: *6.30 your time.* Please. As if he had to calculate time zones. Like he was going to call from bloody Bhutan.

She hoped the romance was a deliberate, manufactured illusion, hoped he was, in reality, writing from his dead-end job or cramped bedsit. She should have paid attention to the postmarks over the years, except that sometimes Sophie made a point of casually collecting the mail around her birthday and Christmas before she did, so she didn't have a chance.

She'd laid the whole thing on the line for Sophie, early on.

'He walked out on us when you were just a tiny baby. So don't go expecting anything from him. Put him out of your life, like I have.'

And for years Sophie had given her that inscrutable child's look and shrugged, even though Sandy was sure she kept all those cards, with their pathetically non-committal messages, hidden away somewhere. Hanging onto something. Some possibility. And then last year, when Sophie had been turning a scary fourteen, she'd stunned her by saying, 'If you've put him out of your life, why are you always talking about him?'

She had felt herself blustering, hot suddenly. 'I don't.'

'Yes, you do.'

'No, I don't.'

'You do. When all your friends are here. You're all shouting to get a word in about who's got the worst ex.'

Just doing her obstinate best to get under her skin about something that was patently untrue. She imagined all those cards somewhere, wrapped up in a box under a journal, maybe. Although Sophie had become so coolly cynical this last year it was hard to imagine any shred of sentiment surviving; it would be hanging on like a tiny gasping plant, clinging by its roots to a crack in the barren rock face of withering teenage contempt. Maybe she'd thrown away the lot. Maybe she'd incorporated them into some weird art installation at school, lying slyly in wait for Sandy to come across at the next parent–teacher night.

And she would have to smile brightly, her face stiff with mortification, and pretend she knew all about it. She was still getting over innocently strolling into the IT lab last term and having the teacher enthusiastically show her the website Sophie ran from her school computer ... no, not website, one of those blog things: BigPage, or MyFace, or whatever it was called.

A wildly popular site, apparently. A cluster of teachers had stood around her, enthusing.

'She's brilliant, really,' the headmaster had said excitedly, clicking away with the mouse. 'Such a thinker, and such a subversive sense of humour, wouldn't you say?', and he'd brought up Sophie's blog. And smiling, still wondering what, exactly, he meant by subversive, Sandy saw that it was called *My Crap Life*.

'This has had thousands of hits,' the headmaster was saying. 'Even the staff read it each week. And the goth twist is what makes the whole thing so exceptional.'

'Emo goth,' corrected the IT teacher, mystifyingly, leaning proprietarily over the back of the ergonomic chair.

Sandy nodded, grimly trying to memorise the web address. 'She's certainly full of surprises,' she said faintly. There was Sophie's face on the screen, indisputably hers, glowering out from under a curtain of black fringe, so it must have been true. Fourteen years old, and this other life going on, a secret parallel universe served up here now in a fait accompli, something for Sandy to accidentally stumble across when it was all too late.

Like that tattoo. Sandy remembered the shock of first glimpsing it, the sensation of the rug being smartly whipped out from under her. Not even a nice tattoo either, the sort that she herself had contemplated — those cute butterflies in the small of the back, say, or a Celtic band honouring your cultural heritage or some small, significant endangered flower on the ankle.

No, Sophie's tattoo was pushing heavy metal, like an AC/DC album cover.

They'd been sitting at a barbecue, and Sandy's eyes had wandered over to her daughter's shoulders just as Sophie had leaned forward to pick up her drink. It was a hot day and she'd uncharacteristically taken off her black hoodie, leaving her bare pale neck and shoulders exposed. Sandy's heart jumped into her throat and hammered there a few times. Oh Jesus, it couldn't be permanent, could it? It was illegal to tattoo a minor, she was sure of it. Wasn't it?

'Oh my God, what's that? Sophie?'

'What's what?' Sophie turned around, her jet-black hair scraping against her singlet. What did she put in it, glue?

'You know perfectly well. That thing on your back.'

Her daughter took a swallow of Diet Coke before answering, and Sandy watched her eyes flutter closed, as she gulped, through the thick sweep of black eyeliner.

'It's only a temporary tat,' she'd said wearily.

'Thank God for that. I thought for a minute ... Sweetheart, what induced you to stick that on there? And what on earth is it? A bat?'

Sophie pulled the singlet down with her black-painted fingernails. 'I'm trying out what I'm going to get when I turn eighteen, OK? So calm down. It's just a bird.'

Spread wingtip to wingtip between her shoulder blades. That pale delicate flesh that she remembered pressing her face to countless times when Sophie was a baby, inhaling that scent of innocence and ayurvedic soap, that skin she'd kept so carefully from sunburn and injury. Now her daughter was planning to scar it indelibly with a ... black carrion bird.

'You've got to be kidding. A *crow*? Right across your back like that, as if you're some kind of ... bikie's moll?'

That slow-motion, long-suffering blink again. Where did she get that sneering contempt?

'Take a chill pill, will you? I told you I wouldn't do it permanently till I was eighteen.'

'As if those studs through your eyebrow aren't enough.'

A snort of laughter. 'Jesus, Mum, you sound like Grandma.'

That shut her up. Made her stand, suddenly, and go over to refill her wineglass at the trestle table, then wander shakily to another seat under a tree where friends were having a long and circuitous conversation about the local council. She did sound like her mother, awful to admit. More and more, when she forgot herself, that voice came rising out of her own throat, Janet even down to the querulous inflections. Please God, not that noble self-martyrdom next. Anything but that.

My Crap Life. Honestly, when had Sophie ever wanted for a single thing in her whole life? You did your best, you were everything to your kids your own parents weren't, you put them first in everything, and they still thought their lives were crap. Their lives were *paradise*, she thought bitterly, picking at the red wax.

Her mother's voice burbled faintly but persistently out of the ether telling her to warm up the iron and find some absorbent paper and do the job properly, and Sandy tuned her out before she could go on to add that there was still a load of wet clothes in that machine that would soon be starting to mildew and a vinegar rinse would get that smell out but why let it happen in the first place?

When are you going to shut up, Sandy whispered savagely to the hovering apparition of her mother standing in the doorway delivering this litany, *and just leave me alone?* The apparition turned stiffly on its orthopedic heel with the outraged offence that would take months to repair, if this was real life.

Here she was, an intelligent woman with a daughter almost fifteen and she still felt — with that small, landslide jolt of shock when she glimpsed herself in the mirror sometimes — that she hadn't yet quite gotten her own life started. As if she was still waiting here in Ayresville, her foot patiently hovering on the accelerator, for her chance to get going. She'd do it soon, though. She'd enrol in something, once Soph had finished school, and didn't need her there every day. Something that would bring all her short courses together, all her skills areas. Alternative medicine, maybe. Or comparative philosophies.

For goodness sake, snapped the spectre of her mother impatiently, as it clicked out of the house in its sensible shoes, *stop your moping around and get up and do something; it's disgraceful.*

Sandy turned Alison's mug again, took another unsatisfying sip. No, it would be *get up off your fat behind and do something.* Never *arse*, or even *backside*. And Janet, her mother, never mentioned Sandy's weight unless it was in mean little parting asides like this one, designed to both deny her the right of reply and to leave her with the unpleasant lingering impression that the reason nobody mentioned it otherwise was that they were all too polite to bring it up.

Not *that* overweight, she thought defensively. Five or six kilos at the most. All she had to do was cut out the wine and it would melt off her.

What had possessed her, all those years ago, to drop out of her Arts degree?

Rich, probably. He could talk her into anything, back then. She'd find out how much of her old degree she could get credits for, anyway, and start to focus on herself for a change. Become a practitioner of some kind, or a consultant. Then, finally, all the pieces, all the little things here and there she'd done — which her mother insisted on calling *dabbling*, as if she was a bloody duck or something — all of it would make sense as elements of the wisdom she'd gathered on the journey. Diverse fragments of a whole. Healing insights.

She brushed the pieces of wax into her hand and tipped them into the bin, then drifted back to the couch and unfolded the local paper. Still three-quarters of an hour to go before Sophie came home.

An auspicious day Wednesday for Aquarians, her stars said. *Watch for a sign that will signal your way forward through a doorway you weren't expecting. Lucky number eight, lucky colour orange.*

She considered what had come in the mailbox that morning. Rich's postcard and a brochure, from her belly-dancing mailing list, inviting her to a week-long residential workshop to reclaim her Inner Goddess.

Isn't it time you allowed nature and tranquillity to nurture you at Mandala Holistic Wellness Centre? the brochure had asked, and she had thought, with a small grim smile, *you bet your arse it is*. She scrutinised the photos with longing — women doing yoga on a hillside in the sunset, women laughing around a table at a candlelit dinner, looking scrubbed and pampered and serene. Yes, please. Slap bang in the middle of the school holidays, needless to say, the hardest time to try to get away. Was a mailbox like a doorway? It would be the right omen, an invitation like that; a sign for the path ahead. Belly dancing was tonight; she might just ask around to see if anyone else was thinking of going.

Maybe she could convince Sophie to spend a few days at her grandmother's. Sophie could use the time to reconnect with Janet, build some bridges after last year's disastrous Christmas lunch at that golf club, where she'd hardly spoken all day. God knows Sophie and Janet were both difficult, but it would be nourishing for them both, she was sure of it, to take the time to explore a little intergenerational common ground.

Just before seven o'clock, she heard her daughter tugging open the screen door at the back of the house and the sound of her school bag dropping to the floor. Sophie came into the room like she always did, as if everything exhausted her, pulling off her jacket as she entered.

'Hi!' Sandy said. Her daughter's eyes gave her a brief, heavy-lidded acknowledgement, a muttered hello. She went straight to the fridge for a can of that horrible zero-calorie cola.

Mere months ago, it seemed to Sandy, her little girl used to come running in with her face alight with news, holding a painting she'd done or some story she'd written to show her. Only five years ago! Well, seven, max. Didn't kids realise that was barely a blip on the radar? You blinked your eyes and suddenly you went from being the centre of the universe to someone over there on the sofa.

'There's some of that chickpea casserole in the fridge,' she said.

'Thanks. I'll have it later.'

'Aren't you hungry?'

Sophie shook her head, screwing up her nose. 'I had something at Tegan's.'

Sandy watched the fine column of her throat, the can raised to her lips as she drank. So beautiful, her daughter, with those huge dark eyes — if only she didn't rim them in racoon black eyeliner like that. If only she wore some jeans with a waistband, instead of those black stovepipes that left her whole midriff exposed.

'You shouldn't just have that, though. That stuff's not good for you.'

Sophie swallowed, then gestured languidly to Sandy's wineglass on the table. 'Look who's talking.'

'Two glasses of wine. Two.'

'And you smoke dope.'

She bridled. 'Once in a blue moon! And never in front of you.' That sounded lame, even to her. 'Anyway, that's not the same. It isn't full of caffeine and carcinogenic artificial sweeteners.'

Sandy's friends had almost talked her out of her bad-mother paranoia over the occasional joint. It was healthy, they said with conviction, for your teenagers to see that it could be no big deal, just something adults did occasionally. It went with the theory that you took the illicit thrill out of something if your kids saw you doing it yourself. Like getting your own navel pierced. Roll up a joint at home, and it would work like reverse psychology. Sort of.

Now Sophie was eyeing her phone for messages, scrolling through with her thumb, not even looking at her. Sandy closed her eyes and gave a little amused chuckle. No response. She laughed again, a bit louder.

'Sophie?' She waited, smiling. 'It's kind of funny, isn't it? I mean, you'd think it would be the other way round, wouldn't you? The teenager drinking and smoking and the parent being all disapproving?'

'What have I said that makes you think I'm disapproving?'

'Oh, I can tell you are. That critical look on your face.'

Sophie gave her a long, opaque look. She was a steady observer, her daughter, so steady it was as if she was watching you think. It never failed to unnerve Sandy, that feeling that everything was going in and so little was being revealed in return. *No, I don't. Yes, you do.* Watching everything, waiting for her to slip up somehow.

'So?' Sophie said finally. Those eyes like two coals, and Sandy feeling the light-heartedness going out of the moment, flailing and exposed.

'Well, don't you think it's funny?' Floundering now. Feeling like an idiot.

'Yeah,' Sophie answered flatly. 'Hilarious.'

Putting her can of cola on the bench, then picking it up again to read the list of ingredients on the side. Lifting it to her lips again, gulping it down as though she'd spent the day in a desert.

She'd tell her later about the postcard. She'd let her know it had arrived, but she wouldn't show it to her, because there was no need for Sophie to know Rich's mobile number. Sandy wanted him ringing on the landline, thank you very much. At a time she specified, when she could monitor the call.

Because even though Sophie never showed it, she was still impressionable. That's why you had to position yourself, like your instinct told you, as a buffer between your child and the absent adult they might have mistakenly idealised; you had to be the protector.

She recalled one of the phone calls from Rich, on Sophie's seventh birthday, one she'd mentally replayed so often it was like the tape was stretched and the sound had become gluey and muted.

'How is she?' he'd said.

'How is she? Great.' Her voice too tight. 'A beautiful carefree little girl who has everything she needs.'

'Is she having a party?'

'Yes.'

Savouring the sound of him waiting, the thudding click as he inserted more money. She imagined a stack of gold coins on a phone box somewhere.

'Has she still got dark curly hair?'

Exhilarating to hear that hinted-at pain.

'It's straight now. She's looking less and less like you.'

'Right.'

'In fact, the less she turns out like you, the happier I'll be.'

Click. A faint hollow creak on the line, or it could have been an indrawn breath.

'OK. I'm going now.'

'Yep. That's what you're good at.'

She would just curl up and die, thought Sophie as she gazed at herself critically in her bedroom mirror, if she ever got that soft flabby skin under her arms that her mother had. She would absolutely die. *Tuckshop arms*, they called that at school, cool voices filled with contemptuous scorn. And it was like her mother didn't even realise, or care. She just went ahead and wore those sleeveless dresses like nobody was supposed to notice all that fat vibrating every time she moved her arms. Sophie raised her own wiry arm and flexed it. She loved the way that little muscle jumped up when she squeezed her fist; the definition of her bicep sinewy and taut under the skin. She could almost do ten chin-ups on the bar now. By about seven she had to really start exerting herself, her legs pumping to kick her up, but she was getting there. Each night she put a pillow on the floor and did a hundred sit-ups, listening to her iPod thumping the first three tracks from her Dogland playlist while she alternated elbows touching on each knee, feeling the air forcing itself out of her lungs as she rose in time with the music.

If you were hungry you could do sit-ups and it took away your appetite. It squeezed your stomach somehow. Her PE teacher said you should stop if you felt nauseous, but you just had to have a glass of water and it went away. Sophie was increasing the difficulty of the sit-ups, not by doing more but by elevating her legs against the side of the bed. You felt a whole other set of stomach muscles lock in then, and grab. A slow burning. When her mother was off on one of her rants about back when she saved the world, Sophie would run her hands slowly down her front to calm herself. Past the rock-hard muscles of her stomach and the loose line of her jeans and over the two protruding bumps of her hipbones. They soothed her, those sharp, delineated bones, the concave flesh between them tight as a drum.

'See, what we were doing, even though we didn't realise it, was paving the way for all the other protests that came after,' Sandy would say, pummelling a cushion and tucking it under her head, gearing up for the long haul. 'We took all those risks to save the wilderness, and we organised. God, did we organise. Meeting after meeting, they went on for hours until everybody felt they'd been heard, you know? That's why we did the training workshops, so that every single protestor understood the power of non-violent resistance.'

'Uh-huh.'

'Then when we finally started the Blockade our solidarity was so powerful it all just came together and nothing could stop us. The whole world was watching.'

Sandy would gaze off into the distance and Sophie would nod, her hands smoothing slowly, slowly down her front. Across the gratifying hardness of her abdominal muscles, down to those trusted, comforting pelvic bones. Back to her taut ribs and down again, keeping her face blank.

Other kids had *The Three Bears* every night of their childhoods; she had the Franklin River Blockade.

'What people couldn't believe,' Sandy would continue, as if the thought was just occurring to her for the first time, 'was that we were prepared to put ourselves on the line for a place. For a river. That's why we got the world spotlight.'

Palms flat then, fingers spread against her thighs. She could have got a real tattoo, if she'd felt like it. She had a friend at school, Lucy, whose mother didn't mind at all, who was quite happy giving her permission for a permanent one around Lucy's ankle, didn't see it as a problem. *If you want them*, she'd apparently said, *you go right ahead. Just don't get a tramp stamp, OK?* No going off the deep end.

They could have used that consent form for Sophie to get hers too. Pretended she was the daughter. Or used a fake ID. The point was, it wouldn't have been hard to do, but she hadn't done it. She'd just seen the way opening up, there, like a tantalising detour, something to keep secret.

Sophie would stand there, knowing she was a substitute for want of a better audience, as Sandy picked up another familiar thread of reminiscence, and she'd start humming in her head. Humming, and watching her mother's mouth opening and closing pointlessly, oblivious to her. It was like pressing the mute button on the TV.

Her mother, she thought, was like one of those old jukeboxes, with the same small selection of scratched old songs, playing and replaying them as though she'd never get sick of them, everything merging into a kind of sentimental mush of karaoke. That's why she loved meeting new people, ones who hadn't heard her stories. She'd sit them down and you could almost see her waiting for her chance to turn the topic round, eagerly pressing the buttons that would let her slip a few old favourites into the conversation.

She never got tired of saying the same thing over and over again to customers at her stall at the Sunday market either. As if she was reading it off cue-cards. In fact, the market was when Sandy was totally focused, laying out her necklaces and smiling her sweet earth-mother smile to the punters. 'Go off and explore,' she used to say to Sophie when she was smaller, giving her a few dollars, flapping her hands to shoo her and her friends away. 'You girls can have a good look round for an hour or two, can't you?' Trying to get rid of them.

And they'd wander through the market that always felt the same — her mother's friends setting out their stripy hats and tea-cosies, unwrapping from newspaper the same old picked-over antique stuff they'd culled from clearing sales and church fetes and placing it onto their trestle tables. Sometimes the man who sold fudge gave the girls a bag of offcuts to suck on as they meandered, the cloying sweetness hitting the cavities in their teeth, puckering their throats with sugar.

Sophie had begun to notice, lately, the people who really made money at the markets. The new people, the ones who moved with a different kind of purpose, setting out the fire irons and hall runners they knew the weekend visitors would snap up, displaying their organic bread and olive oil in regimented rows, tying on clean aprons with their business name embroidered on the front.

Sandy, as Sophie watched her uneasily, lacked this entrepreneurial drive. She smiled too much. She took ages to arrange her jewellery on the crimson velvet cloth and pin it down, and string up the crystals, and set out her little handwritten sign that said: *Shoplifting is bad karma.*

She was an amateur, Sophie could see, even after all these years. She had this too-bright attentiveness, a gratitude when someone actually bought something — it was like watching a dumb round-eyed goldfish in a piranha pool.

And her mother's jewellery looked weird and dated now, anyway. Hippie bling, Sophie and her friends called it privately, scornfully. Earrings and matching necklaces that looked more and more like amusing conversation pieces and less and less like anything you'd actually buy.

For years, when Sophie was little, Sandy would take her on weekly op-shop forays to buy up old jewellery — old strings of beads and synthetic pearls, mostly — and then she'd take them home and restring them into quirkier designs. The year Sophie had started school, her mother had even had some of her jewellery featured in a big craft magazine under the heading *What's Hot*, and the page had stayed pinned to the noticeboard at home for years, slowly curling and yellowing. Sophie could still recall exactly the text underneath the photo: *What's hot are these funky pieces made from restrung beads by Ayresville resident Sandy Reynolds. Chunky and colourful, they're bound to turn heads with Sandy's inspired take on recycling!*

Turn heads was right. Turn your own head, when they snagged on your sweater or in your hair, earrings so heavy they dragged your earlobes down.

'They make a statement,' Sandy would say to potential customers. 'They dress up a plain outfit and show your individuality.' She wore them herself, of course, the earrings jangling like little chandeliers as she bobbed her head, smiling, smiling.

Sophie hated going now, seeing Sandy there, bright and hopeful. She'd fight the urge to walk over and rip that dumb velvet cloth off the table, full of cringing irritation. Didn't her mother see the new stallholders setting up, laying out bracelets and earrings from Bali and Africa and India? Didn't she get it, that nobody wore this recycled shit anymore? No, she'd just stand there behind her trestle table with an invisible neon *Loser* sign over her head, just about, reaching out to polish a crystal now and then, still telling customers the necklaces were *funky*.

Or talking to her friends in the living room, all of them rationalising and self-justifying and nodding encouragement at each other for doing nothing with their lives. Sample, her mother: 'I really just enjoy being an artisan. And I can't register the business because then I'd have to declare everything and it would just eat into my supporting parent's benefit. I just like making art, that's all.'

Cue a careless theatrical shrug, as if she was so helpless to change anything that she was off the hook. Nods all round. *Making art.* What crap.

In her room, Sophie tucked her heels into the steel base of her bed and laced her fingers behind her head. *Up.* The first few were always hard, till you got warmed up. Left elbow to right knee.

The bassline of the Dogland track started through her earpieces. 'Katabasis' — the best song on the album *Elysian Eclipse*, her absolute all-time favourite. She liked *Nosferatu* too, their first CD, and she'd heard the new one *Vermin Kiss* was fantastic — she still had to download that one. She wanted the whole collection, so she would have been happy to buy the CD, but Dogland wasn't the kind of band a music shop in a town like Ayresville just carried automatically. Which went to show how woefully wrong they were about nearly every teenager in town. It was just like the chemist shop not stocking black nail polish.

'Oh,' Sophie sang along softly as she felt her shoulder blades touch the carpet again, '*spiral down into this angelic darkness, this boundless place of my black tomb ...*' Up. Touch. Fourteen. Tonight she'd do sixty, then take a breather and do sixty more. Her mother had gone out to her belly-dancing class, swishing from the house in her embroidered orange dress.

'This one, or this one?' she'd asked Sophie, bursting into the doorway to stand indecisively holding up two hangers, as Sophie sat there trying to finish her science homework. She'd held up the orange dress and another equally bad one in blue brocade with a dropped waist. Both sleeveless, both one hundred percent rayon, made in India. She had a wardrobe full of the things. And the way she scrunched up her hair into those clips then spent ages pulling out wispy tendrils so it all fell artfully down again, hair dry at the ends with that henna red colour so she looked like a sort of bedraggled mad witch. Then when she put her glasses on, a bedraggled mad librarian. Sophie had tried to tell her.

'You should get your hair cut like Sal's,' she'd suggested one afternoon.

'What, in a bob? Yuk.'

'Sal's looks good. Short like that.'

'She cuts it like that because she works for council.' Her mother's tone joking and dismissive, not hearing her. The fake-red strands frizzing down over her shoulders.

Tonight she'd gone out with three chopsticks stuck in her hair, the orange dress, one of those jingly belly-dancing belts with bells. Those heffalump arms. No way was that ever going to happen to Sophie. Ever.

Twenty-two. Twenty-three. She breathed out with each lift, every tenth sit-up touching her forehead to her knees and holding it.

Oh, sang Dogland inside her earphones, *my penance must begin, and hunger, such hunger, spins my tainted requiem ...*

The burn spread, through her hips and down her thighs. A good ache. That was fat burning, she told herself, melting away into nothing but more hard muscle. Just focus on that, and a drink of cold water at the end, then spooning a hearty meal-sized portion of her mother's curry out of the fridge and burying it in the compost heap before she came home. All done.

Two

Dead-end jobs, people called them. Rich just didn't get it. More like means-to-an-end jobs. You took one on, you earned what you needed, and took off again. Perfect freedom, making the system work for you, instead of the other way round. Those jobs that locked you in for life — sucked you in, bled you dry then spat you out at the end — they were the dead ends, if you wanted his opinion. Selling you a superannuation scheme and a few miserly days of annual leave a year. Forget that.

He liked contract work, where he could do odd shifts — starting in the dark and finishing up by lunchtime, like this one, or working through quiet Sundays. Night shifts were best. He liked being able to concentrate on his editing at the dead quiet of 2.30 in the morning with only the machines humming, no supervisor, no colleagues to annoy you except for the other graveyarders and the security guy downstairs who worked till 3 a.m., when the early news crew arrived.

'I work in television,' he told people when they asked, 'just to support my photojournalism. I'm an editor.' He'd leave it at that, mostly, let them think he made documentaries or *60 Minutes*.

He sat back now and viewed the tape for the Leg Magic segment, watching the girl who was going to demonstrate the machine adjust her spandex shorts and frown in concentration as if she was about to take to the balance beam at the Olympics. He fast-forwarded to the music cue, and the point where she lay back and began the repetitive knee flexes, tossing her blonde head and making a little moue of pretend effort. 'I can really feel it working my ... thighs,' she said, gazing meaningfully into the camera.

Rich raised an eyebrow. He'd long since stopped being surprised at any of this stuff. It just kept managing to hit new lows, so all you did was show yourself up if you started complaining about it.

Everybody groaned at advertorials, but say what you like, it did take talent putting them together, and nerves of steel sometimes. Like the morning show that time when they'd done the cooking segment live to air, showing off the Power Shredder Plus, and the actor doing the spot, who should have been sticking to the script and putting carrots or apples through the thing, instead picked up a big cube of rock-hard parmesan cheese and pushed it into the chute. The crappy little motor had made a sick noise and stopped with a chug just as the screen showed a close-up of the cheese jamming the blades. Rich had caught the guy's panicked and desperate eye as he fumbled to flick the off switch with the other hand. They'd cut away to the other camera angle within two seconds, and the talent had recovered himself beautifully.

'Look how easy that was,' he'd said jovially. You had to take your hat off to him. That was the art of it, sometimes — recovering your footing and carrying it off. The art of life, really. Whatever happened, pretending you'd meant it to happen.

Thank God they hadn't used the morning-show host that day; a man so thick he spent the commercial breaks doing the junior crossword. Or studied his script, the poor dumb bastard, anxious not to improvise since he'd been rapped on the knuckles that time for getting carried away and responding to the talent's excited announcement with an incredulous: 'Wow, you'd have to be a *moron* to miss that offer!' No wonder they didn't use the hosts now for the advertorials, and no wonder nobody liked doing them live anymore.

The morning-show host's face unnerved Rich now, since the botox. When he turned his head to listen to something, he looked as blank and chiselled as the cyborg in *Terminator*, and when he laughed heartily at a guest's lame joke there was a sudden startling rush of bleached-white canine teeth while the face itself stayed expressionless. Jesus, it was like a wolf smiling at you.

And the way the guy was so obsessed with a few laugh lines. Men in their forties, Rich had decided, had never had it so good. Twenty years ago, sure, he'd dreaded reaching this particular decade, couldn't imagine what he'd become or how he'd look. But who would have thought it would turn out so well and get so easy? Something had happened about ten years ago that had taken them all by surprise; the number of women looking for men seemed to have increased and with it a simultaneous spike of anxiety about missing the boat altogether, while the number of available, unscrewed-up heterosexual men seemed to have shrunk drastically. If he was ever to write his PhD, it would be on the gender-scarcity principle.

You didn't even have to try too hard. In fact, the opposite was true — the less you appeared to try, the more appealing you seemed, and with every passing year your appeal increased notch by notch. He would have to take the host aside one morning, and explain it to him: *Mate, stop trying.* You could be like one of those brown bears in Alaska. All you had to do was stand in the right spot over the river with your mouth open and a salmon would just jump in. They were hardwired for it, desperate to spawn whatever the odds. They couldn't help themselves.

He rolled the next package, trimmed the introduction. The woman they always used for this segment sat at a coffee table, animation leaping into her face at the floor manager's cue, a mixture of concern and enthusiasm she could flick on like a tap.

'Have you ever wondered what would happen to your family in the event of your unexpected death?' she began. 'With all the trauma and grief of illness or accident, the last thing they should be worrying about is whether they have enough funds to pay for your funeral. And those expenses can really mount up!'

Rich edited in the cut-away: a page of figures. He could see why they kept employing her; on the other tape she didn't even use the ten seconds to glance down at her notes, just kept looking straight to camera with that fixed expression of sincere concern. They called her the one-take wonder. Her suit was a bit loud, he thought absently. Cerise would be fine for moisturiser or appliances. Too bright for funeral insurance. The director should have picked that up.

'It can all come as quite a shock,' she said to the camera now, then her sadness suddenly turned to winsome relief, 'but luckily help is at hand. For the price of a weekly cup of coffee, you can give yourself real peace of mind.'

Rich checked the script against the time. Easy. He'd get this down to four minutes then he'd go across the road to the café and buy some of those gourmet cookies and a decent coffee. He just had the diet-shake promo to do and then he'd stick them in the producer's in-tray, be finished at 11.30 and the day would be his.

'That's right,' the talent said warmly, speaking like a nurse to a patient in shock, 'for no more than you'd pay for a cup of coffee. And you can rest assured that your loved ones will never need to experience financial hardship to pay all the unexpected expenses associated with their loss.'

Rich grimaced. How did the advertorial producer come up with this stuff? Who could possibly believe it was real, this stilted, android jargon-speak?

Macadamia and ginger, he thought idly. Or maybe choc chip. The girl who did the protein shakes had told him last week she couldn't resist chocolate, and given him a big I-just-can't-help-myself smile, an open invitation. A definite come-on. You'd never think she indulged in chocolate. She had abs to kill for. He'd tell her that when she came in, admiringly, just giving the loosest of impressions that he occasionally worked out. See how it went from there.

The advertorial cut to a wide shot. Faking a casual discussion now, right down to the two prop cups of tea.

'Family,' agreed the co-host, nodding sagely from his chair, 'there's nothing more important.'

Rich recognised this guy from a game show broadcast many years ago, in an era when a new washing machine and dryer were enough to whip a studio audience into a frenzy and have a lucky housewife jumping with euphoria. His mother had liked this guy. She'd watched him every afternoon. Rich remembered his big pointy collars and platform shoes, eyes twinkling like a jovial red-haired Scottish elf. He seemed wizened and browned now; a shrivelled elf, carved from an old apple.

'You're so right, Jim,' the cerise-suit woman was saying. 'There's nothing more important than family. And imagine how it would be for *your* family if you were to pass away unexpectedly, leaving them with funeral expenses that can add up to as much as six thousand dollars!'

The co-host looked sincerely pained. As if he'd settle for a six-thousand-dollar funeral, thought Rich. And as if he had a family, instead of living for years now with a Chinese drag queen thirty years his junior. Common industry knowledge.

'Well, we're definitely not buying that ·brand,' Sandy said decisively. Sophie trailed behind, wishing she'd remembered her iPod, as her mother wheeled the shopping cart up the aisle past cereals. 'That's the one we're boycotting.'

'Who's *we*?'

'The Consumer Action Group.'

'What — your book club? You think you're going to make a multinational corporation go under because you don't buy their muesli bars?'

'You know what, back when you were about five, for your information, consumer pressure forced companies to only produce dolphin-friendly tuna.'

Sophie stopped, looked at her. She didn't know why she was pushing this, it just felt good, getting her mother defensive. It felt reassuring.

'What do you mean? How was overfishing tuna friendly to dolphins?'

Her mother made an impatient gesture, exhaled an irritated breath. 'We boycotted particular brands that ... ah ... used a certain kind of drift net, which used to catch and drown dolphins.' She moved the cart further up the aisle, towards the desserts. 'And they bowed to consumer pressure, and stopped using the nets, and look, even now if you check on cans of tuna, you'll see ...'

'OK, OK. So the book club ...'

'I wish you'd stop saying we're just "the book club" like that, being so ... negative. We were meeting as a book club when the G8 Summit was on and that's when we organised the train to go down to the city to the protest.' She glanced angrily at Sophie. 'That's funny, is it? Protesting for social justice?'

'No, no.'

'So what are you smirking at?'

'It's just funny that you've gone from attacking global capitalism to boycotting muesli bars.'

Her mother ground her teeth. 'Well, I'm not arguing with you anymore, and I don't appreciate your smart-arse attitude either.'

There was a silence. Now her mother would go off on another tangent, try to change the subject. Suggest they buy something dripping with fat and sugar as though it was the biggest treat in the world and then try to cajole her, later, into eating it with her. Like they sat up, the two of them, eating gourmet ice-cream out of the carton on the couch in front of the TV together, telling secrets and gossiping like two room-mates in an American sitcom.

'Hey, Soph.' Here it was. 'What do you say we get some of this chocolate mousse mix and make up that birthday cake recipe, see if you want it for your party?'

As if Sophie hadn't told her a hundred times she didn't want a party. She pretended to look regretful but earnest as she handed back the box to her mother.

'We can't, though. Look at the ingredient list.'

'What?'

'Gelatine. That's horses' hooves. We'd have to have a vegan cake, wouldn't we? So that nobody feels left out?'

She watched her mother consider this, really seem to give it thought, with that dumb pious expression like when her group planned their agenda and spent half an hour deciding whether coffee and chocolate in themselves were oppressing Third World workers, or just certain brands. That eager, earnest light in their faces, as if they really believed they made the slightest bit of difference either way. That's what she found most ridiculous and pathetic — the idea of her mother and her friends thinking they had some kind of power and influence. Even when the bloody ordinariness of their lives stared them in the face, they still couldn't give up on the idea that they were special.

'Do you really think that's an issue?' Sandy was saying cagily, toying with the box of mousse. 'I mean, it's not as if horses are *endangered* or anything, is it?'

They made these places overwhelming on purpose, Rich knew. He'd read about it. They employed consultants to make the layout as disorienting as possible, so that when you finally got to the register you were softened up with dazed gratitude. Walking around the huge camping megastore was like tiptoeing into a hushed and vaulted space, like a cathedral, or a biosphere. Somewhere around the middle of aisle three, where earth-toned clothing was stacked head-high all around, he reached into a rack and unhooked the hanger of one of the charcoal grey t-shirts and held it up enquiringly before the sales assistant.

'So this one's got the same concealed, side security zip ...'

'Yes, in the tank, not in the base-layer thermals, obviously ...'

'... and it's quick-dry and in the same colours ...'

'Pretty much.'

'So what makes this one better? Why is it so much more expensive?'

The salesman gave him a confiding smile. 'Wicking,' he replied.

'Come again?'

'This one offers moisture wickability. This one is good, but it's only a polypropylene mix, but this one is wool so it's aquaphobic.'

Rich picked up the t-shirt and inspected it again. 'Sorry, what do ...?'

'It wicks sweat properly away from the body, so that sweat

evaporates from the clothes, not the skin. So you don't get so cold when you're sweating.'

'I see.'

'So, for example, if you're wearing the base-layer thermals with long sleeves, then a shirt then a windbreaker over the top, then obviously you can go for something in the microfibre in the outer layers.'

'Right.' Jesus, it was like doing an engineering degree.

'Or the other thing I could suggest is these — they're a brand new line. Anti-microbial and they impregnate the fabric with hypo-allergenic insect repellent.'

'Are you serious? What happened to just spraying yourself with Aerogard?'

'Well, you might be in a place, for example, where you don't have any repellent. This is really something for your more serious hard-core experiential wilderness adventurers.'

Rich glanced at him sharply, but he was straight-faced, reeling it off with the same unnerving sincerity as the actors that morning in the studio.

'So, repellent-impregnated shirts?'

'That's right.'

'And with all that technology, they can still only make them in orange check?'

The guy shrugged. 'Bright colours are a safety feature in the bush.'

Rich picked up the one with the wickability. 'You know, when I was down in Tasmania at the beginning of '83,' he said, smiling reminiscently, 'we just took flannelette shirts, woollen jumpers and a japara. And jeans. A few people had those waterproof ski pants, but not many.'

The salesman hardly hesitated. 'There's a sale on in those waterproof mussel pants at the moment, if you're interested. They're four-way stretch with welded seams and I think there's a few left in camo as well as the black, charcoal, dark moss and maroon.'

'Yeah, but the thing is, my point is, we all just got wet and cold and put up with it. There wasn't even polar fleece.'

The guy nodded pleasantly, his eyes shifting momentarily past him and back again.

'Well that's — what? — twenty-five years,' he said. 'The outdoors industry has come a long way since then.'

'That was for the Blockade,' Rich said.

'Like tents — talk about leaps and bounds there,' said the salesman. 'Have you had a chance to have a look through? We've got Everest, Safari, Alpine and Hunter. It really makes camping a luxury option now.'

'It wasn't then, let me tell you,' he replied with a laugh. 'Sheltering under the dripping trees there on the bank, rainforest all around us, putting your wet clothes back on the following day. And I mean thick, virgin forest. No designated campsite there.'

The salesman picked up the anti-microbial shirts and smoothed them on their hangers and tucked them back onto the rack. 'Anything I can help you with, just give me a hoy,' he said, stepping away.

They must train them, Rich thought sourly, in the art of deflection. Or else they make them in a lab out the back, and just hang them up in the cupboard at night with the recharger on.

He went to look at the tents.

Sophie would've received the card by now, he thought. So when her birthday rolled around — he had the date in his diary — he'd ring her and just sound normal. Just cool. Say she was fifteen now, and what with one thing and another (he'd address this later, obviously) they hadn't been in touch much, and he was feeling the lack of it. No ... that he could understand if she was feeling the lack of it. Thought it was about time they got to know each other, adult to adult.

He'd read about the six-day walk through the national park in Tasmania in one of his travel photography magazines, and thought immediately it would be something that might work. A father–daughter hike, something to give them both a week of focus while they got to know each other, lots of other people around to take the pressure off. One thing, he mustn't seem awkward, or over-eager. He'd just suggest the walk and leave it with her until the next school holidays; give her a chance to think it over.

He came to the end of an aisle of tents and turned left into a street of packs. He stopped and stood looking up at the battalion of backpacks hanging overhead. A giant mural-sized image showed a snowy alpine scene in which an impossibly pretty male climber in designer stubble stood gazing into the distance, kitted out in daypack and snowboard, with an expression on his face like he was trying to remember where he'd left his keys.

Rich studied the image thoughtfully, his chin in his hand. *Hi, Soph, it's Rich*, he could say. Or, *Hi Soph, it's your dad here.* No.

He remembered with crystalline clarity the shock he'd felt when Sandy had told him she was pregnant, shock that had swerved quickly sideways into a braced sense of challenge.

His mind had sprung to an image of himself — almost ready-made, it seemed, and waiting there in ambush — carrying a baby (boy or girl? he couldn't tell) in all its detail. He saw his handspun jumper, the baby in the striped legwarmers someone at the market knitted back then, both of them in no-nonsense beanies against the crisp morning air.

Women always gravitated towards a man holding a baby, he'd noticed. Well, a certain kind of man. A man confident in his masculinity, unflappable. It must have been something about the aura of nurturing they found so attractive, or perhaps in a town like Ayresville any man who seemed like decent father material was appealing.

Parenting, Rich thought idly as he wandered along another aisle, noting packaway Frisbees and carabiners and polycarbonate dinner sets, *parenting* was a verb now. You had to watch yourself with language; it warped and morphed all the time, as if it wanted to catch you napping. At a dinner party once at their place, years back, he'd said 'homeless kids' and Paul's bitch of a wife had said, 'Don't you mean "disadvantaged youth"? Don't you think "homeless" is such a pejorative assumption?'

And he'd grimaced, made a joke of it, and said of course he did, although to tell the truth he had only the haziest idea of what 'pejorative' actually meant. Then before he knew it, just as he'd got used to that mouthful, someone had corrected him again, telling him the term he really wanted, if he was really serious about being inclusive and non-judgemental, was 'marginalised young people'.

You couldn't be careful enough with language; you could be turned on and criticised for everything, even things you didn't really mean. Like the woman in that self-actualisation workshop Sandy had dragged him along to once, itching to find something to be the centre of attention about, tearfully protesting that she felt *disempowered* by how articulate he was. See, it got you coming and going, you couldn't win. There was offence everywhere.

And poor people, surely, just called themselves poor. Didn't trip over themselves saying they were 'socioeconomically disadvantaged'. Rich just wanted to have a serious conversation that didn't have to contain the word 'socioeconomic'. That, he thought, was the surest indicator of any that the speaker was middle class. Well — that, and using 'lifestyle' as an adjective.

So. Now you *parented*, you didn't become a parent, although you didn't want to spend too long with people who used that one with a straight face. 'I was home, parenting my daughter, when it happened ...' All verbs. *Impacting. Empowering.* He'd even heard *dialoguing* at one meeting. But *fathering* — that was in a different league to *mothering*. One suggested conception, the other, everything that came after, and in Rich's view no amount of consciousness-raising in the world was going to change that for a good long while. *Hi — Soph? It's your biological father here. Your bioparent.*

'Can I help you with anything?' asked a different salesperson, another clear-skinned clone from the lab out the back.

'Um — backpacks.'

'Rucksack, hybrid, trekking or travel?'

'Just get that one down for me, will you?'

Sophie, lugging the shopping back to the car park, felt her feet crunch on something plastic scattered on the bitumen, and she looked down at jagged orange and red fragments. Both the tail-lights of her mother's car had been smashed. The bumper bar of the car was scored with two long dents, pushing it in so far the boot had popped open. It sat there now, like a slightly gaping, stunned mouth.

'Someone's hit you, Mum. Bastards!' She put down her two shopping bags and ran her hand along the dents. 'Some wanker in a Landcruiser, probably. See how it's like the two steel bars in a bullbar?' She glanced at the front of the car to see if there was a note or phone number left under the windscreen wiper. Nothing. Of course. And still her mother stood there, staring stupidly at the damage, not moving, and then turned to look at her.

'I'm not insured for this, I'm almost positive.'

Surprise, surprise, Sophie thought. 'Well, there's no note,' she said out loud, feeling the low-grade thrum of irritation start up in her again. That helpless, dependent look her mother shot her, her indecisive dithering. It would be Sophie who'd find the insurance company number in the phone book at home, and who'd end up phoning them too, while her mother hunted pointlessly for papers. (*Very organised*, her school reports said. *Shows a maturity beyond her years.*)

She watched Sandy now, putting out her hand and tentatively attempting to close the boot. It clicked back open and rose again on its springs.

'Will you look at that?' breathed her mother softly, almost conversationally. Like she was just waiting for the real adult to come along and sort things out.

'I know,' she snapped, exasperated. 'It's broken.' (*Sophie has no trouble identifying priorities and following through on tasks. She demands an extremely high standard of herself.*)

'No, not the boot. That.' Sandy was pointing, mesmerised, at the crumpled bumper, at the one single section that remained unscathed, exactly the length of the purple and silver glitter sticker that adorned it. The sticker that proclaimed: *Magic Happens*.

'That's incredible,' Sandy whispered.

'What?'

'The whole bumper is crushed, but that one small message isn't even touched. That's a sign.'

'Wait — you're saying that someone crashes into your car and drives away, and because your bumper sticker's still OK, that's karma?' *Please God*, Sophie thought, *don't let any of my friends be hearing this conversation.*

'It's still driveable. Look, the globes in the tail-lights haven't even been broken. I just need to get some more covers from the wreckers. They'll have another Datsun bumper lying around, and I bet they fit it on too if I ask them nicely.'

See, right there — that was the way she handled everything, as if life was one long, messy series of favours. People being forced to take pity on you if you just proved you were hopeless enough. Sophie jerked open the door. She couldn't relax even for a minute, she had to be looking out for her mother all the time. Her and her stupid, flabby, wafting *uselessness*. (*Sophie has trained herself this year to work unsupervised with diligence and focus and is self-reliant in achieving her goals and objectives.*)

Another thing. This was really starting to freak her out lately. If she gave her mother an order in a voice like a teacher, Sandy obeyed unquestioningly, like a meek, submissive child. She tried it now.

'OK, fine, get in.'

And her mother did it, without even noticing.

'See something good in this, Sophie,' was all she said as she fumbled for her seatbelt. 'You're getting so cynical.'

'Aren't you even angry?'

'Imagine how the person who did this is feeling right now.'

Sophie slung the shopping bags in the back seat and dug for her chewing gum.

'The person who did this? They've stopped thinking about it, Mum. They probably barely noticed.'

'Well, that's their bad karma, not ours.'

'Right. Magic happens.'

'It does. You just wait and see.'

They drove home, Sophie wincing every time she heard metal

scraping on metal. That's right, she thought. Home in their shitbox car to their crap TV and dial-up computer that was so slow it was like watching paint dry. Home to a miserly water-saving shower with biodegradable hippie shampoo that didn't even wash your hair properly and a house full of garage-sale junk. Then another morning at the markets tomorrow where her mother would tell everyone about the sticker miracle in hushed tones, like it was a weeping statue. She groped for her phone.

OMG sum prik hit our car, she texted to Ariel. *its almost totalled.*

She opened the paper bag from the music shop and checked the title of the new ambient music CD her mother had bought: *Spirit of the Loon*. God, you couldn't make this stuff up. She looked askance at Sandy, who returned her glance with a defiant shrug as she changed gears.

'It's a bird,' she said.

'Right.'

Bouncing over the potholes down the drive, the car's boot sprang open from its broken lock with the sound of gnashing teeth, never to close again without a rainbow elastic strap haphazardly tying it down — a temporary solution, Sophie knew with dull certainty, that would go with the car to its grave.

Rich made his way to the checkout with a pile of wicking microbe-killing clothing, a sleeping bag called an Odyssey Pathfinder that looked eerily like an Egyptian sarcophagus, a backpacker butane stove, a high-performance geodesic tent and a honeycomb self-inflating mat loaded with customised comfort features. He could make do with the backpack he already had, at those prices. And he thought he could probably live without the frisbee.

He got his credit card out ready and tapped it on the counter, keeping his eyes studiously away from the digital price display on the register as each item was added up. If he could get some really topnotch photos in Tasmania, sell them on to someone, he could claim the trip on tax and maybe claim some of this gear as well. In fact, he should find out where this store sourced its wall-sized images from and see if they were interested in some Cradle

Mountain shots. Pay for it all that way. And she'd want to come. He was almost sure of it.

He did a quick check of the tally. OK. A shade under two thousand; that wouldn't quite max him out, and he could transfer some money from his savings account in the interim. It felt good, anyway, buying a stack of brand-new clothing from this high-end chain, in the latest colours and styles. After all, he'd have his teenage daughter, soon, judging him on his fashion sense, his knowing what was what. It didn't hurt to splurge occasionally, if it meant making the right impression. Anyway, no going back now. The cashier tapped another button and the figure reduced itself slightly. Rich looked surprised.

'All the clothing's ten percent off,' she said, flashing him a smile. 'Our new season's stock is coming in next Tuesday.'

Three

Sandy drove down the main street, praying the cops wouldn't notice her crumpled bumper bar and pull her over. Early Saturday morning, and the place was jammed with tourists. *Terrorists*, her friend Annie called them disparagingly, but even Annie had to grudgingly admit they kept the whole economy going, and even she was talking, now, about re-borrowing on her house and building a bed-and-breakfast weekender in her back garden, which was a licence to print money, according to the real-estate agents in town. They couldn't keep up with demand.

Sandy recalled the town when she'd first seen it, nearly — what? — twenty years ago. She and Rich, coming up to Ayresville for that all-night solstice party. They'd stayed in a room someone had built in the garden, a *yurt* — whatever happened to yurts? — and the next morning, nursing a vicious mulled-wine hangover, she went with the host of the party to the arts and crafts market up the hill to stock up on provisions, and had a long look around at the stalls selling pottery and honey and jewellery.

It was nice jewellery, she'd thought with a rising sense of excitement and yearning, but nothing she couldn't make herself, given half a chance. If she came to live here she could have a stall here too in the green sunny park and drink chai tea with these new friends with the same familiar ease, and maybe Rich could sell his photos or make cards out of them.

'You know what? I reckon we should move up here and out of

the city,' she'd said to him when she got back to the party house, where he was lounging on the verandah. Her idea, originally. Hers. She'd had to talk Rich into it, however much he tried to rewrite it later to friends when it turned out to be such a great move. They'd scraped together the deposit on the old house on Runnymede Street, and she was the one who'd made it special. She'd found those big windows at the second-hand timber yard and sanded the floors, and even though it had taken a long, long time, their friend Daniel who had aspirations as a builder had eventually built on the verandah and put in the French doors.

And she did start up the jewellery stall at the market — she had a natural flair for it, and there were always customers from the city in a good mood and ready to buy an original string of beads and earrings. The crystal pendants she made threw prisms of light that hit the ground in rainbows, and what with that and working part-time at the wholefoods shop, they'd made enough to pay their mortgage, something they couldn't have believed they would ever have.

That mortgage. Bloody Richard always had to make such a big issue out of it every time they had people come up and stay; over dinner he'd never fail to mention that they were turning into a cliché of some conservative middle-class couple. Opening another home-brewed beer and talking about subverting the dominant paradigm. Everyone used to come up, back then, and crash at their place.

She'd felt again a glimmering of the same exhilaration and purpose she'd felt at the Franklin Blockade, the same impassioned talk about ideas and possibilities. Everything had seemed so much in ascendancy, then. Going upwards on a rising wave of energising purpose.

Where had that all gone? Things changed so fast it was a blur, like a huge, hulking vehicle roaring past you on the road, overtaking you when you least expected it and leaving you in a gritty swirl of dust. Cruisy, sleepy little Ayresville suddenly a boom town, filling up with freelancers and designers and garden landscapers, and the new-age therapy practitioners who eschewed hands-on massage and just hovered their palms over you, or placed stones along your spine. Taking a quick, confident look at your tongue then telling you that your problem was you had some heavy *qi* energy on your spleen. You couldn't keep up, thought Sandy, who had only just enrolled in an expensive shiatsu course when kinesiology came to town. You got left behind. It was as though you nervously traded your hard-earned money for one currency only to wake up and find there'd been a new revolution while you slept, and now your notes were worth nothing, and people looked at you with the kind of pity that said: *Get with the program.*

A bunch of academics discovered the town was commuting distance to university if they left early enough in the morning, then the road was turned into a freeway. Cottages around the town that had sat vacant for years started being advertised as 'weekenders', and one day she'd driven past the old weatherboard house where they'd first come up to the party all those years ago to see it had been sold and turned into a wedding and convention centre. Where the backyard yurt had been there were now three Tuscan-style villas. Then one by one the shops on the main street began to close and reopen transformed, and at first it all seemed like a great thing to have so many good cafés. No matter what you asked for — a double decaf soyaccino, a skinny moccalatte — they had it. It was all vibrant, all eclectic, all booming. Then suddenly you turned around and saw the old butcher shop was a day spa.

They'd lost it, she lamented privately now as she swung into a vacant space. She hated to admit it, but they'd let it spin out of control, and now it was changed forever. The market had swelled, to accommodate other people who also loved the idea of making pottery and turned wooden bowls during the week, and the new artists rolled their eyes at the craftsworkers' collective — which, admittedly, was a bit lackadaisical — and started up a new chamber of commerce, which ran the annual Solstice Party now at $45 a ticket.

Council built a gym and an indoor pool, and meanwhile the

house that she and Rich had bought quadrupled in value and then, ridiculously, just kept on rising.

That was after Rich had left, thank God. She would never have been able to afford to buy him out now. Not that she'd bought him out — he'd just left. And then her father had died and in a gesture that denied a lifetime of aloofness, left her that money just exactly when she needed it, like a sign, to pay out a chunk of the mortgage. It was her house, anyway. Her energy, her vision, her impetus. Rich had just come along for the ride.

She was sure the thought of the house's value gave Rich pause as he was walking out, but equally, she'd been standing on that verandah, which Daniel had finally finished, holding a wailing Sophie in her arms, and perhaps to Rich in that moment it had seemed a fair-enough bargain. Sophie, red-faced and black-haired like a foundling child, something left by the fairies, her tiny Sherpa hat tied securely onto her head and her handspun jumper chafing at her drooly chin, bundled up ready for a day at the market. She had wanted to scream too — had in fact done quite a bit of screaming the night before as they'd fought for hours, which really went against her principles — but she'd kept her temper and spoken firmly and quietly. The one who raises their voice loses the argument; she remembered that from the non-violence workshops at the Blockade.

And to tell the truth, she had been stunned beyond belief. How had it gone so absolutely pear-shaped — the ten years of cohabiting happiness, all those years of carefree unencumbered adventuring, the understanding that didn't need a marriage licence, the whole shebang — how had it become such a skidding wreck once the baby was born?

Because Sandy couldn't remember changing. That was the thing. She'd stayed the same person, so it had to be Sophie — and the idea of Sophie — that had made him bolt. That's what she couldn't forgive, ever. She'd stood there holding her baby, appalled with the indignation of it, and every second that passed seemed to make Sophie infallibly more hers, and less his, as if their true colours were at last being revealed now that push had finally come to shove. As if she was growing roots now, down from her feet placed squarely there, revealed as the solid one.

He'd packed a few boxes of gear, grim-faced, into the Kombi ('and take that guitar you never play,' she'd called to him, emboldened and powerful ... Why couldn't she feel a surge of that righteous energy now?) and reversed the old van expertly out of the driveway. That was one thing that remained as a lasting impression, she thought stonily; his expertise in backing out of things.

The baby had squirmed in her arms to be let down and she, dazed, had let her crawl haphazardly across the verandah, where she'd screamed again as a wood splinter stuck itself into the heel of her little hand. Sandy had broken down and wept then, after all, seeing with sudden clarity the position she was in — left alone with a baby and no support except from the government and that which might come from useless, dithering, drug-frazzled friends like Daniel, who couldn't even sand and finish off a deck properly.

And yes, she'd called out something vicious and hurtful as he'd started up the van, it was true. It was one of those things you shout when you're furious and desperate, when someone's leaving you, unbelievably, in the lurch. Something about him never seeing Sophie again. Not a threat, though. Just to try to remind him that he was the one walking out on all his responsibilities, and that kind of breach didn't mend just like that.

She'd meant it as a wake-up call. A warning. She couldn't have predicted the expression of baleful coldness falling over his face like darkness, like a door slamming and locking. *Never.* She shouldn't have said never.

But once she had, there was no going back.

At home, Rich read that his new sleeping bag had a curved trapezoid baffle which optimised loft. Loft — another one of those co-opted words — was calculated by measuring the volume an ounce of down occupied in a climate-controlled test cylinder, and his model provided an optimum baffle-wall angle. Well, thank God for that. And sure it cost a week's pay, but he'd been well overdue for a new one anyway. A good sleeping bag was still an asset to pack sometimes if you were heading for somewhere remote. Last time he'd been in Turkey he'd just about frozen to death one night under a miserly cotton blanket, even though he'd been in a three-star guesthouse. He'd heard it was cold in Afghanistan at night, and that's where he was thinking about travelling next. He'd seen *The Kite Runner*. The country would be perfect for a series of photos. Handsome people, the Afghanis. All those good-looking sad-eyed kids, playing in monochromatic stony streets. He'd go and see Andrew at the café, where he'd hung his Brazilian series, and see if he was interested. Really, the sleeping bag was an investment.

Why was he even justifying it? He hadn't bought a new one for probably thirty years — his old one was shoved in the back of the hall cupboard behind the spare pillows. It could go down to the op shop now, to be piled with all the other last-century paraphernalia. He found it — so ludicrously, shamefully bulky! — and unrolled it. Faded khaki green on the outside, tartan brushed cotton over lumpy dacron inside, and a trapped scent that came billowing up at him of wood smoke and damp mist and bracken.

God, the way a smell could bloom like a blown ember in your brain, fresh and sharp as turning over a log to expose all the dark life that swarmed beneath it. Sight and sound had nothing on smell. You unzipped your old sleeping bag, opened an old book, lit a mosquito coil, and it was like stepping on a mine. It made you realise everything was stored, nothing was forgotten, just waiting for the saturation of memory to overspill and flick some switch.

He must have used this since 1983. Must have pulled it out to throw over visitors staying the night on his couch, or loaned it to someone, sometime, so why did it still smell, so precisely, of the river?

Rich took the lumpy end again in both hands and began to reroll it, resisting doing the thing he most longed to, which was lower his head onto the tartan fabric and inhale slowly and deeply, with his eyes closed. He had a new sleeping bag now in breathable, water-resistant windproof nylon taffeta that smelled of chemicals and money, and he was lucky he hadn't got hypothermia trying to brave Tasmania's cold in this sorry half-arsed excuse for a bag which was probably older than him. But still, his head sank weakly towards it, like a supplicant. He rested his forehead on the soft material and inhaled a great savouring gasp of it. Breathed in fog and smoke, sweat and mud and ylang-ylang.

That was it. The scent that would always, always come around to snag him. In behind her neck, at her warm hairline, when they did the group hug. Such an intimate thing to smell on a stranger. She'd been in one of those Nepalese sweaters with the patterns across the front that prickled you like a hair shirt here in the Australian heat. You needed the icy winds of the Himalayas for those sweaters; snow-capped peaks and sub-zero gales. Yak wool, or something. He'd hugged her, felt her fine and fluid shoulder blades moving under his hands as he released her. Regretfully, it had to be said. Nothing wrong with being enveloped in a soft and fervent female embrace at 9.30 on a sunny morning, breathing in a sweet gust of ylang-ylang. Oh, it wasn't just Sandy, he knew that. He wasn't making that mistake. It was Sandy in that place, at that time. The click and the fit.

That's what he'd felt when he'd first shown up; the sense he was in the right place at the right time. They'd surprised him. He'd expected a disorganised shambles, couldn't believe it when he'd stepped into the Info Centre and been asked to register, the businesslike focus of the people there. It had sobered him up, that and the mainstream journalists and photographers queued up respectfully, ready to go upriver. He remembered filling out his details as if he was signing up for the army, that prehistoric telex machine humming in the background, the sense of serious battle being waged. And then setting up his tent at Greenie Acres, where they had to do the training if they wanted to go up the river to be arrested. The whole atmosphere of the place, the banter as they dished up meals in the food tent while he stood in line, like it was an episode of M*A*S*H.

At the workshop Sandy had patted him lightly on the back as their hug ended, smiling. You could never read those sorts of invitations then, not reliably. They were in the 1980s, and men were learning to walk on eggshells. Women he'd met actually liked that reticence, he was coming to realise; they seemed to warm to a certain lack of confidence and hesitation, as if it suggested the man hadn't yet been irredeemably warped by the patriarchy.

'How about a break?' the facilitator had called, and Rich could have hugged him too, for his sense of timing, as though the music had ended in a progressive dance just when he was face to face with the right person.

'Coffee?' he said to her, and she screwed up her nose.

'Caffeine's the last thing I need. Dandelion coffee for me. Or herbal tea if there's any there.'

He poured them both a yellow tea, smelling its aroma of hot wet peppermint, dank as hay. He would have to be dying of thirst, he thought, before he drank another dandelion coffee; it tasted like it was made with burnt potting mix.

Beautiful skin, she had; freckles across her nose and the beginnings of lines that showed she had a sense of humour.

'Where are you from?' he asked.

'Melbourne.'

'Me too.'

'Bit different, isn't it?' She blew on her tea, sipped it.

'It's great. And important to be here, obviously.' God, what a pompous idiot he sounded.

She nodded. 'Oh, absolutely.'

He took a swallow of tea. How did she drink the stuff? Even instant coffee, even the big tin of caterer's blend there on the trestle, would be better than this.

'I've just finished first-year Arts at uni. A bunch of us have been watching the campaign progress and came down to be part of the protest,' she said. 'Are you studying?'

'Well, sort of. I'm starting this year, if I get accepted. I just applied before I came down here,' he answered, then hesitated. 'Just after I got back.'

Her eyebrows rose enquiringly. 'Back from where?'

'Nepal.'

'Oh, wow. I'd *love* to go to Nepal. It sounds like such a spiritual place.'

'Yes, it is. Very much so.'

He waited again, wanting her to ask him more. He had a copy of the magazine that had accepted his photo, back in his tent, and if she asked he could offer to show it to her later, and he had a Dolphin torch and a bottle of port in there too. Not that he'd been planning anything.

'Were you just travelling, then?'

'Not exactly. Doing some backpacking, yes, but I was really working on a photographic essay.'

'Wow. Was that for your uni course?'

'No, no. I'll be studying forestry. But I'm also a freelancer.'

'A photographer? Really? So you get to travel around and take photos?'

He smiled, swigged a bit more tea. 'Yeah, but you know, I'm starting to prefer to say *make* photos rather than *take* them. Because —'

Then the facilitator's voice was braying at them to come back to the circle and reconvene. Share any new insights, reach consensus. He was already pinning a piece of butcher's paper to the A-frame board, Rich remembered with a grimace, ready to write up keywords, draw some arrows, make circles in a different colour, come up with some obscure sense of achievement, it seemed to him, before they broke for lunch.

Sandy had finished her tea, and touched his arm. 'I'm Sandy, by the way.'

'Yeah, I remember from the introductions. I'm Richard. And look, I've actually got a travel magazine with me, if you're interested in seeing some of my photos. I had one of the Nepalese ones published, so —'

'Let's refocus, everyone,' called the facilitator, clapping, and Rich could have drowned him in a bucket of cold peppermint tea. But Sandy looked pleased, her attention still with him, and nodded eagerly. Always eager for something. The next thing, the new thing.

'I'd love to. I'll catch you later, then.'

'OK. Great.'

'And you should take some photos of the Blockade, don't you reckon? They're going to be such an important part of everybody's shared histories.'

'You're right.'

'Oh, sorry,' she added with a smile as she moved back to the workshop, '*make* them, I mean. Document what's happening.'

And she pulled off her hot woollen sweater, crackling with static, to reveal a blue t-shirt underneath. He loved that easy, single, graceful motion. He'd appreciate it all over again in the darkness of his tent a few nights later, when she'd kneel, the sleeping bag falling away from her, this very sleeping bag. She'd pulled her cotton shirt over her head with the same careless certainty, the pale fabric glowing a little and her hair sliding back off her face to reveal her eyes watching him, her faint smile. It was a guilty pleasure, watching her undress, and worth hearing the photography magazine crumple and crease and finally rip under her knee. His hands went to rescue it, but reached for her instead.

Ylang-ylang. She never wore it much later, but that didn't matter, it still managed to hook him long after they'd separated. Years later, absently sniffing bars of homemade soap at a craft market, he'd caught the scent again and, in a sudden floundering clench, memory had reached up and grabbed at his throat in a tight and unexpected grip, and to his astonished horror he'd almost sobbed.

It irritated him no end, the lurking residual power of it. Between that and the nag champa incense no share house was complete without, the world now was an obstacle course booby-trapped with nostalgia scent-bombs. You could still buy nag champa, he'd noticed, in exactly the same red, blue and white box. Health-food shops still reeked of it. Put your nose to any outsized batik cushion and catch a whiff of it ingrained there like ancient dust. Archaeologists of the future, Rich thought, would be able to do nag-champa counts like they did pollen counts now. And ylang-ylang, more flowery, more heady than patchouli, still there at the Body Shop and in the occasional redolent miasma around a dreamy teenage girl he passed on the street. He even smelt it wafting off the aromatherapy candles so many women he met seemed to keep on their bedside table, in preparation for a long and exhausting session of extended foreplay, occasions that would leave Rich jittery and vagued-out the next day, as if sex was a plane trip somewhere, crossing some crucial dateline, and you always got jetlag.

Rich slept now, inhaling and exhaling evenly, sunlight shifting inexorably across the floor, another afternoon closing down.

Four

'Mum, I really, really don't want a party.' She tucked her fingers into her fists, and pressed. The pain throbbed in her fingertips, on her chewed hangnails, the raw swollen ridge on her middle finger where she'd torn the nail down to the nerve bed. Why had she done that? She'd just started gnawing at it and somehow couldn't stop. She'd gone to pick up the soap the next day in the shower and knocked her outstretched hand against the tiles, and the blinding flare of pain in her raw bitten fingers was like when you hit yourself hammering something.

'But, Soph, you're fifteen. Let me do something special for you.'

It was always like this. Couldn't just leave her alone or do what she asked. Couldn't *listen*. She'd made the mistake of having three friends round for a sleepover when she turned twelve. Her mother had taken over then too. Getting stuff out of her wardrobe and asking Sophie's friends did they want to try anything on, pretending she liked thrash metal, and then finally giving them a big, earnest lecture when they got *Nightmare on Elm Street* out of the video shop. Wrecking everything.

And each year since she'd lost this argument, so why should turning fifteen be any different? On Saturday afternoon over they would all come for a party — her mother's friends, not hers — the gang of eight women she socialised with. Her tribe, her posse, her pride. They did everything together, never moving until they'd checked with the others, more obsessive about it than the girls at school, even. They'd sit outside and drink cheap champagne and start talking like they'd been apart for months. They would talk like they'd invented it, like it was an Olympic event.

When she was a bit younger Sophie had called them Aunty for a while, but now she wasn't expected to, thank God. They'd bring their younger kids if they had them and expect her and whoever of her friends had turned up to babysit them; a whole swarming gang of hyped-up feral kids who'd never heard the word 'no', putting nits all over her pillow, probably, when they jumped screaming on her bed.

She was totally over it. She picked at the side of her thumbnail with her teeth, fuming inwardly, as her mother tried to get her to contribute to the list of party food she was writing.

'Tabouli?' Sandy said hopefully.

Sophie held a shred of nail in her teeth and began to pull her thumb away slowly from her mouth. The pain as the hangnail stretched and tore was drenching, exquisite. She tasted the coppery flavour of blood mixed with her saliva.

'Roast pumpkin salad,' Sandy said, scribbling it down.

Sophie sucked her thumb, feeling the raw spot with her tongue, searching for a new ragged corner of nail. Saying nothing.

'Houmous,' said Sandy thoughtfully, and Sophie felt her throat tighten with a suppressed retch of nausea. She could just see them, her mother and her friends on the night, gobbling down dip and crusty bread and all that fattening soft cheese, shrieking with laughter and calling each other *girlfriend* like they thought they were Beyoncé or something. It was too pathetic.

Just three more years, she thought grimly as she bit a tiny clear edge of fingernail and eased it sideways, straight into the cuticle, the nerves popping like an electric shock. Three more years and she could be out of here for good and go to the city and have her own life at last and never have to look at another bowl of burghal ever, ever again.

Saturday, that was the day to ring her, he thought as he leafed through a script. Five more days. He avoided checking in his diary for the spurt of nervousness it gave him. No, not nervousness — why should he be nervous? It was the strangeness of the situation, the formal awkwardness.

He'd have to speak to Sandy, there was no escaping it. When had the last time been? That misguided afternoon meeting in the Botanical Gardens, when Sophie would have been seven or eight. Excruciating. Big mistake. He'd wondered why he'd done it, what had compelled him. The way Sophie had looked nonplussed and skipped off uninterested when he'd given her that handwoven billum from Papua New Guinea, and Sandy's scornful, triumphant smirk that said *don't you know ANYTHING about children?*

Somehow eight years had fallen through the cracks since then, nearly a decade he'd lost without really paying attention. God, you had to watch that; had to learn to steel yourself each year on your birthday so it didn't hit you like a ton of bricks.

Like the ten years that had inexplicably run through the tap before Sophie was born, the decade he and Sandy had spent doing ... what, exactly? Pleasing themselves. Wasting time. A few good holidays, that blissful long drive up the coast to the Daintree, a trip or two to Bali. Going down to the city for film festivals and both of them working part-time in the food co-op that had run for a while in the town, and suddenly he was thirty-three years old and a father, and Sandy was nagging him about buying a better car and couldn't they get another loan, and Rich had felt like some middle-aged buffoon, that his prime years had somehow, impossibly, slipped from between his fingers. He'd been marooned there in Ayresville, pushing a pram back and forth over a bump in the rug to get the baby to sleep, seething with restlessness.

One night he'd come across his passport in the filing cabinet and he saw with a jolt that it had expired the year before and he hadn't even noticed. That's what had set it off, really; the talk of a trip somewhere, all three of them. Sandy had gone off the deep end as though she was just waiting for an excuse.

It was him who'd jumped off the real deep end, though, down and away. Hardly time to take a breath, just pushed over the edge. Resurfacing spluttering fifteen years later to just gape, sometimes, at the thundering progress of all that time, the stop–start rush of it, the illusory slowing down then swirling on, the way it careened you greedily forward.

Because just last year, it felt like, he was in his early twenties and knew all the chords to 'Moondance' and the world was undisputedly, gloriously, his oyster. Now he would be hard-pushed even to remember the second verse to the song, even if he could find the cassette, and even if he could find a cassette player to play it in.

Or he'd experience a moment like today, at work, hearing some scratchy kind of blurting discordant static going off like a distant car alarm and glance up in annoyance to see, to his utter bewilderment, that someone was listening to that sound by choice, through tiny bulbs embedded in their ears. Through a portable device the size of a stamp. You'd need a pair of surgical tweezers to program it. An iPod. That'd be right. For pod people. Everyone under the age of thirty seemed to have one implanted permanently in their head.

'I know that the time will be just right, and straight into my arms you will run,' he hummed to himself. That was a bit of it.

He gazed at the video screen blankly, letting the tape roll, waiting for the ad's start point. He could hear the recorded voices of the floor manager and director in the gallery, over the talkback. Flat voices, bored.

'Just bang, bang, bang through one and two and have two ready for the close-up on her hand when she gets out the brush,' the director was saying. 'If it looks too sparkly, just keep going and we'll cut away to the footage of what's-her-name.'

'Cara St James,' muttered a woman's voice. The assistant director.

'Never heard of her.'

'She was in that soap in the US. The hospital one.'

'And we're all meant to know that, are we?'

'Total D-list.'

'Anyway, keep going and we'll fix it in post.'

Well, it was A minor to start with, for sure, Rich thought,

watching the digits run on the clapper graphic, waiting. A minor, E minor, then some kind of bar chord in the bridge part. He'd never mastered those, though. Mind you, all he'd have to do would be find his guitar and it would all come back to him.

The Eagles, now. 'Hotel California', he had that one down pat. Verses in minor, then major for the chorus, just like the Police always did. Mind you, there were a lot of verses in that song. Better to stick to 'Desperado', probably, or 'Take It to the Limit'.

He'd ring lunchtime Saturday, definitely. Five days' time. Tell her about the walk, what his plans were, ask her if she felt like getting to know her old man after all this ... no, wait. Not 'old man'.

'OK, roll record.' On the tape the guy stuck on the lounge suite in front of a fake wall unit leaned forward to his co-host, his voice filled with sudden animation.

'We're hearing so much about mineral make-up,' he said. 'What makes Glowing Wonder, with its radiant sheer coverage, so different?'

Rich had done a photography course when he was twenty-one, where he'd learned how to process film in the darkroom and slide those pages of expensive light-sensitive paper into the chemical baths, watching them develop. It had never ceased to be a miracle to him, watching those images darken and form in the swirling liquid. The sharp smell of fixative, a smell always on his hands later because he couldn't help reaching in with his fingers even though you were supposed to use tongs, the little rim of dark sediment that would eventually develop in the solution like fine black sand in a wave.

He loved the secrecy of the safelight, people's faces bathed in red, the irrevocable snap as the timer went off. It wasn't anything like messing round with digital, manipulating mistakes with the computer, faking it. There was nowhere to hide in the darkroom, it was just you and your skill, everything you'd caught on film revealed to you.

He'd had a girlfriend who shared his passion for photography and one afternoon they developed a bunch of photos with low-gloss paper, and it was hard to tell under the safelight sometimes — after you'd withdrawn a sheet carefully from its black plastic packet and sealed the box again — which side was light-sensitive and which side was just the back.

And the girl had grinned and said, 'Don't tell anyone but I'll show you a little trick', and had taken his page from him and tested a corner with the tip of her tongue, to taste which side had the coating of chemical emulsion. Just one small exquisite touch. That moment was still the most erotic memory of Rich's life.

The photographer he most admired, after this girl introduced him to his work, was Henri Cartier-Bresson. HCB, they called him. That photo of a man frozen in mid-air as he jumped over a puddle, everything in the world perfectly poised around him, hanging there. Foot over the water. Capturing the second when it all hangs suspended. *The defining moment*, Cartier-Bresson called it. Everything just an extension of your own eye.

Rich believed in that. Getting that moment seized and in the box. That's why he loved his Olympus, and refused to buy a digital. The defining moment spoke for itself, it didn't need any Photoshop trickery later, didn't respond well to technical tweaking. It separated the purists from the pretenders.

He'd had photos in exhibitions, a few dozen in magazines over the years, and even a couple selected for compilations. *The Year in Pictures* — four years in a row there, that looked pretty good on your résumé — until that particular publishing house went bust in the early nineties. A couple in *Fine Print*, the good quarterly. His negatives and contact sheets were stacked along his bookshelves next to the compilations, the only ordered thing in his life.

He kept his favourite prints framed on the walls, just a few from each exhibition — the Guatemalan series of women in doorways, and the south-east Asia collection, a couple of black-and-whites of the prayer wheels from the Kathmandu trip. One bookcase of books, mostly out-of-print stuff worth hanging onto. Contained within those few shelves and on that wall, he often thought, was the only evidence of what he'd spent two entire decades dedicated to. He looked at the places and the dates like swells and troughs; a long exasperating game of trying to coast a wave, beginning with that headlong flight to Borneo after he'd left Ayresville, where he'd taken some of the best photos of his life of those orangutans and laboured over the article till it was perfect. And he'd got the envelope returned to him from *Natural World* magazine, the transparencies and pages stuffed back inside. With a note saying *nice piece and lovely shots but we just did something like this six months ago.* He'd stood there at his post-office box, incredulous. That was typical of this business. You had to be prescient about the Next Big Thing. Be ready to jump at the chance to sniff out some quirky corner where nobody else had been, and aim your camera and make it your own, find the defining moment.

That's what he should have been doing in that ten years before Sophie was born, instead of letting the whole decade drain away like dregs in a beer, treading water in a place like Ayresville. Letting the ease of it numb him into a pleasant oblivious stupor, instead of being out there making a name for himself, before the backpackers and the gap year Eurotourists and this whole generation of restless rich kids started colonising every unexplored inch of the planet till all of it felt like one big overrun strip mall. God, he hated them — pointing their hand-held digital recorders at everything, every second, and racing to upload it onto their Facebook pages. Sitting at the breakfast tables in the backpacker hostels with their laptops open in front of them, nobody talking to anybody else. He'd seen one German guy once, sitting in an internet café in Istanbul drinking iced chai and reading *The Rough Guide to Vietnam*, and that just about summed up the whole sorry shebang.

After he finished his shift he found himself, back at home, running his fingers along the spines of the negative folders, and wondered about putting all this stuff into storage somewhere. His fingers rested on a big soft-cover book wedged in tight, its spine turned in. You'd have to be looking for it to even notice it.

The People Who Saved the Franklin. Its cover had been everywhere once, before the print run sold out to the people who'd been there. Sometimes, lately, he'd see copies at markets and garage sales, as people culled it from their lives. There it would be out the front of the thrift shop stacked incongruously in a bin next to all the old well-thumbed copies of *Zen and the Art of Motorcycle Maintenance* and *Chariots of the Gods* and *Linda Goodman's Sun Signs* and Lobsang Rampa, that old charlatan. Lobsang Rampa and Nag Champa: there it was, the whole era, defined in one rhyming couplet, strummed on A minor and D minor on a nylon-stringed guitar ...

Leave it, he told himself. But it was like a scab.

He pulled the book from the shelf and flipped to the page that mattered, the photo opposite the text on page 29. It showed a grainy black-and-white image of one of the very first protest marches against the dam — the big ones held in each state capital city that made the Tasmanian government really sit up and start sweating.

He'd been in it, and here was the evidence. In the photo a line of people strode along defiantly, the front line of the march, a huge billowing banner over their heads. It was easy to see why the photographer had chosen this one split second as the defining moment. They all looked so young and resolute, ready to meet any resistance head-on, all eyes focused straight ahead into the future.

Everyone except the guy at the end, that is, who at that crucial defining moment had stopped chanting, just for that *one brief second*, mind you, and been caught in the act of raising a salad roll to his mouth with both hands — and wasn't that just so typical of this shitty world? The historic picture captured him mid-bite, a flap of white paper flattened against his cheek, one eye blurrily half-closed as if he was drunk, but still recognisable if you really studied it. Still identifiable.

Rich flipped the book shut with a disgusted snap and replaced it, spine first, back into the bookshelf.

Then his mobile rang, jolting him out of reverie, and when

he answered it distractedly, he heard a voice he didn't know. A woman. Young.

'Sorry, who is this again?' he said flirtatiously, then his heart dived and wallowed like a boat as he realised.

Her. Sophie.

Five

The plumber frowned down into the cistern. 'How long's it been leaking like this?' he said.

Sandy grimaced. 'Oh, a little while. Usually I take off the lid and jiggle the float and it stops.'

She watched it brimming, feeling a flutter of anxiety. People would be here in an hour or two. They'd know she'd wasted all that water.

'Thanks for coming over on a Saturday,' she added.

After he'd repaired it she showed him how she wanted a fixture to let a hose run from under the house to let the grey water onto the front garden. As they stood on the verandah, the plumber tipped his head and checked out the big tree towering over everything else in the front garden.

'Tassie blue gum,' he observed laconically.

'Yes. And don't tell me it's taking over. I hear that from everyone.'

'Well, not just taking over. Sucking all the ground moisture out for ten metres down as well. That's why nuthin's growing underneath it. Didn't they tell you when you bought it, how big it would grow?'

'No. I put it in for ... sentimental reasons. I've got a special connection with Tasmania.'

When Sophie was born and they'd come home from the hospital, Sandy had realised with dismay that they'd totally forgotten to bring the placenta home to bury in the garden. They'd meant to plant a tree in the spot, something that would flower on Sophie's birthday in years to come. Instead the whole thing slipped her mind in the crazed and sleepless few months that followed, so that it wasn't until the following spring that she found herself standing at the native tree stall at the market one morning and deciding that what she should plant was, obviously, a Tasmanian blue gum. It was part of Sophie's heritage, after all, how she and Rich had met in Tasmania. Part of what had brought them together. At home she selected a spot not far from the house, in front of Sophie's window where she envisioned the tree might provide some deep and welcome shade in the future, and dug a hole for it.

God, she couldn't believe how fast that tree had grown. It was like a triffid. By the time Rich had left it had doubled its size and within three years it was higher than the house. Rather than flowering on Sophie's birthday, it sent a shower of leaves, gumnuts and dried crisps of curling bark onto the roof all year round, debris that slid into the guttering and clogged it until Sandy crawled up there shakily on a ladder and cleared it all out before winter each year, swearing to herself.

'It's really taken off,' she said now, and the plumber nodded sagely again, commiserating, so she pressed on. 'At least it's a native.'

'Not really,' he said, and she stopped and looked blankly at him. 'I mean,' he went on, choosing his words, 'it's a native in the Tassie forests, sure, but it's really an invasive species here, don't you reckon? It's not' — he searched for the word — 'actually endemic, so it may as well be an introduced tree. Like a pine or elm.'

Sandy pushed her hair behind her ear, annoyed. 'It's providing ... um ... habitat,' she said finally.

'So does the cypress hedge at my place, though. You see my point?'

'It's still a native Australian species.'

'Bet it sheds a heap of crap onto the roof.'

She sighed resignedly. 'Yeah. It really does. It's just so ... tall.'

He gazed up at it speculatively. 'I've got a mate who could come and cut it down for you.'

'I don't want it cut down, though. Just trimmed, if anything.'

'Pollarding. That's what it needs. They take out the middle trunk there and the tree springs up again, only smaller and more manageable. Less wood and more green growth.'

'So it doesn't kill the tree?'

He laughed humourlessly. 'I don't reckon anything could kill one of those trees. Even if you cut it off at the base a whole lot of suckers would come back again. They're indestructible.'

She hesitated doubtfully, torn in her loyalties, gazing at the tree.

'And what if it fell on the house?' he added.

She snorted. 'Thanks a lot.'

'I'm just saying.'

She chewed her lip, staring at the window to the verandah and Sophie's bedroom beyond the tree. 'OK,' she said finally.

'I'll put him onto it. He's looking for work at the moment, since he got laid off.'

'What was he?'

'A logger.'

She felt her smile stiffen on her face. 'A logger. I thought he'd be a tree surgeon.'

The plumber gave her a look. Muffled a disbelieving snort behind a cough before continuing. 'He'll have to hire a cherry picker too, obviously. Or a scissor lift. Do it properly. But this bloke, he's got one of those on-site chippers, so he could turn all the offcuts and debris into woodchips as he goes. It'd save you some money; you wouldn't have to pay someone else to come and remove it.'

'It seems so brutal somehow,' she said, grimacing.

She felt his eyes taking in the loose planks in the verandah, the way it dipped off on the western side of the house where she still hadn't gotten the restumping done. The row of spider ferns in the hanging baskets she'd forgotten to water.

'Well, you planted the thing. I guess,' he said finally with a dismissive gesture, 'you have to deal with it.'

Implying she was irresponsible, obviously. Or just stupid. 'Pollarding, is it?'

'That's right. That's my advice. Take the bastard out at head height before it comes through your roof in a storm.'

She stood there for a while after he left, leaning on the flaking verandah post, trying to work out whether he'd been having a go at her or not. Then she shook herself, irritated. Of course he was having a go at her. They all were.

Sophie kept her iPod on, reading a textbook, as her mum's friends began to show up. She waved casually, keeping her face preoccupied, as they entered bringing plates and dragging their unwilling children with them. She felt a small surge of satisfaction surreptitiously watching their faces drop as they realised they'd have to keep an eye on their own kids for once.

That's right, she thought vengefully, no dump-and-runs. She ignored her mother when she came in to drag the stereo speakers out onto the back verandah, until she waved dramatically in front of her.

'What is it?' she said sweetly, lifting out one earpiece.

'You're not really going to sit in here, are you?'

'I'm studying for a test. I'm fine,' she answered coolly. 'Go and have your party.'

Her mother stood staring at her for a few seconds, her face set in a struggling mask of tolerant patience. 'I would really like you, Sophie,' she said evenly — ah yes, 'I' statement time — 'to come outside and have a good time with us, and celebrate your birthday. It would mean a lot to me.'

'I'll bring out the dip and chips in a little while,' Sophie replied, turning a page. 'Go on and have fun with your friends.'

Her mother grabbed a pile of CDs and stalked outside, her jewellery jangling. She'd gone all out today; she even had ankle-chains on. And the 44-gallon drum was ready in the back garden, piled high with scrap wood for when it got dark, so the posse was obviously planning on settling in for the long haul. Sandy might have been cueing up Norah Jones now, but by 8 p.m., Sophie knew, it would be Fleetwood Mac, and they would be doing that dancing that looked like someone had put ice down their backs.

It was just as well she hadn't invited any of her own friends. She threw down the textbook, restless with submerged, embittered rage, and grabbed a platter of something someone had brought; a dip an unappetising shade of brown, surrounded by pita crisps. This would be bound to infuriate her mother, she knew; her acting as waitress at what was meant to be her own party. Good. And if Sandy thought she was going to eat any of this poxy junk, she was mistaken.

There she was, sitting back in a deckchair with a tumbler of that totally disgusting wine, gossiping away with the others. Sophie caught her eye and a brief challenge passed between them.

'I'll keep the cordless phone out here with me, Sophie,' Sandy said, holding up the handset, 'and I'll come and get you if there's any birthday calls.'

'Who from? Rich?'

She saw her mother flinch, quicker than a blink, then her bright smile.

'Well, yeah, Rich will be ringing you a bit later to wish you a happy birthday. And then I want you to ring Grandma to thank her for that gift voucher, alright?'

Sophie watched her, using that loud, fake voice to tell her what to do and who she could speak to, surrounded by the armoury of her gang. Sophie savoured the moment.

'Oh, I'll ring him in a sec.'

Sandy's eyebrows flatlined with her smiling mouth, like a plug had been pulled.

'What?'

'It's my free hour on my mobile, so I'll give him a call.'

Such beautiful, pure power. Such a soothing cool thing to hold, to listen to the voices trail away and that uncomfortable silence descend. Sophie remembered how it had felt, tearing away at her nail, and how she'd just closed her eyes and ripped. Incandescent pain, blooming and sizzling. The way you could float above it.

'How did you get his number, if you don't mind me asking?'

She caught that warning note, and volleyed back a smile.

'Who — Rich's? I've had it for ages.'

'From where?'

She widened her eyes, comical and patient. *Listen to my stupid mother*, her look said, *so totally out of it.*

'Mu-um! Whitepages dotcom.'

Look what I put up with, she telegraphed to the silent watching women on the grass. *You think you know us, don't you? You don't know jack. We're all way ahead of you.*

'We've rung each other a bunch of times,' she said in that tolerant, slightly scolding tone. 'We're planning on going on a bit of a trip. To Tasmania.'

Her mother's mouth worked. That nerve-end pain, Sophie saw it there, the naked hurt when your unthinking fumbling hand collides with something hard. She felt a flare of vindictive pleasure, something savage with a deep, bitter quick. That would have been enough, just that moment. She would have left it there, except that Sandy recovered herself, rallying in front of her friends.

'You're certainly not going anywhere with *Richard*. I can tell you that right now.'

She wouldn't like that, Sophie thought with glee, not the sound of her own prim surly mother-witch voice betraying her in front of them. The mothers who pretended they never shouted, who said they talked with their kids like real friends, who knew how to communicate so there didn't need to be conflict. Using those phrases they got out of books from the library. They were witnessing this now, their faces still and avid, and Sophie felt invincible.

'Anyway,' went on Sandy, trying for a little levity and failing, 'you can't tell me you actually want to go on a holiday with the guy? What's he planning?'

'We're going to walk the Overland Track. The Cradle Mountain–Lake St Clair walk.'

If Sandy had snorted with derisive laughter, trying to make a fool of her in front of everyone, it would have been better. But instead she made her face go soft and sympathetic.

'Oh, *Soph*. Listen. You don't really think he's going to come through on something like that, do you?'

'Well, you tell me. He's already booked and registered our names.'

Sophie felt the air tighten between them like a wire as her mother struggled to maintain her poise, reaching up and smoothing her hair behind her ear, that maddeningly understanding smile still playing on her lips. She didn't think Sophie could go through with it. Couldn't believe she wouldn't back down. There was a grim sourness now underscoring that smile, something you wouldn't see unless you lived with her.

'You're not seriously telling me you want to go bushwalking with a total stranger?'

'Yeah. Believe it or not, I do want to.' She couldn't show doubt now, or pretend to change sides. 'I'm borrowing my gear from the bushwalking club at the school. I've already checked it out. So, I'm gonna ring Rich back and get the dates set.' She nearly said *Dad*. So nearly. That would have blown her mother out of the water, witnesses or not.

'I thought you'd be pleased, Mum,' she remarked innocently. 'You're always talking about Tasmania and how it changed your life. Seeing the wilderness and everything. Didn't you and Rich do that while you were down there, really appreciate the place? I mean, you saved it, didn't you?'

'We were there as part of the Blockade,' Sandy said mechanically. 'Not *tourists*.'

I know what you're doing, said her eyes. *Don't think this is finished with.*

'I think that's a great way to get to know your father a bit better, doing a physical challenge together like that,' piped up her mum's friend Margot, smiling encouragingly. Margot who meant so well, who didn't even know that her sixteen-year-old daughter had slept with just about every guy in school.

Later that night, after everyone had gone, she came out of her room to find her mother sitting bent over her desk lamp, making earrings. Sandy's eyes were red and smeared with crying, and as she screwed them up frowning short-sightedly for the holes drilled in the gemstones she was using, she looked old and crabby and tired. If she went on the attack, Sophie was going to say *gee, thanks for a great birthday party* and walk straight out again. But Sandy just glanced up at her and sighed, and fresh tears swam in her eyes. It looked as though it was going to be a crying jag punishment, not an anger one.

'Why, Sophie? Why be so hostile in front of all my friends?'

'I wasn't hostile. I was just telling you I already had Rich's number. I'm allowed to make plans without getting your permission first. Next year I'm allowed to leave *home*, if I want to …'

'Just don't even start that.' Sandy's hands searched in one of the plastic dishes for a piece of stone, digging fretfully. The gesture reminded her so much of Grandma Janet, looking impatiently for something in her purse — her heart pills, or her shopping list, or some improving little item she'd cut out and kept to make a point.

'I don't want you to go there with him,' said Sandy, sniffing through her blocked sinuses. 'I'd worry myself to death.'

Sophie picked up pliers and tigertail wire and an earring hook, and threaded a piece of amethyst on. 'It's only seven days. I want to meet him. It'll be good.'

She looked down at the tray of stones. Rose quartz, maybe. She wasn't going to weaken, no matter what Sandy did or said. No matter how much she cried or tried to make her feel guilty. She kept her head down, sensing her mother wiping her eyes.

'Fifteen,' Sandy said, her voice high and strained with more tears. 'I can't believe it. Soon you'll just turn around and walk out of here.'

'No, I won't. What do you think: rose quartz or a seed pearl?'

'You can't use the seed pearls, they're too expensive. Or just use one, then pile on a few of those glass ones.'

Sophie threaded them on, and waited.

'How does he seem, to you?' said Sandy.

'Nice.'

'Did he bother to ask how I was?'

'Sure. He said he's going to call you to talk about all this.'

'So he bloody should.' Sandy sniffed again, put down what she was working on and put her head in her hands. 'I must be insane to even be considering it,' she muttered. 'Absolutely insane. Everyone's been telling me all afternoon I have to try and be rational about it because he's still your father — someone even quoted some bloody UN declaration. As if the UN could care less that I've raised you alone without help from anyone. And what's he ever done for you? Nothing.'

'There'll be hundreds of people walking along with us.' Sophie wasn't sure of this, but it sounded right. 'I'll meet people from all over the world. And Mr Boyd at school said I could count it as my Community Challenge unit, if I went.'

'Did he? You've really thought this through, have you?'

She nodded. She picked up a piece of tourmaline and found the hole drilled through it, pushed the wire inside. Her mother was gazing at her now, her hands flat against each temple, holding her hair out of her face.

'You know what? I was going to call you Melantha,' she said wistfully. 'I don't know why I didn't. I had it all planned.'

'I'm glad you didn't.'

'It means "deep purple lily".'

'It sounds like medicine.'

'What?'

'You know — Mylanta. That stuff you take for your stomach that tastes like chalk.'

Their two heads bowed over the light, choosing gemstones, Sophie permitting herself a secret smile as she heard Sandy laughing dryly in spite of herself.

'You could go on your Goddess workshop,' she said, still not looking up. 'It's on at just the same time.' Placing the idea there like a small shining stone in her mother's path. Setting it all in motion as she held her breath, sensing Sandy glance up sharply, a half-finished necklace cupped in her waiting hand.

Six

Sunday evening, Rich was walking along the street with Genevieve, the protein-shake girl. Make them laugh, Rich had found, and you were home and hosed.

'It's no ordinary duster, though,' he was saying. 'It's the magic duster.'

'Yeah, magic's a word they use a lot, isn't it?'

'It's a world of magic. Magical solutions to everything. This one, you put a battery in the handle, and so the duster spins round.'

'Fabulous! Where's the Nobel Prize for that man?' She had a great laugh. And a body as finely muscled as a deer, strolling along easily in her cotton sweatpants with that fit little bounce in her step.

'Yep, you press the button and it spins. Good for startling animals. So if you were to combine that, say, with the Magic Swivel Sweeper, which spins itself around corners and has a light so you can dust in the dark, well, *then* you'd have yourself a product.'

'Would it have to be made of plastic?'

'Genevieve, you've seen the things. They're all made of plastic.'

'So they break in three weeks.'

'Why do you think they always give you two for the price of one?'

They got to the Thai restaurant and stopped outside.

'Is this the one?' she asked.

'This is it.'

'Looks busy, for a Sunday night.'

'We could just get takeaway. I only live round the corner.'

He felt the unsaid thing enter the space between them; something speculative and knowing in her raised-eyebrow smile.

'Have you got a magic swivel sweeper with the dust-at-night feature?'

'What have you got in mind?'

Janet. Another unwavering stress in her life. Another judgemental, negative millstone, her own lifelong personal Mother Superior. No wonder she needed to go on a retreat.

'You're not serious,' her mother said when Sandy told her about the Tasmania trip. 'You haven't seen Richard in — how many years? — and now you're suddenly sending Sophie off on a holiday with him.'

Sandy took the cordless phone and walked out onto the front verandah.

'It's not like that. He invited her, she wanted to go. What would I have achieved by saying no, really, Mum?' She kicked crossly at the litter of gumnuts and leaves on the porch timbers with the side of her shoe.

She could hear her mother exhale with exasperation on the other end of the phone. 'Sandy, I really can't understand how you make these decisions. Honestly, it just seems so ... arbitrary.'

'Well ...'

'So spur of the moment. You were never even married to the man, after all. I always warned you he'd only stick around as long as it suited him. And surely it's going to be disruptive for Sophie, at a time when she should be concentrating on her studies.'

Concentrating on her studies. That had always been Janet's favourite mantra. *We don't think you should even think about going out with boys, Sandra, while you're still at school and concentrating on your studies.* Sandy could remember her, hovering pointedly in the kitchen as Sandy tried to talk privately to some boy on the phone, some innocent, normal phone call made agonising by Janet's cold glances of disapproval. And Sandy's throat seizing up with self-consciousness, every word she uttered listened to and judged.

Concentrating on her studies, because her mother kept telling her how much the school fees were costing and what a sacrifice they'd made sending her and her brother to *private school*, even though the schools were only ordinary Catholic secondary colleges. It wasn't until Sandy got to university that she realised just how cripplingly bad an education it had actually been. How warped and limited and hopelessly timid she was now in practically everything important about life.

She'd never even told her parents she was going to the Blockade. How could she, when she went home from student residences on the weekend to eat chops and three veg in front of her parents' television? *Just the veggies for me, if that's OK*, Sandy would say, and her mother would sigh and roll her eyes, and her father, curling his lip at the Wilderness Society rallies on the evening news would grunt and say: *Look at them. Bloody rent-a-crowd.*

She'd told them she was going on a bushwalking trip with the walking club at uni. The Catholic walking club, she'd said in a flash of inspiration, as if such a thing existed. By the time she'd come back for the new term in March, transformed into a different person, the whole thing had clearly passed them by. They didn't see the change in her, either, even though Sandy felt it must have been shining out of her face, freshly minted. There was no need even for the elaborate lies she'd prepared about the trip. That had been a big lesson to her, she reflected; how much time she'd wasted worrying that they'd suspect something when they never even noticed. She'd been free, then, to reinvent herself behind their backs.

Nobody had paid uni fees in those days, she remembered, it had all been free, but her mother still referred frequently and fretfully to how much Sandy was costing everyone. Even now, years later, she still brought up the school fees every chance she got. It was a permanent, outstanding account, forever in the red.

She felt she'd been paying back those fees, really, ever since. Paying them back in assiduous stiff-faced gratitude every time her own education was mentioned — which was still often, since Sandy insisted on sending Sophie to the local public school and Janet never shut up about it — and in her silent, fuming stoicism in the face of criticism, which was the only real skill the school had taught her. None of it did any good. Her mother, she was convinced, still believed she'd frittered all of it away. Janet was still waiting, somehow, for a return on her investment. *You're so casual about work*, she'd say wonderingly, as if she'd spent her own life holding down a full-time job. *Mum*, Sandy would say, *I'm passionate about ideas*, and Janet would roll her eyes with derisive, long-suffering weariness.

'Sandy?'

'I'm here. She's doing fine at school, Mum.'

'Be honest now, Sandy, you hardly know what she's up to, do you? Getting around looking like a vampire, out with the children of all those hippies. And I'm sure she's not well — she looked like death warmed up last time I saw her.'

'She's fitter than you and me put together, Mum.' Sandy went down the verandah steps and kicked with her shoe at a nettle she noticed growing out of the path. She could just see her mother, sitting on that fat re-upholstered couch gazing out at the manicured courtyard of her townhouse, not a thing in the world to worry about but how to interfere in her life.

'It just seems so *lax*, Sandy, and haphazard. She hardly knows him.'

'Well, this might be her chance, now that she's old enough to judge for herself.'

Lax, she thought venomously. Remembering her loneliness, all through her tightly wound, subjugated adolescence, when she'd lie in her room and vow to herself: *If I ever have children whatever happens I'm going to do the exact opposite of what she's done.*

And the thing was that despite Janet's continual attempts to undermine it, she'd done that. What a wonderful childhood

Sophie had had, full of broad-minded, colourful people and ideals. No pointless sterile rules. No warping, guilt-laden repression. The exact opposite of her own, and that was the one good thing she'd managed with her life, one glowing result after fifteen years of effort, and did her mother give her the slightest bit of credit for it? Sandy kicked at the nettle till it was a wet green smear on the paving stones.

'Well,' Janet finished with a sigh, 'I suppose you'll go ahead and do whatever takes your fancy regardless — you always have. Can I have a word with Sophie, please?'

'I'll tell her to ring you — she's not home at the moment.'

'At this hour, on a Sunday night? Where on earth is she?'

Sandy walked back into the house, towards the wine in the fridge. Her jaw was forced down tight. Breathe, breathe.

'At a friend's house.'

She pulled out a glass and stood it on the table, still piled with all her stock from the market waiting to be sorted. She imagined her mother putting a hand to her temple, shaking her head slightly in genteel disbelief; her face, so unlined and well maintained, flinty with that familiar, martyred tolerance.

She's not your daughter, she wanted to spit. *You had your chance with yours, and look what a disaster you made of it. She's mine, so butt out.*

'She's got her own webpage she's working on,' she heard herself say brightly. 'Her teacher says she's one of the smartest girls in her year and the best thing I can do is just give her her head and let her do her own thing.'

'You wouldn't hear that sort of nonsense if she was at a decent school,' her mother said. 'And now she's going off with Richard when you have no idea what sort of person he's turned into. Honestly, Sandy, sometimes I despair, I really do.'

'Well, just rest assured we're all fine here,' she answered inanely. Her mother rang off and she stood there with the phone handset, feeling something corrosive and sour in her chest that had to be swallowed down. '*I* despair,' she muttered savagely to the phone. '*Me*.'

She poured a glass of wine and went back to the couch, glancing at the clock. Honestly. What a ridiculous judgemental overreaction — it was only 9.30. Sophie had her own life to lead, her own friends, and one thing Sandy was determined about, she was never, never going to put onto Sophie the shit her mother had given her. Never. If she wasn't home by ten, she'd do a casual ring-around to a few houses. Trust — that was the important thing. Wasn't it? Freedom.

When, at last, she heard the back screen door scuffing open as the handle turned and Sophie came in, she couldn't believe the traitorous words that leaped suddenly, jerkily out of her own mouth.

'What sort of a time is this to be coming home?' And — shit, how did this happen? — in her mother's voice exactly, the exact same icy tone she desperately wished to exorcise.

'I mean,' she amended hastily, 'I'm not hassling you about it or anything, but you have to let me know. Phone me or send me a text or something. That's what that phone's for. But I get worried when I don't know where you are, you know? Does that seem fair to you?'

'What's the point of sending you a text? You can't switch on your phone to read them.' So flat and tired, somehow, her daughter's voice, with that look that would shrivel you in your tracks. Scare you to death.

'That's beside the point. Anyway, I can read them. I just don't see the sense in taking ten minutes to make one up and send it when I can just ring.'

'I've been studying.'

'Where?'

'At Skye's house.'

She felt her hands start going triumphantly to her hips, and she stopped herself. Folded them. No, even worse. Where on earth to put those hands?

'Well, that's very interesting, because I was talking to Annie and she said Skye was at the library tonight.'

'OK, then, I was at the library.'

The low, sullen monotone of her apathy. Awful. A thin silence between them, like two fencers, waiting on the balls of their feet. When did things get so ... adversarial?

'I think I'm pretty open with you, Sophie.'

'Here we go,' she heard her mutter.

'I don't impose too many restrictions, I hope. But you need to tell me where you are, and I'd appreciate it if you didn't lie, because I know the library closes at 6 p.m. on Sundays.'

'OK, then. I was at Jesse's.'

'Jesse? Boy or girl?'

'Jesse the boy.'

'Well, you don't have to hide your relationships from me, do you? When have I ever not welcomed your friends?'

Sophie swapped her bag to the other arm and glanced longingly at the door. She took a breath, sighed it out in a gust of frustration as though whatever it was wasn't worth explaining.

'You haven't ever not welcomed them. It's not that.'

For all Sandy knew, she could have some of that crystal meth in that bag, waiting for her chance to go into her room and smoke it or cook it up or whatever they did. Someone's kid had overdosed last October, seventeen years old and out cold at the bus stop, right here in Ayresville, none of them could believe it. What was wrong with these kids? She willed Sophie to face her, so she could have a look at her eyes.

'How long has this been going on, with this Jesse person?'

Sophie gave her a long, level, amused look — plenty of time to check out those pupils. Normal.

'Since his family got Bluetooth.'

'What?'

'Wireless broadband.'

'I don't get you ...'

'God, what is this? I was in a *chat room*, OK? Just surfing the net and downloading some music. Nothing else.'

'Well.' Floundering again, on the back foot, her indignation log-jammed with nowhere to go. 'Well, anyway, dinner's in the oven.'

'No, thanks.' Sophie was searching in her bag now, for something. 'I'm on the forty-hour famine,' she said indistinctly.

'I'm sorry?'

'You know — raising money for charity. I told you already.'

Sandy took another mouthful of wine, feeling a quick loosening slip of relief. Had she told her? Maybe. Probably.

'Well, good for you. That's great. Is Tegan doing it too?'

'No,' said Sophie. It was taking up all her attention, whatever she couldn't locate in that bag. Her teased, matted hair fell in a dark sweep across her face. 'Just me.'

'You can't tell me you got these muscles using the AbCruncher Pro.' Rich rested a shot glass on Genevieve's stomach. 'See, look at that. You could probably drink it from that glass without using your hands, couldn't you?'

She smiled, shifted her hair behind her ear. 'Probably.'

'Now why can't they put that on daytime TV? Really though, are you an athlete? A professional dancer?'

'No, I do a lot of yoga.'

'Yoga doesn't give you biceps like that.'

'Yes it does. And don't try challenging me to an arm-wrestle as some kind of awkward flirtation.'

'OK then, I'm on warning.' He felt light-headed, even at the thought of them struggling fully clothed in an arm-wrestle. His mind was racing ahead making a scattergun inventory: how old the sheets on the bed were, the state of the shower recess ...

'Why do guys always do things like that, as if they're the first ones to ever try it on you?'

He was instantly on the alert. 'What's that?'

'Oh, you know. Pretend they've just had the great idea of offering you a massage, say. All those dumb underhand excuses for foreplay.'

He swallowed. Throat suddenly cotton-dry. 'No idea.'

'Like the way they just happen to be carrying a condom.'

'Hmm. Must be annoying.' *Shut up, you clown.*

She sat up without using her hands and downed her drink,

glancing speculatively around his place. Over at the wall, he thought. That's right. Look over there.

'They are *great* photos,' she said finally, and he felt a rush of relief, of new firepower.

'Thanks.'

'You're not saying *you* took them?'

'I did, yeah.'

'Wow. Where are those women from?'

'Thailand. They're tribal women from a particular group up in the north, and they fit those rings around their necks from a really early age.'

'My yoga instructor would have a fit. She says the neck vertebrae are the most fragile in the whole body.'

'It's a cultural thing.'

He remembered booking that tour in Chiang Mai, the street of touts selling different trips. *BEST PRICE FOR VISITING LONG-NECKS*, one blackboard had said. *Visit Hill Tribes With Us Then Best Price Handicraft Factory*. The one he recalled most sharply said: *If You See Any Other Tourist Group On Our Trip, We'll Give You Refund.*

He wished, now, he'd thought to get a photo of that sign. He imagined the repeated complaints that must have motivated it: a noisy group of German eco-tourists coming face to face on the track with an equally earnest troupe of Canadians, both sides lowering their camcorders with stiff resentment, then a third chattering group tramping up the jungle track like Dr Livingstone. And up around the bend, the tribe checking their watches and yawning and getting into position in front of their traditional huts.

'What are you thinking about?' Genevieve asked him curiously.

'Oh, I was just thinking about the day I visited that ... ah ... indigenous community. There they were in the middle of the jungle miles from anywhere.'

There had been a jovial tour guide who'd confided to him that the Thai nickname for *farangs* was 'long-nose'. 'That's my job!'

the guy had said, chuckling and wiping tears of hilarity from his eyes. 'Taking long-noses to visit long-necks!'

Rich started to tell Genevieve this but stopped. 'You know what I feel like?' he said instead. 'Chocolate.'

'Do you have some?'

'Sure I do. Always got some in the fridge.'

She must have forgotten she'd told him about her weakness for it. But when he brought out the block of plain milk chocolate he'd bought, a shadow of disappointment crossed her face, the first he'd noticed that night. He felt a second of doubt. Hoped she wouldn't start spouting on about *carbs* and *trans-fats*. Talking about what she ate as if it was her religion.

'Oh, OK. I don't want to sound picky or anything, and I'm a sucker for chocolate, but I really only like the dark pure organic stuff.'

'Do you? Next time I'll know, then. I know the stuff you mean. The eighty-percent cocoa kind. It's like having four espressos, isn't it? Like a hit.'

He was starting to gabble now, he could feel it, trying to rescue the moment.

'It's actually quite good for you,' she said. 'Full of antioxidants.'

'I've got a bit of a soft spot for this brand, though,' he went on. He couldn't stop himself. 'When I was on the Blockade for the Franklin we were camped upstream in the forest for days on end and it was so bloody cold and wet, this chocolate was a godsend. Someone had brought a family block of it and you would have thought we were in a concentration camp, the way we hoarded it.' He paused, waiting.

'I know it's cheaper, but it just tastes too salty to me,' she said.

'I've got some photos of the Blockade somewhere, if you'd like to see them.'

'That was — what? — a protest blockade?'

'Yeah — the big one. Where we saved the Franklin.'

'That's a river, right?'

He eyed his glass. Another couple of mouthfuls in there — he'd pour them both another one and change the CD; this African one had been a miscalculation.

'The battle for the Franklin River, in Tasmania,' he said lightly. 'Thousands of people went. We all got arrested and went to jail. You must remember it: '82 and '83.'

'Rick, I would have been about two.'

He smiled brightly, feeling the air start to go out of the room, feeling the blades jam.

'Well, anyway,' he said. 'Next time I'll get the gourmet chocolate. And it's Rich, by the way.'

She was looking at him differently. It wasn't just his paranoia — she definitely was. Then she yawned, stretching her glorious, suddenly unattainable legs, and his heart slumped as she climbed to her feet.

'Oh, sorry. Better get going, anyway,' she said. 'Work tomorrow. Doing a big shopping-mall promotion. Thanks for dinner.'

'Sure,' he said, still smiling like a moron. 'See you round.'

Giving her a casual wave at the door, after she'd slipped out nimbly from under his arm, took everything he had. The chocolate, he thought bitterly as he snapped off the CD player, that's how much it meant to these Gen Y-ers. Just a different bloody brand of chocolate would have swung it for him.

He flipped through the channels on the TV dispiritedly, then tossed the remote control onto the coffee table, where it skittered into the others. He seemed to have acquired an arsenal of the things — TV and DVD and VCR and digital box and CD player — he was always looking for the right one, always pointing and pressing impatiently, wondering why the channel wouldn't change. His phone was lying there amongst the remotes and takeaway Thai food containers. On an impulse, he leaned forward and picked it up, scrolled to his phone contacts. He'd text Sophie. Ask her how she was going with her packing. Let her see her old man was still up and doing late on a Sunday night.

Sophie's mobile phone played the opening bars to 'Katabasis' as the text arrived. Sophie, oblivious in stereo headphones, cracked the spine on the book she was meant to have read by first period tomorrow, her hand at her mouth and her teeth absently searching for a rough edge of fingernail. She scanned the first page, her brain troubled, full of the images of the Amazon basin she'd coasted over using Google Earth that afternoon, mesmerised, at Jesse's place. She couldn't stop thinking about it. Floating like an angel, abseiling down to get a closer look at the dieback and soybean plantations and human roads crisscrossing it like unhealed scars on a body, soaring up again, thinking how small and vulnerable it really looked from above, and Jesse saying *hey I thought you were going to help me with this essay*, and her answering, *yeah, in a minute, in a minute.*

Sandy, sitting in a pool of lamplight in front of their own computer, was thinking that it just felt like last week she'd had the guy in the shop install Windows '98 on it; surely it wasn't the dinosaur Sophie claimed it was, surely she could still use the dial-up to ... well, whatever, to downpod what she needed. Instead of all this eye-rolling, pissed-off secrecy that flourished beyond her control. The stuff she felt herself brushing over uneasily, like that CD of Sophie's she'd come across this afternoon — a three-headed dog glowering out at her from the cover. Just another one of those incomprehensible goth things, like the black crow tattoo and skull rings. She felt a furtive relief at the satisfying series of chirps as the modem connected her when she clicked on the right icon, thinking that swimming into the world wide web wasn't as hard as she'd been telling herself. In fact, she was sort of struggling now to remember the principles that had kept her so determinedly opposed to it. Then, hesitantly, she clicked the cursor in the search engine box and typed: *Elmo Goth.*

Seven

What would she look like now? Rich had a photo of her from when she was about eight, one of those school pictures with hair neatly combed and a sweet scattering of freckles across her nose. Pierced ears, he'd noticed, scrutinising the photo. That'd be Sandy's leniency. Way back then (seven years, he reminded himself wonderingly, half her lifetime, gone like blown smoke), he'd debated about taking the photo to show his parents one Sunday when he'd gone over there for lunch, and decided uneasily against it. They hardly spoke about Sophie by then.

It had been awkward, those initial few years after he and Sandy had broken up. They'd grill him about whether he ever saw her and did he have an address where they could send her Christmas presents, and on and on till he felt leaden with grainy, exhausted guilt. Then one year, something shifted. His mother, he suddenly noticed, didn't say Sophie's name. Just called her 'the little girl'.

'You never see her now, do you, the little girl?' she'd said in a voice so quiet and distant he almost asked her to repeat it, then checked himself.

'No, she's basically just with her mother now,' he'd answered. 'I didn't want to drag her through some kind of custody battle. You see enough of that around to see what damage it does.'

He'd glanced at his father — nothing. Just that mouth drawn tight over his teeth as if he was perpetually disgusted with everything.

Showing his mother another photo would have been a mistake. He'd given her one early on in the piece, of Sophie when she was barely two. She'd taken it in both hands and gazed at it, her breathing shallowly heaving through her nose as she kept her mouth clamped shut, and Rich knew what that meant. Sure enough within thirty seconds she'd been weeping and he hadn't known where to look. And his father staring at him with that *see what a fuck-up you've made of things* look on his face.

'I know you don't see her, but she's still our grandchild,' his mother had whispered through the ball of tissues she held to her face. His father had cleared his throat abruptly and got up, and his mother raised a helpless, placatory hand, almost as though she was fending him off. 'I know, I know, I know ...' she had sobbed, and Rich had turned the handle carefully on his teacup resting in its saucer, and itched to make his escape.

'Mum,' he'd said finally, sitting uncomfortably in her lounge room that day, 'try not to upset yourself too much.' He thought, uneasily, about phoning his sister, joking with her to get moving and pop out a couple of kids, get herself home from Washington and give their mother something to devote herself to. His sister was the steady married type; she should be the one his mother pinned all her hopes on, not him.

Anyway. Years ago now, and everyone was over it. He'd eventually sent a copy of the photo of the eight-year-old Sophie on to his parents anyway, as a sort of appeasing extra in a card when he hadn't been in touch with them for a while.

Ludicrous to be even thinking about it now, really. He should be focusing on the seminar he was attending; it'd be over by lunchtime and his boss would want to know what they'd covered.

He stretched his shoulders. In front of him, the Workplace Motivator presenter seemed to be winding up his introductory spiel. Rich could glance through the notes later. He rolled his eyes at a colleague as the consultant launched a PowerPoint presentation, pointed a red laser at the screen and clicked. Nothing. Nobody dared snicker as he aimed it instead at his laptop and data projector on the desk. The screen flashed its familiar rich royal blue and Rich waited as the first message came cartwheeling in across the screen accompanied by an energetic soft-rock soundtrack.

CORE COMPETENCY it read. That vanished to be replaced by the next slide, where the text raced in from the left so fast it leaned forward, only to jerk upright as it arrived, like the Road Runner. *WHAT DOES IT MEAN TO YOU?*

He waited to see whether they were going to use every option on the 'slide transition' list. Yes, they were. The slides flashed in from above, appeared out of a stippled chequerboard, arrived in a slow fade then a pinwheel, marched in from diagonal ends of the screen. Figures and statements accosted him, challenging him with the questions senior management liked to think it asked. He yawned a big jaw-cracking yawn, and checked his watch. *WHO ARE THE KEY STAKEHOLDERS?* flashed the screen. Rich had a sudden mental image of a bunch of besuited zombies, staggering towards him raising stakes in their clammy hands, the walking dead.

K.P.I.s proclaimed the next slide, then dissolved — the lazy editor's tool — into an image of a high, snowcapped mountain that spun disconcertingly offscreen to be replaced by a page which demanded to know: *WHAT GETS YOU TO THE TOP?*

He was sure they had this same theme music in their royalty-free CD archive at work. He'd used it himself, he was almost certain, on an ad about doing your degree by correspondence. They all sounded the same, anyway. It'd be called something like: 'Starburst Success' ('driving uptempo beats, Mozart strings and groovy bass with a euphoric vibe'). Just modified Led Zeppelin riffs, really. *Mountaintops*, thought Rich tiredly. *Give me a break.*

He wondered if they'd catch some good weather on Cradle Mountain; that rich, transitory kind of saturated sunlight that made every photo something special. Magic hour. One thing, the deciduous beech they had down there would be changing colour — he'd make sure he caught plenty of that in his shots.

On the screen, letters began to skid in from the left, flipping as they fell into place like mahjong tiles. *A. T. T. I* ... and he thought lethargically: *let me guess.*

At last it was over and the facilitator stepped in front of the screen holding textas and a roll of white paper. 'We might take this opportunity to break into small groups ...' Rich whispered to the guy next to him, and the two of them had to stifle a bout of gasping schoolboy hysteria when that's exactly what the poor sap said.

He'd go and visit his mother. Before the Tassie trip. Definitely.

It was all a matter of posture, Sandy thought as she explained her story to the mechanic. Your posture was different in the bank, say, than it was in the health-food shop, different when a customer was unconvinced compared to the one who nodded along with you, fishing for their wallet.

'So I came out and someone had just smashed into me and driven off,' she finished.

'Yeah, that's happening more and more.'

'Town's really changing,' she added, and he nodded.

'So I was wondering if you had another one that would fit. One for a Datsun 180Y.' You needed to get the tilt of the head right — apologetic but kind of flirtatious. Appealing.

'Probably got something out the back.' He jerked his own head towards the yard behind the workshop where rusted cars sat mired in waving weeds.

Appealing, yet a little helpless.

'OK, thanks — I'll go back there and see if I can find something.'

'I'm in the middle of a job here.'

'Of course you are. I've got a set of screwdrivers in the car — I'll be right.'

Helpless, and yet a tiny bit brave. 'Because I need to look for some brakelight covers as well — he smashed them up too.'

She was rummaging in the boot before he called her back.

'Look — probably best if I go and have a dig around. OHS,

you know; the boss would kill me.'

He flashed her a quick tired grin; he had a nice smile.

'I don't want to take up too much of your time.'

'Nah, that's OK. Quicker if I check.'

'Really? That's so nice of you.' Now she should stay out of his way until he brought back a bumper bar, and then, when he saw her trying to heft it into the car, he'd offer to put it on for her with the hydraulic drill thing he had in the workshop. She could almost see him now, waving her money away when she brought out her wallet. If she visualised that clearly enough, it might happen. Then she'd say with surprised gratitude, *I'll have to buy you a drink sometime*, getting the posture just right, and who knew? Nothing wrong with a mechanic. They made good money.

Sophie fitted everything into her pack, unpacked it again, repositioned things. Took out the drink bottle and slid it into a side pocket instead, then took all the clothes out and laid them on her bed, debating with herself. *Carrying unnecessary or inappropriate gear*, said the bushwalking guide she'd downloaded, *is one of the major mistakes inexperienced walkers make.*

Well, that wouldn't be her. Tent, poles, sleeping mat, all wrapped inside the two waterproofing green plastic bags Mr Boyd had said would be bound to come in handy. Her online guide agreed with this. *Put all your gear into plastic bags to keep everything dry. Some camping shops sell waterproof plastic pack liners. Modify your plans as necessary depending on weather conditions. If you do become lost, stop, stay calm and set up camp. Signal for help — three blasts on a whistle, three lines stamped in the snow, three yells. Any pattern of three is a standard distress signal in Tasmania.*

She would be totally self-contained, self-sustaining. She'd be carrying everything she would need. *Preparing physically and psychologically for the walk is of utmost importance*, said the guide. *Many beginners overestimate their fitness and stamina levels, and end up exhausted and overwhelmed by the rigorous demands of a six-hour walk carrying a heavy pack.*

Yeah, but how many beginner walkers setting out on the

Overland Track, thought Sophie, could do two hundred sit-ups and twenty chin-lifts? She patted down the plastic boxes stacked with PowerBars, packaged tightly with sachets of electrolyte drinks and ziplock bags of isotonic rehydration powder. She'd found the energy gel bars on the net. Orange flavoured. This would be like doing one of those endurance courses, where you paced yourself, tested your real stamina.

The language of it, it was great. *Protein carbo complex. Predigested hydrolysated protein. Whey protein isolates. Bonded glutamine. Creatine.*

Like a mantra, really. A mantra for a marathon.

Six-thirty, speaking of sit-ups.

Her heart hammering solidly away in her chest as she counted, her breath pulling in and out like a bellows, hot in her throat and chest. Forty minutes of it, until she could smell the sharp scent of her own sweat. A chemical smell. Like her mum and her friends, always on about releasing the toxins.

She bet Rich wouldn't be sucked in by that stuff. She could tell it from his voice, even, over the phone, despite how nervously stilted both their phone conversations so far had been, full of the awkward pauses of strangers. She was relieved when they'd slipped into texting instead. And really, she only had those two old photos of him to go by, the ones in the envelope at the back of one of her mum's photo albums. She'd looked at those blurry pictures thousands of times, at odd moments. One was an old round-cornered snapshot from an instamatic camera, of people standing in front of a big arching tree-fern, the light gloomy and green. Her mum really pretty and slim in her Indian shirt, and Rich a bearded, tanned face in the background, smiling behind sunglasses so that it was impossible to tell whether he was looking at the camera or looking away, thinking his own private, hidden thoughts. The other snapshot was square and shiny with a thin white border, the glaze on its surface, when you turned it into the light, reduced to a maze of tiny cracks. A polaroid, her mother had called it once, and Sophie when she was little had heard the word and thought *polar*. Seen the faded bluish skin tones on the smiling people in the shot, gathered in someone's garden at night, and imagined coldness, numb fingers, frost. Imagined Rich in a cold place, a white world.

He sounded fine on the phone. He really did. Nothing creepy. And she had all the gear she needed, in any case; she wouldn't be relying on him for anything.

She touched her forehead to her knees, panting, resisting the urge to go to the bookcase and find that photo album right now and pull those two pictures out, stare into them as if they could offer her anything more than a shadowed face in a forest somewhere, a person living in a blank, polar world of missing detail.

She could hear her mother's car pull up as she paused to catch her breath, then she heard Sandy call down the hall.

'Sophie? Guess what? The mechanic replaced the bumper for nothing! What did I tell you?'

She dropped her dizzy, thumping head back to her knees, wondering if her mother expected her to answer. Yes, she wanted a response — she could hear footsteps tracking up the hall towards her room. Sophie tucked her legs under her and smoothed her hair back and tried to regulate her breathing.

Here came her mother's standard customary glance as she put her head round the door; buoyant and preoccupied, the cursory absent-minded smile as she waved at Sophie cross-legged and shiny-faced on the floor.

'What have you been doing?' she said, and Sophie rested her palms on her knees, still panting.

'Yoga,' she answered.

Feeling a droplet of sweat break from the back of her neck and run like a raindrop down her demurely straight spine.

Sandy was humming, kicking off her shoes. A good week, some new stock ready for the market, party at Margot's tomorrow. And a car fixed through thinking positively, refusing to let negative thoughts cloud her judgements. She put on her Annie Lennox compilation CD and sang along.

You're pleased with yourself, Janet's voice observed inside her head, not encouragingly. A dampener on her good humour, the usual rain on her parade, but tonight, she wasn't going to pay any attention. *There's nothing stopping you getting a new car, a more reliable one,* her mother's voice scolded in the same old undertone as Sandy stepped into the kitchen and picked a couple of sweet potatoes out of the vegetable box, singing that sisters were doing it for themselves.

Not tonight, she thought sunnily, *and my car is perfectly reliable, I'm just refusing to buy into the whole culture of conspicuous consumption. And in three days I'm going on a retreat to nurture that powerful core of myself whether you like it or not and there's not a damn thing you can do about it.*

There now. Why couldn't she be as articulate as that when her mother was actually on the phone? Nothing bitter or hysterical, just calm assertiveness, just *centredness.* She should get out her yoga mat, come to think of it, and do some yoga with Sophie in the living room. Together. Where was that mat? The phone rang, and she put down her knife and answered it.

Rich's voice on the other end drained her goodwill in one cold swallow. She'd reconciled herself to Sophie going to Tasmania, but her mind kept skittering around the solid fact that it was Rich she'd be going with.

I still have some issues, she'd say sombrely to her friends when they enquired about the trip. And she'd sneak into Sophie's room when she was at school, and look at her pack and equipment laid out in neat piles on her floor, and feel better. Sophie, she could tell, was organised and prepared, determined to get through it. She wouldn't need him as much more than a chaperone. A walking companion, like a teacher on a school trip — you didn't have to be friends with them, you just had to be more or less supervised by them. She'd come home at the end, tired and dirty and aching in every joint and complaining about sleeping in a tent or on a bunk bed, and maybe then, finally, she'd look at the cosy and welcoming home she had here with a whole new appreciation.

Of course Sandy had issues — who wouldn't? — with him muscling in like this, as if everything could be just swept under the carpet. Issues that would have to be expressed, she knew, in order to be transcended.

'Sandy?' she heard him say now. 'Is that you?'

He always sounded quieter than she remembered, less dogmatic. He laid out the planned schedule to her and she stood stiffly, listening, taking notes on flight times. There was a chair there, next to the table, but for some reason she didn't want to sit down. Standing made her feel more empowered. *The anger is justified*, she said to herself. *Go into the anger, and own it.*

'I don't want it just to be at the airport,' she said coolly. 'I don't want to be in the situation of just dropping her off somewhere assuming you'll be there to meet her, and then you go and catch a plane.'

'But that's ... I mean that's pretty much what ...'

'Listen, I haven't seen hide nor hair of you now for seven years and I'm her mother and it's up to me, not you, alright? I need to see you and assess things.'

A silence. 'OK. Fine. So we meet in the city? Catch up there, before the flight?'

'Yeah. Then we go out to the airport together. I'll drive.'

'Great. OK. That makes it a lot easier, actually. That's a good idea.'

Her hand went to the bottom of the phone handset, the fingers seeking a cord to twist. Nothing. She toyed with an earring instead.

'I'm really not happy about this, Rich.'

'No kidding.'

'I've had to think about this very carefully and work through some very conflicted feelings here.'

'OK. Fair enough.'

'You can't just step back into someone's life when it suits you, you can't just cancel out everything that's happened.'

'But see, Sandy, that's just it. What's "everything"? I haven't been around for her growing up, I've missed the "everything". To me it's just a big blank. And that's why I want to catch up, just make an overture of friendship, now that she's about to become, well, an adult ...'

She remembered that reasoned tone, the way he was always able to explain himself calmly and make her feel like she was the irrational one.

'Abandonment,' she snapped, cutting him off. 'That's the everything.'

That shut him up. She heard a sniff, an indrawn breath of someone summoning ... what? Patience? Tolerance? Antagonism?

'It's been fifteen years,' was all he said. Her fingers sought something to twist again, went to the spot between her eyes, and rubbed.

'I just want you to know I'm doing this for Sophie's sake,' she said finally. 'I see it as her chance to test if you're a person she can trust to let into her life. That will be her decision, obviously. But I'm doing it under great duress. I'm feeling a lot of pressure and that seems very unfair.'

'For fuck's sake,' she heard him mutter. 'Not everything's about you.'

How strange, not to have a cord to connect this handset to the phone, tethering you securely to some kind of solid electrical connection you could get your head around. How weird, instead, to imagine their two voices travelling into space, bouncing off a satellite somewhere, bleeping out these little coded messages into the silent, pitiless dark of some black hole.

'Coming from you, that's pretty funny,' she replied, fingers descending for touchdown on the good solid edge of the table, 'the patron saint of selfishness.'

She waited for the flare of temper that would break the connection, like a symbolic door slam, her thin pleasure at knowing she held the last word and the high moral ground. But he didn't hang up. She waited, nervously taken aback.

'What café?' he said evenly. 'And what time?'

She made him hold on while she got out her diary and flipped through it. Annie was singing *Thorn in my side, you know that's all you ever were*, and Sandy held the receiver into the air, hoping he was listening.

OK, done. It was all going ahead. He could feel it. At work, Rich tilted back in his chair to chat to Martin, one of the young guys working on post-production whose shifts sometimes coincided with his own.

'MP3 players,' he said.

'What about 'em?' Martin was about twenty-three, he guessed, and went to a lot of those music festivals held in paddocks around the country. Had those new tattoos they all seemed to get, in rings around his biceps and big curlicues down onto his forearms, and that weird hair brushed forward round his face, like he had a wig on backwards. Played in a weekend band too, Rich thought. Perfect. Martin was his zeitgeist broker, his key into the right demographic. He grinned back at Rich now.

'You finally weakening?' Martin said.

He smiled back. 'Maybe. Call it peer-group pressure.'

'Mate, they're so cheap on the net they're practically giving them away. Once you've got one, you won't be able to live without it.'

'I'm not sure exactly what I should get, though.'

Martin fished something out of his pocket the size of a matchbox. 'See this? I can hold two thousand songs on this, whole albums, other people's playlists, the works. Even your standard MP3 can download movies now. You'll never pay for a CD again.'

'Yeah, but do you have to listen to them through those earpieces?'

'What? Of course not. You get a dock. You sit this unit in the dock and get yourself some good speakers and listen all day ... Hey, why am I telling you this? You work in TV, Rich, you know the technology.'

'I'm avoiding it.' He smiled as he reached across the desk for Martin's player. 'I have this theory, see, that everyone jumps on these fads and thinks the new stuff is totally indispensable and just a few people resist the impulse to leap on the bandwagon ...'

'You are so full of it.'

' ... and after a while the people who've resisted, who've never owned the new gadget, they're the ones who come to seem really cutting edge.'

'Nah, they just seem really weird. OK, so you set this into the dock and buy a couple of speakers, and I can get those off eBay for you for probably $100 all up, and off you go.'

Rich thought of the sound system he'd saved for months to buy just a few short years ago, his stereo that took up a whole tabletop. He couldn't get over how small the CDs had seemed when they first hit the market, compared to LPs. Thought vinyl would soon become collectible, and was still waiting.

'So I can burn all my CDs into the computer ...' he began.

'Yeah, but why would you? Just download everything you want off iTunes.'

'I wouldn't need two thousand songs. But I thought it'd be good, you know, I've got this trip coming up ...'

'I've got just the thing for you,' Martin said, scrabbling in his bag. 'Hardly use this now. I got it last year for the car, but since I got this job here I really only ride my bike. It's only got one gig capacity though.' He handed Rich a black plastic gadget on a key ring. Cord with a lighter plug, like a recharger.

'There's about 150 songs downloaded onto it off my playlist. I'll leave them on; you can delete them when you do your own. You just plug it in and tune it into the car radio.'

'Miracle.'

'Nah — you can have it.'

'Seriously? You star.'

'Let me know when you want to upgrade to something decent.'

'Thanks, but this is great — all I need. And the sound system I've got at home is fine.'

'Let me guess — one of those big black empty boxes with a million wires and cables everywhere?'

He hesitated, then shrugged. 'It's got great speakers and I can record from CD or do tape-to-tape dubs.'

Martin gave a good-natured guffaw, looking at him with something like wonder as he zipped up his bag. 'Tape-to-tape dubs?' he spluttered, shaking his head. 'Mate, what planet have you been living on?'

Rich grinned back, his jaw tight, and turned again to his script. Underlined, the client's strict instructions that the text saying *Three easy payments of $49.99* was only to flash onto the screen for three seconds in total. Rule number one: disorientation. Then pause on the second part that offered an extra gift for the first two hundred callers, as if the switchboard was going to be swamped for a crappy walking machine. *Don't be left out!* the voiceover would add urgently. The illusion that you were missing out on something unless you jumped right now: rule number two.

Disorientation and urgency, thought Rich, inserting tapes, turning back to the screen. Disorientation and urgency. Get those two elements working together, and there wasn't a single miserable thing human beings weren't capable of falling for.

Eight

He was such a big presence in the car, so relaxed the way he draped his arm over the bucket seat to catch her eye and include her in the conversation. And her mother was so clearly rattled by him, nervy and over-talkative by comparison. Sophie was feeling pretty keyed-up herself, seeing him at close quarters like this, reminding herself, disbelievingly, who he actually was. The radio was fuzzing along with static the way it always did in her mum's car and he reached down to adjust the tuning dial.

'That won't do anything,' Sandy said. She pointed to where the aerial should have been. 'That's the best I can get without an aerial. Got snapped off.'

Sophie tried to read the precise tone of her voice. Not apologetic — accusing, almost. Defiant. As if Rich should have divined she needed a replacement, and provided one.

He reached into his bag. 'How about I just use this instead?'

An in-car iPod. Sophie blinked. When he pushed it into the cigarette-lighter cavity, and tuned it in, she felt another nudge of astonishment as the first song started.

'Korn?' she said finally, leaning forward in her seat. 'You like Korn?'

'Sure.'

'How many songs fit on there?'

'Oh — about a hundred and fifty I think ...'

'About one gig then?'

'That's right.'

'The radio gets AM, no problem,' said Sandy suddenly. 'It's just FM that gets the static.'

There was a pause.

'What kind of car do you have, Rich?' said Sandy.

'A car? I don't have one at all.' He turned his head again to include Sophie in the exchange. 'If I'm not on the road I'm living in the inner city, and it just seems like too much of a carbon footprint, you know? So I just use public transport.' He paused. 'Or my bike.'

Sandy snapped the indicator and changed lanes. 'Easy if you live in the city, yes,' she commented.

Sophie heard the tone again in her voice, had lived with that tone and its wounded, aggrieved subcurrent all her life, but Rich didn't recognise it, or else he ignored it. So that when her mother started on an elaborate tirade about voluntary simplicity and working within your own local community, Rich tilted his head back at Sophie and made a face. He raised his eyebrows a little and let his eyes go glazed and slightly crossed so that Sophie had to hide her grin behind her hand and pretend to look out the window to stop herself laughing.

'For example, I've had this one car for fourteen years now,' Sandy went on, still with the same voice, and Sophie knew it wasn't just her, that other people heard the self-righteousness in it too, because Rich shifted in his seat and said, 'Well, hang on a sec. Just for starters, there's a false kind of logic working there', and fearlessly, calmly, ignoring Sandy's face mottled with surprise and anger, he started talking about catalytic converters and old engines spewing lead into the air. Just straight out contradicted her. And he knew what he was talking about too.

'Not that I'm judging you,' he was adding now to Sandy. 'A lot of people think they're doing the right thing, driving round in old cars, and just don't realise they're creating five times the heavy metal pollution of newer vehicles.'

Sophie could see, from the back seat, her mother's furious profile. She shook her head and her bead earrings swept against her neck, and she chewed on her lip for a moment before answering.

'Nothing like as bad as air travel,' she said shortly. 'Ironic, isn't it — here I am driving you to the airport and you're lecturing me about having to drive an old car.'

'I'm not lecturing you. You insisted on doing the driving, remember? And I realise I do have to work hard to offset my carbon footprint with all the air travel I do.'

'Where do you go?' Sophie blurted.

'All over the place, really. Out-of-the-way places.'

'Still taking photos, then?' said Sandy.

'Oh, yeah, that's what I mean. Photojournalism pieces.'

'And what funds all this gadding about?' asked Sandy. *Gadding.* Didn't he hear that tone again, that warning note of buried contempt? Didn't he know to back off?

'I work in television. I'm a freelance editor.'

'Is that right.' There was a flat note to her mother's voice now, like someone who's heard it all, like being a television editor was the worst sort of trivial sell-out. And Sophie realised he'd been aware of the tone all along, because he stretched out his legs and replied just as coolly.

'Yep, that's my other job. What about you, Sandy? What do you do to make a living?'

Leading her right into it, so that when her mum started reluctantly explaining about the jewellery stall he didn't even need to have a come-back, he just raised his eyebrows and said 'Still?' and let her bluster on digging herself deeper and deeper, listening almost kindly, nodding encouragingly, until even Sandy seemed to realise she sounded like someone who'd done nothing but sit in the same place and do the same mundane crap for years and years, and trailed off into stung silence.

Sophie looked at the two of them in the front seats, amazed that they could both have been the two halves of her. Her parents. It hardly seemed possible. Here was Rich, this stranger, a TV editor who probably knew tons of famous people. And he was taking her, Sophie, to a world-famous place, treating her like an adult, assuming she could manage the six-day walk. And there was her mum, going on a retreat to commune with her past lives, or something. Rich was calm and good-looking and he had Oakley sunglasses and listened to Korn; her mother had a shirt that was too tight under the arms and a car with a bent coathanger for an aerial.

Sophie groped for her phone and scrolled down to Tegan's number. She wasn't even sure what she wanted to say. A song by Foo Fighters came onto the radio from Rich's cool little MP3 player as her thumb hovered over the phone and she half listened to Sandy start in on Rich again, reading him the riot act about how he had to be back at the airport on Tuesday at the exact time they agreed on, no last-minute changes, as if he was some slow-witted eighteen-year-old taking Sophie out on a date and she had a curfew. And as she glanced up at them she saw he was nodding seriously, agreeing, then as her mother turned back to the traffic he swivelled his eyes back at her and smiled conspiratorially like he sympathised with her, and understood. Earlier at the café he'd gotten Sophie a double skim latte without even questioning it and hadn't asked her a lot of bright-eyed crap about what she liked at school and what she wanted to be when she finished.

In fact he wasn't like any of Sandy's friends at all, or any of the adults at school, or anyone else's parents. She'd never thought about it till now but of course Rich would know Sandy as well as she did; he of all people would understand what she could be like and what it was like having to live with her. He was an ally.

Rich likes The Vines! she texted surreptitiously. *He is cool as. Stay tuned. :)*

She pressed 'send' and watched the little animated envelope twist on the screen and disappear, then looked back up to see they were leaving the freeway for the airport.

'I mean it,' her mother was telling Rich in the front seat. 'I think this could be a great experience for Sophie, but I want to be kept in daily contact and know exactly where you are and what's happening. Are we on the same page about this?'

'The same page? Absolutely,' Rich answered. He glanced again at Sophie, and she saw, through the calm sincerity of his voice, that he'd crossed his eyes again, just for a second — a message of mutual forbearance just for her. They were in this together.

Sandy kept the slim packages hidden in her bag until she parked.

'I'll get your pack out,' she said to Sophie, and while she was bent over the boot she patted a side pocket that felt empty, slid open the zip, pushed the packets deep inside behind a flap of Velcro and zipped it all up again before pulling the backpack out. Soph would find them in a few days' time, like a surprise present, she thought, and know she was thinking of her.

'All set?' she said as she helped Sophie put her pack on. 'Are you sure you've got everything in there? It seems kind of light.'

'I've got everything I need. Mr Boyd's helped me and I showed you the list Parks and Wildlife puts out, didn't I? I've got just what they recommend.'

'I wish I'd brought the camera,' said Sandy.

Sophie pulled her hair free from under the pack and rolled her eyes. 'Calm down. It's only a week.'

'Eight days,' said Sandy. She felt bruised. Foolish. Concentrated on putting her keys in her bag, to stop herself reaching out and stroking her daughter's hair.

Rich kept sneaking covert glances, mesmerised. He couldn't believe it was her, the little girl in the photo. All that metallic blue and black around her eyes, that fringe hiding the combative scrutiny that missed nothing, and those black shrunk-wrapped clothes and outsized boots. She looked like one of those Bratz dolls. Or like a groupie at a Marilyn Manson concert, pale as paper, ready to cut you dead with a sidelong sneer. Next to her Sandy looked like a middle-aged tour manager huffing along with the paperwork, her shoulder bag slipping off her arm as they waited in the boarding queue. It was OK. Once they went through security and into the departure lounge, Sandy wouldn't be able to follow; it would be just Sophie and him.

'I'm surprised you're flying to Hobart instead of Launceston,'

Sandy said, scrutinising their flight printout. 'It's further to drive to Cradle Mountain, isn't it?'

She was right, and it hadn't occurred to him until he'd already booked the flights.

'I wanted to show Sophie Risdon Prison,' he said. 'Our own personal memory of Tasmania's convict past.' He glanced at Sophie. 'Has your mum told you we both spent some time at Her Majesty's pleasure, in jail after the Blockade?'

The girl took one gnawed black fingernail out of her mouth. 'Only about a million times,' she answered.

'Well, I thought we'd do a drive-by, for old times' sake.'

'A drive-by?'

He grinned at her. 'Not with Uzis, obviously. Just with a camera.'

God, she was so cool, with that sullen, round-shouldered apathy all the teenagers seemed to have perfected now. She was putting it on for him, he could tell. He'd seen that smile bloom across her face in the car. Sandy folded her arms and hitched her bag again as they moved forward slowly in the queue. She'd been furious with him since the car trip. Just a few more minutes, though, and she'd have to leave, and take her bad mood with her. They checked in and weighed their packs, and Rich turned to Sophie.

'Only fifteen kilos?' he said. 'Wow, I'm impressed. That's fantastic. Have you got a sleeping mat in there?'

'Of course I have.'

'And a fuel stove and everything?'

'She's spent weeks packing,' Sandy interjected. 'One of her teachers gave her lots of pointers. She's borrowed most of her equipment from the school.'

'Great. See, mine's twenty kilos. Extra camera gear, mostly. Can't do without it.'

Their packs disappeared down the conveyor as they got their boarding passes and of course Sandy walked edgily with them all the way to the security gates.

'Eight days, then,' she said stiffly to Rich. 'I'll see you back here, in the arrivals lounge, at 11.15 Tuesday morning.'

'We'll be here, won't we, Sophie?'

He watched her turn and seem to straighten her slouch a little as she saw the expression on her mother's face. She raised her arms and gave her a hug. 'Don't worry,' she said. 'I'll be absolutely fine.'

Sandy angled their bodies away from him as she embraced her daughter.

'I can't believe you're actually going,' he heard her say. 'I want you to ... well, take such care, Soph ...' Her voice going high. Red hair stark against a snarl of jet black as their heads dipped towards each other.

'Now you just go and have a great time at your workshop,' Sophie answered. Rich heard, in her voice, the level tone of authority, the voice of a parent.

'Yeah, you too sweetheart. Be inspired.'

Sophie looked embarrassed. 'You too,' she muttered, smiling stiffly. 'Be inspired.'

Then Sandy was turning towards him as Sophie rummaged in her bag for her mobile. She reached up to draw him to her and Rich thought with a flash of surprise that she was going to hug him too — present a united front for Sophie, maybe, or put a lid on this animosity. He put his arms on her shoulders, a bit taken aback, and she tilted her chin to bring her face close to his ear.

'If you harm one hair on her head,' he heard her say softly, 'believe me, you will pay.'

He pulled back his hands, affronted, and she turned without looking at him again, giving Sophie one more kiss before walking away. Sophie was already moving towards the security doors but he stayed a moment and watched Sandy hurrying off, his nostrils still registering her new and totally unfamiliar perfume.

She'd be OK. She would. She'd be absolutely fine. She was fifteen now and God knows she could stand up for herself. Sandy sped, throat squeezing, breathless, towards the car park. If she could just get to the cashier before 1.40, she wouldn't be charged another $12. All the way there it was as if her mother was floating effortlessly along beside her, giving her the usual white-noise monologue. *Couldn't you have worn a decent pair of shoes?* said her voice as Sandy jog-trotted across the zebra crossing, pushing her hair out of her eyes. *When are you going to get yourself a proper haircut, Sandy? I mean, if it's money, just ask, because frankly, darling, a good haircut would make all the difference. Cut all that colour out, don't you think? It's a colour for a much younger woman, I hope you don't mind me saying.*

Sandy put on her sunglasses as she hurried. She saw her own reflection elongate and slip by through the tinted side-windows of the cars she passed. He looked just the same. Just the same. Same long hair in a ponytail, hadn't gained an ounce of weight. Patronising her with that amused patience, and Sophie lapping that up of course. Making her, Sandy, into the frumpy boring killjoy by default. She'd been in a rush this morning, otherwise of course she would have thought about her appearance more carefully. She was just out of the shower when the guy had rung about the tree, asking her when she'd like him to do it, and she'd clutched her towel around herself impatiently, saying, 'Yes, sure, whatever, whenever suits you.' She'd thought she looked good, anyway, before they left. Something indefinable had happened since then to make her appear shorter, and wider, and more crumpled.

Just being conscious of your posture can really disguise a few extra pounds, said Janet's cool hard voice. Sandy scrabbled in her bag for the parking docket as she ran, fishing for coins for the machine. 1.37. Sandy, she heard, *don't take this the wrong way, but is that a properly fitted bra?* She felt some scattered two-dollar coins along the seam and shook it on a tilt to find them all. 1.39, and there were already two people standing at the cashier's machine getting their exit tickets, and she was puffing and flushed and blinking away tears now. She wasn't going to make it. She slowed down, feeling herself give up.

Sandy, you wouldn't look so disorganised if you kept your coins in a purse.

OK. Thanks very much, great advice, yes.

No point hurrying now. Seeing she was already charged for the next hour, she spent some minutes, her tongue between her teeth, composing a carefully light-hearted goodbye text message to Sophie and writing the return flight details in both her diary and address book before feeding her money into the machine and leaving.

The wellness retreat was an hour away on the southbound freeway and during the entire journey she concentrated on her breathing. On being centred and driving out this creeping, panicked paranoia. She was a powerful being with a limitless capacity for seeing the divine in herself and others, and she'd better banish this negative shit and get into the right headspace if she wanted to harness that properly over the next seven days.

When she drove through the gates, finally, of Mandala and heard the bellbird CD in the reception area, she made a conscious effort to stay tranquil and devote herself to being in the moment. *Accept that both your struggle and your quest to heal has brought you here*, said a sign on the desk, before which burned some top-quality sandalwood incense in a to-die-for metal brazier. After she registered and was shown her room, she breathed in the cedar smell of the ceiling beams and touched the single gardenia in a vase before the small, polished Buddha on her study table, and knew it was going to be just what she needed. Maybe that Chinese herbalist she'd talked to was right, and she had some heavy *qi* energy on her spleen. Something that would explain this sensation of being weighted down in her internal organs, something that she could renegotiate up to the top of her head, and release out of the crown chakra. Or whatever.

In Hobart, Rich took Sophie up from the wharves into the museum. Something normal and neutral to do with her, till they both got to know each other a little better. They both halted at the same place, staring at the video loop running over and over.

Thylacine, said the placard. *Tasmanian Tiger.* The scratchy old film footage showed a tiger, pacing its cage in 1936, waiting only for the oblivion that would come when the keeper forgot to open the door to its enclosure on a night when temperatures dropped below zero. Trapped without shelter outside, it had frozen to death. *This was the last tiger to die in captivity*, read the caption. Nobody knew when the last one had died in the wild. On the piece of footage, the animal opened its extraordinary jaws, shook its head. You saw someone's hand tease it outside the wire, and it sat back on its haunches and powerful tail like any other marsupial, the stripes on its back delicate and uniform. Then it turned to the camera and gazed directly at him with black, uncomprehending eyes. After a few unnerving seconds it turned again to pace with the same panicky misery at the wire.

The grainy footage of the thylacine restarted, and the animal again turned its heavy head to look at them with that sunken, fathomless stare.

'It's like it's saying *Why?*' he said finally, breaking the silence.

'No, it's like it's saying *I don't get it*,' Sophie replied.

'Get what, though?'

She paused, looking past the video at the stuffed tiger exhibit in the glass case behind, those shadowed eyes removed and replaced with fake yellow glass ones like marbles.

'Don't ask me,' she muttered. She shook her head and moved away from the diorama, hunching her shoulders defensively. 'This whole place is a bit lame.'

'It is, isn't it? Not even any interactive displays. I went to this museum once, must have been San Francisco, you could stand in this replica room and feel what an earthquake feels like. Right through the floor.'

He was losing her, he could tell. He couldn't afford to lose her.

'Wait here a sec,' he said, and went and had a word with the lady on the front desk, who fetched one of the curators for him. He gave her his best smile and a story of a documentary he was making, flashing her his television station ID and his card which he'd had printed describing himself as a freelance photographer, here coincidentally with his daughter, wondering about the possibility of any other special materials not on exhibit, for research purposes.

He turned on all the charm he could muster, apologising for not contacting her in writing in advance, and finally she checked her watch, smiling, and agreed to let them view the thylacine remains they kept locked away.

'You can see why, can't you?' she said, hurrying them down a corridor. 'I'd have every man and his dog in here wanting to look at them, and really when you think about it they're amongst the most precious remains we have on the planet.'

'Still a lot of interest in them, is there?' he said, buoyant with gaining special access, with Sophie's surprised, impressed eyes on him.

'I would say, of the requests I get about the museum, ninety-five percent of them are about the Tasmanian tiger,' she answered, inserting keys into a lock of a vault. 'The international interest is overwhelming. We get letters from people all over the world, wanting to know if they can be part of search expeditions, asking about the reward money.'

'What, there's a prize if someone finds one?' he asked, and the curator nodded sadly.

'Oh, yeah. A few years back, someone offered a million dollars for evidence of one, and that really stirred up the interest again. It's like it taps into something for people. And that offer's still standing, I guess.'

She snapped on a dim fluorescent light as the cool air in the vault hit them with a blast of formaldehyde, old fur, neglect. In a case to their right were two more taxidermied thylacines; before them on a bench were stacked several large flat boxes.

'These are the pelts,' said the curator, pulling on some cotton gloves and opening a box. 'You can look at them, but please don't touch them.'

The faint sharp smell of something wild. Dark brown stripes, as delicate and precise as if they'd been painted on with a Chinese brush, dark sable on sandy fur. The marble eyes of the stuffed animal beside him stared like the deadest, coldest thing on earth.

Rich suppressed a shudder. You could see the bare skin on the forelegs where it must have rubbed itself raw in a wire snare. On a shelf was a box with *Thylacine bits and pieces* written on it in felt pen. He felt an overwhelming sadness dissolve into his limbs, a terrible sinking heaviness. He wanted to get out of there, now.

'Thanks for your help,' he said to the curator. 'You've been very generous with your time, having us turn up out of the blue like this.'

'Oh, that's alright. What about the documentary? Will you be approaching the museum to make another appointment to interview anyone, or do you want to see these?'

She indicated a box and opened it.

'What's in there?'

'Oh, various testimonials.'

The sheaf of papers was hundreds of pages thick. As she flipped through them Rich saw fountain pen, ballpoint, typescript — then computer-printed pages. A sedimentary layer of the twentieth century.

'The more promising sightings were pretty much all before the end of the 1950s,' she said, thumbing back through the pages. 'There's some evidence there were probably still thylacines in the wild, surviving, until then. They even developed a kit, you know, something for rangers to take out with them, some plaster of Paris to get paw-print mouldings, bags to collect scats, that kind of thing.'

She patted a cardboard box. To Rich, it looked wildly naïve and optimistic, something the scouts might put together, with its assortment of bags and wooden sticks and little packets of plaster. Something you'd give an eleven-year-old boy for Christmas. He could sense Sophie backed up against the door. Watching him.

'So, nothing hopeful, then?' he said.

The curator hesitated. 'Well, you can see the attraction, can't you? Up in the Tarkine, on the north coast; that's 3800 square kilometres of wilderness. Imagine that.'

'Jesus.'

'And 2000 square kilometres of it's rainforest. Lot of people point to that and say a population could still be surviving there, and it's so remote we'd never know. They hold onto that.'

She dropped the papers back into the box with a sigh. 'And there's plenty of sightings, still,' she said dryly. 'Thousands. Especially on the tourist trails. There's lots of feral dogs now, in Tasmania. Lots of feral everything, really.'

'Yeah.' He felt Sophie move impatiently. He didn't blame her. This cold little room like a mausoleum. Like a morgue.

'Everyone wants to see one,' the curator went on. 'Or join an expedition, like I said. Or clone the poor buggers from the DNA inside those preserved foetuses upstairs. Nobody wants to believe they're really extinct. They want to believe that somewhere out there in all that wilderness, they're still managing to hang on.'

'But you think they're gone?'

She hesitated, weighing her words. 'Nothing would make me more excited than someone finding real hard evidence of one. But for me, I have to say ... they're gone.'

He was glad to get out of the building, relieved to be back in the warm air and surge of life, the reassuring sunshine.

'They knew,' Sophie said suddenly and passionately as they stood waiting for a break in the traffic. 'They must have known, and they still let that one freeze to death. Let it have that horrible death, something as unique and precious as that.'

What could you say to that?

'You're right,' he answered. 'People are idiots. The more valuable and irreplaceable the thing, the more careless they are with it. I'll show you photos of Lake Pedder one day, before they dammed it. You should see what it was like. A paradise. And all under water now.'

He hesitated as the traffic moved in a flank before them.

'That's what started the whole movement to save the Franklin — just the idiocy of people who had the power to make decisions for everybody else.'

He was having to raise his voice now to be heard, turning his face away from an approaching truck and the noise it made changing gears. It was a logging truck, an eighteen-wheeler carving its way through the city on the way to the wharf to unload its timbers, and they both glanced up as it roared past them with its chained-on cargo of huge felled trees, some trunks still covered in shreds of moss and bark.

A pocket of cool air seemed to hit Rich as the logs flashed past his eyes, the momentary smell of damp, silent forest. There was a whole world of memories, he knew, still embedded intact in some fold of his brain. Then, as he turned his head sharply to watch the truck coast down the hill away from them, all he could see were the pale, efficiently sliced cross-sections of the stacked trunks — Christ! The size of them! — still breathing out woody moisture, the exposed concentric age-rings jolting away like an ebbing, barely noticed reproach.

'There's nothing you need? No last-minute supplies?' Rich asked her as they wandered through the pedestrian mall up to their hotel. She liked the way he didn't mind if she walked along without saying much. Her mother could never do that. Always talking, no matter how inane the topic.

'No, I've got everything. My teacher at school, he belongs to a bushwalking club, and he helped me list all the stuff I'd need. Just need to buy fuel for the stove once we get there.'

'Those boots going to make it OK?'

She looked down at her Timberlands. 'Yeah, I've had them for a while, they're really good.'

She wondered if he was gearing up to ask her about her clothes and hair, or comment on the studs. Sophie thought her look was pretty understated, but adults, especially shopkeepers, eyed her sometimes as though she was going to stab them.

Her grandmother Janet always looked in pain when she visited.

'Is it the Addams Family?' she'd say. 'Is that the fashion?'

And she had a way of undercutting you, even if you were prepared for her.

'It's not hairspray, is it, Sophie, it's something else — gel or wax, isn't it?' she'd add, touching Sophie's fringe carefully, like it was upholstery. 'Because that would explain, darling, why your skin's broken out on your forehead like that. Not to mention all that foundation you've slapped over it. Soap and water and a few bobby pins is what you need, sweetheart.'

Darling, sweetheart, while she stood there giving you a look that told you there was no way you were up to scratch.

Sophie dug her hands into her pockets. She couldn't stop thinking about those tigers. She'd bought some postcards in the museum shop. One was a reproduction of a sepia photo; a man in a hat and old-fashioned checked jacket and waistcoat, sitting with a gun and gazing at what he'd shot — the dead thylacine hanging upside-down beside him, strung up by the back legs. Its long strong body stretched in dead defeat from the rope, the powerful tail curved back towards the floor, the forelegs reaching down through the air, never to touch ground and run again.

Native Tiger of Tasmania shot by Weaver, 1869, said the caption. Mr Weaver looked lifeless too, stuffed and vacant. He was staring sideways past the thylacine, preserving a profile rather than looking at the camera, as though his lofty thoughts were elsewhere already. Staring right through the thing he'd killed.

The other postcard showed a thylacine-skin rug, four sets of the chocolatey stripes making a wavy pattern. Like ripples of sand after the tide's gone out, thought Sophie. Or those ridges of shadow the wind blows sand into, in an empty desert. Beautiful, really, until you remembered what it was.

Now on either side of them, along the mall, stood souvenir shops and gift emporiums, their stands pushed onto the pavement. And on every stand hung tiger key rings and tiger t-shirts and beer holders and baseball caps, tiger stuffed toys and fridge magnets; everywhere, all anybody seemed to be flogging were mementos of an extinct animal. Tigers that looked cute and harmless as teddies, tigers stylised like cartoon characters. Their image was on every numberplate; beer ads on billboards showed two tigers in an unspoiled, idyllic jungle by a waterfall, something you might stumble across anytime. Everywhere you looked, that foxy face and striped fur.

Sophie shuddered, a familiar tremor of panicky horror. This was what lay ahead, and she'd be alive for it, probably. All of it. The last panda. The last polar bears. All those poor orangutans poached in Borneo. She could almost see how it would go: the display of solemn public regret as the last ones died, those awful bits of footage of polar bears floundering and drowning across melting ice floes, starving to death, that bloody Enya music as a soundtrack. Then this would come, for all of them — a boom in snowdomes and key rings and drinks coasters, a million toy versions made in Chinese sweatshops. Nylon fur. The real thing gone forever.

Terrible, wrecked world, she thought. All of it sinking and melting and going under, the patches of green turning brown. Nothing good left, everything torn up and eaten and destroyed, everything dumped in the next generation's lap.

'How about a coffee?' said Rich. 'Or a juice or something?'

'I'm OK. Thanks.'

He stepped into a confectionery shop. 'Come and check this out.'

She took a deep breath, and saliva sprang into her mouth — oh, the sneaky betrayal of a watering mouth! — as she smelled licorice and butterscotch, musk-sticks and milk bottles and jelly raspberries, all the soft sugary things of her childhood she'd cram her mouth with and let slowly dissolve. She and Tegan, friends even back then, sitting idly on the swings in the park eating their way slowly through bags of caramels and lurid jelly snakes, so different in flavour from the all-natural fruit juice ones her mum bought her. Here, the chocolate was arranged in big seductive slabs behind the glass counter, ranging in colour from pale coffee brown to almost black, so rich its sheen looked almost buttery. She pointed to it and smiled, her finger tapping the glass accusingly.

'Look at that. That's the hardest thing to resist, chocolate.'

Out of the blue. She couldn't believe she'd said it. She pulled her hand back, shut her mouth and swallowed. A single strong peppermint, that's what she needed. Or a no-sugar chewing gum, with that foamy bitter aftertaste of the artificial sweetener killing your appetite.

He was looking into the display case, counting out some coins.

'I like it too,' he said, glancing across at her. 'I'm a sucker for chocolate, actually, but only the really good, pure, dark organic stuff.' He smiled. 'It's full of antioxidants.'

'That's what they say. Just an excuse to let you weaken and stuff yourself with it.' She blinked, shocked again at this dangerous urge to mindlessly blurt something, confide something. She'd have to watch herself.

'I'm surprised you can't get a chocolate Tasmanian tiger,' she said disparagingly, to change the subject.

'Yeah, they sure are keen to milk that for all it's worth, aren't they?' He bought some chocolate-coated coffee beans and when he went out she lingered, and then hurriedly bought an expensive thin bar of seventy percent cacao dark chocolate and slipped it into her bag. She'd give it to him later, when he wasn't expecting it. All this time in her life, she thought, fifteen years of wondering, and this was the first time she actually knew something he liked.

Back at the hotel, Rich lay on one of the beds and flipped through the black hospitality folder. God, what a relief to take off his walking boots, still stiff with newness. They were the only footwear he'd brought, which was probably an oversight. His feet felt weak and tingling, as though they'd been squeezed out of shape.

'Can I use the gift soap and shampoo in the bathroom?' asked Sophie, poking her head around the door.

'Hey, that's what they're there for. Use all of them. Use all the towels, and we can phone down to reception for more.'

She grinned. 'Cool.'

'I thought "sick" was the word of choice now.'

She kept grinning, glancing at him almost shyly as she pushed at her hair. 'Yep. Sometimes.'

'So have a shower. Then we'll phone in some takeaway for our last night in civilisation before we start roughing it tomorrow, OK? And watch a movie on cable. Whatever you want.'

'Can I have a twenty-minute shower?'

He looked over at her, smiling, and made a regal gesture towards the bathroom. 'Knock yourself out!'

That would be Sandy alright, he thought suddenly, that old Catholic schoolgirl self-denial finding its way to the surface in rationed two-minute showers and virtuous misguided principles like driving a twenty-year-old clapped-out car. 'Stay in there for half an hour, if you like,' he said. 'Then you can come out and eat all the Pringles in the mini-bar.'

'Fully sick,' she said, and he was sure there was a glint now, something happy and excited, in those watchful black-rimmed eyes. It was all that make-up that made her face look so much older than she really was, he decided with a little lift of hope. He wasn't too late.

Nine

She knew what the problem was. She never responded well to pressure, and being told to choose a Goddess card on the spot like that had thrown her.

'Cast your eye over the cards,' the instructor had said to the workshop participants, 'and select one you feel drawn to, and that Goddess will act as your guide to reconnect you to the archetypes within you during the guided meditation.'

All very well, but how did you *know*? She'd wanted to choose Isis — her picture on the card showed a willowy woman lifting a beautiful jug of some sort, a woman with just the sort of hair Sandy wanted: thick and coiled up in a braid with a few careless curls framing her face. Mermaid hair. But some other woman had swooped down and picked up Isis, and Sandy had been frozen with indecision. It was really important to get it right. 'Choose a card that intuitively appeals to you,' the instructor had added serenely, and at that everyone else had snatched up cards like seagulls grabbing bloody chips.

And so she, Sandy, was left with the dregs, as usual. She'd grabbed Hera, checked the back of the card quickly to scan through the personality features and dropped it horrified — that Goddess was her mother to a T, down to the imperious pointed finger. Finally she'd settled for some Goddess she'd never heard of. She wasn't even sure how to pronounce her name, so how on earth could she commune spiritually with her and ask her to enter her life and awaken the Divine Feminine within her? Sandy sneaked another look at her card. Demeter. Sounded like something the mechanic tells you has gone wrong with your car. *Sorry, love, the timing chain and the demeter both need replacing.*

And she looked much more crone than maiden, if you wanted the truth. Not the person you'd want along with you on a guided initiation journey. Even a car journey would probably really start to grate.

By rights, she should have been led to Athena, warrior woman. Extroverted, practical, intelligent. Or Artemis, who shuns the busy city in favour of wild and natural places, Athena's closest sister on the Goddess Wheel, protectress of flora and fauna. But she hadn't been assertive enough, she'd let others reach in before her and pick up something that was rightfully hers, and that was going to change everything.

Some participants, the leaflet explaining this particular session had said, experience past-life memories of when the Goddess was dominant in their spiritual lives.

Of everything Sandy wanted now, she wanted some past-life memory to resurface. Wanted that sudden swooning rush of whatever it was that let the woman to her left slump to the ground and have the nurturing arm of one of the facilitators support her as she remembered. If she could just let go of these vestiges of doubt and actually get a glimpse into one of her past lives, she'd be totally committed, she'd give it her all.

God, though, her legs were aching. And only the half-lotus too. She needed to do more yoga, make an everyday practice of it. Clear her mind of the small, distracting anxieties niggling at her now. What was irritating her at this moment, for example, was the smug smile on the face of that thin woman in the front row, twisted calmly like it didn't hurt, her expression like one of the prefects at Sandy's high school, the ones the nuns were always nodding their approval at. Those sugary beatific smiles, hitching up the sides of their mouths with that fake simpering piety like the plaster statues of the Madonna herself. Then out to the quadrangle during recess to make everyone's life a misery again.

That's the kind of smile this woman had, with her green leggings and wispy purple top. Thin as a rake. Probably a vegan too. Probably made a point of asking the staff here to buy in her macrobiotic soy milk specially.

But if she could just turn off this distraction, if she could only *shut up* and *concentrate*, she could surrender herself to the interior question of this moment and have a past-life memory and reconnect with the Goddess like she was supposed to. Otherwise she'd get behind. It was just that every time she tried, Sandy felt her mind slip, like a screw with no thread. She remembered that time she did the Women's DIY class at the community centre, and they'd all had a go at sharpening tools on a grinder, and every time she'd lowered the chisel onto that spinning wheel, it had kicked back with a vengeance and jarred her wrist.

'Press down with a bit more force,' the teacher had said. 'You need to make sparks fly!' But she couldn't press down, it intimidated her too much, and that's all there was to it, sparks or not.

'I honour, heal and forgive my past,' said the workshop leader in a voice just like those nuns reading morning prayers.

Focus, Sandy admonished herself. *You're paying for this*. Bloody hell, she'd been thrown so far off-kilter over the last few weeks, she was all over the place. She had to focus on what it was that had made her feel intimidated in the past, and own and reclaim that thing, then rejoice in her awakened power over it. Her Goddess Power. Otherwise she'd feel like an idiot when they started the chanting and dancing, and they'd all moved forward in the cleansing and reclaiming except her. It was hard to fake something like that. Sandy closed her eyes, and repeated, 'Honour, heal and forgive.'

'I release old patterns that no longer serve me, and awaken to the new liberated self beneath,' said the leader in her serene monotone.

Old patterns, thought Sandy. Yes. They were there alright, spinning away under the surface, kicking back at you when you least expected it. A new liberated self beneath? There was a universe under there. An entire lived existence.

She wondered how much credit she had left on her Mastercard. She could buy a piece of the gemstone she'd seen in the giftshop, called Angelite. The note on it said it opened the lines of communication to your angels and guides. And that drum for sale in the foyer, outside the room where they did the Circle of Welcome, she could just imagine that in the corner of the lounge room.

'We're going via the freeway, so you can't actually see it,' Rich said on the coach the next morning. 'But just there, across the water — that's where the jail is.'

He pointed over the bay, and Sophie ducked her head to catch a glimpse through the window.

'I thought we might have been able to at least see the watchtowers from here,' Rich went on, 'but never mind. The Pink Palace, it got nicknamed. They must have thought painting it pink would have a calming effect on the prisoners. First they took us to the holding cells at Queenstown then brought us here to go before the magistrate. Some protesters had been in prison for Christmas. Some of them hadn't even told their folks where they were. Or else they were here on holidays, saw that the Blockade was planned, and just got swept up in it.'

Tassie had been a different state then, he remembered. The butt of uneasy mainland jokes about inbreeding and hillbillies, a wild, insular place ruled over by the state Hydro-Electric Commission. He recalled the wharf at Strahan, that smell of fish and diesel, and the stiff-faced locals muttering abuse to them in the streets when they'd turned up. Protestors sitting at Greenie Acres, relating their reasons for coming, some of them saying they'd been spat at, and some tearful and scared. That was a 'sharing'. And when other people comforted them, putting their arms around them, that was a 'caring'. Caring and sharing, he thought idly — both used as nouns, strangely, while they used the word 'consensed' as a verb. Jargon took off like a virus, first chance it got. And if he told Sophie about it he knew 'caring and sharing' would sound like the worst kind of Hallmark card cliché, and yet somehow, then, it had all seemed authentic and energised.

'Have you ever done one of those ice-breaking games,' he said instead, 'where you stand in the middle of a circle of people, close your eyes and just fall back, and they catch you?'

She nodded. 'In drama class.'

'Yeah, well. We did those, when we did the non-violence training.'

Total strangers promising they wouldn't let you fall. And that jokey game where the whole group wrapped hands and tried to disentangle themselves without letting go. And again, at the time, it had felt purely fun. It wasn't until later that he thought about them and speculated that they were things designed to make you look foolish in the presence of others doing the same thing, to forge a bond.

'Mum says what she remembers is the meetings.'

'Oh, yeah. We loved our meetings. It was very important that we all felt a sense of consensus.'

His euphoria hadn't lasted long; he'd soon begun to feel an undercurrent of doubt he'd had to stay vigilant about pushing away, so that he didn't let it show. All he wanted was to be arrested, like they planned. Instead there were meetings about meetings about meetings. Meetings while the forest was getting hacked away, meetings that went on until people agreed to strategies, it seemed to Rich, out of sheer exhaustion. Sitting talking until the reason for the meeting was overtaken by actual events, so that another meeting had to be convened. Tactics briefings, role-plays where they practised getting arrested.

We're wedded to the principles of non-violent action, the facilitators kept saying. Welded to it, more like. And all the secrecy and dramatics, that's what had started to get under his skin. Calling a car a 'surveillance vehicle', the earnest whisperings over the secret radio transmissions sent from the Info Centre into camp. Even the constant hugs were starting to wear him down at the end. He was just impatient, he told himself, to get upriver and actually do something, rather than just talking about it.

'We all formed ourselves into affinity groups,' he said to Sophie. 'You had to decide what kind of action you'd do — how you'd be arrested, when the group would act. That decision to be arrested, it was seen as the ultimate sacrifice because it meant you'd be removed from the river. The HEC, the Hydro-Electric Commission, they sent their first huge dozer on a barge up the river to start destroying the forest. Protesters were out trying to blockade the river on rubber dinghies, just small inflatable duckies, and the boat and barge just went straight through them. It was a miracle nobody drowned.'

She'd been looking vaguely out the window as he spoke, but she turned to glance at him now.

'Were you there, then?'

'In the flotilla? No, I was upriver, in the forest.'

'How long had you been there?'

He'd spent two days there. Thirty-eight hours. He shrugged casually. 'Oh, you know, a week or so.'

Getting ready up there at Warner's Landing, waiting for the bulldozer to arrive. Although he hadn't believed it would, really. He'd been certain protesters in Strahan would have stopped the barge somehow from leaving the wharf, surely all the people still at Greenie Acres would have raced down to block it by clambering aboard, or something. That's what he'd imagined. An *action*, after all that interminable preparation. But they'd just stood there and let it leave, he heard later, as paralysed with indecision as he'd been when he'd seen it arrive.

'I saw photos later of the barge, though. Just ploughing through the duckies as if they weren't even there. Then it got up to Warner's Landing and they unloaded the bulldozer onto the site.'

It had roared into the mud-slicked rainforest, saplings cracking beneath it. *NO DOZER IN NATIONAL PARKS* one of the banners had read, and yet here it was, with a police escort in life-jackets, and suddenly that banner had seemed a puny, foolish thing, a misjudgement, a frail little nuisance.

'We stood there and we heard the police PA system calling:

"Clear the water. The barge will not stop." We believed them too
— we knew they wouldn't. And then up the river came this ...
cavalcade. All the protestors still in their boats.'

They'd been paddling, holding their oars aloft, chanting. Like
a ragtag tribe, singing and shouting.

He remembered how cowed he'd felt, flushed and trembling
and overwhelmed, by the sheer purposeful roaring force of
the bulldozer. He'd been holding someone's hand, he realised.
Gripping it.

'We saw that flotilla of rubber rafts coming, and we all moved
together. Well, anyway, that's where I got arrested. We were
totally non-violent — they arrested us for trespass, which is like a
technicality.'

'Did they just, like, take you away then and there?'

'Yep. We'd planned for it to happen that way, so I'd already
packed up my tent. The cops stuck us on the foredeck of their
boat and I heard the bulldozer start up again as we pulled away.'

'How many of you?'

'Over forty.'

Still singing. *Like a tree that's standing by the waterside, we shall
not be moved.*

Except that they were being moved, of course, and the trees
weren't standing, they were falling, you could hear them cracking
and pitching. Then being herded into the bow with the others, all
of them realising it had actually happened and they'd finally done
it. Pumped with adrenaline, hugging. He'd stood a little apart
from the singing, wishing they'd chosen some other song, and
tried to feel the momentous triumph of the occasion, something
of the exhilaration of the whooping people on the banks and the
camp boats cheering them on, all that holy zeal. Telling himself it
was a victory. Nothing. Numb.

She was watching him, eyebrows raised expectantly. He
couldn't tell her that.

'It was the most overwhelming moment of my life,' he said
instead, and she nodded. 'You know what — I turned around and
there was just a single person in a duckie left on the river. He was

standing upright in it, saluting us, as we went around the bend. And then when we got back to Strahan, all the other blockaders were there cheering us as well, clapping as the police escorted us off the wharf and into the vans. We were singing all the way. Singing until we ran out of songs.'

The others had been singing, not him. He'd watched, cut off, unable for even a moment to step back into himself and the moment. Her eyes slid away from him now, looking back out the window, veiled with private thoughts.

'The thing is,' he said, on safer ground now, 'those locals, the ones who spat at us and demonstrated against us, saying we were taking away their livelihoods, I'd just love to find a few of them now. Strahan gets 200,000 visitors a year these days — they'd all be rolling in dough. Every tourist wants to go there. So sometimes, you know, I wonder what they'd have to say, meeting one of the Greenies who saved their cash cow for them when all they wanted to do was hound us out and destroy it forever.'

She nodded again.

'A real peak time, that was,' he said finally. 'You had to be there, I guess.'

She gave a short laugh. 'That's what Mum says.'

He sat back against his seat. Twenty-five years ago, if you could believe that kind of time, he'd been travelling along this road in the other direction, shivering and wet, eyes aching, wretched with confusion.

And those games. Stupid, but they'd stayed with him, locked away and crystalline. Those hands holding yours tightly as you tried to disentangle yourself, the object of the game being not to let go. Those same hands held out waiting, needing you only to close your eyes and trust, to permit yourself to fall.

It took them nearly an hour to check in and collect their Overland Track Passes from the Cradle Mountain Visitor Centre. The place was a crush of backpacks and rustling rain jackets and walkers shuffling as they waited to register and queue for the shuttle bus that would take them to the start of the track. The car park was full of cars and coaches and tour-group minibuses, unloading stack after stack of outdoor gear, and queues of people lined up at the cafeteria for one last cappuccino. They could have bought all their gear right here, thought Rich as he queued to buy stove fuel. They could have arrived empty-handed and walked out of here, kitted up to the nines with state-of-the-art top-of-the-range everything, still flapping price tags as they buckled it all on, trying the look on for size.

It was nothing like he'd expected; this hive of serious industry. It was as though all these walkers, young and old, had been called up for service somehow, and were arriving at headquarters for final solemn briefings before marching out into the field.

He and Sophie joined them, dutifully filling out their forms and tucking brochures and official information sheets into the side pockets of their packs, nodding when a ranger asked them if their fuel stoves and food and sleeping bags were all going to last the distance, because they could always stock up now, before they left.

'After all, it's not as if you can phone for a pizza delivery,' the ranger said, smiling at Sophie.

'No,' she answered him uncertainly, looking a bit confused.

'You realise there's practically no mobile phone reception at all on the track?'

Now she stared at him, her mouth open with horror. 'What?'

'There's sporadic CDMA coverage, but any other kind of mobile won't be any use to you at all. Apart from telling you the time, that is.'

Sophie turned back to Rich with dismay.

'That's not the end of the world, is it?' he said. 'You look like he's told you he has to amputate your arm or something.'

'I won't be able to call Mum.'

'No. You'll have to text her before we get started and let her know.'

She was fumbling for her phone as he spoke, scrolling and checking for messages automatically. They're addicted to the things, he thought. It'll do her so much good, getting away from all that for a few days.

'Ready to hop on the bus?' he asked her, and she nodded, preoccupied, her thumb punching out some incomprehensible code.

'Good luck,' said the ranger. 'It's a brilliant experience, just stay safe.'

'We will. Thanks,' he answered.

'Do you have a lightweight torch and spare batteries?'

'Yes, we do. Thanks.'

Then onto the bus with all the other walkers in their new gear, listening to a babel of German and Dutch and English in accents he tried to place — Canadian, Scottish, Kiwi — then efficiently deposited in the car park at Ronny Creek, which let them step straight onto the famous track, not a worn-earth track as Rich had imagined, but no-nonsense duckboards augmented with a strip of non-slip mesh. Signs and maps everywhere, and a brisk blustering northerly wind sharpening up his senses. His pack feeling suddenly real now that he was about to carry it further than the length of an airport terminal, feeling like a serious weight pulling at his shoulders. And people everywhere he looked, Sophie and him just two in a giant processed conveyor belt of humanity all shouldering their own packs and pulling up their socks, all pitting themselves against what was up that track.

He actually heard one guy say to another, 'Well, up and over!', as if it was a fusillade of enemy gunfire they were facing out there. Then the shuttle bus reversed and took off in an acrid cloud of diesel fumes and another one pulled into its vacated space. There was a brief silence.

'Well,' he said dryly to Sophie. 'Here we are, in the great uncharted wilderness.'

'I guess so,' she replied, with a shrug that showed she was as flummoxed as he was.

'Care for some trail mix?'

'No, thanks.'

He tried to time it, waiting to get started on that wide, safe boardwalk in a quiet moment when nobody else was near them.

It was like trying to step onto a city pavement. Onto one of those moving airport walkways crowded with fellow passengers.

'You ready to get started then?' he asked.

'Of course I am.'

Still he hesitated, wanting the crowds to disperse and leave them alone.

'Do you want to go first?' he asked, and she shrugged again, shyly diffident.

'No, you.'

The raw, untried stiffness between them, unyielding as his boots. He gave her a reassuring grin and set off.

Later it struck him that they could have started out walking side by side, across that first generous section of wooden planks. It just didn't seem to occur to him at the time. Or to his daughter either, watchfully, warily acquiescent behind him.

Sandy couldn't help staring, under lowered lids, at the woman on her left, supported now by two workshop leaders who were murmuring soothing words, trying to calm her down. If she was having a past-life regression, Sandy thought, she'd regressed into someone having an asthma attack. Or perhaps a Goddess worshipper finding herself about to be burned at the stake.

Focus, focus, focus. Who did she identify with, and how could she enter the sacred inner space to channel the Goddess's voice calling her to offer spiritual guidance?

'Have you received any messages this morning?' one of the facilitators had asked her in the break, and she had answered, 'I'm not sure, I'll just check', scrabbling for her mobile phone, and the woman had cried 'Too funny!' and laughed delightedly, clapping her hands as if Sandy had made a witty joke. Laughed for much longer than was necessary, actually, since it was an honest mistake.

Sandy had tried laughing it off herself, but the message from Sophie (*hey there wont b reception on walk till Mon talk then*) had wiped the smile off her face pretty fast. There was nothing she could do but focus on deprogramming herself of this anxiety and accepting what was clearly a lesson for her in relinquishing control.

She covertly studied the moaning and writhing woman, and she tried, she honestly tried, to empty her mind and clear it of judgement, but frankly if that woman was in a shopping mall, or in a car park, or her workplace, or a bank queue ... in fact, if she was anywhere other than at a workshop endeavouring to awaken the Divine Feminine, someone would be calling an ambulance by now. *Honestly, if she knew how ridiculous she looked*, said a small but withering voice from the back of her head. Janet. Great. Don't even start, Sandy thought despairingly. Shut up — I can't hear the Goddess.

'I honour the challenges of my past, when I have allowed myself to go deeply into the strength of my inner core,' said the workshop leader.

She closed her eyes. This was better, challenges of the past, and it was much more comfortable lying on her back with a cushion under her head.

Strength of inner core, yes, something to be honoured. She'd been to prison for her beliefs, after all. OK, remand, whatever you wanted to call it. They were still locked up for a night while they waited for their court appearance. She remembered her apprehension, as they'd climbed out of the police van, slowly, slyly evaporating into a strange kind of exhausted, reckless triumph. In fact, they'd all felt high as kites. After they found out they were entitled to it, all the blockaders had asked to be given writing paper with the 'Risdon Prison' letterhead on it, so they could write to as many people as possible to tell them where they were and what had happened. There was a rush for that paper.

'And with this inner core of strength I will now empower myself to heal and nurture my present,' she heard, but the workshop room was drifting away now, growing faint and unnecessary.

Jail wasn't like she'd anticipated. In fact, secretly she felt just a little deflated, like she'd been psyching herself up for something gruelling that didn't happen.

The police, for instance, processing the women as they were registered, asking them all what they wanted for dinner. Then a hot shower, clean clothes, prison issue or not, and a hot cup of tea, followed by a real bed with sheets — after camping at Strahan in the mud and rain, it all felt a bit surreal.

'I'm a vegetarian,' she said to the policewoman taking meal orders.

'No problem,' the woman had answered cheerfully, and she'd felt, again, the odd, thwarted sensation of having been outgunned. Still momentous, though. This would be something to tell her children, she told herself — jailed as an environmental activist. Something to tell her children, while somehow keeping it secret from her mother, forever.

There was a lot of discussion and sharing that first night, she remembered. Some singing started up at lights out, but she felt too tired to join in — and besides, secretly, she was getting a tiny bit tired of those one-size-fits-all solidarity songs: *Onwards righteous Greenies, marching into Strahan ...* She was already hoarse with singing, anyway, and it wasn't as if she needed support to keep her spirits up. Her spirits had never felt higher.

The next day, though. This was her favourite memory, the secret comfort food she could bring out and savour when she felt hungry for something now, twenty-something years later. It was a hot morning — which was a turn-up for Tasmania — and after they had a sharing in the quadrangle where she could feel the eyes of the other curious prisoners on them as they hugged, there was nothing to do but mill around the yard, talking.

She had requested her writing paper and had six sheets ready to write to someone, but sitting in the sun made her soporific. She couldn't remember now which protestor it had been who'd had the idea, but she'd turned to the others with a grin and said, 'Let's take off our tops and sunbake.'

Within minutes they had pulled off their sweaters and shirts and bras, Sandy included. She could feel a new atmosphere in the air suddenly, as if there was a snake in the yard, and she opened her eyes as a shadow fell across their seated bodies. A warder, or whatever they were called, and she was looking right at her.

'I'll have to ask you to put your tops back on,' the warder said.

Sandy felt the other prisoners listening, to see how activists trained in non-violence would respond. She felt a sudden surge of responsibility — everyone else in the group was deferring to her, letting her answer. 'Why?' she said politely.

The woman put a hand across her forehead, she remembered, to shade her eyes. And to get a better look at her.

'It's against regulations.'

Speak pleasantly and clearly, when you challenge authority, Sandy recalled from the training.

'Can we see the regulations?' she asked, and a delighted, suppressed laugh went around the yard among the other prisoners. Even now, remembering it thrilled her. Because there weren't any regulations, of course. She'd asked exactly the right question. Impossible to describe the triumph bubbling up as the warder gave an exasperated shrug and turned away, shaking her head.

And then, heady exhilaration skating through her as one by one some of the other women prisoners, grinning, started taking off their shirts too, and their bras, and settling in next to them.

'I reckon I'm going to be a Greenie for a day,' one said.

It was a great moment for sisterhood and for solidarity, Sandy recalled later at reunions and parties. It was exactly as the information book at Strahan had suggested: *Non-violence is dependent on reason, imagination and discipline. Victory should not be in terms of victory by one side over another, but victory over injustice.*

It was almost like a planned action, like everyone in authority could suddenly see there was no stopping them. And she'd made it happen, knowing just what to say at the right moment, not losing her cool. She'd been the one.

Holy *shit*, it was straight uphill. They'd passed through some buttongrass plains, a bit of rainforest, and suddenly the path had gone vertical. He was knackered within the first hour, not that he let that show, and he couldn't believe how difficult it was, trying to climb up rocky inclines with twenty kilos of solid weight on your back. Just when he thought they were over the worst there came one bit — he'd actually felt an adrenaline bolt of real fear here — where they had to scramble across a dolorite rockface on the side of a mountain, hand over hand, wedging their boots into the rock, gusting wind headbutting into their faces, and Rich wished fervently he was back with the wooden duckboard and the safety mesh. There was even a chain installed on the steepest sections.

Before he'd come Rich had pored over photos of mirror-still lakes and pandani rising out of mist — nobody had said anything about pulling yourself straight up the side of a bloody mountain with a chain. Some small part of him hoped desperately that Sophie would grab his arm when they stopped for lunch and tell him she'd changed her mind, it was too hard and she wanted to go back on the day-walk loop. He'd be solicitous, understanding; book them both in to Cradle Mountain Lodge for a few days and kick back. Bond over a game of Scrabble or two.

Just as he was thinking this, she overtook him. He watched her legs working metronomically up that mountainside, never hesitating, and his heart sank like a stone. Sure she was thin, but so were those Ethiopian marathon runners who wiped the floor with everyone else at the Olympics.

Stopping for photos and a breather, then up again. Endlessly up, with the pack slumped on his back like a dead animal and his knees feeling full of hot gravel.

'That's the steepest part of the whole track,' a guy at Marion's Lookout commented as Rich staggered sweatily to the summit, his breath heaving in his chest.

'Is it? Thank Christ for that.'

'Unbelievable view, though.'

He looked up and out. Of course it was an unbelievable view: they were 1223 metres above sea level on a pre-Cambrian glacier; what did you expect? But he still took the lens cap off his camera and aimed. Dove Lake far below looked dark as a pool of ink. What was it with humans and their insatiable desire to get up high to look at bodies of water underneath them? His eye was caught by a black bird, a crow, alighting carelessly on a dead tree nearby. He turned the camera lens to it, but it spread its wings, eyeing him, and disappeared over the edge in a careless swoop.

'Lovely view,' he conceded. He'd just about had a heart attack, coming over the ridge of the crater, the exposed rock plunging on either side of him. Sudden vertigo. Scanning anxiously for Sophie up ahead, and seeing her doggedly tramping in a line of other walkers, he'd been sidelined by a complicated disbelief. He hadn't expected her to be clinging onto his hand, but still. You wouldn't put money on it, looking at her, that she'd take the mountain quite so literally in her stride. Wobbling over the crater, he'd taken his life in his hands and paused to get off a couple of shots of it — the tiny figures dwarfed by the vast wilderness in all directions — but some idiot had spotted him, and waved. Thanks, moron. He had recapped his camera lens, and laboured on.

'Telepathic communication with your spirit guide,' intoned the facilitator, 'is a spiritual enfoldment, a pathway towards our truest work as we are gifted with the talents of insight and intuitiveness.'

Sandy floated, dreamy. The first time she'd read about the Blockade, she knew with absolute certainty that she had to go. Someone in her house had been to a fundraiser for the Wilderness Society, a film screening about the river and the Tasmanian government's plans to dam it, and they'd brought back a leaflet that Sandy had idly picked up. She'd kept that leaflet for years.

People will soon be in the region of the Franklin River preparing to defend it and thereby keep it safe and inviolate. They will cut their ties with their normal life, their jobs, family, and customary pursuits and will stay in the South-West as long as is necessary. Theirs is a peaceful non-violent strategy and will result in HEC work (vandalism) being curtailed and delayed. It will focus world attention on the Franklin and South-West Tasmania. We know that you'd love to be with us. But if you can't ... there's no need to feel left out.

You would have had to be living on the moon, she recalled, not to sense the rising pitch of emotion surrounding the dam as the uni year finished and the imminent Blockade began to dominate the news. Fifteen thousand people marching in Melbourne on the Walk for Wilderness. The federal government announcing it would not intervene to stop the dam. Support rally after support rally until the area was officially declared a World Heritage Area and then it was never off the news; it was a constant hum on the wires. Seeing the headline: *Premier Warns Franklin Guerillas*. She, and everyone else she knew, writing *No Dams* on by-election ballot papers. She wanted to go. She could feel the pull of it, like a current. Then in the new year, two hundred people who'd already been arrested were remanded but refused bail in solidarity. *They will cut their ties with their normal life, their jobs, family and customary pursuits and will stay in the South-West as long as necessary.* Heroes.

The nuns at Sandy's school had always gazed fixedly over the class during Religious Education, foolish apologetic smiles on their faces, and talked about *vocations*. Sandy had sat like everyone else, face blank with scorn and boredom. But now she felt fired with something conscientious, unavoidable. A crusade and a calling, and anyone with a shred of ideological courage was down there already. She'd bought a ticket and arrived in mid-January, one of fifty people a day pouring in by then. It was possible, you could cut your ties with your normal life, and become the thing you believed in. She was an activist, she thought firmly, ready to step up and testify, even if it meant stopping a bulldozer. Soaked in true faith. She would step off her safe shore, and be willingly swept away.

It was a perfect small world they created at Greenie Acres. A microcosm of the way society could be. That's why she allowed herself to sob openly as she stood on the wharf singing and cheering for the other protestors, and why she cried again after the police marshalled them all together at the Kelly Basin Road, the day she was arrested herself. It was because on one level she already knew: this was it. This was as full as a heart could get, and she would never feel this kind of euphoria again.

Turned out she'd been right too. She'd been searching for that first sweet hit ever since. At the beginning the feeling of it coursing through her system was still there, magically replenishing itself in those early months after they came back from Tasmania. First the election, and the stunning idea that if you could change the minds of enough people, you could vote out one party who'd let you down, and elect another who shared your ideals. The new prime minister stood on the dais and his first words were, 'The dam will not be built', and Sandy remembered a roar going up, and dancing with her housemates, all of them with arms round each other, high kicking like cancan dancers, engulfed in a wave of triumphant joy.

Then the Supreme Court decision that overturned her trespass case so that all charges were dropped, when she'd gone to another rally and miraculously, out of the blue as they were assembling at the Wilderness Society building, she had spotted Rich.

That kind of life-changing synchronicity wouldn't happen now, Sandy thought wistfully. There was no way you'd ever find yourself on a street corner these days and catch sight of a person through a sheer twist of chance. And you'd never be able to take that as a sign, the universe stacking up all these odds to show you who you were meant to be with. Because now you'd be in mobile contact, you'd just text each other (*r u here? c u in frt TWS :)*) and it would all just seem ordinary and predictable. You'd be deaf or immune to those signals, there'd be no room for the magic to happen.

Back then, it was fate. They'd gone together to a huge spontaneous party when the High Court ruling came down, when they knew they'd won and nothing could change that; history was going to show who owned the moral victory and always had. *Let the Franklin flow, let the wild lands be, the wilderness should be strong and free, from Kutakina to the south-west shore, has to be something worth fighting for ...*

That magnificent, untouched river. Sandy was in it, floating effortlessly, connected forever to that promise of change, alive in a beautiful current where she reached out and grabbed Rich's hand, beaming, thinking they were swimming together.

They'd moved into a share house together in the city and

traces of that blessed drug, something eager and vestigial and amenable, meant there was no talk then about needing privacy or other people driving you nuts. They had a food kitty and a weekly meeting where they amicably worked out the housework roster and everyone had been the best of friends, staying up late and smoking joints and laughing themselves sick telling stories. Rich and her, happy just to have their own bedroom which seemed big enough then for two people and all their belongings, with the poster of Gandhi looking a little reproachfully from the wall (no matter how many material goods you tried to relinquish, it was never enough for that guy) and being so busy with all those groups — the Environmental Collective and the Rage for the Forests and the student magazine collective (whatever happened to collectives?) — and she and Rich finally agreeing, when they bought the VW Kombivan to travel up the coast, that it wasn't necessary to actually relinquish material goods, just not care about them unduly.

They'd fended off the itching, flat sense of anticlimax for months. Whenever they could they got together with other Franklin Blockaders and discussed over long, reminiscent dinners how it had all happened and ways to incorporate their non-violence training into further activism. What they might do next.

But the slow and subtle withdrawal pangs had crept up slowly, the fended-off realisation that nothing was ever going to be that good again.

She remembered when the US invaded Grenada — October, it would have been, just as she was starting to question her whole degree course at uni and whether it was worth continuing. She could still see the spark of excitement alight on her housemate's face as he'd run in to tell her about the invasion, how everyone was assembling for a demo in the city and how they needed to paint a banner right away. She had jumped up to find a bedsheet, pulling open the hall cupboard, thinking guiltily that she wasn't even sure where Grenada was. She hated the glimpse she got, as she searched for an old sheet to paint on, of her eager, hot craving for that old exhilaration, the need to taste, again, a pure and qualm-free certainty. She hated the way that craven need made her feel — pressed airless beneath the surface of her life, utterly unmissed, while it rushed on, churning and oblivious, over her head.

There was a girl in Sophie's basketball team at school who walked like Rich did: stiffly but quickly, as if she had something to prove. She'd walk back to her position when the other team had the advantage with the same agitated, no-nonsense pace. There was no pleasure in it. The basketball coach sometimes made them do exercises called 'Californians' for training, a combination of running and stooping to touch the floor, a quick test to see who was fit and who wasn't. Watching Rich, she thought he could probably handle about twenty Californians. But he'd never let a stitch show. He was like her; he'd walk it off, say nothing. Her pack hung off her like a big sweaty unconscious child, an unyielding weight cutting into her shoulders.

He must know best, waving away the maps like that at the information centre, whispering to her what a rip-off they were. Then he'd taken her into the wilderness photo gallery, full of hushed people gazing at big landscape photographs that made everything look mysterious and majestic. He'd walked around with her, making suppressed noises of irritation and disbelief.

'Look at this — this is meant to be the showcase of Australian contemporary photographic artists — but see that? They've Photoshopped that, I bet you a hundred bucks. Whoever's running this place wouldn't know a good photo if it bit them on the arse.'

She'd watched him stride around the gallery, his arms folded. He knew about tons of things, she could tell. Like the way he'd shown that card to the woman at the gallery in Hobart and she'd taken them to that special vault. Not open to the public. He'd just spoken to her for a few minutes and she'd given them a private tour.

Now he was walking as though she was just a friend he had with him, not continually asking her if she was alright, which she liked. Not ignoring her, but just letting her find her own pace and not expecting to keep talking endlessly all the time. It was hard, climbing these long, steep inclines with a pack on, into the wind — a lot harder than she'd thought when she'd packed it and tried it on in her bedroom before she'd left. It had felt, then, like something she could heft easily, but now, especially when they'd had to slog up the mountain out of the valley to Crater Lake, it seemed full of bricks.

It was funny thinking she was carrying everything she needed on her back, that she could put up her tent and crawl in and be warm inside her sleeping bag.

It was better now they were higher, and the track had flattened out; she could catch her breath and concentrate on her walking.

She looked up at the track ahead, and the brightly clad walkers strung out along it, all of them made tiny by the hugeness of the landscape around them. Sophie had never seen anything like it. It was just hugely, gobsmackingly vast. No point holding up your phone to get a picture, the place overwhelmed that tiny screen. You couldn't capture even a fragment of its detail. Up at the lookout, grateful along with everyone else to let her pack slip to the ground for a break, she'd gazed out over the vista rolling into its vanishing point and the lake far below them, and felt dizzy. The sky seemed to press down and the ground seemed to press up, jamming her in the middle like a tiny speck, like something tossed by a huge frozen wave. One step off that fragmented rock edge and you'd bounce like a speck too, all the way down to infinity.

She'd felt a weird momentary sensation of wanting to. The sloping distance below her tilting up in sly magnetic invitation, reaching up to pull her over and down. How would it feel? Not clean like a building or a bridge, swan-diving through empty air. You'd connect, over and over, breaking with each impact, the agony real and unstoppable, and you would have gone into that voluntarily, that's what would stun your friends and family, you'd have had the unflinching courage to step off. *Down just once and down to stay, through the door that opens just one way.* She loved that song. 'Persephone.' Thought the title rhymed with 'bone' when she saw it listed, then heard the singer's voice whisper it and realised she had it wrong. *Inside the earth I feel no pain and I'm never going home again.*

Sophie ran her thumb under the aching shoulder strap of her pack, easing its bite for a second. Wads of drifting cloud slid across the sky like shorn fleece; chopped, ribboning white tinged with dirty grey. And it was like there was nothing in any direction, apart from that jagged-edged mountain in the distance like a fairytale giant sleeping on its back, the undulating stands of pencil pines, the other mountains rising and falling all the way to the horizon, their windswept peaks bare of vegetation.

All of it empty; just this little track winding through it, puny as a dropped piece of cotton thread on a gigantic rumpled picnic rug. And the humans in their fluorescent hiking jackets tramping along its rucked-up surface, like ants at that picnic.

Sophie thought about Ayresville, where nature was kept curbed and human-scaled. The recreational walk around the lake was paved, with a track set aside for mountain bikes, and at the end was a café and wrought-iron park benches. When you reached a steep section of hill on the Heritage Walk, council had installed handrails and there was gravel spread diligently on the muddy parts. Even the trees had signs.

Here, she felt as though she was in that show *Walking with Dinosaurs*, like a pterodactyl was going to suddenly wheel overhead, and the plunging ridge itself like some worn prehistoric spine, scaled with rock and sprouting sparse, prickly hair. Her pack was sunk hard into her shoulders, catching at her hair when she turned her head, until she reached up and pushed it in under her hat. There was no one there she knew to see her, so it didn't matter how lame it looked.

They stopped for lunch at an old hut that had a toilet behind it, and just beyond it she could see the track started to divide, with a smaller trail heading up the mountain. Quite a few walkers who'd stopped to eat were getting ready to ascend the mountain as a sidetrip. She caught Rich's eye.

'You don't want to slog straight up Cradle Mountain to the

summit, do you?' he said. 'You're not a peak-bagger, are you?'

'No way,' she replied, staggering to a sheltered spot and dropping her pack. She lay there for a while, breath burning, getting her energy back. When she shut her eyes sparks tumbled behind her lids, and she could feel the blood sucking back and forth in her trembling legs like a tide.

'It takes hours,' a woman near her said, also lying on her back with her eyes closed. 'It's the hardest kilometre you'll ever walk, believe me.'

'Zero interest,' she replied, and the woman laughed.

'You did really well on the way up to Marion's Lookout,' she said. 'That's a pretty tough ascent, especially for walkers on their first day, if they're not prepared for what's coming.'

'It's like a week's worth of workouts.'

In a minute, Sophie thought, she'd unzip her backpack and take out the container of PowerBars, and she'd have one and a half. The berry and guarana ones with extra protein.

'Would you like a piece of fruitcake?' the woman said. And before she could stop herself she'd said, 'God, yes please', and reached out for a slice.

'I'm Libby,' said the woman.

'I'm Sophie.'

'Are you walking with your dad over there?'

'What? Oh. Yeah.'

Her mouth was full of sultanas, but it was OK because dried fruit was good; you were allowed dried fruit to replenish energy. And she had some rice cakes in her pack too, which were bulky even though they weighed nothing, so the sooner she ate those, the better, really.

'Have another piece,' said Libby.

'No. Thanks all the same. That's really good cake.'

'Aren't we lucky to get this bit of sunshine?'

'I guess. Is the wind always this cold though?'

'This is nothing! Did you see that old hut we passed just back there? That's an emergency shelter on the walk and it's got a door set two metres from the ground, in case the snow gets that high.'

'Jeez.' She could see Rich sawing away at some cheese and tomato with his Swiss Army knife on a rock, balancing some slices of rye bread. Making enough for her, expecting she'd be having something with him. Assuming the responsibility of getting her lunch, like that was something they could both take for granted. *Dad*, she thought. Experimentally, cautiously, then dropping the thought hastily like something hot. She felt her hand reaching automatically for her phone, and remembered she was out of range.

'This is my first real bushwalk,' she confided to Libby.

'Is that right? Well, you seem really fit, I must say.'

She felt a small, warm rush of pleasure.

'It's always the way, I find,' Libby continued. 'The ones built like greyhounds are the ones who turn out to have the real stamina. I mean, look at you, you've got an athlete's physique. My dad used to say you can't fatten a thoroughbred. But Russell always says I've proved him wrong!' Libby smiled and gave her thigh a resounding slap. Sophie winced. The way the woman owned that solid flesh, like she claimed it and didn't care.

'Hey,' Libby went on after a pause, 'I hope you don't mind me interfering, but I couldn't help noticing your pack looked a bit awkward before, when you were walking.'

She shrugged. 'It's OK. Just feels a whole lot heavier than I thought.'

'See, I can see the marks on your shoulders where it's going to start chafing you soon. Has anyone adjusted it for you?'

'Adjusted it? No. I borrowed it from the school.'

'Well, listen, stick it on for a sec. I'll show you.'

She stood up and pulled her pack off the ground, feeling her back protest when she slid it over her arms. The woman, Libby, stood her up straight and pulled the straps tighter at her chest.

'I'll just shorten these, and then we'll see if it's better when you adjust the hip belt too. That's really where you want to carry the weight, so it fits your individual back length, here across the hipbones. Especially for us women. Otherwise if you're carrying it all in your shoulders ... See, is that better?'

It was. She felt the load of the pack shift a little, off the aching tendons of her neck.

'Thanks a lot. I didn't even think I needed to adjust anything.'

'That's OK. It's a good pack, but even the good ones can sit wrongly and make you fatigued early.'

'Hey, thanks.' She slid the pack off again, gratified and surprised. 'Um, would you like a rice cracker?'

Libby blinked at her and laughed.

'Thanks, Sophie, but no. Eating those things, it's like chewing on a piece of polystyrene. I'll stick with the cake. Hey Russell,' she called to a guy setting up a fuel stove, 'come and meet Sophie.' He stood up and came over to them just as Rich approached her holding out a sandwich.

She didn't want to do introductions, so she let them all say hi to each other, and it was easier just to take the sandwich with a smile, and wrap it in a plastic bag when she dug in her pack for the rice cakes. Pretend to brush crumbs off her lap if anyone looked her way, like she'd already eaten it. One-and-a-half PowerBars, then when they got to the hut for the night she'd reward herself with some two-minute noodles. Reload just enough carbohydrate. And no trail mix, since she'd already eaten that fruitcake. *An athlete's physique.* She felt for her phone and remembered again; a stumble of automatic reflex. Then she just lay there on the grass, gazing at the shifting acres of dark shadow that crawled restlessly over the mountain ranges all around them as the clouds scudded across the enormous sky allowing intermittent sun. The massive stony peaks stood bone-bare, like eroded islands left after some monumental flood had advanced and retreated, leaving only the hardest parts behind.

She let Rich go first again as they came down the track from Cradle Cirque into Waterfall Valley — all of them descending now, thank God, so much easier — and he slowed down so that most of the other walkers disappeared ahead of them. He was talking to her about photography and how he'd got into it when he stopped a little way in front of her and lifted his hands into a frame in front of his face.

'What?' she said, halting behind him.

'Just check that out, for instance. What a classic panorama shot,' he replied, indicating the vista ahead of them. She looked. It reminded her of a couple of the photos she'd seen in the Photography Gallery that morning — wide and empty, the duckboard track winding down into the far windswept distance.

'Just run past me again what I'm supposed to be looking at?'

He grinned easily. 'Just all that wilderness — the cushion plants either side of the track, the dead trees, that huge blank sky. Can you wait for a sec while I get out my wide-angle lens?'

'Yeah, sure.'

She watched him. How certain his hands were, screwing and unscrewing, twisting dials, drawing lenses out of bags. She tried to remember the last time she'd seen her mother so ... intently focused on something, so confident in her movements. The beads, maybe, choosing stuff for necklaces. But the beads didn't count; they weren't like this.

'See, this lens will accentuate the sense of space, it'll stretch the horizontals and make you look really small in the landscape.'

'Me?' she said, blinking, feeling instantly flattered.

'Sure. If you wouldn't mind walking on ahead and I'll take it when you get to a good distance. Let's try it before someone else comes along and wrecks the shot.'

She hesitated. 'Are you sure you want me to be in it?'

'Of course I'm sure. You'll look perfect. And I'll send you a copy too. It might even be in an exhibition, or in a magazine.'

'Wow. OK.' She started walking, then turned to glance doubtfully back at him. 'It'll just be my back, right?'

He grinned again, made a gesture of submission.

'Just your back. Nobody will know who you are,' he promised.

Thrilled, she tried to walk normally down the duckboard, waiting to be captured as the single human being in that landscape, walking steadily straight into it. From behind her came his voice, low with concentration.

'Except me,' she heard. 'I'll know it's you.'

Already special, to him. She could hear it. Her heart jumped nervous and slippery as a fish and she heard the shutter snap once, twice; sealing her there.

Russell and Libby were already at Waterfall Valley Hut when they arrived.

'We thought we'd try the luxury of a night in the hut,' Russell said with a grin. Sophie took a quick look inside and wondered if he was joking. About twenty people seemed to be crammed in there, and the ceiling was hung with damp jackets and leggings like colourful piñatas at a party. Everybody was cooking on the tabletops, yakking away with each other, rolling out their sleeping bags on the bunks. But they weren't bunks, really, she saw with dismay. There were no mattresses, even. They were just wooden platforms. Like sleeping on a storage shelf.

And there were boots everywhere. Scanning the room, she sensed an unexpected atmosphere like a classroom before an exam; nervousness amongst all the camaraderie. People were a bit too loud, a bit too animated, or else they sat looking drawn and shocked, just gathering their composure and resting. They all must have felt the way she did, even the loud jovial ones, cracking jokes like they wanted to break the tension. They must have been conscious of the molten burning in their leg muscles, tightening and aching. Wondering uneasily about the next day, and what they'd got themselves into.

'We'll be camping,' Rich said firmly, taking a look inside.

'Lovely tent platforms, you should grab a good one so you can wake up to the view of Barn Bluff in the morning,' said Russell. 'But you should leave your food and perishables in the hut, really, if you don't want a visit from some nocturnal wildlife.'

'Really?' Rich, crouched on the verandah, was unpacking stuff out of his bag. Crackers. Cheese. Sophie felt saliva flow into her mouth.

'Possums, wallabies, Tassie devils sometimes. Friend of ours got his tent ripped by some persistent little wombat one night when he was doing the track. Tore the fly to ribbons. They're pretty good at working out how to get inside.'

'Right, we will. Thanks for the tip.'

'And have you got a headlamp?' Russell went on. 'There's no moon tonight.'

She could tell from Rich's silence that he didn't.

'You can borrow mine,' offered Libby. 'You forget how dark it gets out there.'

Rich nodded. 'OK, thanks. That's very nice of you.' His voice was short, but he smiled at Sophie; a weary, hollow-eyed smile. 'Let's go and bags ourselves a spot. Then dinner and into bed for you, I reckon.'

'I'm alright.'

'Well, I'm not. I'm totally buggered. I'm just using you as an excuse.' He laughed but she saw his guard drop as he turned away, the tiredness like a curtain as he mustered the energy to pick up his pack again and drag it to the camping sites. That walk again, defensive, as if the ground was hot and strewn with burrs. The smile that promised he'd cook dinner, and see her safely into bed, the weary, vigilant responsibility she saw briefly in his features. A parent's face, thought Sophie, noticing it with a pleasure that felt strangely embarrassing. Ready to look after her.

She unrolled her tent on one of the wooden platforms, singing along to 'Velvet Sepulchre' as she did. It was great, seeing the landscape around her in counterpoint with music she knew so well. It made her hear Dogland in a whole new way.

'Hey.'

She could faintly hear Rich talking to her, and took out her earphones. 'What did you say, sorry?'

'Do your guy ropes reach all the way to the hooks?' He was tugging at his tent-fly, trying to stretch it more tightly towards the spot where you were supposed to attach it.

'I've got extra rope in my bag,' she offered.

'Have you? Great. I'll sort it out later, then. No wonder everyone in there was already making dinner — I'm starving, aren't you?'

She ducked her head into the tent, pushed her sleeping bag and roll inside.

'Not really,' she answered.

'Bloody hell. You've just walked nearly eleven kilometres, you should be chewing off your own leg. Let's go and cook dinner. I reckon it's time for some serious carb loading.'

'Sure.'

'Rice or pasta?'

She paused. 'Pasta.' She could have pasta instead of the two-minute noodles. That would still be OK.

'Carbonara which tastes nothing like carbonara?'

'Sure.'

Her tent was ready, and she slipped her earphones back on. *Icarus lies weeping, and I shun those wings*, the singer whispered. *Icarus lies weeping for all those childhood things.*

She unzipped a pocket of her pack, and took out her plate, her knife and fork, her cup. The ziplock bag of chocolate malt Sustagen. An orange-flavoured isotonic energy gel bar. She followed Rich up to the hut.

Ten

What animal was it? Sandy wondered. She sat cross-legged in the morning Circle of Welcome, trying to meditate using the candle flame, as instructed, to focus her thoughts entirely on the single unifying fire of life, but in her peripheral vision was the drum she wanted, placed outside the gift shop.

The piece of skin stretched over the drum was black and white and hairy. Probably a goat. It was important to know — she didn't want to find herself back at home with a drum made out of some endangered species, and have to bear the brunt of the shocked judgemental silences of better-informed friends.

And where was the drum made? Out of what timbers, and by whom? Indentured labourers? It was a full-time job, keeping yourself from accidentally being an oppressor. She had a beautiful set of enamel bracelets she couldn't wear now since someone had informed her earnestly at a party that everyone was boycotting those bracelets because they were made by child slaves in northern India. *Everyone.* Like they'd had a meeting without her.

And that woman last week, who'd stopped in front of her stall and complimented her on her earrings, and then, when Sandy thanked her, had frowned. 'Oh — you made them yourself? I thought you might have imported them from somewhere. India, maybe. Pakistan.' She'd gestured vaguely. Glossy expensive manicure, Sandy noticed. Probably cost enough to keep a third world village in clean water.

'Well, I get some of my beads from India. They're imported glass ones. And I get some from Africa too. But I make all the jewellery myself.'

'So it's not an aid project, or anything?'

'No.' The woman's mouth had made a disappointed little smile. As if Sandy had let her down, for crying out loud. An *aid* project? They were coming up all the time now, these women, flipping through her stuff with one hand as they talked on their mobiles like they owned the place. The kind who didn't want a necklace, they wanted a story. They demanded something exotic they could buy along with it, something they could recount as they gave it to someone, a little way they could claim ownership. Bracelets handmade by refugee children in Azerbaijan. Earrings made from glass bottles picked up by a women's collective off the UN rubbish tip in the Philippines.

This kind didn't buy things, they *sourced* them. Like shopping demanded some kind of special expertise, or a qualification, like shopping was your *job*.

Sandy had felt a teary, defensive tightness in her throat. Ridiculous. That woman couldn't care less about her. And she'd just walked away then anyway, off to slight someone else. What was wrong with people, that they couldn't just buy something they liked, and leave it at that?

At home, in the top of her wardrobe, she had a boxful of wire, feather and bead trinkets she'd made a year or two back. They were called dreamcatchers. She'd seen them around for a long time in crystal and aromatherapy shops, often with a little tag explaining they were a traditional Native American craft. That was good; Native American was always good. You put them in your window and they caught your dreams, or stopped bad dreams getting in, or attracted good energy to you, that kind of thing.

She hadn't thought she'd be treading on anyone's toes to make some for the stall, but someone on the very first morning she'd had them on display had seen fit to give her a lecture about cultural appropriation. She'd been mortified.

'What about your batik shirt?' she'd called as the woman walked away. 'What about your Indian bag?'

Well, not *called*, exactly. But she'd said it, whether the woman heard her or not. The whole thing had left a bad taste in her mouth, an awful anxiety she was offending someone she didn't even know. She was secretly relieved to see a pile of them one day outside the $2 shop; cellophane-wrapped dreamcatchers made in Malaysia and heavily discounted for a saturated market. Anybody could feel ironically scandalised by that sort of cultural thievery.

You couldn't predict these things, anyway. Look at chai soy latte. She wished she'd gotten in on the first wave of that.

Or the gemstone stall that often ended up next to hers. Gemstones really appealed to people. Gail was a great saleswoman too; you had to give her that. Very intuitive.

'That's a black obsidian massage stick,' she would tell someone. Or, tuning in somehow to their specific needs, it seemed, she'd pick up a similar stone off the velvet cloth and say 'This is a Reiki healing wand.'

Sandy would watch the customer, weighing the stone carefully in their palm, nodding slowly and gravely, as if they were being given directions about taking some medication.

'What about this one?' they would say.

'That's a tiger's-eye palm worry stone,' Gail would answer serenely; or 'that's a smoky quartz healing generator.'

Sandy herself had bought one of those. You held it in your hand and used its energy to enhance your business creativity and boost your endurance to facilitate the completion of worldly activities. Idly, she wondered if she could claim hers on tax. But when was the last time she'd put in a tax return? No idea.

Anyway.

The candle.

Christ on a bike, he felt like he'd been on the rack all night. Rich had spent some uncomfortable nights in his time — in airports, across benches, on living-room floors — but despite being dog-tired the night before, it was as if he'd physically absorbed some of the unrelenting essence of what he'd lain on. Now it felt as though his own body was constructed from wooden boards covered with the thinnest layer of cushioning foam. He tried to walk off his stiffness. On feet that felt like they'd been wrung in a vice. Tenderfoot — that was him. Thank God today was only three hours. A mere seven-point-seven kilometres of track under Barn Bluff then across the open exposed ridge, all the way along the dotted line on the map in the hut that made it all look so benign. At least the weather was holding out. And at least walking warmed up the chill that had seeped into him overnight too, despite his superior loft sleeping bag.

He'd talked to everyone last night, made the effort to get to know them, conscious of Sophie watching him and taking her cues from him. They were a mixed bag alright. Not exactly what he'd expected. Mind you, that guy Russell was already starting to get up his nose. *Gaiters — you mean you haven't brought gaiters? Well, heavens, take my spare pair* and *what you need, Rich, is a micro towel — haven't you come across these? Oh, they're magic, mate; here, use this one, I can share Libby's.* Doing everything but slapping him heartily on the shoulder, jumping out of his skin with glee that he had something Rich didn't that he could brag about. Knew everything. Been everywhere. Like a bloody scout master.

Wondering how many days of rain the park got a year? Russell was your man. Two hundred and seventy-five, since you're asking. Unsure whether you needed to boil the water out of the hut tank? Here, have a few of these water-purifying tablets, so you don't need to waste your stove fuel. Mildly interested in knowing what bird it was you'd seen that afternoon? Why, let's take a look in Russell's handy pocket field guide.

Rich kept a teeth-gritted smile fixed on his face as they sat and ate gluey cheese noodles, then tried to remember the rules for 500 when Russell and Libby asked if they felt like a few hands of cards. Sophie picked it up like she was born to it. Sitting there shyly calling trumps in a hut in the middle of the Tasmanian wilderness, her half-finished plate of pasta congealing on the end of the table.

'She's a great girl,' Libby had said to him when Sophie had taken the headlamp, giggling, and gone out to brave the composting toilet. 'She's a real credit to you.'

'Thanks.' He'd paused, then thought: *it's going to come out sooner or later*. 'But I can't take credit for her. I've only just really met her, actually. Her mum and I aren't together. Haven't been for a long while now.'

He felt her keen eye. An uncomfortable moment.

'Well,' she said smoothly, 'she seems very well adjusted.' A kind thing to say about a girl with a ring through her eyebrow and a silver skull pendant.

'Hey,' Russell had said, breaking the ensuing silence, 'do your guy ropes reach the platform hooks, Rich? Because you should take this — perfect thing to extend them.' Giving him a neatly rolled length of white builder's line tied with four strong elastic bands. 'And you can use those elastic bands to extend the length of the elastic on your tent-fly too.'

Well, Rich wanted to say, *you've certainly earned all your badges tonight*.

'Great for clotheslines too,' Russell added, a juggernaut of handy hints.

'Thanks,' he said, smoothly gracious. 'I appreciate it.'

Now he was trudging along in Russell's gaiters, which it pained him to admit did keep his socks and boot tops a bit dryer, still feeling like he'd spent the night on an ironing board, or strung up in a few lengths of Russell's white twine. Nearly at Lake Windermere, which would mean they were almost there. He'd decided against the side-trip to the other lake. Three extra kilometres he didn't need — he was already starting to ration his energy and time for the photo opportunities — and let's face it you've seen one cold lake fringed by pencil pines, you've seen them all.

He didn't take his boots off when they stopped for a breather at the lake. A few other people who'd been walking ahead of them had, and they were lounging and splashing their bare feet in the freezing cold water. He longed to join them, but knew that it would just make it worse trying to put his boots back on again, easing his feet down through that hard leather curve. When he stood up to start walking again, bracing himself mentally for more pain, he felt his right sock pull away with a little tear from the flesh of his heel, skin he'd never before realised was so unbearably tender and sensitive. That meant a blister that had broken, and the sock had dried to his foot. Only a little further to go now until the hut, he urged himself.

He began to walk, gingerly, but as briskly as he could. That feeling of ripping away, like a bandaid, the same little sharp gulp of pain.

He remembered his mother trying to pull a bandaid off his foot once, when he'd overdone it in a basketball game at school. She'd winced and made little pained noises as she picked away ineffectually at the strip, then finally jumped up and ran him a bath, saying he could soak it off instead. He recalled his father grunting with derision as he made his way obediently into the bathroom.

Rich pushed one foot in front of the other, his jaw set. He hadn't a single recollection of his father administering any sort of first aid to him or his sister, not a dab of disinfectant, not a bandage, nothing. He couldn't even remember him putting a hand to his forehead to feel if he had a temperature. No, that was the province of their woefully ill-equipped mother, who would have taken them to the doctors for a bee sting if she could. Every cough was asthma, every admission of tiredness was glandular fever.

He remembered drawn-out, tedious days in bed during primary school, long after the novelty of missing school had worn off, and his mother rousing him from his book, as if preparing some great treat for him, and sitting him down to watch a daytime soap opera with her. He saw enough episodes through the years to basically follow the storyline, and make a sort of sense of his mother's worrying running commentary. That's one of his clearest memories of her; pressing the pillowcases and tea towels on the ironing board as she talked back at the telly. Telling Julie she was mad to leave Doug, and telling Mickey whose the baby really was, despite what that scheming Jacinta said.

He remembered her disappearing into the kitchen mid-afternoon one day as he lay on the couch covered with a quilt, feeling drowsy with sleep and boredom, and reappearing with two glasses of dry sherry. One for each of them. He'd been eleven at the time, and taken in by her complicit smile. It didn't seem a long distance between that day and coming home from school to find her on the floor of the pantry, out cold, her head down under the shelf where she stored all the jars. Jars she kept for jam, she said, but he couldn't recall her ever making any. The kitchen smelled of the dinner in the crockpot, a slow cooker which had the effect of tenderising everything down to generic mushy casseroles that would fall to pieces off your fork. You didn't see those around much anymore, but his mother had professed to loving hers when she'd got it for Mother's Day.

He'd dropped his school bag and said her name a few times, practising getting his voice steady, then stood for as long as it took to convert his shocked incredulity into something approaching manageable. Something that allowed him, finally, to stop saying her name, to make himself a glass of chocolate milk, in fact, and go into the living room and change channels on the television till he found the shows he always watched. *Scooby Doo*. Then *The Brady Bunch*.

On the dining-room table the washing had been all folded and pressed into four neat piles, one for each of them — all they had to do was put it in their drawers. His sister was at her jazz ballet class, so there was no one else home — only him, and his unconscious mother lying there with laddered pantyhose and no shoes, quietly breathing in the other room. He made the chocolate milk last a long time, because he was hungry, he realised as *Gilligan's Island* started, but there was no way he was going back there into the kitchen until she woke up and pulled herself together. He'd liked the new hardness in his voice as he said that to himself. *Useless,* he mouthed sneeringly at the screen. Sitting there, he tried on his father's habitual barely concealed derision, and to his surprise found it fitted like a glove, like a garment that had been lying there waiting for him for a long time.

He took off his hat and scratched his scalp as he walked, pushed the heels of his hands momentarily against his eyes. The wind was making them sting. No point dragging all that stuff up now. That was just growing up, it was what you went through. Nothing more tedious than middle-class dysfunction.

The hut was just up ahead. He'd give the tents a miss tonight and find himself a quiet bunk in the corner, lay some of his clothes flat under his sleeping mat, maybe. See if he'd left an odd valium by chance in his travelling first-aid kit, because a decent night's sleep was all he needed; otherwise he was fine. He'd wad up the cotton handkerchief he had in one of the side pockets of his pack, and wrap his ankle in that. Cushion that small blister. That's all it was, really. New boots, and a blister that was starting to burn like a bastard. You couldn't buy a great pair of boots without having to break them in, after all. If you couldn't tough that out, then forget it. Give up. They moulded themselves to you and you moulded yourself to them, and then they'd last you a lifetime.

It was probably goatskin, and in that case would be OK, because goats were domesticated and occasionally a feral nuisance, so she should stop worrying. One of the things that made her so chronically tired and possibly a little edgy, Sandy thought, massaging the pins and needles in her ankles, was just the task of constantly having to be on guard against everything. That's why she had to check the drum out carefully, because there was always the chance of someone coming over to your house, flipping your drum over, finding a little sticker that said *Made in Pakistan* or whatever, and starting to talk about poverty and human-rights records to make you feel bad.

And there was so much to feel bad about — whether you were exploiting somebody, or whether an animal was suffering because of you, or whether you were taking away the jobs of other drum makers somewhere else, or whether the wood had been taken from a rainforest you were helping deplete ... for crying out loud, it never stopped. You tried, endlessly, to tread lightly on the earth, to take only photos and leave only footprints, to buy locally and reduce, reuse and recycle, and all you got was tired. It took up so much of your energy. She hesitated, then untucked her legs and lay down. Amazing, how a mat this thin could be so comfortable once you lay on it. You just settled your head back onto the cushion and made sure your whole spine was touching the floor. Then practise thinking of nothing. Breath going in, breath going out.

Trying to do the right thing. To not just give in to it all, and switch off your conscience. She knew it drove Sophie crazy, sometimes, but then Sophie was a teenager and teenagers thought you were oppressing them if you made them get out of bed in the morning.

'Who's going to notice?' she would say, exasperated, as Sandy refused to drink orange juice that contained pulp from imported oranges. 'What do you think's going to happen — the fruit juice police are going to storm in here and arrest you?' And Sandy would laugh, but a little uneasily, truth be known, because Sophie was right — everyone was kind of policing each other, everyone was under surveillance.

She'd been a vegetarian for many years, for instance, but when she'd given birth to Sophie and started breastfeeding, a terrible, insatiable urge had come over her. She'd needed meat. Big slabs of roasted red meat, oozing juice.

This need hadn't occurred to her until she'd walked past the Rotary fundraising sausage sizzle at the market, then suddenly her feet had turned her around and walked her back as she'd fished four dollars out of her pocket and found herself saying, 'Two, please.' Her voice seemed strange to her as she spoke, firm and guttural with someone else's resolve, and her eyes had watched the guy pick up the sausages with tongs and put them in white bread (*White bread! Empty of nutrients! With margarine from the supermarket stuffed with dye and polymers and known carcinogens!*), watched every move he made as she said yes to onions and yes to tomato sauce and it was all she could do not to salivate down her own chin. Then she went and sat under a tree and, staring into the middle distance at nothing in particular, had eaten the sausages in three short minutes, every tastebud on her tongue crying its thanks.

She licked her fingers, and contemplated having two more, and it was only the baby in her sling waking up and starting to cry with hunger that stopped her. As she put Sophie to her breast she was calculating what the time was, and if she had time to get to the butcher's before it closed, and if she did, what she would say if someone saw her.

'Iron depletion,' she began to explain, when people looked at her with disapproving surprise, with that infuriating wounded disappointment. 'It's for the baby.'

And it was true, a large part of her exhaustion seemed to vanish once she started eating what her friend Carlie distastefully referred to as 'flesh'.

It was gleeful, she thought now, shifting more comfortably on her cushion, taking a breath to join in the Energising Hum. Gleeful, the smug catching out of others, the chance to know better. People came awake when they saw an opportunity for it. Their faces actually brightened.

When Carlie had had her baby, Sandy had felt a miserable, envious swoon. A textbook home birth, in the tub, with aromatherapy oils and gentle music, culminating in a baby boy Carlie had named Jarrah.

She thought, not for the first time, of Sophie's chaotic arrival in the world and how she wished she'd come up with a more imaginative name. Carlie had a sling based on a Mayan design and she'd invited her to hold Jarrah in it one day, about a week after his birth. Attached to him, she noticed bemusedly, was a small fabric-wrapped parcel.

'What ...?' she'd said nervously, holding the baby carefully and letting her eyes travel from the bag to the baby. Joined by a wizened sort of cord, she observed guardedly, her eyes hadn't been deceiving her.

'Lotus birth,' said Carlie. 'It's a very ancient tradition.'

She had sat very still, not wishing to reveal her ignorance, but her face must have given her away.

'Umbilical nonseverance,' Carlie had gone on. 'It's the practice of not cutting the umbilical cord at birth, letting it fall away naturally.'

'So that's ... that's the placenta?' said Sandy faintly, gesturing to the bag.

'Yes, the fabric's from Rajasthan, because that place is very significant to me, of course, after spending so much time there. You dust the placenta with rosemary powder and lavender seeds, then later you plant it under a tree, at a ceremony when the time feels right.'

She kept her eyes away from the cord after that. No saved placenta, at Sophie's birth. The whole birth plan out the window. The final, humiliating failure of a caesarean she still tried hard not to refer to, her ultimate cowardly abdication, the absolute hospital takeover. She vaguely recalled an injection of something, the midwife lifting something away as the doctor got ready for the stitches, but frankly, seeing the baby safe and breathing, and with a good hit of pethadine, it had all felt like something happening miles away she couldn't care less about.

It was only afterwards she'd been blindsided by the nagging persistent thought that she'd given away control of everything. Just given up and let it happen.

'We planted a tree,' she said finally. Carlie, on a roll now, explaining how empowering the home birth had been away from patriarchal obstetric intervention ('You're so right,' Sandy said) and showing her how she'd even made her own baby powder for Jarrah out of chemical-free cornflour ('Wonderful,' she exclaimed), on and on until Sandy had gone home to roll a big fat joint and wait for five-year-old Sophie to come back from school to lift her out of her debilitating, dispiriting sense of inadequacy. Sophie, at five, could cure her of anything.

But, see, the karma rolls around again. She'd come unexpectedly across Carlie eight months later in the hypermart Big W in the next town up the highway, an economy box of disposable nappies clearly visible in her trolley and Jarrah howling like any other ordinary kid in his papoose, two ribbons of green mucous dribbling from his nose, pulling at Carlie's hair and straining to get out.

'They get illnesses whether you want it or not,' Carlie had said hurriedly, wiping a snail trail of snot off her shoulder. 'It builds up their immunities naturally.' Her face had been scarlet and she'd made a quick excuse and escaped to the checkouts.

Ridiculous, she thought to herself as she watched Carlie's retreating harried back, ridiculous, this tiny surge of triumph.

'Sandy?'

Bloody hell, the yoga instructor was bending over her.

'The meditation is over.'

'I know,' she answered, mustering a serene smile. 'I'm just gathering my thoughts.'

She got up (*For goodness sake, don't scramble up off the floor, Sandy, you're forty-five years old. Sit in a chair like a grown woman*), hearing reflective strings and birdsong fill the room as someone pressed 'play' on the CD player. Sandy took a while to straighten up. She'd pulled a muscle, she thought, doing the Downward Dog. She'd buy some tiger balm in the shop.

She loved the shop, here at the Wellness Centre. She'd slip in there during breaks to drink in its atmosphere of assurance and tranquillity. Why couldn't home be like the interior of this shop? Sandalwood burned in the oil burner, a waterfall burbled soothingly in the background, lovely quilts and kites and tribal pillows were hung from the ceiling. Textiles. Maybe that was what her place needed. More textiles. She drifted to the bookcase, shifting the collection of marble elephants to browse. A book would be an investment, something she could read and learn from later, pick up the fine points of what they were covering. She selected *God Has Gifted You*, *Sacred Path Medicine Cards* and *Questions for Your Spirit Guide*, and took them over to the register; $79.50, but that was OK. She had a lot of questions.

No mirror here either. Just the unadorned composting toilet and the walls of the Windermere Hut covered in maps and photos, everything but a simple mirror she could use to fix her make-up in the morning, and she should have thought to just bring a small compact one in her toilet bag, but it hadn't even occurred to her. And Rich with his camera, probably wanting to take photos of her; she'd come out looking like some twelve-year-old idiot with tiny eyes and bad skin and her hair tucked up under a moronic beanie, that's what she'd have to live down, and there was no way she could go up to a total stranger and ask them if they had a *mirror* to loan her, what sort of up-herself loser would ask that on a bushwalk? Sophie opened her packet of make-up wipes and rubbed savagely at her eyes. It would all just be black smears now, anyway, better nothing than that deranged look. She'd pluck up the courage and ask someone. That woman Libby, maybe. She might have one. There was no way she could go out in public just with *nothing*. It would feel like being naked.

Rich moved on auto-pilot. Score a sleeping space on the bunk platform, roll out your sleeping bag. Amazing how relative comfort was, he mused, how little you were prepared to settle for. What he really wanted was a hot shower and a lingering read of the paper in an armchair, listening to the ice sigh as it melted in a double scotch, but he was prepared to settle for a wooden platform like something in a Malaysian prison cell, and just about as crowded.

What's more, he was grateful for it. Full of nothing but unutterable relief as the hut had come into view, knowing the interminable trudging was finished for another day, that he could at last slide off the backpack and experience, for an odd, false moment, the sensation of being as light as air without it. As he fumbled through cooking dinner on his fuel stove on the packed tabletop, he watched from the corner of his eye the young dreadlocked Israeli couple doing the same thing. Or perhaps not a couple. Perhaps just two people who hardly knew each other, doing the walk as some kind of army endurance exercise. They were pretty much silent, glancing with stolid coldness around at other walkers and speaking to each other in short, low monosyllabic exchanges.

'How are you finding it?' said another woman stirring something in a pot next to him.

'The walk? Fine.'

'You're with your daughter, aren't you?' A Kiwi, he thought.

'Yes, how about yourselves?'

'Old schoolfriends. Promised ourselves we'd do this when we all turned thirty. So here we are.'

'Well, good on you.'

He scoured his brain for something else to say, and failed. He was too tired for this. Too tired to do anything other than measure out the water for this packet of artificially flavoured crap and boil it up then shovel it into his mouth then hit the sack. Hit the boards. Hit the wall. No need to get dragged into a conversation, anyway. The woman was listening now to the Germans at his table as they discussed Tasmanian wildlife.

'The devils, yes, but they are not so numerous now, after the facial cancers.'

'And the quolls. We saw so many of them on Bruny Island. So beautiful. And once all over the mainland.'

'I read somewhere that fifty percent of all native mammals originally on the mainland are extinct now,' the New Zealander said.

That can't be right, Rich thought, poking at the rice. They've all got the wrong end of the stick there. He was too exhausted to intervene.

'So why not, the biggest mammal to live here still surviving, with so many thousands and thousands of square kilometres of unexplored territory?'

This was an earnest girl talking now, whose tan suggested she'd just spent a month or so in Cairns.

'For me, I believe they are still here. We've met now, two tour operators who believe it still exists. It was still only classified as an endangered species up until 1986. And the Parks and Wildlife officer who saw one in 1995 — why would he lie?'

'Yes, I remember reading this too. In the remote wilderness,' said another.

'Pyengana would be where they are,' said the Kiwi.

They were talking about the tiger, he thought, tearing the corner off a packet of Surprise Peas'n'Corn. The good old mythical beast. He saw, fleetingly, those yellow glass eyes, the smell of mothballs, that giant yearning clump of testimonials.

'And here, in this park, the German tourist who photographed one in 2005. I think many, many people still do believe, but are afraid they will be laughed at. Many scientists. And the tour operator is offering $1.75 million now.'

'They say the photos might have been faked.'

The girl shrugged. 'For me, I still believe. I still hold out a hope. For this I come halfway across the world.'

'Is there a bus to Pyengana?'

Bound to be, Rich thought dully. Get out there and thrash the bushes, folks. Secure the territory in a coordinated pincer movement. Operation Tigerhunt.

He looked up and waved at Sophie, shouldering her way into the hut.

'Sit down,' he called. She looked so spindly and fine-boned, he thought as she picked her way through the tables, compared to the strapping outdoorsy Germans. So wan and worried. And younger, somehow, although he couldn't put his finger on why.

'Have you seen those girls from Melbourne Uni?'

He had to think. What girls? 'No. Don't think they've arrived.'

'What about Russell and Libby?'

'Not sure,' he answered, heaping a huge serve of rice onto her plate. 'Tonight's gourmet treat, brought to you from Continental Rices of the World.'

'Thanks,' she said, taking the plate carefully.

'Risotto à la Richard,' he added. 'Sit down here, we'll eat together.'

She flashed him a look. A stricken look, hunted. He watched her lower the plate self-consciously, take her eyes from its contents back to him again.

'Sit down,' he said. 'There's enough for seconds too.'

What was her problem? Who was she looking for, her eyes darting round the room? 'If it's OK by you I think I'll go and eat mine outside. Watch the sunset.'

He kept his face expressionless, covered up the hurt quickly. 'OK, then. Whatever you want.'

It took him a few moments to gather the energy to turn back to the table alone with his own plate. Feeling like an idiot, like he'd asked someone to dance and been snubbed. The Germans were sketching maps now, flicking through their guidebooks with an expeditionary air.

'So,' he said jovially to the New Zealand woman, mustering a warm smile, 'all of you have been friends since school, have you?'

Once he'd finished he went out to look for Sophie. OK. So she was moody. No need to worry. Just try to think back, see if he'd said or done anything out of the ordinary today that might have put her nose out of joint. Nothing — he was totally in the dark. So, let it go.

She saw him and approached with her own empty plate, and they stood, the tension hanging between them making him feel a rush of confusion.

'Here,' he said. 'I'll wash up.' He touched her spoon and felt dirt on it, grit moving beneath his fingers.

'Well, I know I'm not much of a cook,' he said lightly, 'but did you really have to dig a hole for it rather than force it down?'

Her eyes snapped over to him, and she sucked in her lip. 'You're meant to. It says in the camping book — you have to bury the leftovers. Because of scavengers.'

'OK, OK, keep your hair on.' Jesus, this was impossible. He'd never realised how instantly defensive a teenage girl could be.

'Give us your plate, then,' he said, gesturing. 'I'll wash them away from the water, OK? Like you're supposed to. I bet that's in the book too, right?'

'Yeah, it is.'

'Us humans, we're just a bunch of filthy old polluters, aren't we?'

She wiped the spoon clean of dirt on her jeans. What was wrong with meeting his eye once in a while?

'Yeah,' she muttered. 'We are.'

It had been going so well, those first few days. A bit shy, maybe, but he'd done nothing to warrant this kind of cold shoulder, he was sure of it. He'd caught her looking at him sometimes over the last day or so, speculatively. God knows what went on in a fifteen-year-old girl's mind — it was as though she was still waiting for him to do whatever it was that would live up to her expectations. But — he acknowledged this with a flutter of panic — she didn't seem to be smiling quite so much now. What was she waiting for? What cues was he supposed to read?

Less than a week, now, he thought tensely. To ... what? Make her love him?

No, not love him, he corrected himself hastily. He didn't expect that. But at least respect. At least not to look at him with that expression of bland, polite lack of interest, *enduring* him. And to want to see him again, sometime. The thought of seeing that look on her face when they said goodbye on Tuesday was intolerable.

It'd drive you insane, having to live with that. The thought that whatever it was that had disappointed someone, it was something in you that you couldn't see.

His calf muscles ached as he crouched to wash the plates, his sore ankle stiff with raw heat.

She was under his skin, now, whether he liked it or not. And he had till Tuesday to work out how to do it. How to see what she wanted, and win her over.

Eleven

She was up early, restlessly wakeful in the hut with all that strange unfamiliar breathing going on around her. She'd dreamed she was organising a music festival, feverishly responsible for everything, every single detail; showing cars where to park and doing sound checks and finding clothes racks for the performers and hanging all the lights, and just as she was about to meet some stars she heard her mum calling her from the ticket booth where she was supposedly trying to help, just one tiny simple responsibility, calling her to say, giggling, that she'd forgotten to bring any change, did Sophie have change so she could sell some tickets? And in front of her, a huge queue of Sophie's friends waiting, staring at her accusingly.

She had woken up with her jaw clenched in rage, and gone outside. Smelt the forest, inhaling the rich scent of so many woody fragrances — soil and leaves and cinnamony dampness. She'd sleep outside in her tent from now on. She liked it much better, waking up hearing birds calling to each other instead of humans snoring.

She should have told Rich she was on a special diet.

Or in training.

For what, though? Something at school. Some inter-school athletics event. She could invent something. She had found that the trick of lying to her mother was inserting a couple of specifics to distract her with. That, and knowing that Sandy wanted things easy and frictionless and made a point of not seeing anything she didn't want to see.

With Rich, maybe she could let her guard down. She'd eaten nearly half of it, anyway, making herself chew each mouthful twenty times, but even despite the walking, she'd had no appetite for the rest, and scraped her plate clean quickly. She was fine. Just hated people watching her while she ate. And the protein bars were really filling.

He'd ask her about herself soon, she was sure. He'd say *Boy, you're ten times fitter than I am, that's for sure.* And *I guess you've got a lot of questions about why Sandy and I split up, so go ahead.*

She thought about what he'd said in the bus, about doing that trust game, relying on strangers to catch you as you fell. All her life, she felt, she'd been relied upon, the stable counterpoint as her mother muddled through, her unwilling confidante and vigilant, uneasy sidekick. *What would I do without you?* Sandy would say, only half jokingly, as Sophie remembered to bring in the washing and prioritised the overdue bills and showed Sandy again how to program the video and use the printer and record a message on the answering machine. *What would I do without you?* in a voice that could turn clingy in an instant, in that holding pattern of perpetual needy hopelessness.

Well, she wanted a turn letting go. She didn't want to fall, just to see how it felt to lean, rather than be the one leaned on. To be able to step into the circle, and stop having to brace herself, automatically, for someone else's weight.

It was worse. He was conscious of that the moment he woke up.

He unzipped his sleeping bag, peeled back his sock and had a look at his ankle, wincing involuntarily at the weeping redness of it. It looked a bit like the start of a tropical ulcer he'd got one time when he was in Bali. He'd gone out stoned on someone's kayak and scraped his leg on some coral, and by the time his holiday was over it was an angry festering mess, the centre like a tiny angry volcano on a shiny crimson plateau. It had taken a course of antibiotics that time, which had really done his stomach in after all those magic mushrooms.

He got up stiffly, ducking to avoid the wooden bunk above him, and went outside onto the verandah, where two parties of walkers were already ensconced with bowls of muesli and unfolded maps, talking routes and side-trips. They wished him good morning and he smiled distractedly, trying not to limp as he found a spot to sit on a fallen tree nearby. He soaked a handkerchief with cold water from his drinking bottle and applied it to the heel. The relief was instantaneous and he sat there for a few minutes, immersed in it, only opening his eyes when he sensed someone standing over him. It was that guy Russell again. Jesus, was nowhere far enough away?

'Just out watching those brown scrub wrens,' Russell said. 'Did you see them?'

'Nope.' The only birds he had really noticed on the walk were the crows, hanging around as though they were waiting for you to fall in your tracks so they could peck your eyes out. They'd cluster on bare branches, making that cawing, croaking sound like they were catching their breath after a bout of helpless laughter.

'I saw a dusky robin yesterday too. And a couple of flycatchers.'

Fabulous, Rich thought darkly.

'Got a few blisters there?' Russell went on. 'Couldn't help noticing you were limping a bit.'

'Yeah. Just the one, really.' He glanced at Russell. 'Actually I'm not sure it's a blister — I'm wondering if I've got a bite from somewhere.'

Russell squatted down. *Rack off,* he wanted to say. *Rack off and go and read your fucking bird book.*

'Let's have a look,' said Russell.

Rich removed the wet fabric reluctantly. He bet Russell never got blisters — no, he'd have skin like a bloody elephant's. His heel would wear a hole in a boot, not the other way round.

'Actually,' he said, 'it reminds me of a tropical ulcer I got once when I was sailing. In Flores. Took a catamaran through the archipelagos there.'

'This might help,' said Russell. He held out a little jar. 'You can have this.'

Rich worked hard to control his voice, keep himself friendly and reasonable. 'What is it?'

'Golden Seal ointment.' Russell rose and stretched. 'And try two pairs of socks. If you need some sterile dressing to cover it with first, let me know.'

'Right. Thanks very much.' No, this guy wouldn't have antiseptic cream, would he? He'd have this stuff, like something out of a medieval apothecary. He sniffed it. Christ, it was like axle grease.

'Sure this goes on the inside of the boots, not the outside?' he said jokingly, but Russell had gone back to the hut, no doubt to prepare some gourmet breakfast out of freeze-dried lichen.

'Golden Seal,' he muttered, smearing some on. 'Made with real seals.'

He looked around for Sophie to share the joke, but she wasn't around either. Probably still asleep, he thought. But then he spotted her, up and dressed and sitting on another tree stump, staring into her mobile phone like it was a bloody oracle. She obviously still couldn't believe what the ranger at the centre had told her, and the evidence in front of her own eyes. See, they were addicted to the things, they couldn't live without them.

'Ready for some breakfast?' he called to her. She glanced up from behind that screen of lank, black hair, blinking, dropping her hand from her mouth where she'd been distractedly gnawing a fingernail.

'I've already had breakfast.'

'Eh?'

'I had two GoBreakfast bars.'

'Hey, you need more than that to do today's walk. It's almost seven hours today.' As he spoke, determinedly cheerful, he felt a shudder of horror at the thought. His heel, inside that boot, for seven hours, rubbing over and over and over on that broken skin as he trudged fourteen kilometres straight. 'I thought I might cook up some porridge,' he went on, sounding to his own ears as relentlessly, inanely upbeat as one of the phoneys at the TV station, adding a bonus temptation of an added attachment to the slicer-dicer deal.

'I had some protein bars.' Steel in her voice.

He had to get back to his pack, dry his heel, put on this ointment, then two pairs of socks, then somehow ease his foot into his boot. Then get up and walk, and walk, and walk. He let the smile slide off his face — she was looking back at her phone, anyway.

'You're telling me you're going to walk till lunchtime on nothing but two muesli bars? That's bullshit.'

She flashed him a quick look. No smiles now, from either of them.

'Just watch me,' she replied mutinously, digging for her earphones.

Muttered it, really — like she didn't care if he heard or not. The day stretched ahead of him, bleak as certain pain, an image of pushing himself forward with every step along a desolate cold moor that went on as far as the eye could see, not even a place to stop and shelter for seven more hours. No way out of this now but ahead.

He was composing the rough sketch of an article in his head as they wound across Pine Forest Moor. It took his mind off the inescapable reality that with each kilometre they covered he was walking more deeply into a landscape he'd then have to walk out of, because they weren't even halfway. It felt, when you stepped back from it, like the height of stupidity, to be voluntarily ploughing pointlessly onwards only to plough out the other side again. It felt like an elaborate practical joke someone was playing on you, that you hadn't got yet.

The track was stony and crisscrossed with roots, and although the day was clear they still had to traverse deep, squelching bogs, and this deteriorated into a veritable marsh once they'd crossed the base of Mount Pelion West. Composing the article (*a landscape scattered with massive boulders left by receding glaciers and gnarled old* trees, war veterans of the weather's dramatic battles) helped him not think about the thing, whatever it was — a golem, a gremlin, a succubus — that hung onto his foot inside his boot and hit his Achilles tendon with a tiny red-hot hammer every time he took a step. A few thousand steps, he thought through gritted teeth. Then a few thousand more. It had to toughen up soon.

Miles of stiff yellow buttongrass, tufty and strawberry blonde, like a glam-rocker's hairdo. Duran Duran grass. And the pandani, those big clusters of grass trees like something Dr Seuss would draw. A solid headwind hit them as they toiled around the low boggy ground, a whole line of walkers now bent into the wind, trudging forward like a party of sherpas trekking across Everest, Rich thought, hunched against the elements, setting their jaws and staggering on. And when he looked ahead he couldn't quite believe it but they were actually going to slog back in the direction they'd already been in a big, depressing loop, they were going to *double back*, so they'd get to experience this wind from every possible angle. Sophie was up ahead, he saw, making heavy work of the mud and roots, like everyone, and he looked back down at where he was putting his feet again when suddenly the wind seemed to gather itself and expel a whistling blast that almost tore his hat off his head. He glanced up again, staggering, eyes streaming, and saw it had actually blown one of the walkers off the track; they were on their back in the mud. Sophie! He jogged awkwardly, stumbling, to the spot, the tiny hammer going *crash crash crash*, pounding rivets into his ankle. She was trying to scramble to her feet, hampered by her pack which kept her, turtle-like and helpless, in the bog. He couldn't see, for a few seconds, whether she needed help getting up or not.

He hesitated. She'd been so pig-headed that morning, snapping at him about breakfast, maybe she'd swear at him now if he reached out a hand. Maybe she was humiliated that she'd fallen over and he should just pretend ... By the time he'd moved forward, torn by indecision, somebody else was already there, one of the group from New Zealand. The woman braced a foot against a tree root and held out a hand to Sophie.

'I'm alright,' he heard her say. 'I can get myself up.' Her legs kicked again, straining for purchase against the tussocky grass, and she raised herself onto her elbows, her pack coming free and sucking out of the mud like a mired tree stump. He caught her eye as she paused there, panting, and she looked straight through him as if he wasn't even there. He stood frozen as she hauled herself up onto her knees.

'Good on you,' said the Kiwi woman, taking Sophie's outstretched hand and hoisting her back upright again, dripping mud and water. Just as she did, another gust of wind made them both stagger and clutch each other and Rich winced, expecting tears. Or a scene — sitting down on the track and refusing to go any further, maybe, or screaming at him for dragging her through this, making it his fault. He waited, cringing, for the outburst, but instead Sophie and the other woman laughed. They sat on the cross-laid logs of the track and wiped their faces and tried to brush themselves off as the wind whipped and belted around them, and laughed, speechless with helpless hilarity. As he watched, still rooted to the spot, the other walkers who'd stopped smiled too, exchanging a few words, stepping over them. All laughing, now, at the weather, making light of it, making a little Kodak moment of instant glowing camaraderie. She was incorrigible. Sitting there giggling with the Kiwi woman, covered in mud.

He crouched down. 'Are you really OK?'

'Yes, yes. My fault — I wasn't watching where I was going — I was looking at the light changing on the mountain there.'

'Mount Oakleigh,' said the New Zealander. 'I was looking at it too. You can't go through this beautiful scenery watching your feet every step of the way, can you? Good thing you were wearing your raincoat.'

'Yeah, it's just my pack really that copped it, and everything inside's in plastic bags, anyway.'

She was turned away from him; there was nowhere he could put a reassuring hand on her now without seeming clumsy and awkward. He'd missed his moment. He glanced up at the mountain she'd pointed to — just a big grey outcrop that looked like a burned, badly risen soufflé. And he still had kilometres of agony to go, with nothing but dead trees and bogs, and across this track made of these slippery split logs that were killing his feet. Russell had told him there was more than likely going to be a Parks and Wildlife ranger or warden at the next hut, so he'd make sure he'd ask them whose brilliant idea it had been making a track out of rounded logs, and did they realise how much more arduous it made the walk. How it had nearly caused a serious accident with his daughter. And he'd have something to say about it in his article too. He let the indignation mount and seethe in him.

'Are you sure you're alright?' he said again.

'Yes. I'm good.'

Still not looking at him. Later he wished he'd made more of a deal of it, wished he'd trusted that shred of instinct, because he was sure he saw a tear glittering in her eye, despite her tone of dismissive nonchalance as she re-shouldered her pack and wiped mud from her forehead. He realised in that moment what was different about her face — she wasn't wearing all that eyeliner and pale foundation anymore, and her features looked undefended somehow, strained with a new rawness.

By the time they'd slogged through the last gruelling kilometres of wet forest and dripping tree ferns, and emerged exhausted and sweating at the other side, it was clear she must have been at the end of her tether. He should have seen that, but he was too preoccupied with his own exhaustion, too cut off. So that after they'd dumped their packs on the big wrap-around verandah of the hut and all gone down to a creek Russell had told them about, where she could wash the mud off or even have a swim if she wanted to, Sophie had stood there unbuttoning her raincoat with weary fingers and Libby, with a startled grimace of distaste, had cried, 'Ugh, Soph, you've got ... wait ...'

And all of them, Sophie included, had looked down at the pale, mud-smeared skin on her chest to see a necklace of leeches, seven or eight of them, blackly shining and fat with blood, just where the collar of her raincoat had been, and Sophie had sucked in a breath and screamed and screamed.

And it had been Libby she'd turned to, her arms outstretched like a child's. Libby who'd taken her hand and let her scream her revulsion out till she was spent, leaving him to stand there, drained and jangled, redundant. Whatever her tether had been, it was clearly snapped now, he thought, seeing her ashen and hiccupping, still clinging to Libby's hand. Secret relief rushed through him like a bitter anaesthetic. OK, he'd thought with flat finality, all over bar the shouting, the whole idea. Now let's find the ranger and get the fuck out of here.

My God, she'd never seen a real bloodsucking leech in her life till now, and they were totally disgusting. But there was a Parks ranger at the hut called Jen and as soon as she saw Sophie arrive back on the verandah with Rich and the others, she knew just what to do.

'Welcome to Pelion Palace,' she said, 'just let me get some salt for your visitors there.' As she sprinkled it onto the leeches she muttered, 'Take that, you little pricks', so that Sophie had to smile, and within a minute the leeches were writhing in satisfying death throes on the ground and Sophie was inside holding tissues to the uniform little trickles of blood on her neck.

The whole vampire thing — totally freaking horrible. She kept thinking of how they'd wriggled in there, their gaping little mouths sucking her blood out, and she hadn't felt a thing. A circle of them. She sat there shuddering, waiting for the bleeding to stop.

Then Jen made her a hot chocolate and heard about how she'd come a cropper off the track in the wind, and she found Sophie her clean dry clothes in her pack and brushed off her jeans and hung them up to dry in front of the stove.

'Have you got other pants?' she asked.

'One pair, yeah.'

'That's alright then. Are your feet cold?'

'They sure are,' she answered. She could hear the tiredness

in her own voice, the shake in it, embarrassing tears hovering somewhere threatening to spill. Jen lent her some great bedsocks and she couldn't work out why she felt like crying when she handed them to her. It was her mum, she finally realised with a start. That was just the kind of thing she'd do. Russell and Libby pooled their food with Rich and her and they made dinner, and Libby somehow put together an apricot crumble that Sophie ate without even admonishing herself, without even thinking about it. She felt brittle and weak, shivery with fatigue. Lactic acid, she thought vaguely. Should have an isotonic electrolyte replacement drink to buffer it, one with calcium and magnesium she could quickly absorb, but her eyes watched Libby spoon out another helping of apricot crumble and pass it to her and she ate it gratefully, mechanically. Carbohydrate and fruit, some sugars. Not so bad. She'd earned them; it was fuel. Even though the hut was huge there were too many people here to deal with; she wanted to be back in her quiet house, lying on her bed, doing normal things, not sitting here listening to Rich tell Jen about the time he'd got a leech on the Franklin River. She found an empty bunk space up the end of the hut and crawled into her sleeping bag and watched an episode of *CSI* she had downloaded on her iPod, her eyes focused on the tiny screen and blotting out everything around her, and as long as she didn't think too hard about the leeches she felt OK.

'How's she now?' asked the ranger, and Rich raised a wry eyebrow as he came back and said, 'Doesn't want to talk to anyone. She's bundled up in her sleeping bag watching a movie on her iPod, if you can believe it.' He raised a hand and let it sweep. 'Here in the middle of the wilderness.'

'Hopefully she'll feel better after a good night's sleep,' said the ranger confidently, as if anyone could sleep on those bare board beds. 'She's just a bit upset about the leeches.'

'I don't blame her. That time on the Franklin, I had to burn mine off with a cigarette lighter, and it was right in my ear too.'

She grinned. 'I looked down one night and found one between

my toes, and I just about had a fit too.'

He hesitated. 'I think she's finding it a bit tougher than she thought.'

'Yeah, that stretch today is a hard one; a lot of people feel they've maybe overestimated their fitness levels by about this point, especially in bad weather. We get people staggering in here, nearly in tears.'

'Well, she'd never say anything to me, of course, but I think she's struggling with it.'

She nodded thoughtfully, and he ploughed on. 'The problem is that there's no turning back, is there? Once you're on the track, you have to keep walking till you get to the end.'

'Not at all. In fact, if you're going to call it a day, this is a good place to stop.'

He kept his face calm, his expression somewhere between surprise and resignation. 'What — you've got a vehicle or something here?'

'Well, no, it's all on foot, but you can walk out from here without too much backtracking. I'll show you on the map. You head out along the Arm River track.' She paused. 'That is, if you really think she's reached her limit.'

He blinked. It was like a weight lifting off him, a stay of execution. 'Really?' he said.

'Yeah, it's a much easier walk than trying to head back over Cradle. You just go east instead of south.' She indicated a guy across the room. 'See that bloke over there? That's Andrew — he's out here doing some volunteer track work with us. He could probably go with you.'

'How far is it?' He could hardly keep the joy out of his voice, the incredulous relief.

'Oh — a few hours walking, then you reach a sealed road. I can probably organise a lift for you back to Mole Creek if you don't mind waiting round a bit once you get there. There'll be someone from Parks heading down to the Outdoor Ed Centre, I reckon, who can come and pick you up.'

He sat still and felt pleasure creep up on him, gave himself over to it. He lifted his palms in a gesture of acquiescence.

'Well, it seems like a shame, but I reckon that would be for the best.'

'If you think so.' Deferring, just like that, to his parental authority. Of course.

'I really think she's ready to call it a day,' he added.

'No worries. I'll sort it out and confirm it with you in the morning.'

'We'll be ready to go any time Andrew is, then,' he answered. 'Thanks for that.'

A graceful abdication, a tactical retreat, dignity intact. It was perfect. He could feel the accumulated stress and dread of the days ahead slide off him like rain off a roof.

When he unrolled his sleeping bag and climbed onto one of the wooden platforms he actually slept, and when he rose to consciousness the next morning, the dragging weight of queasy trepidation that had settled on him each morning till now dissipated smoothly as his mind sharpened to wakefulness.

The dread was gone. It was over. Just a few hours walking, penance for the whole folly, then a road. And a lift in a car that would turn the last three days slogging on foot back into half an hour. And then they'd be dropped somewhere they could catch a bus from — up to Deloraine maybe, or the caves at Mole Creek; somewhere with a B&B, anyway, that took credit cards, and Rich was sure that he and Sophie would laugh about this in the future. *That time we went to Tassie,* she would say, *back when we hardly knew each other, remember that, Dad?*

He climbed laboriously out of his sleeping bag, so grateful now that he wouldn't be walking too much further on his ankle, and limped out onto the verandah. Sophie was already up, her hair pulled back today out of her eyes and under her hat, and she was rolling and repacking her stuff into her backpack, which had dried out overnight in front of the fire.

'Hi,' he said, magnanimous and calm now, feeling — yes — almost fatherly.

'Hi,' she answered. 'I made tea, the water's still hot.'

Remember that final straw, Dad? she would say, grinning. *When that headwind blew me straight into the mud?*

'Listen,' he said, 'I was talking to the ranger last night, and she said that considering what a shit day you had yesterday, there's no need to keep going. Nothing to prove, and I agree with her. You've been amazing, getting to this point. We can walk out today along a special track and the Parks Service will give us a lift back to the nearest town and we'll go somewhere good for our last few days, OK?'

He kept his voice gentle, admiring. She lifted a hand suddenly and swept the curtain of hair out of her face, and gave him a searching look. His heart knocked at his ribs like a dull desperate fist under her scrutiny because, Jesus Christ, he needed her to smile and concede, needed to see her eyes fill with grateful childish tears of relief, because God knows he couldn't do it. Couldn't face another day of it.

Then she lifted her chin and gave one decisive shake of her head, and his heart stopped, then sank.

'No way am I quitting now,' she said.

He stared at her, watching her mouth, wondering if he'd possibly misinterpreted what she'd just said. He almost repeated it after her, so stunning was his dumbstruck anger, his shiver of resentful admiration. The cloud of it seethed and shifted inside him, settling into a grim mist of consternation, into a dull joyless acknowledgement that they were going on. There would be no escape east with the likes of Andrew, no reprieve, even if he admitted his own defeat. He was tied to her, bound to her. He stood there swaying slightly with incredulity, sick with rage, and sick with envy; both reactions, he could see, as pure and impulsive as a child's.

Twelve

No way was she going to be anybody's excuse. Rich had wanted to give up, she could tell. She'd seen the pissed-off, floored look in his eyes when she'd shaken her head. He'd been quick to hide it, but she'd been watching.

She was OK now. She'd hit rock bottom there for a minute but, like her PE teacher said, once you'd hit the wall you just had to come back harder next time and the inner reserves would be there.

That was the lesson. Not leaning on anybody. Let go of that childish shit.

She didn't get why he had to be so unfriendly to Russell and Libby, though. Some of the other people on the track were kind of silly, sure, and it was easy to make fun of them, but Russell and Libby had been so nice to him, lending him all that stuff he'd forgotten to bring, and they knew tons about Tasmania too, and had been bushwalking for years. But Rich got that look on his face whenever Russell started to talk to him, as if he couldn't wait to get away.

This morning when she'd got up to do her stretches and repack, Libby had said to her, 'So we're losing you, Sophie?', and she'd shaken her head, puzzled, then heard about the idea to just give in and walk out on some shortcut. Rich's idea.

'I'm not going anywhere,' she'd answered, and Libby had just smiled and said, 'Good.' She'd asked her to come and have breakfast with them, and she'd gone, even though she told Libby she'd already eaten.

Then of course she couldn't stop looking at them spooning up that porridge Russell had made with powdered coconut milk and sultanas. Her stomach growling.

Libby saying, 'Just have a spoonful, you'll feel much better', which was a weird thing to say when you thought about it, like she was sick.

Weird, and it should have put her on guard, but she'd had a few spoonfuls that she'd eaten as slowly as she could, listening to them chatting away about how they were planning to go to Spain to walk the pilgrim trail once their youngest son had finished his final exams for school, and then Libby had looked at her and said, 'Our daughter Ellie, Sophie, she'd love to meet you, she was just like you when she was fifteen, she went through the same kind of thing', and Sophie had shrugged, still chewing slowly. Thinking she meant a goth phase, or rebelliousness, or some dumb thing that adults always thought you did as an affectation they were confident you'd grow out of.

A bit preoccupied, in any case, wondering whether the coconut powder Russell had used for the porridge was full-fat or low-fat. Could you even buy low-fat coconut powder?

Then Libby was looking at her again, with a sad kind of smile, nodding, saying, 'I never knew how to address it with her, to my eternal regret, but she's just great now', and Sophie realised she wasn't talking about dyed hair and piercings.

It took such a huge effort to swallow, suddenly. Down with the mouthful of porridge went what threatened to be a sob. God, no way. No way in the world could she lose it and start crying again now.

Because they'd ask was she OK, they'd need to know why. And how could you ever explain it, that what you were crying for was yourself, for having to worry about a spoonful of powder, having to give something like that so much of your devoted attention? Crying for the sight of Russell's hand giving Libby's forearm a quick squeeze in the silence that followed, a terrible silence full of the potential to crack open?

She'd swallowed, finally, and looked down at her plastic plate, holding it together, the porridge sitting in her stomach like clag, and they didn't ask.

'Anyway, I've got something for you,' Libby said after a few moments, in a brighter voice.

'I don't need anything. That was heaps, really.' The words jerking out of her mechanically.

'Well, I hope you'll think about just rolling these up in the corner of your pack, just in case.' Libby rose and went to her pack and returned with two folded-up tops.

'Couldn't help noticing yesterday your windcheaters cut out a bit early round the bottom,' she said with an apologetic grin, gesturing to her own hips with a wave of her hand.

'You'll have to excuse Libby,' Russell said. 'She thinks every illness begins with a chill in the kidneys.'

'Don't take it the wrong way,' Libby went on, 'and of course don't wear them if you don't want to, but they're thermal tops, specially designed for hiking — they look a bit daggy but they come right down over your jeans.'

Sophie tried to make her face looked pleased and interested.

'You can give them back to me at Narcissus if you like, or keep them, I don't mind, but I'd feel a lot better if I knew that freezing wind wasn't hitting your bare skin. OK, now I'm totally embarrassed, so take them, please, and stuff them in your bag.'

'Well, thanks,' she said.

'Good in an emergency,' said Russell. They both smiled at her, and she smiled back. It was as awkward as Christmas, when her grandmother gave her butt-ugly unwanted clothes as well, a similar strained and sickly silence. There was no way she could wear them. It wasn't as if anybody on this walk could care less about appearances — not one single person had even noticed she hadn't been wearing make-up after the first day, she'd been stressing for nothing — but really, as if she'd ever wear a coral pink polo-necked top. Even to bed. And the beige stripy one was almost as bad. Still, as her mum often said after she'd opened one of Janet's fashion-disaster gifts, it was the thought that counted. She'd keep them, and give them back to Libby later. She'd thank her and say they'd been great.

She still felt shaken. Just three days, and she'd been more or less eating dinner every night, but Libby had noticed. Her mum had never noticed.

Nothing to prove, he'd said unwisely; he might have guessed that would be the exact wrong thing to say. He couldn't believe her renewed stamina. He didn't know where she got it from, because God knows she was built like a bloody racehorse, but whatever it was let her progress up the track now, on the fourth day, in the rain, like a grimly determined clockwork toy. Here she came, her long legs striking out in their black leggings, thin as a couple of licorice straps, eating up the miles. Like a fury.

He'd pulled himself together this morning. Gone back into the hut and averted his eyes from his pack, lying there in the corner like a gloating Rotweiller, waiting for him. After desperately rummaging through for anything that would let him keep walking on his ankle — Panadol, anti-inflammatories, anything — he almost wept with relief when he found the blister pack of prescription painkillers in the bottom of his toilet bag. At last, at last, a lucky break. Someone at work had given them to him, he recalled, after the guy had had a knee reconstruction. He'd taken two and managed to haul that hated, overstuffed weight up onto his aching shoulders, managed to walk without having to think about pain every second. OK, so he was slow, pacing himself carefully to make the distance, but did everybody really have to catch up with him and try to hold some inane conversation with him? Couldn't they just leave him alone with his own sodden thoughts, let him focus, teeth gritted, on one foot in front of the other? Out here in the desolate middle of nowhere, and he still couldn't be left in peace.

'I'd heard about the damage to these tracks,' the walker next to him was saying conversationally. 'I knew it was caused by erosion. All these walkers, one after the other, going around the muddy boggy spots instead of through them. But I had no idea it was getting so pounded.'

'Yeah.'

'Was talking to that guy Andrew last night, at the hut. Out here on his annual holidays, helping them do repair work. Makes me want to sign up to come and do some voluntary work myself next summer.'

Rich snuck a quick glance at the guy to see if he was joking. No, deadly serious. 'They're going to have to cap the numbers soon,' he answered. 'Almost ten thousand people a year, queuing up to do the walk. They're going to have to draw the line.'

The guy nodded eagerly. 'That's what I mean. That's why you get braiding damage like that. Too many walkers, just loving the place to death.' He pointed to the wide marshy mess up ahead, a bog of footprints around a black hole of marshy mud. 'Look at that. Disaster.'

What can you expect? Rich thought irritably to himself. Six-day walk, pisses with rain most of the year, everybody in big boots? It's a walking track, for godsakes. People create it by walking on it.

'Wet-boot walking,' said the guy firmly. 'That's the only thing for it.' He approached the puddle with clumping, square-shouldered determination and strode straight through it. There was nothing for it but to follow him. Rich felt his new boots hit the mud with a squelch. They sank up to his ankles. He thought of the diggers in World War I, toes rotting off with trench foot. The mud around here, he wouldn't be surprised if someone went in up to their waists. There'd be plenty of hikers coming up behind to haul them out, like they were all on some kind of gruelling spiritual test.

Wet-boot walking, he thought contemptuously, tramping along. Even slogging through mud's got to have its own bloody terminology.

Like the way they insisted, now, that you do the walk from north to south, to protect the track. Just to make sure you were all herded along in the same direction, stopping at the same huts and cooking up the same freeze-dried meals and swapping the same stories of how intrepid you were, pitting yourself against nature. And if you ever got a chance to look up to appreciate the scenery around you it was either covered in cloud or driving rain, so you went back to just watching your own feet, right and left, interminably, one after the other, forever unto infinity over the wire-covered duckboards and rutted puddles, on and on and on. You could save yourself the money, thought Rich bitterly, and stick a Fatbuster Pro exercise treadmill into a shower, turn the cold tap on, walk underneath it all day with twenty kilos of weights strapped to your back, and get just the same effect.

Russell was up ahead, springing through the muddy patches in — he couldn't believe it — what looked like a pair of old sneakers. 'Stunning, isn't it?' Russell called back, indicating a rain-washed vista with a wave of his arm.

'Fantastic!' he replied, jerking his head up, away from his feet. They slogged through another Somme trench, Russell on calf muscles that seemed hydraulically powered.

'Mate,' Rich said as he caught up, 'why aren't you wearing proper hiking boots?'

Russell grinned. 'I come from the other school of thought, the one which prefers Dunlop Volleys.'

'Are you shitting me? For bushwalking?'

'Well, they're light, they're comfortable, they've got great grip in the wet, and they're much more low-impact, especially in delicate alpine environments like this. I'd always bring extra boots in winter, of course.'

'Of course.' Sarcasm, though, was no match for Russell's eager enthusiasm.

'I read some research,' he said, 'that showed that carrying a kilogram on the feet is equivalent to carrying seven kilograms in a backpack.'

What sort of person, Rich thought, would come across research like that? Russell strode along the track as though his feet weighed nothing, as though he didn't have a care in the world. Any minute, thought Rich sourly, he's going to start yodelling

'The Happy Wanderer'.

Russell glanced back at him, still grinning. 'Makes you glad you brought other shoes to change into at night, doesn't it?

'It sure does!'

Bastard, bastard, bastard.

He was limping worse now, she could see. Trying to hide it, but it kept making him drop back. Only three hours today, if you just went up and over Pelion Gap. He'd shaken his head dismissively at the idea of climbing Mount Ossa.

'Too cloudy,' he'd said. 'If you're so determined to keep going, there's no point flogging yourself up a mountain as well. Won't get much of a view from the summit on a day like today.'

He was still angry with her, for wrecking his plan. Still sulking, thought Sophie wonderingly, like a little kid. She slowed down to let him catch up, watching him toiling along the valley track through stands of spindly eucalypts shining with moisture after the rain, pinnacles and cliffs of rock rising from the scrub in mammoth vertical slabs. You could hardly believe your eyes, it was so beautiful.

'I'm just taking my time today,' he said when he came abreast of her. 'Just thinking about making some photos, you know, resisting the need to rush ahead.'

He hadn't mentioned the leeches, or what had happened when she'd fallen on the track. Sure they'd all laughed about it later, but she hadn't forgotten how he'd stood, undecided, as someone else had stepped down and helped her up. As though he couldn't make up his mind if he should intervene or not, as if she was some stranger on the street who'd tripped.

Well, she was a stranger, really. She still knew nothing about him.

'How did you meet Mum?' she said after a while. He glanced at her with an ironic, preoccupied smile. She could hear how he had to catch his breath, before answering.

'She's never told you?'

'She said you just hung around till you moved in.'

'What a total crock.'

'Hey, I'm just kidding. She said you met up by coincidence after the Blockade and you moved into the share house she lived in.'

He sniffed and nodded. 'Yeah, that's right. We'd got together briefly in Strahan and then caught up by chance later.'

'She says it was this great communal house and you were all activists.'

'Well, I guess that about sums it up. Then we moved up to the country. Ayresville was a pretty quiet old town back then.' He paused, concentrated on the track for a moment. 'My father always tells me we could have made a packet in real estate if we'd seen the writing on the wall. But I never wanted to buy into any of that stuff. Something in me just needed to keep on the road.'

She waited for him to go on. She wanted to hear him say: *I never wanted to leave,* or *if I had my time over again I'd do it differently.* Anything. But he just walked a little faster as they reached a section of duckboard, stepping ahead of her with that twitchy limp so she couldn't see his face, presenting her with nothing but his blank, uncommunicative back.

She was going to ask him about his mother, Rich thought with heavy, dread-filled certainty as he moved ahead of her, hoping to put her off. That's what she'd slowed down for; to interrogate him, blast him with uncomfortable questions. He could feel the silence building, and wondered how to deflect the question when it came.

Sure enough, it was as if he'd willed it. 'What about your mum?' Her voice hesitant but determined behind him.

'Oh, she's still alive,' he said neutrally. 'Why do you ask?'

'Just wondering. She is sort of my other grandmother, after all.'

'Apart from Janet, you mean? How is old Janet?'

He heard her short humourless laugh as their feet clopped along the duckboards. 'Old,' she said.

'Still going strong?'

'She's only seventy-three. She runs her local U3A group.'

'Oh, I bet she does. I bet she runs it like Colonel Klink.'

'She drives Mum mad.'

'Still? Then again, if she didn't try to run Sandy's life, she'd have nothing to live for, would she? U3A must come a distant second.'

He started to tell her about how Janet used to come to visit them at Ayresville and insist upon staying at the local motel rather than in their spare room. 'Like we had bedbugs or something. And before you were born, Holy God. You should have heard her when we said we wanted a home birth.'

She didn't say anything for a while and he was hoping she'd forgotten her original question. Then he heard her say, almost conversationally, 'Mum says you didn't support her in having a home birth.'

'What? She said *what?*' He turned his head so sharply he felt something in his neck pop.

'No, wait. She said you didn't have the strength to offer her the support she needed.'

'Now hold on a fricking minute there. I can't believe she'd spin that kind of holier-than-thou crap to you. Well, actually I can. That'd be bloody typical.'

He was hammering along now, his blood pressure mysteriously up, fighting the urge to wheel around and grab her by the shoulders, make her see how it had been for him.

'She's the one who couldn't go through with it, Sophie. She was all so gung-ho for it, and I was behind her one hundred percent, believe me, but the first sign of a contraction and she was screaming, yelling at me to get her to the hospital.'

He wasn't embellishing it at all, he remembered it vividly. She'd dropped the idea of a home birth as if it was radioactive.

'OK, OK,' Sophie said, her face pinched. 'I'm just telling you what she said.'

'I'm not putting your mother down,' he said, sounding as calm and reasonable as he could in spite of his indignation, 'but she ...

how can I put this? She liked the *idea* of being an earth mother better than she liked the actual process. I mean, it sounds good, doesn't it? A drug-free birth? Until you're actually in it.'

'She tried, though. To do the right thing.'

Strange, these little flashes of defensiveness from her, that stalwart loyalty.

'Of course she did,' he agreed at once. 'I'm not saying that.'

She'd set him off now, remembering all of Sandy's exasperating contradictions. He walked along for a while, weighing up Sophie's allegiances.

'She was always starting great schemes,' he said finally. 'Making soap. Spinning, that was a big one. Homemade candles. One time she started researching how to build a geodesic dome in the backyard. She'd seen one somewhere. So she started making one out of — I don't know — bamboo or something.'

This time he heard a snort of laughter, and he turned to see her grinning, eyes on her feet, but smiling.

'Well, it's still there,' she said.

See, it wasn't so hard. He just had to coax out her soft spots, and keep it light. Win her over that way.

He clomped along, smouldering a bit still, taking the odd swig of water, the pain on his rubbed-raw heel mercifully buffered. They were the business alright, those painkillers. Keeping everything a little spacey. If he could only take a couple before bed he'd sleep like a dead man. But he should save them, with two solid days of walking still to go. Ration himself.

So. Sandy had blamed him for the caesarean as well as everything else.

He should have seen the warning signs, probably, the inevitable sappy clichés; Sandy talking about how children were the glue that held communities together, offering to babysit for friends, fervently telling them that it took a village to raise a child. Then starting to go quiet when he talked about them selling the house and heading off to live somewhere else for a few years — the South Pacific, he remembered suggesting, or Kerala.

She'd taken the decision out of his hands in the end, of course.

Not long after she'd turned thirty; 1993. Ended nearly a decade of easy harmony and tacit understanding on a whim, on something that looked a lot to him like peer-group pressure, dragged him along for the ride.

'No more joints for a while,' she'd said one night, and he'd said distractedly, 'Really? How long?', and she'd given him a nervous smile and said 'Nine months', and he'd felt his stomach drop through the floor like an elevator with a snapped cable.

You could profess yourself delighted, feel in fact a surging kick of fleeting paternal pride, but there was no hiding that initial stomach-plummet he could recall now, the wave of panic-stricken nausea reaching towards his throat with its sticky, enmeshing fingers.

He'd felt protective, at first, after he'd got over the initial shock. Keen to give it all a go, willing to constantly give Sandy the reassurance she needed, and allay the naked fears she confided to him in their bed in the dark. He couldn't believe how quickly she could go from her blithe serene confidence in front of their friends during the last months of her pregnancy to blind, gabbling panic once they'd left.

'We're having it here at home,' she'd insist to their friends. They'd turn to glance at him for confirmation.

'Right here on the living-room floor,' he remembered echoing brightly, spreading his hands in an encompassing gesture that took in the rug and the throw cushions.

'Maybe starting off in the bath,' Sandy had continued. 'We've got pregnancy bath oil. Lavender.' Her face, when he sneaked a glance at her, was a calm oval of anticipation. 'The midwife's coming over, the one I met at the prenatal yoga.'

'You seem incredibly centred,' friends would murmur.

'Well, it's not as if birth's a medical procedure. It's just the patriarchy that's told us that.'

Then after they'd gone, she'd lie panting, trying to wriggle herself into a curled position.

'Rich, Rich, I can't sleep.'

'Is the baby kicking?'

'Sometimes he kicks all night, sometimes he doesn't, then I'm so scared his heart's stopped. I just lie there praying and trying not to cry, for hours. What if his heart's stopped beating?'

'Maybe he's just sleeping.'

'Put your hand here. Feel that? That's his head. Jesus, I'm crazy. I have to push that out. It's going to bloody rip me in two, isn't it?'

'No, it won't. Women since the beginning of time have given birth the way you want to.'

'What do you mean, the way I want to?'

He hesitated. It sounded terribly like a trick question. 'Like ... well, like you just said tonight. Not controlled by the patriarchy. Drawing on your own ... empowerment. You'll be fine.'

'You think it's going to be fine, you fucking give birth then, you arsehole.' Gah, she was like Sally Field playing Sybil.

'Whoa, whoa. Calm down, and don't worry. You're just nervous. Anyone would be nervous. It's a huge thing.'

'Don't patronise me. Just leave me alone.'

He'd talk her back into it. Cajole her with images of the two of them, birthing their child together, the baby born into candlelight and lavender, the warm bath and her own endorphins providing natural pain relief — he'd recite it all back to her like a litany. After a while she'd relax and sleep the sleep of the dead for the rest of the night. And he'd listen to her softly snoring and the thought would skitter around in his mind like the panic-stricken moth at a window bashing itself to death trying to get out: *this is my life now.* He'd lie there listening to it blundering again and again into the glass, not getting it.

My. *Bam.* Life. *Bam.* Now.

He watched his legs pace one in front of the other across the duckboard. Heard the rhythmic swish of Russell's gaiters with each step. It was like marching, the mindlessness of it making things come into your head unbidden. Sophie didn't say anything else, and after a while, when he raised his head, he realised she'd passed him once they'd reached Kia Ora creek, and had gone on ahead. It must have been when he'd stopped to take his time soaking his foot in the cold shallow water, rewrapping it with clenched teeth, pushing it, excruciatingly, back into his boot.

Sandy shouldn't have built it up like that, the birth. All their friends were expecting something remarkable by the time Sandy finally went into labour. They'd all talk about it and he would feel a queasy, apologetic sort of smile stretching across his face, as if he was suddenly cast in a play and the director had told him to look joyful. It was too much of a burden. After all, he'd totally come around to it, cleared his head of the thought that they should have been spending that cot money on tickets to India. He'd been as wholehearted about it as he'd been about anything in his life. But even after quelling all those creeping doubts, he'd still spent months fighting off Sandy's insane control freak of a mother, defending principles that felt stale before he'd even started arguing them.

'You can't be serious about this home-birth nonsense,' Janet would say by way of greeting when she rang. 'I mean, Richard, being all green and political is one thing, but the day comes when you have to behave like adults.'

'Hello, Janet. We're both well, thanks for asking.' He'd glance across at Sandy, who'd be on the couch with a pillow over her head when she realised who it was on the phone.

'Is it money, is that it? I realise people like you wouldn't bother to have health insurance, but if it's a question of not being able to pay for private care ...'

'Janet, it's nothing about private or public hospitals. It's hospitals *per se*. It's the way they make birth a medical procedure, like a disease.'

He'd listen to himself dredging up, again, words that sounded false and flimsy even as he spoke them, anxious to get her off the phone and out of their hair, but everything he said seemed to galvanise her with more energy.

'I have to say, Richard, that attitude is totally ridiculous, and I'd like to speak with Sandra right now.'

'She's asleep right now, Janet.'

'Well, go and wake her up.'

'What?'

'I said go and wake her up. This thing has gone far enough. I won't have it.'

He closed his eyes, breathed deeply. Imagined Sandy as a teenager, trying to do normal teenage things with Janet suffocating every move from on high, Janet *not having it* at every turn.

'You want me to go and wake her up? Well, I'll try, but it might take a while. Hang on.' And he'd put the phone down and go and sit outside and read the paper, fuming. If Sandy wanted to pick up the phone, she could.

Being all green and political. Where did she get off, the arrogant self-righteous bitch? Trying to make the Franklin Blockade experience into something trivial. They'd captured worldwide attention with that protest — they'd forced a change of government by standing up for what they believed in, and Janet didn't even get it. The old conservative middle-class vanguard, the postwar boomers, with their desperate, scrabbling attempts to stay in power — they were pathetic. Still exerting their atrophying dominion wherever they could. Hoarding it all up.

Sandy still hadn't told her mother she'd been arrested, even ten years later, long after all charges were overturned and their records were expunged. Rich was so determined to make Janet eat her words about the birth that he began to look forward to the due date with a kind of grim pleasure. He'd send her a card with a photo and the caption: *Our Green and Political Birth.* Or maybe: *People Like Us have had a baby.* Pretentious domineering old cow.

So when Sandy stood up one afternoon — heaving herself off the futon in three lumbering stages that were awkward just to watch — and a gush of fluid puddled on the rattan matting, their eyes locked with the same dogged, glittering gleam of resolve.

'Now just stay calm, OK?' he said, thinking: *Perfect, you're already sounding like a Yank sitcom.* 'Where's the birth plan?'

'In the bathroom. But let's not rush into anything. This part takes hours. The book says it might be another whole day. So I don't want to ring the midwife. I want to light the fire and put on the first-stage cassette.'

'Yeah, I know.' They'd made a mix tape, painstakingly, over a week. The first song was one Sandy had chosen, something off a Wyndham Hill collection, and as the opening piano riffs came through the speakers he thought uneasily that there was something a little manic in the way she was tearing up raspberry leaves into a teapot in the kitchen, something beady-eyed and grim, as if she was preparing for a nuclear attack.

'Just slow down, Sandy. You'll be fine.'

'And don't ring my mother, alright? Even if I die, I don't want her to know till afterwards. Because I swear, if she comes over here, I'm going to have to hit her over the head with the axe.' She poured boiling water on the leaves, groped for a cup in the cupboard.

'Shouldn't you wait till that steeps?' They both stared stupidly at the teapot.

'Should I? Jesus, I don't know. How will I know when I go into labour?'

'What did your guide say?'

'That everyone experiences it differently, but the more centred and focused the labouring mother ... Holy *shit*!' She broke off and staggered into the living room, wild-eyed and clutching her back, lunging for her birth book. He, marooned in the middle of the room, felt that ludicrous apologetic smile paste itself back onto his face.

She was going to buckle, he could tell. He was already cast as the stupid fall guy who was going to get screamed at the moment he suggested running the lavender bath. Screamed at, or punched in the head. He watched her fold herself over on the floor, swan-diving onto the rug groaning, riffling with one desperate hand through the pages in the birth book she knew by heart. She would buckle, he knew with a sweet sad certainty, and he would take the rap.

It took less than an hour, he recalled now, looking up from his throbbing feet to squint at some alpine gums and wonder if they were worth a photo. Well, half an hour, really; then they'd had to roll-start the car, that rust-bucket blue Corolla that of course, of *course*, chose that moment to refuse to start. He remembered pushing it down the incline of their street, running to jump into the driver's seat as Sandy lay writhing in the back. Clenching his jaw in silent prayer as he judged the moment and took his foot off the clutch.

When he looked back on the day Sophie was born, he didn't think of the moment she drew her first shuddering breath, lifted aloft like a bloodied seal from the green surgical drapes after the caesarean. He remembered, instead, the thumping jerk as something in the engine grabbed and chugged, and him stepping on the accelerator and clutch together with everything he had, heart hammering with stress. The moment he'd lurched ignominiously back and forth in the car like a crash-test dummy, double-clutching, jamming the terrifying future into gear.

Thirteen

Questioning your spirit guide, read Sandy. *Greet your guide with whatever greeting you choose. Telepathic communication with spirit is known as clairaudience. When you receive an answer, you may feel a physical sensation such as pressure on the top of your head. This is the opening of the crown chakra. Ask your question, then pause. Listen to your thoughts. Connect with the answer. Imagine your frequency connecting with spirit. There is no hurry! Spirit has no timetable.*

She put her finger on the page and closed the book on her lap. What questions did she want to ask? She'd snuck a glance at some following pages and thought she might skip the metaphysical existence questions, but nevertheless what she'd skimmed still nagged her, raising more confusion in her mind than anything. Was her spirit guide only with her in this incarnation? What was their connection? And, perhaps more confusingly, had she ever been the spirit guide's spirit guide while it lived on the earth plane?

No, keep it simple. Personal spiritual questions.

'Is my karma to be just a parental caretaker?' she thought. She paused. No answer. Well, obviously it wasn't going to be as simple as that — it wasn't like making a bloody phone call; you'd need to learn how to listen for that inner voice. She struggled again to empty her mind of expectation, of outcome, of second-guessing a desired response. 'Do I owe anybody a karmic debt?'

It wasn't her tentative expectation scaring away her spirit guide, she thought impatiently. It was the spectre of Janet, hovering there on the edge of her consciousness like a disapproving, silver-haired bouncer, her arms folded and her expression that of a woman whose patience has been tried beyond endurance. Her mother, sticking her insistent foot in the door of everything she tried to do. Now that vision unfolded her arms and shook her head sorrowfully. *Sandy,* she said, *far be it from me to interfere, but do you think your father and I scrimped and saved to put you through private school for this?*

'That's *it*?' the American woman said doubtfully, looking bemused. 'That's the tree we've been hearing so much about?'

A knot of people stood around the sparse little stand of myrtle beech, with its small pleated leaves turning yellow. Rich had heard that particular tone of voice so many times on so many trips; its polite disappointment, condescendingly concealed but not quite enough.

'I mean, it's pretty and everything, I guess,' she went on, unscrewing her water bottle. 'But hey, the way everyone's been carrying on I was expecting ... I don't know, a *beech* forest or something, colours like in *fall*. This one's, well, it's like a bonsai, or something. I have to admit, I'm a little underwhelmed.'

There was a short pause as they gazed at the tree, wondering if it was worth a photo. Wondering, he thought, if there was a better thicket up ahead, something more in keeping with their expectations. The tree did look pretty spindly, he had to admit. But her whiny voice, as if they all owed her an apology!

'What's the proper name for it again?' the girl asked.

'Fagus. And it goes red, eventually,' someone else said.

'It's not the size of it. It's the fact that it's the only naturally occurring deciduous tree that's found here. It's not as spectacular as all those maple and oak forests in North America.' That was Russell, of course, the insufferable voice of reason. 'But further up, into the Du Cane Ranges, it's amazing when you come across forests of it, cloaking all the hills as far as you can see.'

The woman looked doubtful, like he was a spruiker trying to

sell her something.

Rich remembered standing in front of the *Mona Lisa* once in the Louvre, and hearing that exact same tone — one tourist turning to her friend, away from the crowd clustered permanently around the painting, and whispering in a disgruntled hiss, 'Well, *I* don't think she's very attractive.'

'It actually grows in thickets,' Russell was saying, 'and it's incredibly strong and wiry so it can bear the weight of a really heavy snowfall without snapping. The boughs just bend and the snow slides off ...'

Rich tuned him out, remembering another time, the crowd around the newly arrived pandas at a zoo, everyone clutching their souvenir toy pandas and panda key rings and panda baseball caps, and when the real animal came shuffling out into the enclosure, someone near him said with doubtful distaste, 'It's kind of *dirty*, isn't it?'

And then last night, one of the German tourists had said confidingly to him, with that same tone of aggrieved disappointment, that he didn't see why there couldn't be a permanent hut warden stationed at each hut, keeping the stove stoked up for walkers and ready to go out looking for people who didn't return from their daytrips at the time they'd estimated. Staff, Rich thought disgustedly. That's what they want — staff on hand to ensure their every need is met, pull them out of any potential scrape as they play at roughing it, having their *wilderness experience*, floodlights and gravel paths guiding the way to each tent. Pandas washed and brushed clean like big cuddly toys. Trees that guaranteed to impress even the most jaded Bostonian. Sherpas bringing you a morning latte on the slopes of Everest.

'I think it's magnificent,' he said in a low voice to the Americans, moving behind them. 'It demands we experience the landscape on its own terms, not with our own competitive, mine's-bigger Western mindset. It's a Zen thing.'

That, he was pleased to note, put a flicker of doubt on their faces. That's all it needed, he thought with savage amusement;

lodging the idea in there that maybe they'd failed, maybe they'd missed the point, maybe the problem was them.

How can I rekindle my passion?

Well. Now she was at the pointy end of it, alright. Not romantic passion, she had sort of given up hope of that. But her old self, the one who had cared so passionately. The ferocious way things seemed to matter, and her brimming, certain heart, capable of containing it all. Is that what she'd lost? She stood up and went outside, sitting on a bench by the water feature, telling herself she just needed some fresh air. A nudge at her knee made her open her eyes to see a proffered box of tissues.

'Thanks. Sorry.' She kept trying to straighten her back, like those ramrod women in the front row, who must have done yoga every day, but she slumped instead, sighing.

'If we didn't feel pain we wouldn't notice life passing,' said the facilitator.

Sandy blew her nose. 'I know that. I just want to know where it's all gone. All that love and certainty, you know what I mean?'

She stole a glance at the facilitator as she spoke, who nodded. Sandy didn't believe her, though. She'd be, what? Thirty-three? What would she know about losing anything?

'The time I'm thinking about,' she went on, wiping her eyes, 'we all sang together, all held hands, it was like the strongest bond imaginable, like our hearts were going to burst with it.'

'The human will is full of the richness of existence, isn't it?'

'No, you don't understand. What do you do, when you've experienced that? What do you do for the rest of your life?'

The facilitator tilted her chin pensively. She looked, Sandy thought, like one of those prefects at school, about to win a spelling bee.

'Well, we use it as spiritual insight. We gather it to us as our enlightenment.'

Sandy sniffed, studied the balled-up tissue in her hands. 'Enlightenment? See, I've always thought that when you used that term, I mean, in a Buddhist sense, you're talking about nirvana, stepping off the wheel of existence onto another plane.'

'No, I'm talking about personal, day-to-day enlightenment.'

Everything got so watered down here, she thought with a sudden flash of clear-eyed melancholy, everything refashioned from ancient traditions into an opportunity for personal development.

'How are you progressing with your spirit guide?'

'OK.'

'What about visualising your totem animal?'

Sandy gave a bleak, watery smile. 'Well, I've been trying.'

'Because that may help. It may help to understand that you have a companion totem guide with you now, and that it's always been there, assisting you.'

'Yes, I bought the medicine tarot cards; I did read about it. But I sort of wish I'd signed up just for the workshops with the Goddess study, because I'd only just begun to make progress there I think, just scratching the surface. There's just so much to absorb and try to understand in a few short days.'

The facilitator smiled encouragingly at her. 'It's many paths all to the same well of wisdom, whatever tools we use on our quest.' Her long elegant hands described a sinuous path in the air.

'Yes, that's a lovely idea.' What was she doing, sucking up to this woman?

'After all, that's why we're called Mandala, because that's what a mandala is — the Sanskrit word contains meanings for both *circle* and *completion* — a microcosm of the divine power of oneness in the universe.'

'Yeah, um ... thanks. I did read that. It's just that my questions all seem to be about loss, and ageing, and trying to find that passion again. I don't mean falling in love, necessarily, but ...'

The facilitator took Sandy's hand in both of hers. 'Wait till the sweat-lodge ceremony. A lot of seekers find it's almost like a vision quest, doing that ceremony, and those missing answers appear to them out of the blue. As if the discipline needed to seek and go on seeking is the test itself.'

Sandy pushed the ball of tissues into her pocket and tucked

her hair behind her ear. 'OK,' she said, doubtfully.

The facilitator smiled, nodding her head. 'Now back to that cushion,' she said earnestly, pointing into the meditation hall, 'and back to work.'

That's not work, Sandy heard Janet's voice mutter as she stood up. *That's sitting on your behind on a cushion.*

There was plenty of fagus now, enough to satisfy every tourist, Rich thought. All you had to do was walk down from the hut to the cascading creek and there it was, stretching away up the valley, some of it red as a spray of arterial blood. He'd taken some good shots of the Alpine Yellow gum trees on the way, then dumped his stuff in the hut, which was already like a sauna redolent with the smell of kerosene, wet wool and socks. He'd put his tent up later — he wanted some more shots.

Sophie had come down with him, and was watching him. Good. He liked the thought of her seeing him doing something he knew he was absolutely competent at. Letting her see that getting something right takes time. He looked through the viewfinder — the shining pebbles were all good, the exposure was perfect. If he could just wait until this gust of wind shifted the cloud cover and gave him that great silvery light on their wet surfaces again, he'd have the shot in the bag, but it was missing something. He needed a tiny focus in the middle, that's what Dombrovskis's pictures always had, that special little something that lifted them out of the ordinary. A pebble covered with red lichen, for example, or a little orange leaf caught on a twig amongst all that shining grey and white. He had often wondered if such a perfect composition could have been totally natural. It must have been. He just couldn't picture the great man stomping down the beach, looking for a scarlet starfish to place just so, or splashing an alpine gum with water out of his drinking bottle to make those colours more intense.

The depth of field he wanted, you just couldn't get that with these new digital cameras, he was convinced. They were for happy snappers, really. Dombrovskis had used his huge-format camera, lugging it with his tripod through days of wilderness, and you could tell. Those frosty leaves, the focus going on forever, those beads of dew and granules of sand and ice. He'd spent many hours studying those photos. Well, you couldn't help it — they got jammed into your field of vision every direction you looked — every souvenir shop and wilderness shop and bookshop and market stall had them reproduced on racks in all their glory. Nobody else came close.

'What are you taking?' Sophie's voice, clear over the sound of the water.

'Just some leaves. Some studies in contrast and colour.'

He'd so nearly got it, that time. On the river.

Didn't want to think about it. Unbearable to think about it.

Stop. But it was as if some unseen force, sensing weakness, rolled the footage before him; its grainy, damning evidence.

The morning at Warner's Landing when he and his affinity group had been arrested, Rich had got up early. Once they were arrested, that would be it. Back to Hobart, probably, and no more chances here on the river, unless they defied their bail conditions and risked a heavier sentence. Today if the bulldozer arrived it would be the moment they'd been preparing for during all those training workshops.

He'd bush-bashed his way carefully down to the bank with his camera, and had seen the shot of his life. You only got one or two chances like that in your career as a photographer, Rich believed, and you had to be ready there and then in that instant: correct aperture, correct focus, tripod at hand if you needed it, the certainty of your instinct getting everything right.

That morning on the banks of the Franklin, Rich felt his defining moment arrive like machinery clicking smoothly into place. Strung over the bank from some flowering dogwood was a spiderweb and through its sparkling chains of dew the river spilled dreamily, purling the surface, morning mist rising from it. He saw the frame, how it had to be, snapped open the camera case and grabbed the camera. He sank down on one knee, never taking his eyes off that web. The light struck the water at just the angle he needed to see the sepia tint of submerged logs under there, and the spectrum of greens that striped through his viewfinder when he raised the camera to his face made him see even how he would mount this, the gloss of the card. Dombrovskis had taken a photo a year or two before that had been reproduced a million times, at least, on the No Dams campaign. It showed Rock Island Bend, and he'd kept the aperture open so that the water streaming around the rocks took on the texture of cloud swirling through an Arcadia, and wherever Rich went he saw that image, on posters, on placards, in mail-outs and on postcards. That image was going to win them the election, win them the whole fight.

Well, here was another Rock Island Bend, he was certain. Same iconic essence of everything they were trying to save.

He focused, keeping his hands still, breathing deeply at the rippling perfection of it, and his finger pressed down and he knew he had it. He had it, but he couldn't leave it, he'd heard too many stories about that kind of overconfidence, now was the time to stay calm, wind on, and take another one, just to be sure. Sunlight touched the fronds of tree ferns, that primordial light filtered and shifted, and Rich stood to take one last shot and the edge of his boot skidded off a moss-slimed tree root and juddered six inches down the muddy incline. His foot hung over space, over water, over nothing. Suspended.

The gulping jolt of it lasted forever, as something in him made him save himself, and instinctively lurch one way instead of another into caving wet ferns, staggering against them in an ungainly, outstretched sprawl.

Had he let himself fall into the river, he might have been able to keep his arms raised and his camera dry. Instead, he clung to the bank, grabbing at grass with his free hand, clawing it with blind self-preservation, and his hand holding the camera arched backwards out over the water. The camera had fallen sideways from his fingers. And then, Jesus, that knifing sound of it hitting the surface, like a fish escaping a hook and dropping back into the deep. A kind of whimper had come out of him as he gathered the strap around his wrist and jerked it free.

That was the moment that never left him, seeing the camera coming up dripping out of the water. His old Olympus, which had taken him faithfully through a hundred rolls of film in Nepal, Tibet and India, beaded with icy river water in South-West Tasmania, totally ruined, and nausea squeezing behind his ribs so he just wanted to kneel there and vomit.

No other picture he'd ever taken mattered compared to the one he'd just lost.

His own Rock Island Bend, the one that could have been the cover of *Nature*, his own little precious, unrepeatable negative that would make his name. And only he had seen it. Only him. The proof of his talent, his vision, and the loss of it something he'd have to carry now forever, his own private little scarred burden.

'What are you waiting for?' She was still sitting on a rock nearby, swinging her long legs, oblivious. He had to hold the breath in his throat to keep his voice light, lift his sunken head. The painkiller moved like sludge in his veins.

'Oh, just for the cloud cover to move. Pick out these shadows.'

His chest. He remembered how it had felt full of curing, hardening cement as he took off the bayonet lens and saw moisture already beading behind the glass. The river condensing inside his camera, like it got inside everything, curling the pages of your diary with furry damp, rotting your shoes, peeling the skin between your toes, slicking the tent with wetness, till you were practically growing mould out here, the whole riverbank swollen with rot and mist and black clammy coldness like a bloody grave. It had to own everything, it couldn't leave anything alone.

He'd climbed back to his tent, laid the camera lens and body carefully on his towel in some wild unlikely hope it would be alright, and instead of lying there howling, which was how he felt, he'd numbly forced himself to get dressed ready for the action. It was only 7 a.m., and someone in charge of radio communications was going to give them the word if the dozer actually docked at Warner's Landing and he'd have to have all his stuff packed ready for someone else to take it out for him by then. He listened to the camp stirring around him, getting breakfast, talking in low voices, checking he was awake, while all the time he couldn't drag his eyes from his camera, imagining the wrecked roll in there, glutted and sticking to itself, destroyed. Once he pressed the shutter and heard a sluggish calibration, and when he applied tentative pressure on the arm turning the rewind spool it sounded like teeth breaking on stones in there. The failure burning him like a coal.

And then they expected him to sing. Sing that fatuous retread of a song. *By the waters, the waters of the Franklin, we lay down and wept ...*

'Is it that fagus you're taking?'

'Yeah, fagus and moss.'

'That's like that postcard we saw in the visitor's centre.'

He rubbed his eyes. 'Nothing like it. A totally different light and configuration.'

Holding up that banner and the bulldozer straining its huge transmission to get purchase on the bank, and Rich, still numb, catching the eye of someone else in his affinity group and stepping forward with arms linked into its path.

The HEC guys giving him the fish-eyed look of blokes sick and tired of such a bunch of posers. The police giving it a minute or two then stepping up and arresting them so formally and unemotionally — a hand on the shoulder, *you're arrested*, a dead-stern face reciting the lines earnestly — that it all seemed unreal. Another role-play.

He'd lost the faith. He knew it in the yard at Risdon, when the protestors had got together to rehearse what they'd all say in court, and when someone suggested a sharing he'd felt a scalding, mortified horror at the thought of being hugged, back here in the real world. Stuttering and repeating himself in front of the magistrate like an idiot. Back to Melbourne after he'd been released and retrieved all his gear from the campaign office in Hobart, he'd screwed the lens back on and tested the shutter action again. Terrible. When he held it to his ear and tried to wind on the film, he heard a series of small dull snaps inside as the teeth tore through the swollen, stuck roll, so that without even wasting his time with hoping, he pulled the whole mess out of the canister and threw it into the bin.

'I had a great camera once,' he began to tell people when they admired his photos of the beggar children in Kathmandu, 'but it fell into the Franklin River, while I was on the Blockade, and got damaged.'

He'd leave it at that, so they'd imagine a skirmish, a clash with police, the camera torn from his hand and thrown furiously over the edge by an ugly redneck local or vindictive copper. After a while, the odd thing was he could almost see it happening that way himself, like a ghostly double exposure.

Sophie sat on the rock, watching Rich as he knelt over the tripod, then shifted around to the other side and knelt over it again, focusing through his camera, adjusting the tripod minutely, squinting up at the sky.

She thought of all the hours of her childhood she'd spent imagining her father, every time Father's Day rolled around and the hardware stores started advertising power tools and leaf blowers for Dad, she'd imagine him, grinning with delight at an electric drill. Or she'd be on stage in a school production, swishing her dragon tail behind her or running into the spotlight being a forest sprite, and she'd see other fathers in the audience and think about Rich, whether he'd be a videoing father or one who just sat there, hands tucked between his knees holding a rolled program, following her every move. She wasn't the only one. There weren't many fathers around amongst her circle of friends. Their mothers would get together on Friday nights after school and sit drinking beer with their feet in someone's dam, while the kids raced around and paddled, and it seemed to Sophie the conversations would always follow the same kind of worn track — husbands and boyfriends absent, potential boyfriends on the horizon, the limitations and weaknesses of the old ones and the possible star qualities of the new ones. The mothers would let the kids cover themselves with mud and dry out in the late afternoon sun like lazing crocodiles. Sometimes, they'd plaster themselves with mud too, or yoghurt and honey face packs, or they would henna their hair and sit with their heads stiff with red sludge, combing each others' right to the ends and winding it on top of their heads to warm it up in the sun and make their hair even redder. The afternoons stretching into a long dazzle of sunburned indolence and circular talk.

'Don't worry about wearing swimmers!' they would call to the kids, but Sophie always wore swimmers. They were allowed, on Fridays, to have hot chips from the fish and chip shop — proper food, the kids privately agreed; crisp and salty and fried, the big white piece of wrapping paper flapping on the grass as they sat and devoured them, licking their fingers.

The mothers would wade into the dam and rinse the henna from their hair, rubbing in herbal conditioner, admiring the colour in the late fading light, and she always thought how similar their bodies seemed — soft and faded brown and starting to look worn-out, broad across the hips and thighs, swathed in Indian dresses and stonewashed jeans that came off when they splashed into the water.

That's what having babies did to your body. Wrecked it. Gave you a body like theirs — like balloons that had been stretched to the limit of their endurance then left to gradually deflate again, the skin silvered with stretch marks and softly puckered like overripe fruit.

Not for her. She had already decided. Whatever she did, she would never let herself get like that. Just like her mother, the other women didn't even try to disguise it, all that disgusting loose and dimpled flesh, the rolls of fat bulging over the top of their jeans. They had no shame. It was as if they were actually proud of it.

She remembered the time they had arranged for all the girls to participate in a ritual womanhood ceremony with them, when she was about twelve.

'Celebrate the cusp of what you're on!' Sandy exhorted her when she said she didn't feel like joining in. 'Your body's old enough to bear a child now. Feel that power!'

Totally embarrassing. She hardly knew where to look. Their

mothers drank mulled wine and painted their faces with ochre, danced with tambourines and clapsticks around a fire they'd built and fuelled with symbolic items. The dance was meant to be a Native American ritual of cleansing and rebirth. An absolute crock.

'Burn something you reject!' Sandy had cried, wild and elated. 'Something from childhood you're leaving behind, or something negative that you have no more use for, that's been holding you back.'

She had burned her Strawberry Shortcake diary, the one with the dinky little lock that she was sure Sandy had snooped in while she was at school. When she saw her mother's face, she knew she'd hoped to see, instead, the metal box of postcards from Rich. That hadn't even occurred to her, to torch the sparse record of shorthand correspondence from him.

Your father, Sandy used to call him, up until Sophie was about eight. *Your father's sent you another postcard — that was generous of him, wasn't it?* A voice dangerous with contained bitterness, acid-edged, uncontestable.

Then she stopped that, and he became *that guy*. Like he'd run out of credit on his paternity account. Missed his last opportunity. 'I tell you, that guy,' Sandy would say, shaking her head. 'Don't get me started. What a dud he turned out to be. What a total waste of space.'

And once, just once, Sophie had said, unguardedly, 'He's still my father.'

And her mother had said, 'I want you to understand: he was never your father. He was your sperm donor.'

Now she watched him, that stranger. That guy. Her polaroid father. A ponytail, same as in the photo. A camera round his neck, and his hands resting on it, ready, same as then. Every other detail was revealed now as stuff she'd painstakingly invented. There he went, climbing over rocks towards the small tree with the orange leaves, and pulling some off. Back to his camera and tripod, and Sophie watched him lift his hand and scatter those leaves onto the moss. Then pick them all off except for one. Then add one more, and squint through the viewfinder again, then reach down and arrange the two leaves against the bed of moss with his finger. Crazy man. If you saw him with a baseball hat on, hiding his greying hair, and just in his jeans and t-shirt, you'd never know he was middle-aged. And he was still pretty good-looking too, in an older-guy way, if he'd just lose the ponytail. He'd be hunted to extinction in Ayresville, that was for sure. One night at the pub and they'd be lining up to see if he was on the market, all the single mothers tired of sleeping alone and chopping their own kindling. He'd do the rounds, over the months, shifting from one to the next, wrecking old friendships and shrugging it all off with a helpless grin, leaving a trail of chaos in his wake as he stumbled into the next pair of arms — the same thing she'd seen happen tons of times. He'd be just like any of those guys, just the same. Nothing special.

She reached for her iPod, pushed the comforting headphones into her ears, and scrolled down till she found the Dogland track she wanted. Out here it filled her head like a soundtrack to a film so familiar in atmosphere she didn't have to pay attention to it; it just underscored whatever her eyes landed on. A movie you made up as you went along.

My anguish hides, came the lead singer's voice. *Rise up with her sacred dagger, there can be no disguise, my anguish hides.*

Sophie's head nodded slightly in time as she stared out over the patterns of light and shade on the ridges, shifting and sliding as the clouds moved. '*Thorns engulf me*,' she sang along softly, '*and I turn against the flame. I will not see my captor, I will not say his name.*'

Fourteen

What was in those painkillers? Rich was having a bad night; a night of syrupy, chattery, trippy dreams; a night of restless, garbled dozing as he shifted himself painfully on his sleeping mat in the hut, the cold seeping into the woodenly stiff muscles of his neck and seizing up the flaring hot tendons in his leg. He was back in his parents' lounge room, half listening to his mother talk about the boxes of junk they had stored in the shed, allowing himself to tune out her fretful circular monologue. Then she'd said, 'The sooner your father gets those boxes out of there the better, because I can hear them at night, going through them, picking over all our things.'

He'd glanced up. 'Who, Mum?' he'd said, and she'd looked wretched with anxiety.

'Well, you know. They come and go through it. Take things out and sell them. I can tell, when I go out to check. Everything's been opened up and re-taped down again, so they don't raise the alarm.'

He turned to his father, who was sitting stolidly in front of the football. 'Dad?' he said softly. But his father had only glanced quickly at him and looked away again, his face an expressionless mask. Rich had looked back to his mother's hands, twisting in her lap with agitation.

'All my good china,' she was saying now. 'They think I don't know, but I do. I hear them.'

'I think maybe you're hearing mice or possums, Mum,' Rich said. He felt a heavy, encumbering sense of inevitable obligation descending as he spoke; he longed to turn now, like his father, back to the numbing boredom of the last quarter being played out on the TV screen.

'They open them, you see. The cartons. They have a key, because I lock the garage door, but it doesn't do any good.'

He had tackled it with his father, when she'd gone out to make tea. 'How long's this been going on?'

'She's dreaming. There's nothing there.'

'I'm not talking about the bloody boxes. I'm talking about her — getting so caught up in this delusion.'

His father grunted. 'You know your mother. It's been so long I barely register now.'

He'd stared hard at his father, willing him to turn around and face him. 'She seems very distressed by it — have you spoken to her doctor?'

Now his father had swung round like he'd been barely restraining his grievance.

'Listen, mate, any time you want to come and take a bit of responsibility for your mother and take her down to the doctor, you're bloody welcome to. Meanwhile, just leave it.'

She came back in. Teapot but no cups. Then cups but no milk.

'Let me give you a hand,' he had said, feeling heavy dread dragging itself over him, the cold awareness of what was starting to happen.

He watched her set up the cups, position the strainer, lift the pot, and pause.

'How do you have yours again?' she said.

'Milk with no sugar, Mum.'

'Yes. And what about your father?'

Rich twitched through his sleep, turned himself painfully onto his side. His mind felt ephedrine-bright, scoured with the pills, running manic with weariness. A dreaming slide like a wash of water, and he was upside-down, pitched off a surfboard into a dragging undertow, air crushed from him in churning solid seawater, conscious, as he dangled there choking, of a pinching resistance keeping him hobbled.

Ankle strap. The board up there on the surface, and his ankle clamped by a strap. It clamped him, wrenched, shook him back and forth. Twisted the chafed and burning tendons of his heel. All he had to do was rouse himself, bend his body around and climb that connecting rope. Hand over hand, up to the precious air.

Then he was dry again, back in a chair, straight-backed as if it was a job interview. He knew where he was, though. With his father, at the specialist's. He'd sat there listening to the talk about cortical and subcortical dementia, holding brochures about neurological and cognitive warning signs, sat there, his father stony-faced beside him, as the doctor listed on his fingers everything Rich had already seen. 'Loss of memory, loss of intellectual skills, difficulty with personal and social interactions, withdrawal,' he'd said smoothly, ticking them off, and Rich heard the jargon, and bought into it with instant, eager relief. Wading straight in and wielding it like a pro, like a man finding his true calling. Hedging delicately over 'custodial care' and 'comorbidity', galloping smoothly through 'assisted living'.

Then the doctor had scratched his head and hesitated, and Rich could feel them both stiffen, sitting there. Father and son, bracing themselves for it, attuned to avoidance.

'One consideration,' said the doctor, 'is that alcohol can worsen the behavioural and neurological changes people experience in these early stages of Alzheimer's Disease. Long-term alcohol dependence leads to much higher cognitive impairment', and Rich had said with total neutrality, 'Oh yes?'

Oh, it was a neutrality that surely would make his father proud, neutrality so perfectly learned and mastered, and over such a long apprenticeship.

'It's important to be clear,' the doctor went on diplomatically, 'because if we know there is a history of alcohol dependence or abuse that would certainly change the types of treatment we

would use. Some medications actually create more problems —
stomach and intestinal problems, for example, or complications
with delusions. We'd be cautious about prescribing a number of
drugs if there was an alcohol problem.'

In the silence that followed he heard his father exhale beside
him, and clear his throat.

'Nothing like that,' he said decisively, 'she's just always
been a nervous person', and Rich felt himself nodding slowly
in agreement, sealing his mother's fate in this tacit collusion,
this sudden one-off piece of cowardly teamwork that showed
him, once and for all, that he was his father's son. The moment
suspended, outstretched in a little pool still as a mirror. Defining
him.

'No, nothing like that,' he'd heard himself echo. Smiling his
reassuring charmer's smile, wheeling his mother out before him
like a human shield, full of all the deflections in the world.

He pulled his rustling sleeping bag round his shoulders,
not awake exactly but not asleep either, seeing himself signing
pages, his pen an ominous slippery weight between his fingers.
Custodial care agreements, power-of-attorney agreements, all the
signing that was required now to keep the lie humming along,
the regretful conversations with neighbours and friends, the
immoveable unrelenting silence of his father touring through the
'care facility', all the fuel that was needed to push into the lie's
maw and feed its growing appetite.

He'd walked away and left her there, he thought as he ached
and twisted and turned, some slippage occurring in his dream.

Left her there, crying. Off to somewhere. Borneo. Latin
America. Somewhere he couldn't be contacted again for a good
long while. All the best intentions in the world of visiting, of
reassessing, of reinventing, but still leaving. Easy lies. Spinning
himself some bullshit story, all the while backing away, feeling
for the car keys, desperate to be free of it. That adroit stepping
backwards, saving himself.

He opened his eyes, blinking until the dark lines in front
of him resolved themselves into the wooden slats of the bunk

above. Tasmania. The bloody wilderness walk. Still three days from a hot shower, his ankle banging now like a warning drum proclaiming imminent war, and four hours walking ahead of him this morning.

He'd be alright, he thought hazily, if only he didn't have so much to carry.

If only the load on his back didn't feel so much like the clinging, goading arms and legs of some other person riding him, a ruthless and oblivious deadweight wrapped around his neck and hips.

Rich ran a hand over his face, as if erasing it. He licked his lips and tasted salt.

Sandy had meant just to lie on her bed for a short break and read another chapter of spirit-guide questions. She'd meant, a few minutes later, just to close her eyes for a moment and ruminate on those questions. Then it occurred to her guidance might come in the form of a visualisation, or a dream, so nobody would mind if she allowed herself to keep sinking.

She was trying to get passport photos taken, but somehow at the moment the flash went off she'd slip awkwardly on her seat, or jump in surprise. Each polaroid page rolled out of the camera at $12.50 a pop and she'd watch them darken and develop with a sinking heart. There she was, slipping out of the frame, her eyes widened like a lunatic. And there, a blur of head you could count on to move at just the wrong moment. Worst of all was when the last page got ejected from the camera and she stood waving it, waiting to see the image form, the passport office clerk watching the clock, so she knew she was being a monumental nuisance. Waving that sheet and peeling back the protective layer, to find she wasn't even there. She'd disappeared entirely. She hopped urgently from foot to foot, crying with frustration. She needed that passport, or the plane would go without her. Take off while she faded, blurred into nothing, fell off her chair, missed her chance. She could hear it, actually, overhead, winging its way through the air with her empty seat inside, leaving her behind.

She woke up with her head under the white laundered sheet, like something laid out in those coroner shows Sophie always watched. The dream still hovered and receded, a blur of lost hope, of ridiculous rage. On the bedside table, her new books lay in a stack, like homework. *Is this crap,* she thought, *or is it just me?*

So, OK, it was a waterfall. A beautiful spot made impossible to enjoy by other hikers there, quacking about turnaround times from the moment they arrived. Nothing like a gang of people walking into frame, thought Rich bitterly, to wreck a good shot. You'd wait for them to notice and move on, to show a bit of respect for you, then another mob would turn up rustling in their blue and red Goretex jackets, meander straight in front of you and stand there staring at you like bloody sheep even though they could see you were trying to set something up. Whoever invented Goretex, he thought, must be relaxing in his Jacuzzi right now.

The sunlight shone fitfully onto the shining, rain-streaked rocks, and mist rose like a vapour through the cascade. But what was the point of a wilderness photo if it looked like a bus stop?

'This place would be great,' he muttered to Sophie, recapping his camera, 'if only it wasn't full of rubbernecker buffoons.'

She shrugged. 'Well, come back really early in the morning, then. When nobody else is around.'

'The light would be totally different then.'

'Yeah, well, excuse me for making a suggestion.'

'We'll be walking further on in the morning anyway.' He leaned over towards her to whisper. 'Somewhere away from these nutters, anyway.'

No smile. She looked away, back to the falls, watching the complicated manoeuvring as everyone there who held a digital camera waited their turn politely. They all wanted exactly the same thing, he saw with rising, scathing annoyance: the illusion of emptiness, the myth that they were there alone. Nothing he could take here would ever be fresh or distinctive; it was all trampled by ten thousand pairs of boots, uploaded onto hundreds of travel blogs, stored in phones, restlessly sifted over a million times.

'Can I take one?' she said suddenly, startling him.

'Sure. I guess.'

He took the Olympus out of its case, suddenly protective.

'Before you even start, wrap that strap around your wrist,' he instructed.

'So there's no auto-focus on these old ones, right? I have to adjust ...'

'Wrap the strap around your wrist. I mean it.' The command came out more sharply than he intended. Strangled, almost.

She gave him a surprised look. 'OK, OK, calm down. I'm not going to drop it, just going to take a simple shot. I have used cameras before, you know.'

'Yeah, digital cameras that are worth nothing. When you use a good SLR it should be an automatic reflex. Wrap it twice just to make sure.'

She gave an exasperated sigh and lowered the camera. 'Forget it.'

'No, sorry. Go ahead. Just ...'

'Here. If it's such a drama.' She handed the camera back, glowering, and walked off.

Well. If she couldn't handle a few essentials, that was her problem. He'd had a fleeting thought, yesterday when she'd been watching him — a quick daydream — that he could teach her a few things about photography. He could get her interested, and then maybe have a reason to catch up with her sometime in the city. Introduce her to how a darkroom worked, and all the expertise you needed to make an image emerge slowly in a bath of developer instead of having it zap onto a screen within seconds. He saw their two heads together, bent close over the tray. Could he make her appreciate that? Or would she just roll her eyes and sulk, shrug and screw up her nose with that infuriating, apathetic disdain?

They'd left their backpacks with a pile of others leaning against a tree a kilometre away, and when they'd walked back to them again, Rich swore.

'I don't believe it. We've been rolled. Look at that.'

Their packs lay unzipped and the remains of ransacked biscuits and dried fruit lay scattered over the grass, torn from their ziplock bags and prised-open plastic containers.

'It's not people,' said Sophie. 'It's those birds. Wait and see.'

She pointed to a few flapping black birds perched on a tree nearby and as he waited, watching, they wheeled down confidently, landing with a little jounce, and went back to tearing into their food supplies. Those crows again — they were everywhere.

'You're trying to tell me birds can open zips with their beaks?'

'Well, just watch them.' In a few moments one capered over to a packet of crackers and stabbed at it with its beak, eating the contents in a series of jabbing, furious pecks. He gaped as he watched two others jump on his pack and one hold a corner steady while the other tugged at a zip. Bloody *co-operating*. How many packs had it taken them, how many thousands of humans dumping their belongings here day after day, for the penny to drop? He looked down at the ground again beneath his feet, the silted dust marked with patterns of soles. Talk about the beaten track. A deep slow wash of pointlessness tipped over him, a weighty exhaustion. She was waiting for him to speak, though. To keep enthused. And there was his pack, demanding to be shouldered, the pain kept a blurry black smudge by the tablets but constant as breathing. He'd been insane, planning this. Out of his mind.

'Are they ordinary crows, or something else?' he asked.

'I dunno. Ravens or something. Currawongs.'

'Right out here, though? How have they learned, to open zips like that?'

'Hey, don't ask me. They've evolved. Like foxes in the city.'

The birds spread glossy wings so black they looked blue, like oil. Their small hard eyes were the coldest things you'd ever seen, watching and constantly gauging the distance between the humans and themselves. They stropped their beaks and bided their time. It gave him the creeps.

'Let's pick this stuff up and see what can be salvaged,' he said. Maybe he could set up a shot tonight, lay out some sultanas or scraps on a rock somewhere at sunset, get the crows flapping in silhouette against a red sky.

'How do crows teach each other what velcro and zips are?' he wondered aloud.

'Is that a joke?'

'No, I'm just trying to imagine. It must be like the Hundred Monkeys Theory. Have you ever come across that? There were these monkey colonies on various Japanese islands and researchers gave one group potatoes, but not the other colonies —'

'We did that in Science,' she cut in flatly. 'It's been totally disproved.'

Rich picked up an almond from his scattered supply, and chewed on it. She was pushing small plastic containers back into her pack, methodically rolling socks and t-shirts back into tight little bundles and jamming them down into all the corners. He watched the crows squabbling over the strewn crackers, picked another nut off the ground, and tried again.

'You know one time,' he said, keeping his voice determinedly conversational now, 'I was in Bombay —'

'Mumbai,' she muttered.

'Right. Yeah, OK. I was in Mumbai and I heard about this amazing place called the Tower of Silence. It's where they lay out their dead bodies to be picked clean by vultures. You can go there and see it.'

She swung around, mouth twisted into a grimace of distaste. 'How totally disgusting.'

'They don't bury them, you see. Contamination, or not enough vacant ground, or something. So the vultures come swooping in and devour them. It's not disgusting, it's actually really interesting, because ...'

'No, I mean how disgusting that you went there. Like it was some kind of tourist attraction. Did you all go on a bus and buy postcards?'

He concentrated on snapping the lid back on the container he was holding. He remembered buying that container, in the supermarket, before he even met her. Optimistically imagining them sharing trail mix out of it, in a ferny dell somewhere. A ferny dell! More like Jurassic fucking Park.

'OK, fine. Let's just repack this stuff and push on,' he said, still keeping resolutely pleasant. 'Because I don't know about you but I'm not sleeping on one of those bunk platforms again tonight, I'm setting up the tent as far away from the hut as I can.'

'You're changing the subject.'

'What?'

'You did, didn't you? Take photos of it? The vultures eating someone?'

How did they do it, these kids, manage to sneer and snicker at the same time?

It was as though they all trained themselves just to get you riled; putting that abject, scowling defensiveness into their slump, finding that perfect infuriating balance between hostility and lethargy. *Speak UP*, he wanted to snap at her, like he did to all of them. *Sit up STRAIGHT, why can't you? Look people in the EYE when you speak to them!* The irritation peaked in him, like water reaching the boil, fractious pain and weariness pounding in his temples.

'Can I ask you something? How come you never say a bloody word until there's a chance you can have a go at me about something?'

He was expecting her to withdraw, cowed and contrite and apologetic. Her curling lip, the ferocious black spark of her eyes, came as a complete shock.

'That is absolute crap.'

He recovered indignantly, feeling it fraying. 'No, you do. I'm telling you. It's the only time your face lights up, do you realise that? When there's a chance to scoff at me.'

He saw a little tremor of shock cross her features, a little knock like a ripple moves a boat.

'That's bullshit.'

'No, it's not. Here I am, stupid enough to try to tell you something, *share* something with you, about this place, the Tower of Silence ...'

Another sneer. 'It sounds like a name they pulled out of *Lord of the Rings*. Something they made up for the tourists.'

'You know what? I don't care if it was. *You're* a bloody Tower of Silence, yourself. You're a monument to fucking silence. Why have you got to be so *cynical* about everything?'

He was shocked at the pleasure his meanness brought him, the way he saw it wound her.

'You're the cynical one, not me,' she flashed back defiantly, her eyes as dark as the birds, just as mistrustful. 'You hate everybody on this walk — you said so.'

'I ...' Fatal hesitation. 'OK, forget it,' he snapped. 'I'll just remember from now on not to tell you anything, alright? No stories, no observations, no jokes, nothing. Maybe that will make you happy. Then you can walk around confident that everyone in the whole wide world is inferior to you.'

He stopped, taken aback at himself. She's fifteen, he thought. I'm attacking my fifteen-year-old daughter. Pull yourself together, you sorry arsehole.

'We're both tired,' he said hastily, making an effort again to neutralise things. 'I didn't mean to snap at you. I just ... thought you'd be interested.'

Lame. Weak. Conciliatory. He'd dreaded this. She'd smell the need on him, he thought. Hear that pathetic wheedle in his voice. Or else it was already snapped, and over. Irreparable.

'Yeah, about vultures eating dead bodies,' she muttered.

'Yeah, well. They do it everywhere. Even in wonderful magical Buddhist Tibet. They call it sky burial there.'

She actually was listening, he told himself, as she sorted through the unwrapped food and picked up litter. Underneath, she was interested.

'That's one place Mum's always talked about going to, Tibet.'

He jumped eagerly, too grateful. 'Yeah, I know. Even when I knew her she did, a long time before you were born. Of course it would have been much better to go back then, before it got really commercialised and ruined by so much tourism.'

She straightened up, looking at him with guarded, cool amusement.

'What's so funny?'

'Is that when you went? Before it got *ruined*?' She repeated the word delicately, archly, pushing a finger sideways against her teeth to gnaw on a nail.

(*Take your hand out of your mouth!*) He worked hard not to rise to the bait this time.

'I did, actually, yeah. I was extremely lucky to get to witness an actual sky burial there, hardly anyone from the outside world ever sees one. It was a real privilege.'

That much was true — there'd only been three other tourists in the little town he'd gone to, and they all whispered about the ritual to be held the next day, in hushed tones.

Early the following morning, walking up to the desolate, windswept hillside where the ceremony was rumoured to be taking place, he'd felt a thumping, squeamish, nervy excitement.

Until a monk stepped into his path and coolly sold him a ticket.

He still had that ticket, and it was one of the weirdest souvenirs in his collection — a blurry photo of vultures clustered on a carcass. Birds eating a corpse. That's not your average tourist attraction. Not something everyone has the fortitude for.

What he'd been shocked by in the end, though, was not the dead body. It was the leisurely way the workers there had cut up the body and broken up the bones, throwing the pieces to the vultures like fishermen throwing scraps to seagulls. They'd chatted as they worked. It was so casual it was horrible and he couldn't take his eyes off them, waving the hobbling, eager vultures away with a stick until they were ready to step back.

'So did you take a photo that time?' Sophie was saying.

He hesitated. 'I was ready not to, to tell you the truth, because they said, you know, that the locals wouldn't like it and it was disrespectful and all that — but while I was there watching, a Tibetan guy next to me asked to borrow my camera and he took a couple of shots himself. So yeah, somewhere in my files I do have a photo. Imagine what a rare image that must be.'

She picked up the last barbecue shape and crumbled it in her hands for the birds.

'Don't get too excited,' she said, slapping her palms together dismissively. 'I bet you ten bucks there's a video of it on YouTube by now.'

'Forest ravens,' said Russell when they told him they'd been robbed by birds. 'Or it could have been black currawongs.'

'For a hundred thousand dollars,' said Rich, 'what are their Latin names?'

But Russell, it seemed, had endless trumps up his sleeve.

'*Corvus tasmanicus*, that's the little raven. And *Strepera versicolor*.'

He glanced at them and grinned apologetically. 'I don't know all of them. I'm not that much of a twitcher. I just know the common ones.'

'Give us a break,' Rich whispered to Sophie after Russell had left to boil the billy for lunch. 'He'll be handing out scarves and woggles next.'

She looked at him mystified, as if he was the weird one. 'What's a woggle?'

When they'd climbed the dense forested track to Du Cane Gap (1070 metres rising over two kilometres, and Rich feeling every burning inch of it) he stood panting, gripping the Olympus, getting some breath in his burning lungs before deciding which direction to photograph first. The views weren't as spectacular as Pelion Gap, but it was good to just look back to see how far they'd come since then. He could see all the way until it vanished into cloud cover like a delicate Japanese painting, the rocky rises and summits with their tree-frilled silhouettes disappearing and reappearing fitfully through the watercolour wash of white silk.

A long way, he congratulated himself. Bloody tough country. He'd walked nearly forty-seven kilometres with this pack, but they were nearly there. And it was all downhill now to Windy Ridge Hut, and if he could just ration out his painkillers to take tomorrow morning, he'd have the thing in the bag and be at Narcissus in a few hours, then a whole day to rest at the hut there;

a whole incredible, feet-up, boots-off day. Then catch the ferry the following morning, time to sit and talk about the trip with Sophie, patch up those few altercations and misunderstandings. Not burned bridges. Singed bridges, if anything. Understandable.

There was a suspension bridge he'd seen in photos of the Overland Track, hung high over a creek somewhere; he must remember to get a photo of her crossing it. He'd do an enlargement and mount it for her, write a note. Or even a letter. *Here's to many more bridges to cross together*, he could put. Or a quote: *The journey of a thousand miles begins with one step*, or *You can't step in the same river twice* or *Let each person march to the beat of their own drummer*, or ...

'Here come the Roaring Forties.'

Christ, bloody Russell again, bobbing up beside him on the summit, making him just about jump out of his skin.

'The what?'

'The winds — can't you feel them? Straight off the Antarctic ice shelf — Tassie's right in the way. That's why a blizzard can come over in about five seconds flat. I was over in the South-West once — and boy! One minute we were walking along in the sunshine and the next we were getting knocked over by horizontal sleet and the temperature dropped fifteen degrees in fifteen seconds.'

'Is that right.'

Nothing Rich said or did seemed to get rid of this guy. He was like some incessantly cheerful office dork in his big sneakers and the baggy-arsed Target jeans no self-respecting single guy would be seen dead in. He nodded to himself now, digging in his daypack for a pair of gloves, saying with a kind of relish, 'There could really be some bad weather blowing in, now.'

How could he tell — by watching ants? 'What makes you say that?' Rich asked reluctantly.

Russell turned and gave him a puzzled look, then raised a hand to point at the horizon, banked with slate-grey cloud.

He barked a little self-deprecating laugh. 'Oh, right. I see what you mean.' Smart-arse. He stared out assessingly at the clouds building over the stony peaks. 'Yeah.'

He had nothing else to say. Praying fervently it wouldn't start lashing with rain again, not now, when they were almost at the end. Imagining people packed into the hut that night, damp rising off them in a fug, the repertoire of snores he'd have to endure, the smell of socks ripening like cheese, the dawn chorus of plastic bag crunches and whispers and backpack zippers, as some poor gang of fools from Stuttgart or Toronto set out for the next leg in driving rain, freezing their knackers off down that rain-lashed track. Or even worse, if that were possible — the tents sodden with water, bowing sideways in the gale, straining at the pegs, with him and Sophie inside trying to sleep on those mats as wet plastic stuck to them like a freezing shower curtain.

'Once that comes in,' Russell was saying now, with a kind of sombre enjoyment, 'it'll be here to stay. So fingers crossed it blows over us tonight and gives us a bit more clear weather.'

'Uh-huh.'

'We've been real lucky on this walk, with the weather. But if that comes in there won't be any views to speak of.'

'You're right there.'

'Nothing worth taking a picture of then!'

'True enough.'

If he comments on the tripod, thought Rich grimly, watching the clouds roiling low to the horizon like a Steven Spielberg special effect, *I'll shove the thing up his nose.*

He pointed over at the peaks on the horizon.

'Is that still Cradle Mountain National Park there?' he said, for something to say.

'Nope. They're the Mountains of Jupiter; we're really close here to the adjacent park, the Walls of Jerusalem. They're all the Orion Lakes there. Libby and I did a walk through there a few years ago, higher up. We wanted to go to Lake Adelaide but Parks and Wildlife was detouring all walkers around that track, so we missed out. They were working on a dog-eradication program and had all these baits laid apparently.'

'On a what?'

'Trapping feral dogs. There was a pack of them they were

trying to catch. We had a chat to a team of rangers while we were there and they were going to bring in a bitch on heat to trap the males.'

Gosh, he thought sarcastically, *you're a fount of information, aren't you, mate?*

'Libby reckons she heard barking the other night, really faint,' Russell went on.

'I would have thought feral dogs would stick to farming country where they can attack something easy, like a sheep,' he said.

'They get disoriented,' Russell answered.

What was he getting out of his pocket now? A bloody Chapstick.

'How's that blister?' Russell added conversationally, unscrewing the lid.

Rich raised the camera to his face, pointed it to the south where Lake St Clair lay waiting for him like a shining blue reward. 'Never better,' he answered.

Fifteen

He waited for Sophie to catch up so they could begin the descent together down to Windy Ridge Hut. Kept his tone determinedly pleasant and neutral, letting her know he was prepared to put that little spat behind them.

'Who have you been chatting with?'

'That couple from Israel.'

'The ones with the dreadlocks?'

'Yep.'

'They're actually friends, are they? I thought they might have been on some kind of military exercise together. They hardly seem to speak to each other.'

She laughed. 'You know what? They're on their honeymoon.'

'You're shitting me.'

'Nope.'

They were trudging through myrtle forest now, towering and fragrant.

'Their *honeymoon*. I can't believe it. Christ, people are peculiar.'

'After this they're going to Vietnam and Laos.'

'Would it kill them to look like they were enjoying themselves?'

Sophie grinned, tipping her head to catch a glimpse of the forbidding sheer rock faces of Mount Geryon and the Acropolis rising fissured and grey on the western horizon as they walked.

'That looks scary, doesn't it? Like the walls of a fortress. Do you reckon people climb it?' She was making an effort, he could tell. She was sorry.

'They're probably not allowed to,' he answered. 'It's as if we're walking through a sort of museum, isn't it? Can't touch this, can't do that. No lighting fires, no stepping off the track. And those Dutch guys last night insisting you were supposed to strain out your dishwashing water and scatter the dregs around so that it doesn't hit the ground too hard!'

'They make it strict so people don't wreck it, though. Because it's pristine.'

'Pristine! This isn't pristine. It's heaving with people. And I read in the hut last night you get fined if you build a cairn. Wow, one of the most picturesque things about walking in Tibet is all these stone and wooden cairns people have built around the place, on hilltops and mountainsides mostly. They decorate them with all this stuff.'

She considered this, frowning into the distance. 'Do they have those prayer flags hanging on them?'

'Those multicoloured ones? Yeah. Sending all those prayers to heaven.'

'Mum's got them all around the verandah. She reckons they have to stay up until they tatter away naturally, or something. Sometimes I wonder what they actually have written on them.' Sophie paused at the grin sliding across his face. 'What?'

'Oh, nothing. That's just so like the Sandy I remember. Decorates the house with Tibetan prayer flags but hasn't ever actually been to Tibet.'

He was expecting her to agree, to smile conspiratorially with him. He felt a sharp ache for it, that easy camaraderie. But her voice was subdued when she finally answered.

'Well, she was busy.'

'Yeah, she was always rushing round, getting caught up in the latest craze.'

She shook her head. 'Busy looking after me, I meant.'

There was no accusation there. No hidden reproach for him. It just made his sudden hot shame worse. God, the way she looked up at you, raising those downcast lids to give you the full high-beam of everything she was thinking. Nowhere to hide, in that glare. You just wanted to put your hands up to your own face, like a shield.

'I wanted to ask you something else, yesterday,' Sophie said.

A pinch of trepidation. He felt bruised, as though he was coming back in off the ropes, dazed, wavering arms up. Some internal tear somewhere, something to blindside you again later.

'Fire away.'

'I don't know ...' Eyes away from him again now, a hand creeping up to her mouth to anxiously chew a nail.

'You may as well. Now's the time.'

'Did you love me when I was born?'

Ligaments tearing. A rib poking, surely, into his lung; stabbing, sharp-edged. What else could suck the air from you like that? From every part of him, he felt himself gathering breath, drawing in remnants and shreds of everything he needed to answer her. And he couldn't hesitate, couldn't let her see a second of doubt.

'Are you kidding? You were ... awesome. Totally beautiful. You even melted Janet's heart in five seconds.'

'But you, though.'

He couldn't trust himself to look at her now, how she hunched around the fingers in her mouth, teeth tearing, her eyes averted from him with mortification. Him. It was him putting her through this.

'You have to believe that I did.' He hesitated. 'Your mother and me splitting up was ... that had been brewing for a very long while. It wasn't you.'

'Right.'

'I mean, I don't know what Sandy's said, but ...'

'OK. Don't worry about it.'

It hadn't been *him*. Absolutely not his doing. The certainty of that fact savage in him, familiar as a witness statement pared down to its essentials, recited over and over.

I'm promising you now that if you leave you'll never see Sophie again.

He could remember it, the instant fury as it turned in him sudden as an undertow, grasping in that moment that Sandy saw the baby like leverage, like a piece of ammunition against him. He'd looked back at her, wondering how twenty-four hours could turn someone you thought you knew into such a cold and calculating stranger, standing there on the new deck clutching their baby like a hostage, glaring at him with such utter icy *capability*; he knew she would do it, given the chance. He just couldn't bring himself to even answer.

He'd turned around instead, and kept walking. It wasn't like he'd weighed it up, just that something in him suddenly snapped. Now, he thought, she could be like all those others she seemed so enamoured of — all the loud and domineering women who propped themselves in his kitchen drinking wine out of the cask and complaining about how hard done by they were, when as far as he could tell all they did was sit around on their supporting mother's benefits and do as little as possible. Those women! The town was jammed with them — women who looked at you askance, with instant dislike, the moment you dared to disagree with them, women who waved off your contribution to the conversation with smirking, impatient contempt, because if you weren't talking about them, they weren't listening. Sandy's new club.

Hit the road instead. Turn your back on it. Get back a bit of the spontaneity that had almost died in you, hanging round in Ayresville, sleeping through your life.

He had recalled, as he'd driven away, a recurring dream he'd had for years — one of those stress dreams about being inexplicably at some airport, with somewhere vital he had to get to and suddenly without luggage or a ticket. But then he'd find himself calming down, realising that he had all he needed, despite it all, just his passport and keycard. The rest he could manage without. Passport and keycard — the bare fundamentals you'd need to escape with.

'All I want to take is the Kombi,' he'd said to Sandy that day. The new, ice-cold hatchet-faced Sandy, who stood staring at him as he stuffed some clothes into a bag.

'Take everything that's yours ...' she answered grimly.

'You can have everything else — the books, all the household stuff ...'

'... everything that's yours. Take it and go.'

'And my share of the house. You take it all.'

She'd sneered at him. 'Gee, thanks. That's big of you, leaving me the mortgage.'

He stopped, feeling his face contort. There was no reasoning with her. That was the trouble.

'Will you just shut up and listen? I'll ring you, OK? When we've both calmed down and we can discuss this ...'

She raised an arm and pointed down the road, a dramatic, imperious gesture that made him want to burst out laughing.

'There's nothing to discuss. You walk out on us and I never want to hear from you again. No contact, no custody, no nothing. So you'd better pack everything you want now, Rich, because once you go, that's it. That's the ultimate betrayal.'

'You don't have to be such a drama queen. Now's not the time to ...'

But once she'd cast herself in the role, he could see, she had to keep upping the ante. Asked him how his parents would feel, told him how Sophie would grow up now thinking that all men were like him; absconders, never to be trusted or relied upon.

'Sophie can ...' he began again.

'What do you care about Sophie? You'd rather go and sit on a beach in Goa than stay here and be a father to Sophie.'

'I want all of us to go. Jesus, that's what we've always talked about. How a baby shouldn't be a reason to stop travelling and experiencing the world —'

'Rich, just get your stuff and get out of our lives.'

And then that final sentence, *I'm promising you now that if you leave you'll never see Sophie again*, and her face like something carved out of marble.

The driver's seat of the Kombi, the smell of the van as familiar as his own clothes; heat cracks on the dash from thousands of kilometres of happy adventuring together, the gull feathers and shells strung with fishing line hanging from the rear-vision mirror seeming suddenly like a childish craft project.

They hadn't driven that van for months because there wasn't really room for the baby seat, but he'd held his breath and turned the key and the Kombivan, that triumph of German engineering, coughed in Teutonic amazement and started. The ragged sound of the engine turning over flooded him with relief.

He pushed the column shift into reverse, not looking at her there on the deck, telling himself he'd call that night and they'd be able to rationally discuss what to do. She was the one who had burned the bridges, not him.

The few cartons he'd taken he boxed up in a friend's garage in the city, already feeling the restorative powers of ridding himself of all the stuff he knew he could do without. He wrote an ambiguously open-ended note to his parents and drove to Sydney, where he sold the Kombi to a couple of Dutch backpackers who wanted to see Uluru, wished them luck without telling them about the crack in the radiator.

Walked away without a pang. He couldn't believe how light and clear things felt, how unencumbered and exhilarating and vast the world suddenly seemed, full of its old potential. Some people, he thought, were just made to be always moving, always exploring. That was what the desire to travel was about — movement towards an emptier, less cluttered life. Now he was himself again, substance flowing back into him, vital flesh and blood.

He made his way to the airport carrying almost nothing, and thought how the dream had probably been signalling to him all this time, preparing him for just this kind of detachment. Then he was on a plane to Borneo, divested of all of it, shuddering with relief as he leaned back in his seat, the ID photo on his new passport looking at him with the steely eyes of a man who's made a narrow escape but now has got places to go.

He remembered the plane banking over the airport and out across the ocean. It had been raining on the ground, but above the cloud cover the sky was a dazzling blue. He'd closed his eyes against the glare, and shed his nagging doubts like an old skin.

And here she was, that same baby, back to bring it all up again. He'd invited this, he'd plotted it, argued for it, wanted it.

She'd pulled ahead of him by now, her hands appearing from around her backpack to grope in a back pocket for the earpieces to her iPod as she walked. That fumbling defensiveness, the thin delicacy of her wrists, sent a terrible sharpening sorrow through him.

That's not what she wanted to ask him, he knew. Not really. She didn't mean *did you love me when I was born?* She meant *why did you leave me?*

Rich couldn't answer either question, anyway. He wondered if he had loved her. He wondered if he'd ever really loved anybody.

Sandy was perspiring even before she climbed into the sweat lodge. She'd always hated confined spaces, especially dark ones. Once she was inside, settled on the cedar benches with the others around the brazier, she wondered what the minimum time was you could stay in there and still fulfil the requirements. Not that it was a test, she reminded herself, blinking the stinging perspiration out of her eyes. Nobody was making her stay in there — if you had any doubts or health concerns you could opt for an aromatherapy spa instead — but it made sense that the closer you got to the edge of your tolerance, the longer you could endure the purifying heat, the sharper your vision would be.

She was a bit hazy on what kind of vision to expect. She was getting her shamanic animal totems mixed up with her medicine tarot animals, and the Goddesses were all blurring into a composite perfected being with a willowy figure, flowing hair, a jug and a sheaf of wheat. The sweat was pouring from her, though. That had to be having a good detoxifying effect. But with all the steam being generated from the brazier (just garden variety heat beads, a small part of her brain registered; there was nothing stopping her trying this at home) you'd think the air would be moist, but it was scorchingly arid as she drew it into her lungs. Dry enough to shrivel your eyeballs. No wonder they had advised everyone about 'intaking' enough water this afternoon before the session.

'Focus now,' said the instructor, whose name was something even Ayresville residents would have hidden a smile at — Passionflower Windfeather, or Butterfly Eaglemountain, or somesuch — 'focus now, and look down into that sacred tunnel, and invite your totemic animal guide to appear. We invoke you now, O Mighty Ones, we call across the forest and the prairie for you to approach.'

OK, Sandy thought, but *prairie?* She closed her eyes. Should have opted for the spa, she was thinking, when a wave of inspiration hit her. It just blossomed in her head out of nowhere. What someone should invent, it was suddenly clear to her, was a medicine tarot pack using native Australian animals, and Aboriginal mythology instead of Native American. Rejig the whole idea — dingos instead of coyotes, echidnas instead of porcupines, majestic red kangaroos instead of wolves. She could see how the whole thing could be marketed — you could even throw in a dreamcatcher. She'd talk to Gail at the Sunday market about it when she got home. The idea seemed so perfect, so foolproof, she wondered if she was a bit delirious with the heat. The instructor was talking to them now about their breathing, only she was calling it 'breathwork'. Even respiring, she thought fleetingly, was called work around here.

Focus now, on the swimming reddish space before her closed lids. Another minute and she'd climb out, before she fainted, because she remembered this sensation now from kneeling in Mass at school on hot days, when everything went distant and prickly as though she was losing reception on a TV, then she'd keel over. Something small and black wavered tentatively before her closed eyes.

Not a *bat*, please God, she thought despairingly. Anything but that. But the shape alighted and tucked its wings neatly into place, bustling with merry energy.

For a few astonished seconds, inside her head, she saw what she was supposed to. It hopped right up to her and cocked its coal-black head, tapping its beak with businesslike energy onto the ground between them, like it was calling her to attention. She could see its mischievous eye shining. She held her breath. Surely to God the thing wasn't going to open its mouth and speak to her. She saw that shrewd intent eye, the beak briskly tapping again, *here here*, on the earth. Sandy, behind scrunched lids, dropped her eyes to tumbling blackness, the blank ground splitting open. Then she toppled sideways off the bench.

The hut site was on the edge of a rainforest and in the shelter of Du Cane Gap, and the tent platforms were scattered throughout the nearby forest, but it still felt exposed to Rich, the wind outside the hut pouring like liquid ice. There had never been a less inviting prospect than trudging out into that darkness and crawling into his tent, but he couldn't stand the alternative either, of turning back inside and staying in the hut with all the others. He felt a sudden unexpected wallop of restless fear, a blast of claustrophobia and agoraphobia rolled uneasily into one.

Stupid. Ludicrous, really. It was just exhaustion. Out there were hundreds of square kilometres of uninhabited wilderness, this hut floating in it like a tiny ship in space, the only human light and warmth for light-years around. And yet both options felt oppressive. There was nowhere to go. Nowhere comfortable or familiar, nowhere he didn't feel trapped. His agitation bit at his core.

He stepped reluctantly back into the cabin and leaned against the wall surreptitiously watching Sophie, chatting with the three jovial women from New Zealand. She was telling them something, and laughing. He watched, hungrily, the animation on her face, the shy grin that transformed her features.

'I actually brought my phone recharger,' she was saying, covering her eyes with her hand at the thought. 'I thought there'd be power points! In the huts!'

The other women nudged her, laughed along with her, sipped

glasses of port. *Port!* he thought in sullen, irritated disbelief. They'd lugged a bottle of port all this way.

'The thing is,' Sophie went on, and he was brought up short again by the new, relaxed warmth in her voice, the confiding familiarity in it, 'the one other time I went camping, with my school, there were these cabins and there were power points you could plug into.'

'That's a fair enough assumption, then,' said one of the New Zealanders in that odd clipped accent.

'Yeah, but look where we are!' Sophie giggled. They all rocked back in their seats and one of them started telling Sophie, leaning over like they were best friends, about the time Naomi here — she prodded her friend, who smacked her back, laughing helplessly — once took a hairdryer with her when they went camping.

'I thought we'd be staying in a caravan park!' Naomi protested, wiping away tears of hilarity. 'Anyway, you — *you* — took that reading lamp! And a travelling iron! I saw it!'

He watched the four of them, Sophie included, shaking with laughter, and let black annoyance fill him. It wasn't that funny, for godsakes.

He wandered aimlessly to a bench seat, on the edge of another conversation. His ankle was killing him. It sang with pain, hummed with a bright, ringing note of it, clamouring for his attention.

Out there, behind him and separated only by this thin layer of timber, was the chill, the hostile dark, a buffeting wind throwing that smell of freezing wet earth into your face.

He could hear it now, smacking the door with gusts that could knock you off your feet.

Nothing out there for him. Just his tiny tent snapping with wind on the platform, the foam bed-roll hard as a rock. Darkness that seemed to resent you even being there.

And the alternative was in here. The chatter, the exhausting one-upmanship, the carefully worded travellers' tales; the prospect was almost worse than the implacable blackness outside. He got up again, tongue between his teeth at the pain, and pretended to study a map on the wall, as if he'd developed a sudden avid interest in topography. Worse came to worst, he could read the messages in the logbook. Even that seemed to be used as an outlet for frustrated poets. He flicked through the most recent entries.

Here were Russell and Libby's details, and underneath, in small letters, a Latin quote: *solvitur ambulando — it is solved by walking.*

As if they were an institution that had its own motto, or something. Nothing was solved by walking, he thought flatly; it was inflamed by it, rubbed and irritated and endlessly chafed by it. *Time wounds all heels*, he felt like writing. Sophie was right about one thing — he did hate everybody on this walk.

Some people were already climbing into their sleeping bags on the platforms. They looked like bodies on the shelves at a morgue. What was he doing here? Why was he putting himself through this? Why were any of them lugging their belongings on their backs from hut to hut in this glacial wilderness, like a contingent of urban refugees?

'Hey Rich,' called Libby, waving at him from a table in the corner. She and Russell were talking with a bearded guy Rich had already briefly met, who claimed to be a photographer but only had a couple of digital SLRs with him. Unwillingly, Rich waved back and moved over there.

'Have you met Paul, Rich? He's a photographer as well.'

'Yeah. Hi again.'

'He's taking photos of fungi in the park. So he's one person who's pleased it's so damp.' Libby laughed. 'Have a piece of cake, Rich. This is the last of it now — we've rationed ourselves all this time.'

He took a piece of cake and bit into it. The taste of something real and rich, rather than the reconstituted starchy stuff he'd been eating, exploded deliciously in his mouth.

'Thanks. So why fungi?' he said to the bearded guy.

'Oh, it's a commission. Part of an exhibition planned for next year at the Wilderness Gallery here. A few of us are doing different seasonal flora of the park, so as you walk through it will be like the passing of the four seasons ...'

He talked on as Rich swallowed down the mouthful of cake with difficulty. It had turned dry in his mouth, a thousand crumbs that threatened to choke him.

'Great,' he managed to say.

'What about yourself? I noticed you had a fair bit of equipment with you. You working on anything special?'

He nodded. 'Oh, yes, a couple of things. Some one-offs here and there.'

'I notice you don't use a digital camera.'

He didn't need this. Not at the moment. He couldn't summon his usual energy to start a sparring match about this.

'Yes, I'm still a traditionalist, I guess. The day digital cameras can deliver the quality of resolution I want in my photographs, I'll consider buying one. Until then I'll just depend on my own skill.'

'Right.'

Good. Point taken, discussion over. He took another mouthful of cake and chewed balefully.

'Isn't it great to see Sophie having such a good time?' Libby said.

'Yep.'

'I mean, it's lovely seeing her so happy and animated now that she's met a few people. She seemed a bit out of her depth at first, but she's really come out of her shell now, hasn't she?'

'Uh-huh.'

'And such great ideas about everything! She was telling Russell and me today about her website.'

'Was she?' he said, smiling on. He brushed some crumbs carefully off the pine tabletop in front of him.

He remembered his mother doing that, brushing up crumbs after dinner into her cupped hand, and then one night his father and him both watching, blank-faced, as she brushed and brushed at crumbs that weren't there; her eyes roving over the tablecloth getting more and more anxious, as if invisible crumbs stretched as far as she could see.

'And I thought she meant a science project,' Libby was saying, 'but she said, no, it was actually a weekly blog she does. She told me all about it.'

Those prescription painkillers must be messing with his head, he decided. Because he felt, with a wave of desolate, lonely envy, the stinging pressure behind his eyes of imminent tears. Hold it together, he rebuked himself.

'Will you be spending any more time with her after the walk, Rich?' said Russell.

'No, she'll be flying home, I'm afraid, back to her mum's. We'll have a day at Narcissus waiting for the ferry. Make the most of our time together.' Like they confided everything, strolling hand in hand. Like she'd taken the time to tell *him* about her web thing, rather than some stranger she'd just met.

'Straight to Narcissus? You're not doing a side-trip to Pine Valley?' asked Russell.

Rich shook his head.

'Oh, that's a shame. It's a perfect time for the fagus, up in the Labyrinth. Acres of the stuff.'

'That place,' said the photographer called Paul. 'God, you can't take a bad photo up there.' He shook his head reminiscently, peeling an orange, the dense citrus smell of it filling Rich's nostrils. 'Friend of mine — not even a pro photographer, just a rock climber I know — he was doing the south peak of Mount Geryon and just snapped a shot off, you know, with his compact digital, and later it was on the cover of *Wild* magazine.'

'Yeah, it's dramatic, alright. And Pine Valley's beautiful; this really ancient forest of pines and mosses and creeks. And the new hut there's lovely,' said Libby.

Rich looked at the three of them. 'And you're all going, are you?'

'Oh, yes.'

'And it's not actually an official part of the Overland Track?'

'Well, it's kind of the connoisseur's part of the track, I reckon,' Russell said. 'A lot of people are a bit over it by now and just want to get into the home stretch to Narcissus. They don't want to tackle the extra few hours on a side track if they don't have to.'

'So nobody goes there?'

'Oh no, quite a few people go. But it's two hours down to Pine Valley Hut then another six clicks or so into the Labyrinth, and plenty of people reckon they've done the track without it. Done the recommended walk, I guess, and secretly just wanting to get back to the comforts of home.'

'It's not a soft option. But I personally wouldn't want to miss it,' added Paul. 'I love that isolation. Beautiful. Everywhere you point your camera.'

Rich sat nodding. He still had five blue bombers left — he could eke them out. Walk up to this place tomorrow, stay at Pine Valley Hut tomorrow night instead, then back on down to Narcissus, catch the afternoon ferry, and straight on a bus to Launceston.

'You can do the Labyrinth as a day walk, but there's nothing like taking your tent in there and camping beside one of those lakes,' Paul went on. 'I got some shots there once — man! Sensational. Dawn breaking over this valley of ghost gums, mirror images of rocks in these crystal-clear little lakes, and in the middle my one solitary red tent, lit up in the sun like a tiny flower. Nobody else around for miles.'

Or stop for lunch at Pine Valley Hut, he thought, take another painkiller, do the extra six kilometres, and show Sophie what real wilderness camping could be like. Their last night out here. The welling pressure of emotion behind his eyes was subsiding now, thank God. He wouldn't think about the kilometres of walking, he could get himself through that. Impress upon her that he wasn't the kind of man who just stayed on the beaten track and did what everyone else did. Whatever else she went away thinking about him, it wouldn't be that he was ordinary. The idea took form in his head; shimmering, possible.

'I took a great series like that once,' he said now to the others. 'Upriver on the Franklin, back in '83.' He paused, seeing it register in their listening faces, and gave a rueful, reminiscent grin. 'Just managed to get a roll finished,' he continued, 'before I got arrested.'

Sixteen

Pencil pines. King Billy pines. Celery-top pines. All good for the article. (*For over 60 million years, these ancient and unique forests have flourished in the rugged remote grandeur of Tasmania, tucked away and almost forgotten at the bottom of the world*. And a photo of a King Billy Pine in close-up, still beaded with dew.)

'You'll love this,' he'd said to Sophie. 'We won't just do what everyone else does, we'll go on a special side-trip. Russell and Libby are going. Are you up for it?'

She'd wanted to see it on the map. Had to confer with Russell and Libby first, her new best buddies, couldn't just trust him to do something spontaneous and fun. 'OK,' she'd said finally.

And now they were actually on the track, meandering through forest which he had to admit was pretty primordial and beautiful, there was no way she could be disappointed. (*Deep tea-coloured creeks cascade by the carpets of moss and lichen, tinted by tannin and icy-cold*. Photo of brilliant green moss, a long exposure on the water so it had that silky Dombrovskis look.)

They'd skirted the Narcissus River on the way down to the Pine Valley turn-off and then as they made their way through the forest, there it was: the suspension bridge. He'd got a shot of Sophie standing precariously in the middle of it — he'd caught her smiling — and then alongside Cephissus Creek, where the track had been made to wind naturally around the creek's contours. Hobbit land. Fantastic. Huge tree ferns shook dew down onto them (him turning up his collar, pretty paranoid about leeches now), moss-hung beeches and myrtles and pineapple-fronded pandani, all with fingers of dim, arcadian light pouring through trying to reach that understorey — it was all perfect. Much more like what he'd imagined.

'Beautiful, eh?' he said to Sophie.

'It sure is.'

'Glad you came?'

A grudging smile, like he was forgiven. 'Yeah, I'm glad.'

He walked with his camera ready round his neck, pointing and shooting, changing lenses, waiting for other walkers to get out of his shots and for the light to change. (*It's the smell of the forest that strikes the walker most intensely — the rich fertile scent of fallen leaves on the forest floor creating a heady freshness ...*)

They came to the hut in the forest, bunk spaces already claimed with packs and sleeping bags, food caches hanging from hooks in bags.

'Lot of people seem to be already here,' he said as he cut up the last of his cheese for lunch. 'It's going to be crowded tonight, Sophie. Maybe we could camp ...'

'You can never predict how many people are going to be at each hut,' commented Russell. He was ensconced on the verandah, reading. He and Libby were planning on climbing the Acropolis tomorrow, he said, so today was a rest day. Rich didn't know how he could get around in the ridiculous thermal leggings he had on. What a buffoon.

'I don't mind camping,' Sophie said, surprising him. 'I really like waking up and being outside rather than in a hut.'

'Me too,' said Russell. 'There's still some nice platform spots left.'

'Well, OK,' he said, feeling vaguely irritated. 'We'll probably just get on up to the Labyrinth, then, while the weather's so clear. Got your daypack organised?'

'Yeah.' She lifted the one she carried.

'Barometer's looking good,' volunteered Russell. 'Although

you never can tell with Tasmania.'

The guy was carrying a barometer. Soon, thought Rich, shaking his head, he'd pull out a deckchair and a beach umbrella.

'Well, we'll see you back here later this afternoon,' he said to Russell and Libby as they filled their water bottles at the tank.

'Yeah, we'll mind the house, Soph,' said Libby with a grin. 'See you back here for cards.'

'You'll love it up there,' Russell added. 'We've been up three times over the years and it's sensational.'

He felt a smooth relief as he and Sophie finally set off down the track past the hut's helipad. He had her to himself now. Nobody else to distract her.

'Once when I was in Guatemala,' he began lightly, 'haven't thought of this for years, but our conversation yesterday reminded me, I met this American guy at this beautiful lake. It was a phenomenal place, all these volcanic peaks and blue water, and he had this plan to set up a tourist attraction where he'd sell hang-glider and ultralight flights to backpackers, like a sort of adventure tour thing.'

'Uh-huh.'

'Well anyway, he's got it all lined up, and he's wondering how to market it, so he asks the locals: "What do you call those birds up there, the ones that circle up high in the sky on the wind?" And the locals tell him: "Zopilotes, señor." So he goes ahead and designs his hang-gliding brochure with the slogan: "Soar with the zopilotes." And the locals can't stop laughing, because he's thought they were eagles, you see — but the birds he'd pointed out, the zopilotes, were actually vultures. So he was inviting tourists to come and soar with the vultures.'

Rich laughed as he turned back to see Sophie's reaction.

'Soar with the vultures!' he repeated in an exaggerated American accent. She glanced at him distractedly, a dutiful little smile. Not even listening.

He remembered seeing the admiration in her eyes when he'd changed lenses to take that photo the other day, and before that, when he'd talked his way into the museum vault in Hobart. The eager way she'd watched him handle it, and take charge. She'd respected that expertise. That's what he had to get back again.

'Two roads diverged in a yellow wood,' Rich was calling to her now, gesturing, crouching with his camera and taking a shot of the paths curving away from them. 'You know that poem?'

They were already at the two turn-offs past the hut; the one that went up the Acropolis, the one to the Labyrinth.

'Nope.'

'Great poem. "The Road Less Travelled."'

'I'll be sure to check it out. Mum will have a thousand copies in her bookshelf, I'm sure. Or on one of her inspirational desk calendars.' She paused. 'With a photo on it pretty much exactly like that one you just took.'

He snapped his lens cap airily back on his camera, eyebrows raised.

'You see?' he said. 'It's like I told you, there's an eternal spring of cynicism inside you, but I am no longer buying into it.'

He was smiling though, as he said it, a lofty, theatrical smile, and she couldn't help a smile escaping her own lips in return. He hadn't been so bad, really, on this trip. She'd be home in a couple of days and she could think it over more and get some perspective, and sure he hadn't turned out the way she'd imagined, but he was alright, if you just turned a blind eye to what a try-hard he was.

They squinted up the track that rose hard and steep above them, and spotted another couple of walkers in the distance, already toiling up the incline, polar-fleece hats bobbing above their daypacks.

'More of them!' Rich said, rolling his eyes. 'The place is swarming, isn't it? Not an inch of untouched space anywhere. All of it trampled by the jostling hordes.'

Like he was already planning one of those travel articles he wrote, in his head.

'Well, there's no hut there, I read that last night,' she responded. 'It's really exposed. That's why it's so crowded back there, people just come up here for day walks, and stay at Pine Valley Hut.'

'Ah yes,' he said sourly. 'Tucked up safe in the hut. With all the other youth hostellers.' He turned back to her. 'You know what — we could camp up here the night instead of staying at the hut. Then just walk down straight to Narcissus Bay in the morning, get there in time to catch the afternoon ferry. Hour and a half, say, from the Labyrinth back to Pine Valley, then back down to the Overland Track, and straight on down to Narcissus. One real night in the wilderness before we hop on the ferry and back to civilisation.'

She chewed her lip, doubtful. 'So carry our packs and all our gear up there for the night?'

'Sure. It's only six kilometres. Give those tents a proper workout. The real walkers camp up there, obviously. There's lots of lakes and grassy spots on the map. What do you say?'

'It looked nice on that map in the hut.'

He gazed up the track. 'It's up to you,' he said. 'But that's where I'd love to get some shots. And it would be worth it, just to get away from all the other trekkers for twenty-four hours. Off the Overland Superhighway.'

'I guess.' She wasn't even sure what a labyrinth was, apart from a lyric on the Nosferatu album.

And Libby and Russell were back at the hut, saving her a spot. She glanced down the track, reluctantly.

'Unless you think you can't carry your pack up that mountain,' he said.

She felt indignant. Who'd been holding them up so far? Not her. 'No, I'm fine with it.'

'It's a high plateau, above the rainforest here in the valley. Big boulders and lakes and rocks; imagine all those views,' he said. He was looking at her, speculatively, wondering if she was up to it.

'Let's do it then.'

'Find somewhere where there's nobody else but us, just for one night.'

'OK. Yeah.' She smiled briefly at him and pulled her beanie

down, tucking her fringe up and under it. Six k's was nothing. She could probably *run* that now, given the chance. She'd never felt so fit in her life.

They trekked back to the hut and retrieved their packs.

'Changed your mind?' said Russell in surprise when he saw them, and Rich answered, 'We thought we'd give an overnight camp a go', filling a cup with water and surreptitiously pushing a couple of capsules into his hand, gulping them down as Sophie filled in the logbook.

Back out tomorrow to catch the boat, she wrote. It would be good, she told herself as she signed in the time. Not a test. Just something apart from everyone else, like Rich was telling Russell now. 'We don't *want* to join up with anyone else who's going,' he insisted, when Russell suggested it. 'That's the whole point.'

'What is a labyrinth, anyway?' she said as they walked back towards the turn-off.

'A Jim Henson film,' he said, 'starring David Bowie.'

'I've seen that!' she exclaimed, remembering. 'With the Bog of Eternal Stench!'

'They must have filmed that bit on Mount Pelion,' he said dryly, and she couldn't help laughing as they started climbing.

'Don't you reckon,' he went on, grinning, 'that all those tufts of buttongrass look like one of David Bowie's wigs?'

She laughed again. He was OK, really.

They went through a swampy forest track in the valley but then the track climbed sharply and she concentrated on her footing as they walked, feeling for the first time enough heat in the sun to warm the back of her neck. She had on just her short-sleeved thermal top and her pack felt so much better now, lighter somehow. Less food, probably.

They went clambering up, panting with exertion, the landscape's vegetation thinning out into dramatic alpine gums, raising limbs skywards like arms, and huge lichen-encrusted rocks, and the air smelling like cold mossy water. It felt as though they were going back in time.

You could feel the difference when they got up to the plateau and the ground flattened out all around them.

'Top of the world!' Rich shouted, and she nodded, because he was right.

The exhilaration that pumped through her when she looked around her was like nervousness and joy at the same time, like a shock of pleasure. There wasn't actually a clear track to walk on, but the ground was hard and worn so you could see where other people had walked, across the cushiony soft patches of grass. All around them were massive stony mountains, pushing grey fingers and pillars of rock up and up. Clusters of broken boulders, bright with green and yellow lichen, ground tipping off into cliffs and ravines. Rich stopping and crouching, exclaiming, snapping photos.

They walked towards the towering crags of mountains, and Sophie saw a couple of wallabies bounding through the rocks into the vegetation, there then gone.

She slowed down, the wind blowing her head clean, dreamily taking it all in, until they reached a mirror-still lake, reflecting sky and upswelling cloud.

She couldn't tell how long they'd been walking. Their two heads, when they leaned over the water, were silhouetted perfectly, the bowl of sky behind them, the bottom of the lake clear below the shadows of their faces. She could see it there, crystalline under the surface, another world furred with slow, patient algae, dropping away.

'Can we stop and camp here?' she said, and he gazed round assessingly and there was a long moment of contented silence. Then as if she'd dropped a rock into the water, it was broken; Rich yelping 'Shit!' and staggering awkwardly to a boulder, brushing his jeans maniacally as if he was putting out flames, swearing.

'Ants everywhere!' he called. 'Look out!'

As he spoke she felt a stinging bite, and hit at her own jeans, pulling off her gaiters and swiping at dozens of tiny black ants.

'God, the place is infested with them!' he said, stomping furiously. 'Quick, grab your stuff and come up onto the grass.

There must be a massive nest down there.'

She scratched her bites and climbed onto another boulder, watching the ants swarming over the ground, looking for her. Scenting where she'd been.

'That's amazing,' she said, and fished in her pack for a cracker, which she crumbled, fascinated, over the dirt.

'You're not feeding the little bastards, are you? Argh, this is impossible — come on, nice as the lake is, we'll have to find another flat spot where we can set up the tents. Have you got any sting gel?'

She shook her head, hypnotised, still dreamy. She watched the ants grab tiny crumbs of dry biscuit and drag them like cargo off the lake shore, like loot off a shipwreck. Where were they going with it? She imagined a colony underground, a huge warren of tunnels and nests, an ant civilisation, efficient as a fortress. They could just slip through a crack in the earth or down through a fissure in these rocks, she thought, and into that secret hidden world. She could have watched them for hours. Her hand crept to her mouth and her front teeth bit absently at a ridge of fingernail, then she stopped, and let her hand drop. No satisfaction in it. No need for it.

'Let's get going, eh?' he said. 'We're going to be overrun here.'

She pulled on her pack and followed him, her mind miles away, picking her way vaguely across the alpine grass until he stopped and uncapped the lens cap of his camera.

'Look at this,' he said.

Ahead of them stood a sign, an incongruous intrusion, the hand of departmental officialdom. *Do not proceed further unless at least two people in your party are competent at navigation with a map and compass.*

Rich grinned, nodding. 'This is more like it,' he said exuberantly. 'At last.'

He took the photo with a flourish and kept walking, glancing back to check her response, and she saw the challenge on his face, the playful, evasive way he winked at her.

Later she'd remember his face as he turned back to her in that instant, that eye closing in a momentary glitter of anticipation, the sun bathing his face in bright hard light. She'd summon it again and again, trying to divine its intention, but it was still impossible to tell whether it was innocent or not.

'Wow,' he heard Sophie saying behind him as they scrambled across a cold stretch of lichen-bright rock. 'Wow, wow, wow. This really is like *Lord of the Rings*.'

Those glossy, wrinkled snowgums, bent and twisted by weather, the peaty smell of the ground, tarns and clear little lakes. And to the west, as he fumbled for his camera again, range after range peaked into a vanishing point.

The day cold but as clear as gin, that blue air that made every exposure perfect, every reflection a mirror image. He was getting some great shots; shots that pissed all over the murals he'd seen in the wilderness-gear shop that day. He'd send them these, for sure. See what happened. They climbed, scrambling from tarn to hill to see more peaks, down into glaciated folds and valleys, touching the great fissures that ice had split in boulders, and at last it was possible to walk on ground untrampled by other people's boots.

He could tell they both felt it, the jubilant relief of empty wilderness, a place as beautiful as a postcard every way you looked. And maybe that was just a transitory lucky illusion, maybe in a few minutes they'd come across a couple of German backpackers munching cheese and Ryvitas and looking up something in their field guide, but for this minute, at least, he was happy.

His head seemed to clear. Everything, finally, was going the way he'd meant it to.

'See?' he called triumphantly to Sophie, as they came across a pyramid of heaped stones, guiding the way. 'Cairns!' He lifted his eyes from the faint impression of a trail they'd been following on the ground, letting it resolve itself into open ground again, searching for the next heap of stones somewhere ahead.

Patches of sunlight and shadow sifted down and rolled across this vista through breaking clouds. They thinned and tore like gauze, revealing patches of palest blue, like a glimpse of something promised.

Sandy tried to do as she was instructed: empty her mind of all preconceptions and allow a single image of her positive force in the world to rise undistorted by any negative patterns.

Her positive force in the world. Just thinking about it gave her a peculiar shiver of something like grief. She'd lost focus, that was the trouble, from her political activism, her conviction. She'd got tired and burned out.

She thought about Sophie, and the night years ago when they'd gone to a friend's birthday. There'd been a band, and all the kids had been dancing along with the adults. She saw Sophie as she'd been that night, eyes closed with blissful abandon, dancing in that big happy tribe of kids, grinning the big, unselfconscious smile of a five-year-old, radiating nothing but joy and delight. How beautiful to be five, she thought, so free and uninhibited, and so cherished. The image of that child pirouetted and twirled in her mind's eye, jumping and holding hands with the other kids. That's positive force, she thought. Once you've danced like that, once you've felt that collective joy, it lodges in you forever somewhere. Whatever happens, it never leaves you.

She sat, her eyes closed, hugging herself as she watched that small precious child whirl like a laughing dervish. Somewhere in her daughter now, she prayed, was the memory of a childhood in a town where maybe people were disorganised or ineffectual or lax or infuriating, but when the music started, at least everyone got up to dance. She might have got lots of things wrong learning to be a parent, but she'd got that bit right, at least.

Stone-littered hillsides, rocks scabbed with scaly lichen, the afternoon ticking on. He walked calmly, covertly trying to establish his bearings. No panic. The whole basin was only eight kilometres long.

They stopped for a break and took off their packs, Sophie reaching up to pull off her hat, scratch her scalp and untangle hanks of hair with her fingers. Exertion had given her cheeks a high colour against the paleness of the rest of her face.

'I have to ask you,' he said to her, 'what's with the hair?'

'What do you mean?' Tilting that defensive look at him which instantly stirred some memory, something silted and covered over.

'Hey, I'm sure it's the hippest of the hip, but it just looks kind of ... I don't know ... snarled up about halfway down there.'

'They're hair extensions.'

'Eh?'

'They're extensions. They plait them in to give you longer hair. Everyone's got them. Don't you ever wonder how some celebrity turns up one week with short hair and then the next week has got hair down to her waist?'

He looked at her hair again, fascinated. 'Is it ... fake hair?'

'You can get real hair too, but these — I don't know what they're made of.'

'I mention it because it's turning into a big clump of dreadlocks.'

She grimaced. 'Yeah, I know. It's been rubbing against the backpack.'

'They look like they're going to knot up and split off, or something.'

She flicked her hair back over her shoulder, stared pointedly out at the horizon.

'They're gonna get wrecked,' she muttered.

'Pardon?'

She favoured him with an eye-rolling sideways glance. 'They're going to wreck my hair. Because they use araldite, to put them in.'

'Wait. They *glue* these things into your hair?'

'Yeah.' She inspected the ends of her hair, considering. 'Or else they tie them in, or just clip them.'

'You know what, Sophie? I reckon we should cut them off. I

could use the small blade on my pocket knife.'

She turned and glared at him. 'These cost me seventy-five bucks.'

'Yeah, but they're ruining your hair, right? You can't even brush it.' He scrabbled in his experience for another approach. 'You'd look great with short hair. Just up to there, under the chin.'

Before he'd had a chance to think about it, he'd touched her. Just tapping his finger against the side of her neck, under her multi-pierced earlobe, drawing an imaginary line across that tender skin.

And just as suddenly, she reached back and grasped a strand of his ponytail between thumb and forefinger, and gave it a light-hearted yank, and he saw he was wrong about her, of course, and about any lack of fire or spirit in her. She grinned Sandy's grin at him, one eyebrow up, just the same. Oh, that quizzical look, lips parted, puzzling. He remembered it now.

'I'll do you a deal,' she said.

And he nodded, mute, dry-throated. Anything, he'd do anything if she'd give him that mischievous, conspiratorial grin again. If she'd take charge.

'What's the matter?' he heard her say. 'Nervous?'

'Course not.'

'So why have you got your hand in front of your eyes?'

He needed a second or two.

She'd had that little quirk of the eyebrow when she'd been born. They'd pulled her out like they were hauling a tree root, forget this comforting bullshit about *lifting* out the baby during a caesarean, and he'd said, 'It's a girl, Sandy'; and at the sound of his voice the baby had turned her head and given him this baleful quirk, her newborn squashed face searching out his eyes in one long assessing owl blink, the eyebrows saying *well?* with barely concealed impatience, a little Winston Churchill look, wondering if he was the one, if he was going to be up to it. Already finding him wanting. Fully cognisant with his weaknessnes, it seemed to him, even then.

'Here, you'd better do the deed,' he said tightly, passing the knife, blade uppermost, into her open hand.

And that night at Greenie Acres, Sandy retrieved the memory now, with a kind of wonder that she could have thought she'd lost it. Impromptu singing and dancing around the fire, energy fuelled on nothing but adrenaline and joy that she had taken the leap and found herself here, so firmly entire and reinvented.

Seeing the blue and white flashing lights of a police car, sudden subdued disappointment thumping in her. Three police officers had gotten out of the car, and the music had wavered uneasily, the guy on the violin and the girl on the flute faltering, the banjo being lowered uncertainly, and Sandy had thought *oh, no, please don't*. Then the police had asked for an assurance — what was this? — that there'd be no photos, and the protesters had agreed eagerly *of course not, no photos*, and then the police officers had turned off their blue lights and thrown their hats in the back seat and joined in the dancing. Yes. Sandy had felt it then, the overspilling strength of what seems fragile, that unforgettable lesson. For half an hour, as they all hooted and stamped and jumped, anything in the world had seemed possible.

When these facilitators asked her what was making her cry in the meditations, how could she even begin to explain?

'How long have you been growing it?' Sophie asked him, as he ran his hand across the exposed back of his neck with a rueful smile.

'Eh? Oh, I don't know. Had a few haircuts here and there. Usually going into countries where it's an issue, you know — where they give you a hard time for looking like a hippie. A hangover from the old days. But that's my first haircut in about seven years, I'd say.'

She held the sawn-off ponytail like a swatch in her hand, looking at it closely. Her own hair swung at her jawbone now, her lovely neck suddenly exposed.

'When mine's not black,' she said suddenly, 'it's just the same colour.'

Rich rubbed hard at his neck. That feeling again, threatening to engulf him.

'Exactly the same,' she added, and twisted the strands and locks of hair together in her hand. A helix.

'It's like a nest,' she said. 'I might leave it here.'

'Why not?' He was standing with his hand shading his eyes now, scanning the rocks on the horizon. They hadn't seen a cairn for a while.

'Wild birds might use it.'

'They might, yeah.'

All the hills looking the same now.

She curled the hair into a sheltered hollow on the rock. After a minute she reached up to her eyebrow and found the screw for the stud there, unscrewed it and took it out. She remembered the expression on Sandy's face when she'd come home with it, the way she'd bitten her lip. It was annoying her anyway, rubbing against the snug fit of her hat on her forehead. She laid it down on top of the hair. How dead and black hers looked, actually, dulled with chemicals.

She shook her head experimentally, surprised by the absence of hair scratchily slipping across her shoulders and neck. Its weightiness was gone. She pushed the fringe away from its customary spot resting against her cheekbone, and it was like lifting a blind, not having a familiar dark lock of it to curtain her right eye.

She looked up to see Rich watching her, his face unreadable, before he smiled brightly.

'Let's find a good spot to get the tents up, and get one of the stoves on and cook up some dinner,' he said. 'Before it gets dark. Because I guarantee it's going to be black as Hades up here, once that light fades.'

He woke at 5 a.m., lightheaded with anxiety. The best thing to do would be pack up and leave as early as possible to retrace their steps, reorient themselves by yesterday's lake and make it that way back to Pine Valley Hut. Then rejoin the trail, and follow it down to Narcissus, and they'd be out of there. Safe on the afternoon ferry, then a bus up to Launceston, airport in the morning, and Rich would take out a lottery ticket and light a candle to the patron saint of narrow escapes, whoever he was. All normalised, all managed and pretending you meant it. He just had to concentrate, now. Swallow two of the last few precious blue tablets to take his mind off his foot, which felt, after yesterday's extra climbing, as though someone had taken to it with a hacksaw in the night. Forget the roiling bilge of bile he was denying in his gut.

They were moving by 7.30, traversing a low, sinewy forest of some flowering scrub plant, peppery with fresh scent, and then walked up another incline across boulders and cushion grasses. The ground was dotted with little pockets of water, the wind changing direction and blowing them along now, rippling the surface sporadically of the tarns they passed.

That stand of dead white trees clumped with the heath rising behind them.

Another tarn.

Another one.

Pale cloud, a flat fillet of it, obscuring the horizon to the north and east. Wait, no. Think. The west and south.

East and south, yes, but the wind had shifted around again and was edging them along the exposed headland towards another stand of bent white trees rising out of the thigh-high scrub of heath and bushes. Then an empty patch.

A profusion of more cushion grass and bare rock.

Another tarn.

'We've been here.' Sophie's voice. He'd been waiting for it. His skin prickled.

'Yeah, I know. We just lost our bearings for a minute there. This is better though. There'll be another cairn soon to show us we're on the right track.'

There was something appalling about the trusting way she was following him, putting it all into his hands like this. Her footfalls behind him, with their faith in him, the way she wasn't watching that smear of cloud blotting itself around three horizons now, cloud that curled itself up into a heavy diffuse blankness so that he gave up wondering which direction the Acropolis was in, and those tarns, all identical, silvery like they were filled with mercury, the surfaces wrinkling and flattening in the intermittent wind.

Thousands of tarns, literally. The New Zealanders had told him that. But here, this basin of the Labyrinth itself, he was certain they'd told him it was only eight kilometres long, and dozens of walkers a day set off on this track. Dozens, easy. They'd be surrounding them soon enough. That guy Paul, probably, striding around with his digital camera. He craned ahead, his eyes trying to pick out the brightness of a Goretex jacket or the fluoro glow of a distant tent.

'We just have to get back to that lake, where we stopped first yesterday, then it'll be clear all the way out. We've still got plenty of time.'

'OK,' she said doubtfully. But trusting him. Not scared, because she thought he'd take care of her. Believed him. He heard her give a little cough, then sniff, her nose running with the chill air, and it gave him almost a physical stab of anxiety to step back from this and picture them both, him leading her across this vast landscape of repeated landmarks duplicating themselves slyly in every direction into infinity, dampness beginning to settle and everything around them so huge and ancient and merciless, and here was his girl following him, cold and tired, trudging after him believing he'd make her safe.

Sandy heard birdsong and burbling water, soothing sounds of the rainforest.

'Welcome,' said the masseuse, beaming at her.

'Gosh, it's so warm in here.'

'Too warm? I can just turn down the thermostat.'

'No, it's fine.' She smiled brightly. These young girls with their thin thighs and lycra tops, didn't they realise how it felt to be stripping off in your mid-forties?

'You're here for the full holistic bodywork rejuvenation, aren't you, Sandy?'

'That's right.' Feeling absurdly guilty now. Vain and silly.

'A total body pamper. Wonderful. Well, first we have a full-body exfoliation scrub with pure marine salts, cold-pressed grapeseed oil, lime, ginger and lemongrass. That prepares the body to detox.'

'OK. Great.' Sounded more like something you marinated a fish in.

'Pop up on the table for me, Cindy.'

'It's Sandy.'

'Oh, right. Sorry. Heated towel?'

They were high now, buffeted with blustery cold wind, views in all directions of dolerite, silvery trees, anonymous summits. If we just stay here, he thought with that same smothered, fluttering panic, someone's sure to come along. A view like this. But when he glanced reflexively to the horizon he saw a new line of cloud lying swollen and dark as dirty wet newsprint, the charcoal grey soaking through like running ink. Wind licked along the exposed surface they stood on, heavy with moisture, scudding and rippling like waves.

The clouds were moving too, with a speed that made his jaw drop. He swore to himself. It was changing before their eyes, closing in, coming down on them like early darkness. The gunmetal cold, pressing the air flat, and the two of them vulnerable as insects on this huge cold-cracked surface.

Sophie oblivious, crouching looking at something on a rock, for godsakes, still thinking he had things under control. Rich shuddered, fumbling hastily for the straps of his pack. Just couldn't be countenanced now, the knowledge that they'd never make Narcissus in time even if by some miracle he could get his bearings again, and every step after that going awry, the ferry and the bus and the shuttle and the plane all pulling away without them, like shunting cars slamming one after another in a train wreck, and, Jesus, you couldn't do a damn thing without having it all blow up in your face, couldn't even calm down and think because you were so hamstrung by other people and their demands on you.

And then he stopped worrying about those missed connections. Why was he even wasting time berating himself with them, he thought, when he could see what was right there on the horizon boiling towards him? Because, Christ, he could smell that wind and what was in it: frozen sleet and melted icecaps and dank crystallised bog, ready to saturate them, and here it came like a black iceberg, a great gout of bruise-coloured cloud, pulled by some relentless winching tide straight into his path. Then Sophie was grabbing his arm, shouting in the wind, her eyes wide.

'Holy crap!'

'We have to get down into some shelter, OK? We're totally exposed up here,' he yelled back as he pointed down through the boulders. 'We'll get off this rise and find a place to get a tent up, stay sheltered. See how fast it's moving? It might even be snow.'

'This time of year?'

'Yep, bloody oath. Let's get going.'

She slid her arms hastily through the straps of her pack, heaved it up and settled it on her hips, her face incredulous. Together they began to clamber downhill, keeping their footing by grabbing rocks and setting their skidding boots sideways into the descent, gravel and stones tipping and rolling down with them. His ankle humming one pure note of pain, and every plunging step sending his heart into his throat.

She felt the frigid wind lessen as they scrambled down the cliff, but she could hear it shaking the trees behind and above them, its hissing voice. She put out her hands and swung herself between two crooked trees that flexed with her weight, thought suddenly about the whole tough and stunted landscape here battening down the hatches ready for the next onslaught, tightening its grip and hanging on, growing a tenacious inch a year. She was slipping and scrambling, her chin tucked in hard and knees jarring all the way down, and she thought of how she'd turned her nose up at the hard bunk-bed platforms in the huts, and the coal and gas fires that had been burning, and the meals she'd left half finished.

Then they were down, lurching over shale and tussocks, and Rich was pulling her into a rocky spot sheltered by mean little shrubs — impossible, really, to imagine how these stalky, scratchy little bushes would ever protect them from anything — and there was nothing for it but to push her icicle fingers inside her clothes, in under her arms, to try to warm them enough to fumble open the zips and fasteners on her pack. In there was nothing but a few laughable folded layers of coated plastic that somehow were meant to shelter them from this storm, rolling in to drown them.

'Get your tent out,' Rich shouted. 'I'll set up mine as an extra roof', and she heard how much he had to raise his voice against the rising wind and saw him pause uncertainly then start hauling some stones into a circle, pushing them into place with his boot as if he was going to make a fire in contravention of all the park bylaws. Then he stopped that too and began unzipping his pack, digging down the side and tugging out his waterproof jacket which billowed as he shook it out, gesturing for her to grab hers and do the same. Then she came out of her trance as the same gust of wind caught the tent fly she was unrolling and snapped it hard as a whip into her chest and the first hard pellets of hail struck her naked neck, stinging the skin like a needle stippling a design.

'We believe in letting the earth's natural powers do the work of opening the energy centres of the body,' murmured the masseuse. 'The scrub works to slough away the dead cells, extracting toxins and impurities. Assisting in the release of chronic pain and stress and realigning mind, body and soul.'

'Great.' Brochure-talk, thought Sandy. She began to fight against a deep tranquil doze as the massage began. She really should stay awake and respond. But the disembodied voice began to fragment as she let her concentration dissolve, until it sounded like a waitress reciting the menu at a dreamlike restaurant.

Wildflower essence therapeutic oils. Pure shea nut butter. Ginger and apricot kernel. A wrap of Dead Sea rich mineral clay blended with wild Canadian seaweed extracts and hemp oil. And to finish, a wattle husk body polish.

'You must feel like an entirely new woman,' the smiling masseuse said to her as she left, wobbly with pampering. Why not? she thought, feeling her skin tight and tingling all over. Experts say we replace every cell in a seven-year cycle, so we weren't the same physical person at all we'd been before. Why shouldn't that process be hastened by holistic rejuvenation, so that an entirely new skin could be revealed? Replenished. Recreated. Reinvented. Starting afresh, and *sloughing* off the old cells. She'd always wondered how to pronounce that word.

Seventeen

When he felt the initial fury of the rain easing he crawled out of Sophie's sagging tent and scouted around the base of the outcrop for dry wood. He wanted it to get cold; cold was good, because that might clear the cloud and then in the morning he could try to reorient himself from the mountain ranges again and at least know what direction they were facing. If he could just look at the sun, and watch its path across the sky, he told himself, he'd be able to sort it out. But then his eye was caught by something that hung shredded on some brambly shrub nearby. Some fabric, zippered, flapping thing — torn to pieces. His tent, or what was left of it.

Impossible. He'd opened the bag and got the tent-fly out, the string, the bloody extra bits of string. There'd been a wind howling that knocked your thoughts straight out of your head. He'd stuffed the tent back into his pack, he was sure he had. He'd tucked it hastily in there, conscious of keeping it dry. He would swear on a stack of bibles. But here it was, buggered completely, hanging off a tree like a wrecked kite.

Fuck, fuck, fuck.

It was drizzling with steady rain now, the dim sky still crammed with serrated banks of white like the flesh of a fish, like smeared, dense forkfuls of mashed potato, and the ground all around him was fading from its orange-brown hues into monochrome. There was wood he could have dragged back, but it was saturated, glistening with moisture. He should have thought of wood first, when he'd seen the storm coming, just grabbed whatever he could find and shoved it somewhere sheltered. Or at least collected some armfuls of dry kindling together as a first priority. But then that rain, like a typhoon, had bucketed down; he'd never seen anything like it. Like being in a black hole under a waterfall, and he'd run to help Sophie, hammering in tent pegs with a stone, desperately hoping to keep sheltered if they pressed themselves in under the rocky overhang above them.

He'd got her tent up, billowing and ballooning as if it was about to take off, and tied his own fly as best he could, corner to corner, over the top. And he'd got her safe inside, pushed the packs in after her into the vestibule. Finally he'd crawled in too, pulling dry clothes out of the packs, paranoid about taking out the sleeping bags in case they got saturated. He didn't want to think about what they'd do if that happened. Just reassured Sophie, tried to keep it light.

He couldn't believe the turn things had taken.

But now here he was, the light fading so fast he actually felt scared, no dry wood anywhere, and the ferry would probably be pulling up to the dock now and from every moment here on, he was accountable, he was in overtime and would be called to explain. Had to find the track out tomorrow. Get to a phone.

And about five kilometres away, it couldn't be more — this was the irony that really killed him — the next wave of walkers would have the stove going in the Pine Valley Hut and he could've been unrolling his sleeping mat out on one of those bunk beds right now. Borrowing a book, even.

His boots were heavy as hooves. When he stopped and inspected them he saw they were huge with clinging, compacted mud. He stopped to kick each heel hard against some rock to dislodge it, and felt a spasm of excruciating heat jolt up his calf when he knocked his blister. It had almost kept him company, that raw, throbbing heel. He'd felt every heartbeat echoed in it, hammering rhythmically with tightly stretched pain, a pulsing SOS. It had looked a bit better, back at Windy Ridge, but it was a lot worse now.

He limped back to the tent. It was dry inside and holding out OK, and she was in her sleeping bag, sitting staring out at the drenched, glistening valley even though it was almost too dark to see it now, hugging her knees.

He switched on his torch and unfolded the brochure from his pocket, taking a deep breath.

'Well,' he said. 'That took us a bit by surprise, didn't it?'

How ridiculous he sounded, like a moronic officer jumping back down into the trenches, full of fake bonhomie. And she gave him a look too, just like those shell-shocked tommies must have to their commanding officer.

'Tomorrow,' he said, 'all I need to do is reorient myself by the peaks of the Acropolis and the Parthenon — these two mountains on the map — and we can start walking out through this valley, and look, the Pine Valley Hut is right there.' His finger traced a thin line on the tourist map, a sketchy mark fine as a thread.

'I can't believe this is the only map we've got,' she said, her voice tight now.

'Yeah, in retrospect we probably should have picked up another one. Paid the ten bucks.' He tried for a rueful grin, but she gave him that withering look again. He tried harder.

'You know, what we should have bought is a pack of cards. You know that joke, about the cards? In an emergency all you have to do is start laying out a hand of patience, and within five minutes no matter how many thousands of miles you are from civilisation someone will be leaning over your shoulder pointing and saying, "Red nine on black ten!"'

The forced levity was almost evaporated in him, shrivelled into something wooden and hard that knocked in his throat.

She shut her eyes and laid her head on her knees.

'This is where that walker went missing,' she said, her voice muffled. 'That young woman — did you see that plaque in the Pine Valley Hut? They've never found her body. She just vanished off the face of the earth. Out here, exactly where we're lost now.'

He sat back, stretching his aching leg in front of him,

mustering energy. 'Nothing to panic about. Nobody can help a storm, it makes everyone change their plans. It rains seven days out of ten here, Russell told me. We'll just be a day late. Everyone will be. There'll be another ferry.'

She would see it in a second, he thought desperately, the anxiety soaking through him, the brittle confidence. See straight through him.

And here came her voice.

'So where exactly are we, on this map?'

He took his time, moving the flashlight's beam over the page, letting his finger hover.

'Well, this whole area's less than ten k's long, believe it or not. So as long as we don't do anything stupid like climb over a whole mountain range, we can't really go wrong.'

'Yeah, but where, exactly?'

He bent forward to unlace his boots. Tried his never-fail smile. 'Not entirely sure.'

'We're lost, aren't we?'

'Well ...'

'We are.'

'I'm not lost,' he said, trying and failing to laugh. 'I'm geographically embarrassed.' It was something he'd seen the other day on a t-shirt, and sneered at, never dreaming it would return to sabotage him like this. The laugh came out like a dry heave, as though a bone caught in his throat, and his rictus smile died as she looked steadily at him, something draining away from her face until it contained nothing, finally, but emptied-out disenchantment, like he'd gone the way of Santa, and the Easter Bunny, and whatever tender credulity it was that allowed childhood in the first place.

Then she turned away from him and straightened out her sleeping bag, digging for her iPod and untangling the cables.

'Are you hungry?' he said. 'I'll boil up some pasta, set up the stove in the vestibule, OK?'

'I don't want anything,' she said flatly, rolling some clothes into a pillow.

'Well, I want you to have something,' he said. 'What about just some noodles?'

'No, thanks.'

'OK. No problem.' As if being obliging was going to change anything now.

'We're meant to be in Launceston, ready to get to the airport to fly back to Melbourne and meet Mum in the morning.'

'Yes, I know. But we ran into some bad weather, and that's the way it goes. We got delayed.'

'She'll be there waiting and we can't even contact her.'

'It's not the end of the world.'

She hugged her knees and hunched away from him. 'What's stopping you setting up your own tent, anyway? I want some privacy.'

He licked his lips. 'The storm wrecked my tent. I only have the fly left, and it's sheltering both of us now.'

She was silent, digesting this. 'So you're sleeping in here, with me.'

'No other choice, I'm afraid.'

She gave him a look to curdle milk and climbed into her sleeping bag, curling up and closing her eyes. He crouched in the vestibule and made enough continental rice for two, using the water out of his drinking bottle. He had three packs of instant meals left — he wasn't sure about her. And some porridge and dried milk. Jesus. Don't think. The pattering in his throat squeezed and slackened, thick with smothered, acidic dread.

He spooned her share of rice into a plastic container and went through the motions of eating a meal, taking a leak outside, even brushing his teeth to keep the sense of normalcy going. He eased his boot finally off his throbbing foot and saw the dark spread of the bloodstain on his sock in the torchlight. When he peeled the layers of sock away, hissing a breath of pain through his teeth, he saw the shiny raw patch beneath and the strange pink hue of the skin around it, like plastic.

The painkillers had worn off and a hot wire of pain was jiggling up his calf, like some glinting lure with a wicked disguised hook at the end, biting and snagging, holding. With every heartbeat he felt it throb, metronome-like. He spread out his mat and sleeping bag, holding his jaw clenched, he realised, to stop his teeth from chattering.

He wouldn't think about the next day. He'd just get to sleep, and deal with it when it came. He could tell Sophie wasn't asleep, there in the confined chilly dome of the tent. After a while, helplessly, he put his hand on her shoulder, and felt her stiffen.

He'd had no cause really to touch her till now, not really; the time he'd touched her face earlier today had been accidental, he had no right to expect any physical contact from her, or affection.

As his palm rested on her shoulder he felt, even through the layers of clothes, the curving bone of her shoulder blade move beneath his arm. They might freeze here, he thought, the claims of the Odyssey Pathfinder could be bullshit, never designed to be tested. Dead of exposure in their thin tent, like Hall and Oates.

No, you dickhead. Scott and Oates. Hypothermia, thought Rich, what were the symptoms of that? Amnesia, for starters. Stumbling, slowness, irrationality, walking around in a stupor ... tick all of the above, for about the last twenty-four hours. Tick the last twenty-four years, actually.

The cold seeming to hold him and rattle him, like a coin in a cup. He had the better sleeping bag, he reminded himself, the one with the superior loft.

'I know you're awake,' he said softly, 'but please don't worry, everything's fine.'

He heard her take a shuddering indrawn breath, as though she'd been silently crying all this time, and he hadn't even noticed. He would have noticed, though. He was sure he would have.

'Come on,' he muttered. 'I don't care if you hate me, I want you to get into this sleeping bag and get warm. No point dying of cold.' Without speaking, to his amazement, she wriggled in. He unzipped hers and laid it over them, then lay back down and tucked his arms around her. Christ, there was nothing to her, it was like hugging a bird. Bones light as air, coathanger collarbones and those sharp shoulders pressed into his chest, and it suddenly hit him what he'd stunningly, obliviously, failed to notice. What had he actually seen her eating, since he'd met her? Two-minute noodles and half-plates of pasta and those health-food bars, stuff she'd hoarded in the bottom of her pack, nothing you could call a *meal* really, not the five food groups for a balanced diet, or whatever it was. He felt a thump of blinding, painful illumination. What if she had that thing? Not the one where you made yourself throw up. The other one.

Was it possible that he'd been so obtuse? He'd just thought she was fashionably skinny, the way they all were, with their waistless jeans hanging off those boyish hips, revealing their stomachs concave and mushroom white, and the inevitable navel piercing. She'd seemed just like a clone of all the other teenage girls who shouldered past him on the train and dully scanned the codes on his DVDs as he waited at the video store. So how had she found the energy to doggedly tramp down those trails after him, never asking for a break? It was anger, then, that ferocity to prove herself. The energy of anger, the fuel of it. There was probably a self-help book out there called *Tapping into the Energy of Anger*. Some theory he hadn't caught up with yet. One of Sandy's little volumes. *Higher-Plane Anger. Angry Like the Wolf. The Anger Journey.*

As he finally began to approach sleep, something from the non-violence workshop all those years ago came back to him, teasing at the frayed edge of his consciousness, circling and disappearing. What had they called it, after they did the role-play about confrontation, with half the group taking on the roles of people they'd be likely to encounter in a real blockade? He remembered drowsily the police officers and angry workers played with hopelessly nice passivity by sheepish protestors. If real tensions rose to the surface during the role-play and people found it hard to *de-role* (Jesus! That jargon again!) they'd have to embrace each other afterwards. What had been the term for that?

He felt his daughter's sharp unforgiving elbows relax by tiny increments against him as her shivering abated. Warmth — that was what he could give her. He could feel it starting now they were sharing the one bag, making him almost comfortable; his clenched limbs relaxing after being braced stiffly for so long.

The energy of warmth.

Sandy had inoculated Sophie against him. There was no other word for it. Like the other day, telling him what her mother called him, when she referred to him at all. 'A waste of space,' she'd said coolly. 'She reckons that's all you are.'

Well, he wasn't wasting any space now. He was closing the space, tucking his frame around her, finding a spot to rest his hands protectively around her elbows. He opened his eyes and saw the nape of her neck before him faintly in the darkness, fragile as a tulip stem, pale as a bird's egg.

What had they called it, that day, the tension breaker they had devised? They'd all been strangers and it had felt awkward, to him, a kind of sickly Woodstock feeling of instant reconstituted intimacy he mistrusted. Sandy had been there. That's where he'd met her again, after pretending to be an antagonistic bulldozer driver in the game. The feel of her flannelette shirt, the smell of her perfume as they hugged self-consciously.

He fitted his knees into the backs of Sophie's. He had a sudden mental image of her practising handstands and cartwheels on those long legs on a stretch of sand somewhere as a child, and felt a wash of grinding remorse. He'd never seen that happen. That, and everything else he'd missed because he'd been scared he was going to miss something somewhere else.

Now she was a fifteen-year-old girl exercising her dominion over her one thin and furious arena of control. She'd freeze to death before she admitted she was cold. But they were both warm now, inside his expensive sleeping bag; she felt relaxed and solid and he could tell she'd fallen asleep. He lay there with his arms wrapped around her. It was bigger than remorse or guilt, the loss he felt. It was more a piercing grief.

She wasn't a millstone. He'd been an imbecile to feel that, those wasted nights resentfully rocking her pram. More like ballast. Something with its own counterweight, solid against his unaccountable absences and abdications, something that might have actually anchored him.

Hugging the Enemy, he thought hazily as, despite everything, he slept. That had been it.

Early on the final morning, and it was all winding up. Sandy did a circuit of the circle in the final sharing session, embracing everyone in turn, like a new-age barn dance. She hugged each of the other women with genuine affection today — even the ones who'd annoyed her a little at first. She was leaving in half an hour and she could afford to feel magnanimous, soon she'd be cruising down the freeway and then home, replenished.

'All of you in your own ways,' said the workshop leader, 'are set afresh on your individual journeys, sheltering in the light of your own Inner Goddesses to step now into the sunlight.'

She's got that straight out of a book, muttered Janet, tapping her foot at the door. Lighten up, Mum, Sandy thought. She was feeling great. *I've worked through a lot of issues*, she wrote on the evaluation form, *so thanks! I'll be back!*

Ask the universe, and you shall receive in abundance, she thought, discovering just how opportune it was to have a handy elastic strap tying down the car boot, because now she could use it to secure the lid of the boot over her new drum, wedged safe and secure against the spare tyre. Everything aligned, everything fitting together perfectly. Meant to be.

No matter what he tried to pull over her eyes, Sophie thought darkly, she wasn't an idiot. Couldn't stop thinking, now, about how clear-cut the planned route had been at first, the standard walk, nothing risky, everything in place. And yes, she'd agreed with him, more or less, about coming here to camp for a night instead of that hut. Hadn't she? He could make you feel great when he wanted to; maybe he'd just talked her into it, charming her until she'd said yes. Sure, it might have been different if the storm hadn't happened, there was no way he could have planned for that. But still. Still. This, of everything in the world, was the thing that would totally make her mother freak. If that was what he wanted, to really do her head in, he'd chosen the perfect thing.

The more she thought about it, as they shook out the tent the next morning and tried to wring it out before rolling it up, the more possible it seemed. Now when she looked at his face more closely, she couldn't believe she hadn't noticed it before; the set of the mouth, the bad-actor lines of concern between his eyes. And that calculating wink he'd given her as they passed that sign, put there to warn them.

She felt a cold creep of devious possibility, of trickery. He'd used her. She'd been sucked in.

She stood up slowly from the tent roll, more and more details occurring to her now, watching him as he stood there pretending to study that brochure again, with the map that didn't tell them anything.

'All going according to plan?' she said softly. His eyes slid to her first, creepily, then he turned his whole head, and she saw a flash of fear there.

'What?'

'You did this on purpose, didn't you?' She thought she could tell a liar. She watched his face cloud with affront, his mouth going slack.

'What are you talking about?'

'Dragging us out here. Showing off. You wanted us to get lost, didn't you?'

'Come on now. Just think for a second. I mean, I know you're upset, but think.'

She could see it in his face clearly now, the whole bag of tricks he had in his repertoire ready to bring out. The reasonable calm, the funny charisma, the pleasant smile. She'd watched him turn it on at the museum that day, and then on this walk too, whenever he wanted something from someone. That's what he could do, so he did it. Like now, the way he tried to touch her arm, get to her that way.

'Fuck *off*, you total loser,' she spat, shoving him away.

'Whoa, whoa, WHOA!'

She jumped up and walked away, pacing — nowhere to go, no door to slam.

'Give me a single reason why I'd actually *try* to get us lost.'

'So you could impress me. So you could pretend to be a big hero. To get back at Mum.'

As soon as the words were out she could feel she'd hit a nerve. He stepped backwards as if she'd shoved him in the chest, his arms raised in defence.

'You're stressed out and not thinking clearly. That's just ... crazy.'

'You don't *know*,' Sophie muttered, teeth gritted. 'You have no idea how much the idea of me even coming away with you went against all her instincts.'

She sat down on her pack and straightened out her legs, trembling. 'See, she knew. Better than I did, obviously. Knew what kind of a *dick* you were.'

'Look, I know Sandy's got her own take on me. But if you think I'm trying to prove something to you by bringing you here, not being one hundred percent sure where we are, well, you're insane. And I told you, there's nothing to worry about. This is what camping's all about. Or used to be all about, anyway, before they turned it into the bloody package tour they're trying to sell us out there now. You went into the wilderness and just found your way, pitched your tent in spots you chose, stayed warm by lighting a fire, obeying the rules of nature and keeping in touch with the elements. When we camped on the Franklin ...'

She dug her hands into her hair and pulled, groaning in frustration. 'Will you *Just. Stop. Talking* about the fucking *Franklin.*'

There was a silence, then he flared at her. 'You have no idea, you know that? We put ourselves on the line out there, nothing but mud and rain and freezing cold, but we were determined to see it out. We stopped the dozers.'

'No, you didn't.'

He faltered, mouth open as he stared. 'What?'

'You think I haven't been listening to this stuff for my whole life? Mum's got all the books, a bunch of photos and news clippings, everything. She's been shovelling it down my throat since the day I was born — I've done bloody school projects on it. You didn't stop one bulldozer getting in there and ripping up the forest.'

'I can't believe we're having this conversation. We *stopped the dam*. We saved a pristine wilderness.'

She closed her eyes. 'The election's what stopped the dam. You guys were really just a nuisance that held the HEC up for a while, weren't you? You make yourself sound like a big hero, but really, what did you do?'

'Sorry? I thought I'd just told you.'

'You just showed up, when it comes down to it. Someone had to organise everything and have the idea for it, someone had to plan it all out, but it wasn't you. You showed up, someone drove you there, someone told you where to camp, someone fed you. And then someone boated you up the river and then someone else arrested you. Chauffeured all the way, really. What's so heroic about that? Why don't you get over yourself?'

'I went to jail protesting to save that river.'

'Yeah, for what — two days? Listen to you, trying to make it sound like Guantanamo Bay.'

He wanted to start giving her a lecture, she could tell by the way he pointed a finger at her. But his eyes followed hers to the outstretched finger, to the way it waved there pointlessly, shaking. My God. He was crying.

Rich shoved his hands onto his hips. He couldn't believe this, it had to be the tablets, to have him so strung out like this, stretching him to snapping point. A wetness in his eyes. Losing it. Crumbling.

'Hey, they didn't make any allowances for us in prison. We should have been put into remand, sure, but there were so many of us they put us into high security with all these hardened criminals.' He hated the querulous defensive pitch to his voice, the tightening in his throat. And Sophie staring at him shocked, with some little trace of *pity* for him, under her needling sneer. He felt, with dread, all of it coming on now; the temperature dropping on him, the seconds pouring away fast, and he was naked in this cold, flayed and exposed with even his own voice betraying him.

'They tortured you, did they?' That cold, unrelenting gaze pinning him to the spot. 'Beat you up? Starved you?'

'Someone I know was put into solitary confinement.'

'For managing to be an even bigger pain in the arse? Give me a break. There wasn't a moment when you didn't know you were going to get out of there in a few days, was there? Just time to write a few prison blues songs and tell everyone you knew how it felt to be ...' she hesitated dramatically, mockingly '... incarcerated?'

He threw up his hands. 'Jesus, for someone who's walked around like a deaf mute for most of this trip, suddenly you've got a lot to say for yourself.'

'That's 'cos it's true, and I'm sick of listening to you. You and Mum, you're both exactly the same. Sitting back admiring yourselves for turning up to be part of one big thing twenty-five years ago, doing nothing since. Nothing. So just shut up about it.'

The silence that came after that was like the silence in the van as he'd driven away with his stuff that day, when she'd been a baby; full of space and floating dust motes and snapped timbers, something wrecked.

Eighteen

Coming through the glass doors at Domestic Arrivals, Sandy caught sight of her reflection and swept her hair casually back over her shoulder. It had been a tactical error, meeting up with Rich before they'd left, when she'd been so flustered and out of sorts. She'd hardly had a moment to think about her appearance then, but now she couldn't believe how different she felt. How confident. The workshop had done that; had put her in touch again with her inner spirit — she could see it for herself. Her skin massaged with expensive cream, glowing after the body scrub, and her hair glossy with the intensive moisture treatment. Even Sophie was going to approve, she thought, of her Indian cotton blouse in the lovely shade of red she'd chosen. Paprika, they'd called it in the shop. And her linen pants were avocado. Everything edible and delicious. When he saw her this time, he'd look twice. He'd remember. And this time she'd be serene and radiant, focusing on Sophie but casually offering him a lift somewhere if he wanted. She was centred now, and in control. She waited in the arrivals lounge with an apple juice, watching people appearing and being greeted, the dismissive way some of them treated each other. As though they had no love to give.

She checked the clock: 11.10 — they'd be coming through those doors any minute. She couldn't wait to get her arms around Sophie. Now that Rich had met her, how could he not be envious of that bond between them? How could he fail to understand, now, that it was his absence that had actually created that shared, mutual closeness? He'd see how there was no room for him there, she thought, he'd see he'd forfeited that. And he wouldn't be able to help but feel the aching, bitter regret he deserved.

She swallowed. Checked the clock and went to the toilets and brushed her hair. Saw on the board that the flight had landed, and watched every face coming through the arrivals door, heading towards the luggage carousel. Then it was 11.35 and the screens over their heads changed and shifted to other flights and other concerns, and their flight marked *landed* kept slipping up the board until it disappeared, and she felt a shake start in her stomach and she couldn't look anymore at people greeting each other with all that affection and complacency, all that offhand normalcy.

Shaking, bone-chilling cold. She stood rooted to the spot. 12.10.

The plane was in and that clock just kept shifting into new numbers, coolly oblivious, and the day unravelled in front of her. Just wound itself to breaking point and snapped like a string of beads, bouncing hopelessly in all directions. Sandy knew she would have to compose herself and act now, and it took the greatest effort of will to pull herself together to even contemplate doing it.

To gather up these fragments from the white lino and blue-grey carpet of the airport floor, the orderly, rational parts of herself she needed to collect and account for.

Police first, she thought, or ring Janet, or just wait for the next flight from Tasmania that evening, or find the number for the national park in Tasmania and ring the rangers there. The automated voice on Sophie's phone saying *the number you have called is turned off or out of range.*

She squeezed her hands together, wiped them down her new shirt and onto the textured linen of her pants. Impossible to clear the clamouring in her head, the voices that argued about what to do, and nobody to ask, nobody to take charge. She swayed through a dizzy spell and found a hard moulded seat, wiping the back of her hand against her sweaty forehead and smelling the cloying slick of citrus and apricot face cream.

He has her was all she could think. *He has her somewhere I can't find her. Right this moment.* Her mind seemed to lift out of gear and spin there, baffled and sick, feeling around the parameters of that appalling knowledge as if it was a dark box she'd found herself inside. She could not move forward, and break the spell. The clock showed more digital numbers and more flights shifted up on the board, and she sat watching her trembling right leg drumming the floor, going through the motions of movement. For the first time in seven days, she felt herself held like an insect in the sinuous, inexorable present.

They'd gone back to packing up, a thick hateful silence between them, and Rich felt something in him change direction; something that had plummeted seemed to swoop and start climbing, as though he was on the end of a bungee rope, the elastic band holding him there by his ankle, secured with screws drilling directly into the bone. Temperature, that was it. He'd been cold, but now he was hot. Hard to assemble his thoughts into a clear sequence. He finished pulling on the boot, aware of a film of sweat on his neck and chest, and heat from the ankle rising like steam into his head. His awareness of it not muffled anymore — he was light-headed with it. Remembering with sudden needle-sharp clarity his mother's kettle, an old-fashioned one that whistled, which she was forever hurrying to as it reached the boil, desperate to turn it off before anyone had to endure that rising shriek of noise.

His foot was making that scream now, silently. A warning siren of seething, scalding pain. That's what his mother must have found so unendurable too. He began to unzip his jacket, fumbling, as Sophie stood nearby, waiting impatiently, the expression in her face one of pure, unadulterated loathing.

'Well,' she said with heavy sarcasm, 'I guess we missed our plane.'

'You seriously think I orchestrated a storm just to piss off your mother?'

'I don't know what you think you're doing,' she replied, 'but
let's get walking.'

His leg was so stiff and he felt so dizzy that he found himself
floundering to clamber up off the ground. She stood watching
him for a few moments as he tried to lever himself up with his
hands flat on the rock, the sore leg awkward and inflexible as
something prosthetic. Then without a word she walked over and,
with slow reluctance, put out her arm.

Neither one of them said anything. He grasped her
outstretched hand as she braced ready for him and then hauled
himself up onto his feet, not looking at her. Steadying himself,
humiliatingly, against the surprising muscle of her arm.

Sandy steered and changed gears in the cotton-headed daze of
a sleepwalker. She pressed the accelerator and indicated before
turning, stolid as a zombie. Then she was on the freeway. At
home, half an hour away now, was the number for the Parks and
Wildlife ranger at Cradle Mountain, waiting on the phone table
where she'd jotted it off Sophie's notes. The ranger would answer
and she could pass into his lap this terrible burning weight, alien
and sinister as a meteorite, that smouldered now in her own.
Then she was at the turn-off to take her home to Ayresville, past
the road sign she'd always noted with such affection, the FORM
ONE LANE amended, Ayresville-style, to FORM ONE PLANET,
then negotiating her way through town automatically, glancing
up at her house at the end of the street as she turned the final
corner. This was going to be the worst part, going inside the
empty house, but she could get to the phone, her lifeline, call
the ranger, the local police, Annie and Margot and Rachel. Rich's
parents — maybe she should ring Rich's parents, tell them what
had happened. It kept coming to her in tiny gasping reminders,
little stabs of panicked terror like something small and terrified in
your hands, jerking and squirming.

The front tyre hit the kerb hard as she pulled up. Phone, she
thought desperately, inside to the phone. Maybe there was already
a message. She opened the door to run, in her new flat leather

shoes, across the grass, up to her house.

Her house. There it was, but something instantly, baldly wrong with it.

The blue gum in the front yard. Sophie's tree.

Blank bright sunlight was pouring onto the front garden, the beds were covered with — what? — woodchips, strewn thickly with them, and the very worst thing, in the middle, the tree gone.

An amputated stump left, the last fifteen years lopped off slice by slice and every leaf and twig grown there disposed of, turned into nothing but leaf litter, and *debris*. All pushed into the chipping machine, those whirling vicious blades rendering it all down.

She stood with her hands on the dampness of the cut stump, breathing in hard sobs. Minutes were ticking away and she had to get inside and onto that telephone, but she couldn't move. Seeing the tree's base so deeply rooted there, tangled hard into the earth, and this trunk rising solidly, trustingly.

Then chopped.

Oh, the midwife lifting that placenta away, and her bleeding as it had torn from her, tissue from tissue. Seeing the cord, pale blue and shining, that had bound Sophie to her. She'd gone to speak but hadn't, stunned. Hands had lifted it. Clamped it. The scissors opening and snapping shut, that noise as it was severed. As her daughter took a breath, shook with outrage, and howled. Small and terrified in someone's gloved hands.

Move.

She caught sight of herself in the glass panel of the front door as she scrabbled for her keys, looking like she'd aged twenty years during the drive home, her new clothes crumpled like yesterday's newspaper, mouth aghast with bolting fear.

Phone the ranger, phone the police, phone her friends.

You're not going off the deep end, are you, Sandy? came Janet's warning voice. *You're not totally overreacting here? Think before you jump to any ridiculous conclusions; don't make a total fool of yourself.* Her mother, who'd never put herself out to feel panic for her own children, who sat safe and snug in her own complacency, who she hated, really hated; her mother who had no deep end to go into, who was nothing but shallows all the way through. Her mother, who should have carried a sign warning you that you'd break your spine if you dared to put your trust in her, and jump.

Sandy put her shoulder to the front door, which always jammed on its frame since she'd had that partial restumping done, and she should have had it seen to months ago, the whole house was a stuck-windowed, dodgy-floorboarded, tilting, decaying disaster, and she — she was a laughing stock, a failure, a fool. She was sobbing openly now as she kicked and pushed against the jammed door, her slippery new shoes, with their unworn soles, sliding against the porch timbers as she braced herself and put her shoulder to it, uselessly, again.

Nineteen

Ian Millard was on shift at Search and Rescue and took the call on the public dial-in line. It took him a while to calm the woman down and get a sense from her of whether she was next of kin, whether she'd called the ranger at the park first, who was missing and how long they'd actually been lost. When she said they were just a day overdue, he felt himself let a breath out and take the time to turn over a new sheet of paper, smooth it down. Get her back to procedure.

'We're not Parks and Wildlife,' he said. 'You haven't called Parks and Wildlife — you've called the Tasmanian Police Service. We handle search and rescue operations.'

She was meant to pick them up at the airport this morning, she was saying, going a mile a minute as he tried to write; they'd all agreed to be there, but they weren't on the plane, and she'd rung the ranger and he was sending someone to check the logbook at the last hut, but what she wanted to know was when could they send out a search party and how could they find them with no mobile phone coverage?

'Hang on,' said Ian. 'Just take it easy. It's only been a day and there's probably a perfectly reasonable explanation. We had a lot of rain yesterday over the centre of the state; probably every walker on the track holed up somewhere to wait it out. They would have filled in their information when they registered and that's what gets referred to in the event of a walker being reported overdue.' The ranger, he knew, would have already explained this to her

'That's what I'm doing now,' she said, voice cracking. 'I'm reporting two walkers overdue.'

'They're going north to south?'

'How would I know?' she yelled. 'I don't know what the bastard had in mind.'

He paused. 'Who's that?'

'Her bloody father.'

'OK,' said Ian, putting down his pen. 'Let's go back a few steps.'

Ian Millard had liked the interview he'd gone for with Search and Rescue, where they'd asked him, 'So, do you have an outdoors background?', and the next weekend he'd been out diving for abalone with them. He remembered his boss Geoff introducing him to Tim Redenbach, and Tim saying, 'Have a guess what my nickname is', and him answering, 'Spider?', and Tim laughing and saying, 'Boys, you gave the right man the job.'

He'd been with Parks and Wildlife for eight years and the police force for twelve, so it felt good, getting his land search and rescue qualifications and the ambulance paramedic training. Great crews. Great coordination. All twenty personnel involved last year in the search for that Swiss hiker in the same area, liaising with Parks and the State Emergency Service. They'd winched a dog in for that search, the winds wild over Mount Ossa, sleet driving sideways into Ian's face as he waited on the ground to grab the dog, feeling its legs kick convulsively as it registered his arms, its clean warm smell. He'd felt something dip hollowly in his chest, a cold gulp of dread, when one of the searchers found the guy's backpack left against a rock on the summit. That moment there, of unzipping the pack and seeing the guy's extra sweater and his carefully folded raincoat inside, his diary and passport and *Rough Guide*, all of it had come back to Ian in bad moments ever since. That diary. A couple of blank postcards tucked in the pages, ready to be written on. Ian had crouched there feeling the temperature dropping and dropping, that hard painful tug in his throat, thinking that the walker was somewhere near, somewhere within a couple of kilometres in this gathering darkness, and the dog already up to its chest in crunching snow, floundering and crisscrossing its own tracks, as keyed-up and tightly wound as he was.

He'd zipped up that backpack again, full of a young guy's blind, immortal optimism, wondering what protective clothes he had on now, and whether they'd have to ring Switzerland.

Ian had rescued quite a few people — out of caves, from kayaks pulled hastily out of flooded rivers, hanging on in the back of the chopper winching divers down to a holed boat — but what stayed with him, what dwelt on in him, was how utterly forlorn and useless that guy's backpack on Mount Ossa had seemed, the chilled feeling he'd got. The weather had turned that time, so suddenly. That's what worried him now.

Something bad was happening to him, something weird. Sophie could see it and didn't want to see it, the cranked-up, furious pace he was trying to set, like it was an endurance race and he was going to win whatever it took, the manic twitch she could see jumping in his jaw when he turned to check she was still following him as ordered. She hadn't known what to think at first. For all she knew this was part of the plan too — not talking to her, paying her back.

So she'd racked her brains for something to ask him.

'What do you actually do in your job?' she'd said. Just needing to hear him talk normally again, like he genuinely wanted to get them out of there.

But then he'd started. Just one long stream of words, explaining every little technical thing to her, until she stopped listening because it became too confusing and tiring. He kept at it, even though he kept looking back and must have been able to tell she wasn't paying attention anymore. She could have been anyone.

'Then there's the BCC Glow effect,' he was shouting now,

glancing back over his shoulder as if he expected her to be taking notes, or something. 'It increases the picture's chrominance, which means it takes the existing colours and blows them out to the edge of their spectrum. So red will be really red, orange will be really, really orange. I mean, totally over the top. The editor can go into the effect and there's thirty different parameters they can manipulate, controlling how much of the picture glows, whether some colours glow more than others, all that.'

She watched him, tramping doggedly over tussocks and jutting boulders with that freaky limp. Her stomach was tightening. Hurting. About an hour after they'd started walking, he'd taken off his boot and started carrying it, making his way towards the next high plateau they could see, and somehow that was the scariest part, the way he swung that boot casually by its laces like an enemy's head, and his filthy sock flapping as he wove around to avoid the sharp stony sections, trying to keep to the grassy patches.

He'd had some bullshit theory about how they would be able to calculate which way to go next by the angle of the sun and looking for watercourses in the gullies below them that they would then be able to follow. He wouldn't shut up, and she couldn't make sense of it anymore. Just watched him jauntily waving that empty boot, hobbling along as if his leg was made of wood. Freakazoid zombie pirate.

'But if the colours are too bright, the picture will break up on air, because the playback server's chroma tolerance is exceeded,' he panted, glancing back at her again, his eyes glittering. He looked like the lead singer of Dogland, only that guy did it for effect, he wore make-up to make himself look that hollow-eyed and intense, like he was really suffering. He wasn't suffering, she thought dully. It was just another kind of karaoke.

She felt the hot shuddering burn in her thighs, the sour, coppery taste of adrenaline as she scrambled after Rich. Her stomach scoured with nausea.

He must have caught the look on her face.

'Don't worry, no need to be anxious,' he sang with brittle

cheerfulness. 'Once we're back on soft ground we'll find a track again, or a cairn, or something. Leave it to me.'

That cracked smile again; mouth askew, the eyes burning. 'Leave it to me,' he repeated. Nodding firmly to himself, as if that was going to reassure her.

Sandy, head churning with scenarios, stood numbly at the sink. She had nothing to do, nothing to occupy her, nothing but the fragments going round in that swirl. Sophie somewhere with Rich. No phone message from her, so that ruled out just a delayed plane or a changed plan. Still somewhere out in the wilderness, unable to reach her. She had phoned the Tasmanian police and the ranger and the police station in her own town, and time was crawling now, stretching till it didn't seem possible that the hands on the clock could still be moving.

She picked up the phone again to double-check the dial tone. Placed her mobile more squarely on the bench.

It was still only 4.30 in the afternoon, here in this parallel world she'd been shoved into. He was the one who'd forced her here. Rich. Showing her how he could still take away, in a moment, everything she cared about. She should have listened to her instincts, and kept him away, stepped in front of Sophie like a shield, opened her mouth and breathed fire in his path.

She gazed out the kitchen window, trying to keep her breathing slow and regular. There it was — her domain, her garden. She could hardly stand the sight of it now, so overgrown with weeds she hadn't dealt with. When you had an organic garden you had to get out there and pull up every one of those weeds by hand, and she'd let it slide. You could hardly see the raised beds at all. It just looked like ... (*don't say cemetery, don't think it*) ... an abandoned lot. In summer the ground had been too hard and now autumn had brought some rain and the couch grass had colonised everything, rampant and triumphant. She stood there with her hands on the edge of the sink, blinking at the sight. She'd tried. She really had. She'd spent hours on her hands and knees, digging it up with the garden fork, scrabbling in the dirt for the runners, trying to curb it before it took off. Every year was the same, she thought with a sudden flaming sensation of futility; trying to clear the garden bed, heaping it painstakingly with her special compost, making hillocks like they suggested in the magazine, based on what the Hopi Indians did, or the Mayans or whatever. Planting everything out, weeding with all that resolve, putting out beer traps for slugs, avoiding using even pellets. And then you turned your back, you got caught up in other things, and when you glanced around again, look where you were. Up to your knees again in couch grass. Choking everything else, the whole garden bed just a thick green joke of suffocating weeds.

She stood there hating the couch, glad of the diversion. She thought of the way it insinuated itself along, under the ground, the tendrils settling themselves like a web, just waiting for rain. The way it effortlessly strangled all her good intentions. It wasn't as though she was a maniacal zealot about self-sufficiency or permaculture, she didn't pretend that. She just wanted to look out at her garden and see something there that she'd planted and tended, not this, staring her in the face.

And all these years she'd gritted her teeth and gone for the wheelbarrow and the fork again, breaking her back. People drove past, she thought, and sneered at the disaster she'd made of it, her feeble pathetic attempts to get it under control. Well, stuff it. She pulled the plug in the sink, picked up her mobile, found her car keys and drove, steaming with revenge, to the garden centre.

She'd thought she'd just buy a bottle of weedkiller concentrate, not the backpack and the wand. She couldn't stoop to that kind of destruction, could she? But the kit was on special and once she'd decided to make a stand, why not go all the way?

And it was so easy, just wading through in your gumboots, pumping the mixture onto the clumps of couch, and the towering stalks of marshmallow weed, seeing the poison drift and bead like dew. She'd raze it all and start again, without the seeds lurking under the surface, ready to thwart her. You needed to fight fire with fire, Sandy thought savagely.

She'd found some goggles in the shed and tied her scarf up

over her mouth and nose. Coldly, efficiently, she wielded the wand to direct the spray exactly where she wanted it to go, right at the base of the plants. Not that she had to stick to that plan. She was the one with the Round-up, she could kill whatever she liked. Just had to point and pump, like a gun. Once she started in on this track of payback, she couldn't stop herself. There was no bottom to her vengeance; she wanted to kill it all. What had she ever managed to grow, anyway? A few stunted snowpeas and misshapen zucchinis. She'd always been ready, if anyone asked, to explain that this garden bed was totally organic and had never been touched with even a quick sprinkling of chemical fertiliser, far less weedkiller. But nobody had ever asked. Nobody. Who cared?

Well, she was dealing with it now, once and for all. She pumped another mist of Round-up, laying waste to it all, and marvelling at what an idiot she'd been, always trying to do things the hard way. Let it all die, she chanted, swinging with a wild napalming fury, let it soak into the ground and poison it, let it all burn and choke and wither away.

'Ms Reynolds?'

She nearly jumped out of her skin at the voice, staggering a little as she swung around. That 'Ms' — who called anyone 'Ms' anymore? A policeman and a policewoman stood there enquiringly, their shadows throwing elongated shapes up her brick pathway. Sandy knew she'd called them, knew she'd been the one to instigate this, but the thick navy polyester of their uniforms, the businesslike spick'n'span-ness of them, somehow, released a little extra surge of panic in her. The way their hips were hung with equipment, the shiny streamlined late-model squad car in the drive, made everything suddenly, soberly real.

'Yes, sorry,' she shouted through the muffled layers of scarf, hastily unwinding it from her face. Her hands trembled. She was confused too, when she took off the goggles and felt a little suck of pressure as they adhered to her face, and the surprising wetness that trickled down her cheeks.

'You called about your daughter going missing?'

'Yes, I did. Come in.'

She put her thumbs in under the shoulder straps and unhooked the backpack of weedkiller from her back.

'Wasn't sure you'd heard us there. We heard you ... ah, singing, and thought you might have had your iPod on.'

'No, no.' She was blushing to the roots of her hair, she could feel it. She pulled off her gumboots and led them into the house.

Whenever strangers came to her house like this, she was suddenly aware of how it smelled, as if she was entering it herself for the first time. It never happened otherwise, the house smelled of nothing. But now she could detect the sticky, sugary scent of the oil burner, the ground-in dust of the rugs, long-ago incense, burned toast.

'I'll put the kettle on,' she said. 'Sit down. Would you like tea?'

'Do you have ordinary tea?' asked the policewoman. 'Just teabag tea?'

'Sure.'

They were so young. The guy like he was just out of school, the way he laboriously printed something at the top of the page in his notebook.

'So just to get this clear,' he said. 'Your daughter's gone away with her father?'

'Yes. But she's hardly seen him her whole life. I mean, this was meant to be, you know ...' She stopped. She hadn't thought this through.

'How overdue are they?'

'They should have finished a bushwalk yesterday and caught the plane this morning.'

'Was there a custodial dispute?'

'No, no, nothing like that. He's estranged from us. He rang and wanted to take her on this walk and she agreed. And she's fifteen now, and I didn't see ... I didn't want ...'

There was something tightly acrid in her throat, like she'd breathed in that weedkiller after all. She should have bought one of those masks. She took a breath and it snagged and hooked in her chest, noisy and gasping.

'We need to be clear,' the policeman was saying. 'Do you have reason to fear an abduction?'

She heard the kettle reach boiling point and click itself off. Her hands danced across the bench, jerking like something escaped, and now that the word was spoken, hanging in the air between them, she couldn't stop her mind from skittering either, ricocheting through the stories of fathers driving their kids off bridges into rivers, shooting them all in the head on weekend access visits, berserk fathers parking the car and sticking a hose through the window as they all sat eating their takeaways, trusting him, and the noise was unsticking from her throat and keening through her mouth now, a toxic mist of it expelled with each racking gasp. The two cops sitting there waiting, embarrassed and solemn as the fear pumped and pumped out of her chest, buckling her like she was retching.

'I'm not a bad person,' she heard herself say, the voice like something on helium, squeezing through a tiny crevice in her locked throat. 'I don't know what he's done. But he's taken her.'

'You sit down, Ms Reynolds,' said the policeman, rising. 'I'll make the tea.' It almost brought her undone, that 'Ms' again. Just that respect.

Ian Millard looked at the satellite images on the meteorological website, grimacing.

'Check out that cloud cover,' he said to Mal.

'It's always the way, isn't it. How bad, do you reckon?'

'Probably heading towards total white-out.'

'So we can't go?'

'We'll have to sit tight. Same as the ground crew.'

'But all hands on deck tomorrow just in case?'

'Mate, it's Cradle Mountain, who's to know? We could get half a metre of snow yet. We've got Buckley's.'

Mal finished his coffee, scratched his clippered head. 'Well, bags I not tell the mother that. She thinks we're rolling out the whole circus.'

'The thing is, they might be absolutely fine, that's what I've been trying to explain to her. They're barely overdue. Left Pine Valley Hut on Sunday, according to the log, still with tents and sleeping bags and food. Could have made it to Narcissus and forgotten to deregister, could have decided to sit out that storm. So say the meter's on and we've got the chopper out and we're running round like blue-arsed flies tomorrow, they're liable to just walk out of there saying, "What's the story? Can't we spend an extra night or two without you guys having a hissy fit?"'

'I love the way,' said Mal, 'they try to ring up on their mobiles demanding instant assistance because they've climbed up the side of a cliff somewhere. I mean, I imagine them, you know, hanging on with one hand, texting with the other.'

Ian flipped through the ranger's report. 'The ranger headed in to Pine Valley Hut and spoke with a few of the walkers there,' he said, reading. 'In fact, it was a couple they'd met and been talking to who raised the alarm — said this guy told them he'd be spending one night in the Labyrinth and would see them at Narcissus the next day. Says that the girl was emphatic that they had to catch a plane Tuesday. So these two hung around at Narcissus — waited till the ferry left actually — then they walked back to Pine Valley, read the logbook, saw they hadn't come through and notified the ranger.'

'They walked all the way back? That's the kind of citizen we need.'

'The woman said the girl was doing her first big bushwalk.'

'Aren't they all.'

'The guy said her father seemed pretty confident and had told him he was tired of how crowded the track was and was heading up into the Labyrinth.'

'Well, there you are then. I reckon they're not even lost, and we shouldn't be busting our arses. Give 'em another day.'

'The ranger says here he'll try to go in this arvo, just a small ground team.'

'Who is it?'

'That guy Paul Colegate? Used to be up at Mole Creek?'

'Yep. Good bloke.'

Ian looked at the weather pattern again, the cold front stirring in the south-west. 'I've got a bad feeling, though. I reckon this is going to settle in.'

Sandy hadn't had tea with two sugars since before she gave it up for Lent when she was fourteen, but it was exactly what she needed.

'Things may not be as bad as they seem,' the policewoman was saying. 'After all, they're on a wilderness walk, and they're only a day overdue, right? You'd be amazed how many people lose track of the time, then we all go into panic mode and they just walk calmly out the next day, can't believe all the fuss.'

'It's not like that,' she muttered. 'Sorry, but there's something else going on here. We ... there's still a lot of conflict between us, over this. Him just stepping in now, trying to muscle in after ignoring Sophie her whole life.'

The male cop was in the kitchen filling the kettle again, his face unreadable. As she watched he reached up and touched one of the bunches of herbs she had hanging in the window. They looked a bit faded and desiccated now. He picked thoughtfully at something in the dried stalks of oregano. A cobweb. She could see it from here. But hadn't ever noticed it until this moment.

'Did he make any threats to you? Even, you know, guarded comments?'

'No. He was trying to keep it all pleasant for Sophie.' Remembering herself at the airport, reaching up and hissing into his ear. His recoil.

'And he's an OK bloke, is he? I mean, I realise you're not friendly, obviously, but he's got his life in order, has he?'

'Oh, yeah. According to him, anyway. He's a legend in his own mind.' She heard the sourness in her voice. It wouldn't do to sound petty. Or bitter. 'We've been perfectly happy without him in our lives,' she added. 'He just walked out on us. Sophie wasn't even one year old. So you can see why I'd be a bit ...'

She trailed off, making a complicit ironic grin and a circling gesture, but they just kept watching her, expressionless and polite.

'A bit anti,' she finished.

A beam of sun hit the crystal in the living-room window and a prism of rainbow jittered across the tabletop. Awkward with the silence, she reached out and took the tiny bottle of Rescue Remedy from beside the fruit bowl and shook four drops onto her tongue. The young policewoman looked interested.

'What's that?'

'Rescue Remedy,' she explained, relieved to change the subject. 'It's what I take instead of having to use paracetamol or ... well, any medication, really. It's an all-natural calmative and stress reliever?' She heard the rising inflection in her voice, placatory and eager. 'For shock and emotional upset,' she added, more firmly, 'like now.'

'How does it work?'

'Well, it's flower essences. Distilled to their, um, essences.'

The policeman came back over to the table, picked up the bottle and read the label.

'So it's — what? — in an alcohol base?'

Sandy sipped her tea and felt that infuriating piece of grit lodged in the glaze on the mug drag on the inside of her upper lip.

'You just take four drops. It gives you centering energy.' She glanced at their faces. 'Nobody's really sure how it works. But it sure is better than taking some drug full of, you know, chemicals, made by some big pharmaceutical company ...' She was losing them, she could tell by their polite attentiveness.

'And that cures a headache, does it?'

'Not a headache, no,' she answered. 'Symptoms of shock.'

'But how, exactly? If you don't mind me asking.' He placed the bottle back on the table and she picked it up again.

'It's flowers,' she said again, brandishing it, feeling annoyed. 'Homeopathics.'

There was a short silence. She'd ring her friends and break the news as soon as the police left, she told herself. Brace herself and ring her mother too.

'Ms Reynolds ...' said the woman, a bit more briskly.

'Sandy.'

'Sandy, do you have a recent photo of Sophie we could take to make up a bulletin for the police in Tassie? I'm thinking, he could have walked out of the national park with her, caught the ferry from the lake at the end of the track and be somewhere else by now. If the ferry operator can ID them, that helps us focus our search away from the park itself. I mean, then we'd know they weren't just temporarily disoriented.'

She didn't want to open the drawer to the phone table. Inside that drawer was the carved elephant box and last time she'd rolled a joint (which was *months* ago, Christmas, at least) she couldn't remember if she'd left some in the bag and just shoved it back into this drawer or closed it safely into the elephant box. And in that drawer, she was almost certain, was Sophie's last set of school photos.

'Hang on,' she said, and rose. She steeled herself and went into Sophie's room, just trying to keep her mind blank and calm, and retrieved a photo from the pin-board over the desk — Sophie and two friends on the jetty by the dam at Rachel's place just a couple of months ago. She passed it to the policewoman.

'Which one is she?'

'The one in the black t-shirt. Her hair's not really that dark. She dyes it.'

'And how tall is she?' The policewoman put the photo down on the table, glanced up at her with a frown.

'Ah — five foot eight, I think. Whatever that is in metric — I can never get my head around it. A hundred and ... something.' She shrugged with an apologetic smile, her eyes on the photo. The three pale teenage bodies looked so etiolated from this angle, angular and shadowed in the sun glaring off the water.

'What does she weigh, Sandy?'

'Oh, I wouldn't have a clue. Sorry.'

And the woman was looking up at her again now, with an expression that made Sandy stop.

'What? Why?'

'Well, she looks pretty thin. Has she recently been sick? In this photo, I mean.'

'What?' Sandy said again. A flash of light from the crystal slid across the woman's face on the other side of the table. The expression concerned, tactful.

No, that wasn't it. Sympathetic. Grave.

Sandy's hand reached for the drawer handle on the phone table, and jerked it open heedlessly, fingers scrabbling for the plastic bag with the school photos inside, the head-and-shoulders shots of Sophie, the ones she'd complained about buying, saying *can't you smile in these? They cost me twenty-seven bucks...*

The policewoman tapped the other photo again. 'Sandy?'

I am not a bad person, she repeated to herself, eyes back on the dam photo now, feeling something shiver and cave a little, something ahead of her under the surface she couldn't see. 'What do you mean?'

She felt it like a tremor underfoot, as she gazed at the image of her daughter, a time-and-place stumble as if she'd been startled awake, sitting here propped, unaccountably, in a chair. Like a sleepwalker, blinking and bewildered, who'd been asleep for a long, long time.

Twenty

It was incredible, Sophie thought, how suddenly everything had disappeared, the way it had rolled out like a special effect. On the plane she'd wondered how it would feel to slip down into the thick piled meringue of clouds below them; well, now she knew. In Ayresville they sometimes had foggy mornings, but you could feel it start thinning when the sun got stronger and the vapour would rise and tear and you'd see the familiar landmarks again — the cars on the street, rooflines of houses, trees appearing slowly out of the whiteness, all gathering detail and colour and a reassuring density.

Not here. Nothing moved, no sun burned through, although it wasn't cold, exactly. When you breathed in you could taste the cloud itself, tainted like old ice-blocks out of the freezer. She knew she was keeping her brain busy with trivia — thinking about *fog*, for godsakes — to keep herself calm. To not backtrack and think instead about how it had happened, the moment this afternoon when they'd both sort of stopped at a place that looked like an OK campsite, how nothing had been said but they'd both loitered there, not looking at each other.

That was the moment, she knew, when they'd both given up. Just stopped pretending.

They'd dropped their packs onto the ground, and set to work in silence putting up the tent and filling up their water bottles out of the little lake nearby. And thank God they did that, at least, because as soon as they'd finished cooking a starchy meal of pasta

— she was almost too tired to chew — the fog had thickened around them as if some sorcerer somewhere was pouring it out of a jug.

Until it had started closing in, she had been subconsciously running another scenario in her head, one where her mum had alerted some kind of rescue operation that'd go straight into action, and find them. That ranger Jen coming over the rise saying *you're so close, Sophie! Come on, let's get you back in front of the fire.*

Now they wouldn't even be looking. And Rich had just finished eating and crawled straight into the tent and curled up, shivering. Muttering to himself.

Her father, the wilderness hero. As hopeless as every other adult she'd stupidly relied on in her life. A pseudo-adult, him. Crumpled as soon as you tried to lean on him.

And to think she'd believed he was trustworthy. Here they were, miles from anyone else, stuck out here without a compass, without anything, and you couldn't see fifteen metres in front of you, or even guess what time of day it was.

She sat outside the tent, trembling, the rest of the world bleached to fogged white around her. It wasn't cold, she wasn't shivering because of that. It was the way it all dissolved. If you stood up and walked out there, just let yourself get a few dozen steps away ... you'd be gone. It would eat you up.

She wasn't going anywhere. Just behind that boulder and back when she needed to pee, her hand on the boulder all the time, terrified. And bushes and dead trees would swim in and out of vision like hallucinations, like the faintest pencil marks on a blank page. She'd seen another wallaby already, swerving towards her and scaring the life out of her, running headlong back into the mist.

Dogland had made a music clip once she'd seen on MTV set in a swirling misty landscape like this, for their song 'Erebos'. It had looked spooky to her at the time, like a real place, but it was probably just a studio with a machine making all that fog. They probably switched the lights back on when they'd finished filming, and went back to their hotel, or whatever. Faked it.

She was trapped here with him. The longer she'd trudged behind him today, listening to him, the more she knew he was losing it. *Wigging out*, kids said at school when describing someone who'd lost the plot. That's what was happening; and anyone could see his foot was so swollen now that he couldn't pull his boot on to even try to get out of here anymore, so now he was totally useless.

Well, not totally. He was so hot and clammy that if you sat near him it was like being near a radiant heater. So she guessed that was something, at least.

In a minute, when she couldn't stand the damp eeriness of the total silence anymore, she'd crawl in. See if he'd talked himself out yet and finally run flat, like her iPod.

Rich woke rising through thick layers to consciousness, not knowing where he was. Inside a green cocoon, slick with sweat, a swollen ache behind his eyes thumping like a machine. He was in the tent, he told himself.

Outside, when he put his head out dazedly to check, a low, thin twilight mist wrapped them in tissue. Underdeveloped, he thought groggily, and underexposed. Nothing coming through, no true blacks, just that grainy fog of wispy detail, those prickly trees and wet, faint rock faces. No contrast. He blinked a few times, the ache in his head stretching and shrinking as he tried to focus. *Amnesia. Fatigue, irrationality, poor judgement, stupor.*

Not hypothermia, though. Must be his blister. Blood poisoning or something. And no more blue bombers — he'd taken the last of them back there at ... where had it been now? Couldn't remember. But gone, anyway. He felt as feverish as he'd ever felt, even that time with dengue. He had to hold it together. Sophie was sitting outside the tent against a boulder, her raincoat wrapped around her shoulders, her beanie pulled low over her face. He could hear her, the giveaway congested sinuses as she sat there.

'Sophie? What is it?'

'What *is* it? What do you think? Just leave me alone.'

'Are you crying?' He got up and crawled out stiffly, dragging out his raincoat and daypack to lean against on the ground. At least they were somewhere now that wasn't totally sodden with rain. He pulled his own hat down over his ears.

'Imagine what Mum's thinking right now. She gives in to me and lets you take me off to Tasmania and look what you do. Her worst nightmare.'

He swallowed before he spoke, focusing with all his attention. 'I'm sure she's thinking it through logically. Working out we're just a few days overdue.' The words took enormous effort to produce.

'She'll be going ballistic.'

He ignored the tight nausea in his throat. 'Well, even if she is, that's good because she'll be notifying someone and alerting them about it, won't she? They might send some searchers in to try and find us.'

Sophie turned around to face him, shaking her head decisively. 'She said to be on that plane or else.'

'Well, I'm sure she'll quickly realise that things don't always go according to plan when you're out in the wilderness.' He couldn't believe the airy idiocy of his voice, the awful way he just opened his mouth and another platitude leaped out. His brain was baking, inside the booming tightness of his skull.

'She'll phone the police.'

He gave a small dry laugh. A gasp. 'No, she'll phone Search and Rescue.'

The queasiness rippled from his throat down into his guts. Swirled and eddied there, like bitter, swallowed bile. She'd phone the police. What she'd report was an abduction. It would all fit together for her. There was probably a special department for it — insane estranged fathers disappearing without trace clutching their offspring. There'd be a special charge.

And Sophie, this pissed-off traumatised fifteen-year-old fuming opposite him, he already knew what she thought of him. How she'd testify, given the chance.

'Listen,' he said, clearing his throat. 'If I could walk properly, believe me, I'd have us out of here in a couple of hours.'

A blank look of total disdain. 'You are so full of shit.'

'There's no point trying to reason with you.'

'Totally, *totally* full of shit.'

They lapsed back into silence. The dusk was deeper now, grey and felted like damp wool, mist curling up off the ground. They heard something crashing nearby through the bushes; the panicked skittering noise of escape through that tangling prickly scoparia.

'Listen to that.'

'Wallabies. I saw them before. They're spooked.' There was a pause. Another crash.

'It's only been a couple of nights,' he said firmly, determined to have the last word, when something loped into his feverish peripheral vision, an animal he saw duck its head and then raise it nervously, and he couldn't help himself, even if he was imagining it; his body jerked backwards reflexively. His legs flailed and kicked suddenly like in one of those falling dreams, the ankle a single bundle of flaring molten sinew. He heard his own voice and the animal sprang forward, disoriented. *Dog*, his brain stuttered like morse. *Wolf. Coyote.* It veered close to him, he heard its claws on rock and gravel.

His mind lay disordered and agape for a few seconds, like something ransacked. The animal ran past where they sat, twisting itself back again as it encountered the rock face, facing them again, almost cowering. He saw the tail, its curve and weight, and then in the cottony near-darkness, knowing he was awake, and it was real, his hand plunged reflexively for his camera, there inside its bag right next to him, his thumb flipping off the lens cap as he pulled it free.

Stripes. He saw the stripes, patterned along that hunched muscular spine like a branching fern, and knew even as his thumb felt for and found the flash switch that there would be no more misfootings into cruel empty space; he had the camera in both hands, reflexes humming like a sharp note, and nothing was going to be the same now.

Ian got a printout of the cold front and turned off the screen.

'Aren't you going home?' said Tim, who'd come on shift after Mal.

'I am,' said Ian. 'Very soon.' He emailed Paul at the Cradle Mountain office, giving him Sandy Reynold's direct mobile number in case he didn't have it, and left his notes on the desk. A text from his wife on his phone, asking him to pick up a carton of milk.

'Just leaving now,' he said.

Rich pointed and pressed and saw the flash go off perfectly, burning that creature onto his 200 ASA black-and-white film, and thank you God, thank you for making me load that into the camera yesterday morning when I finished the roll of slide film, and now wind on and press again, another flash and the animal perfectly visible there crouching in the frame, then turning as he wound on again, holy fucking unbelievable a third shot as it scrambled across gravel and away. And he had it this time, he had the defining moment there safe in the box. Everything going quiet as he and Sophie stared at each other slack-jawed, blinking blindly in the afterburn of the flash, like they were the last two people on earth.

'Did you see the stripes?' he said. He heard himself whispering it. Had to put his camera on the ground for safety as great rolling dumpers of shock trembled down his arms. She just stared at him.

'They never attacked people,' he whispered hastily, which wasn't even true for all he knew, but her face was paper-white, her eyes blank and uncomprehending.

She started to stutter something, and stopped. Her teeth chattering when she unclamped her mouth. Locked her eyes on his camera.

'I can't believe it,' he said. He needed desperately to get up and move around, the fizz of it coursing in jolts through his body, but his leg ached and throbbed and held him there. He grabbed handfuls of his hair in his hands, gasping, adrenaline splashing back and forth in him with no outlet. It was like being outside of himself, thrown through himself like a windscreen. King hit, and coming to.

'A dog.' Her voice quavering.

'No, Sophie, not a dog.'

'It was a dog. A wild one.'

He shook his head convulsively. Fingertips touching the camera, back off again as if it was hot, as if it was ticking away with half-life like a Geiger counter.

'Jesus H. Christ.' He exhaled a huge shuddering breath. 'Did you see the stripes on it?'

'What if it comes back?'

It was like remembering how to talk again. 'Doesn't matter if it does or it doesn't. I've got three shots of it. What did that woman say? The first hard evidence in seventy years. But it makes sense, doesn't it? Hundreds of square miles of impenetrable wilderness, same ancient landscape it's evolved in over thousands of years, no humans ...' He trailed off and took a gasping breath, recalling stunned witnesses he'd watched on the evening news; gabbling, words spilling, the big jerking, twitching gestures.

She was looking at him. 'Show me the photos you got.'

'See, but I can't. It's not digital, remember? It's on negative film. We have to wait till we get back.'

'So it's inside the camera there?'

'Bloody oath it is. It's just hitting me. This is it. Everyone believing it's extinct, then I get these. A real living breathing one. People are going to go apeshit.'

She just sat there, loose with shock, still gazing blankly at him. She'd get it soon. He'd sit up and wait for the sun to rise, if that's what it took, to make sure they were pointing in the right direction to get out of here. He'd crawl out on his hands and knees now, if he had to. Carrying what he had there, finally, sealed in darkness. Precious as a grail.

Sandy had gone into Sophie's room during the night and lain down on her bed, pulling the doona over her head. She wanted to be cocooned in a dark place. Somewhere without edges or definition, or even time. When she realised it was close to dawn she'd got up feeling stiff and battered, mechanically plumped up Sophie's pillow and remade her bed, and went outside.

She rang the park number again and the police again and then just sat, blank and disconnected, until her friends arrived. It wasn't like any of them to knock — they just came straight in the back door and everything about them, from the plates and bottles they carried to their determined postures, told her they were taking charge.

'Crisis-management meeting,' someone called cheerfully as they came through the door with a bakery box. It would have been wonderful except that she was suddenly struck by the dreadful thought that this was how they would be at a funeral too — in control and brooking no argument, propelling her through the room to sit on the couch and offering to be the bolster between her and the outside world. She pushed the thought firmly from her mind.

'There's no way you want to be alone, is there?' said Margot, holding her at arms' length, passing her to the next person for more embracing.

She started to cry again. 'You're all such good friends,' she said, sobbing. 'What would I do without you?'

'You just let yourself lean on us now.'

'Sandy! Wow, your front garden looks sensational! It's all mulched!'

'A guy came and trimmed the tree while I was away and made it all into chips and spread them around for me.' Her voice sounded like something on the wrong speed.

'I'll have to get you to give me his name. It looks brilliant.'

Normal chat, everything determinedly, decidedly normal. She could hear glasses being taken out of the cupboard in the kitchen; low, organised voices as the tap was turned on in the sink. Her great, reliable friends. Women of her generation, they'd had to create their own kinship networks. Your women friends were closer than your family. Look at them, so rock-solid, mercifully taking it all out of her hands.

She pushed away another small but troubling awareness. There was something a little awry here. She frowned as someone solemnly handed her a small imitation velvet bag and a well-thumbed book of the I Ching. She shifted it under her arm to accept the gifts of massage oil for stress relief and juniper candles that promised clarity.

'We'll just take things one step at a time,' someone was saying to her now, clearing a space in front of her discreetly on the coffee table in case she wanted to lay out runes or tarot cards for answers or roll up a comforting joint or perhaps, she thought, just lay her head down there and weep. All the usual rituals.

'At this moment they're just lost, right? Wandered off the track temporarily, out of mobile range, there could be a million explanations.'

'Yes,' she agreed. It was Rachel talking, who'd known Rich before he left all those years ago, and Sandy was desperate enough to find a shred of absurd comfort in that. Someone else gave her a glass of white wine and she took a distracted sip and there was something wrong with that too; it tasted like white vinegar, a glass of stomach acid. She coughed and shuddered.

'They were meant to walk out on Monday, right? And it's only Wednesday, this happens all the time in bushwalking.' Rachel again.

'Has anyone ever been to Cradle Mountain?' said Margot brightly.

Nobody had.

'I mean, is everything well signposted? All the tracks clearly marked?'

'It's just a long trail, isn't it?' she heard herself say. 'Lots of school groups.' She looked around her pleadingly. 'Walking groups. Huts and cabins where you sleep at night.'

'It's wilderness, I thought,' someone said hesitantly. 'It's hundreds of square kilometres, or something.'

'Yes, but there are rangers, aren't there? Checking who's where, bed allocations ... I mean, it's all a designated walkway, the actual track, right?'

Someone behind her started massaging her head. Her earring snagged on her hair and she removed it impatiently. Lethargy was creeping up on her, cloudy and anaesthetising. The way they were all arranged around her, pumped with solicitous purpose, flushed with excitement. Like the Furies. Alive. That was it. She hadn't seen them so shining-eyed and avidly motivated since ... well, since the last personal crisis they'd all rallied for.

Galvanised with something exciting to do, determined to outshine as the best, the calmest, the most supportive, the most enlightened, the bloody wisest. Then they would turn around if things got worse and vie to be the most outspoken, the most vengeful, the most impassioned. She shook her head to clear it.

'We know he's a bastard, Sandy,' Annie said. 'The question is, is he an evil bastard or just a stupid bastard?'

She stared. 'You can't ask me that.'

'Come out and sit on the verandah,' said Margot, 'in the fresh air and the sunshine. Do some deep breathing.'

'I don't mean *evil*,' Annie amended hastily. 'I mean, has he got something to prove? To you? To Sophie? Or would he just have sincerely lost his way?'

They were standing her up, and picking up their drinks and trailing together out onto the porch chairs, hustling her along with caring pats; a phalanx of bodyguards taking the star from the stage. What was it they coveted? Why were they here?

'I think I really just want a cup of tea,' she said, and they jumped to the task.

She closed her eyes on the old busted-up couch against the morning sun so her vision was bathed in red, and tried to picture Sophie, walking now with other bushwalkers along some well-defined track, laughing about accidentally leaving it. She could visualise it clearly. The bushwalkers would be teachers, reliable and fit, good in emergencies, dressed in khaki shorts and smelling of sunblock. There would be a ranger at the hut. Or experienced guides. Or would there be tracks for four-wheel drive vehicles, even, for people who wanted to get out of there, tracks leading to a sealed road? What had she been thinking, not even researching this?

Annie was holding something out to her and she dazedly opened her palm.

Two coins.

Something, she thought, recoiling, for putting over the eyes of the dead. Or for playing two-up. These ones had holes in the middle.

'Close your eyes and focus for a moment and hold in your mind the question you want to ask,' Annie said, sitting down opposite her and smoothing her skirt. 'Then throw the coins and we can establish the hexagram.'

Something prickly and constraining seemed to be lowering itself over her shoulders, tucking itself across her chest. Someone's pashmina, adjusted with invisible, swaddling hands. God, they were all patting her, competing for a piece of her, plucking at her for attention. At the same moment Margot handed her a mug of tea. That damn mug of Alison's with the wonky handle you could only fit two fingers inside, the lopsided lip with that embedded grit. Was it the only bloody cup they could find in the house?

'Six throws altogether,' Annie said, and Sandy threw the cup, a sudden and impatient toss, off the verandah and onto the brick path, where it broke at long last. A slosh of chamomile tea arced out into the overgrown grass, and she felt jaw-aching hysteria spill from her in the shocked silence. She rocked with speechless laughter, impatiently shrugging off the shawl and gasping for breath, gesturing for fresh air. Holding the coins aloft in the other hand, with every question she had crowding unbidden and unanswered into her mind at once.

Twenty-One

Fog. The only thing that was stopping him.

He couldn't believe it. Seriously, it was like God sat down at his desk and devised this every morning, how to torture him. He'd crawled out of the tent this morning and wanted to pound the sky with his fists.

He just needed one decent look at this landscape for what it really was. All those tarns glittering, the whole landscape as monochrome-metallic as black-and-white film, just glistening, huge 360-degree sweeps of emptiness. And from above no doubt, on a clear day, any fool could see a track out of here, twisting like a ribbon, scuffed bare by earnest tramping feet.

He would be alright if he could just rise above it, float up there like a wheeling *zopilote* and get some perspective. It would all look ridiculously benign then.

Slog it out for a few kilometres, then duckboards leading straight down to the ferry and then onwards out of it all to safety and warmth.

He'd strayed, that's all. A temporary disorientation had become a major loss of position. There'd be people just an hour or two in some obvious direction, people with first-aid kits and top-of-the-range thermal clothing, with food dehydrated using NASA technology that reconstituted into green chicken curry and beef bourguignon, the whole global village there on your packaway plate. They'd have gourmet dried-fruit trail mix and emergency rehydration powdered drinks and superstrength paracetamol and sleeping bags designed for the conquering of Everest.

Such serious dedication to the task of placing yourself at risk. Such expense, shoring up your own puny little carcass against the elements, against the hostile wilderness you'd chosen to enter. They'd all be bolstered and barricaded against it with Goretex and optimum loft and hundred-mile stares like soldiers on a mission. Like he thought he'd been.

The skin around the scarlet raw patch on his heel had tightened and seemed to shrink, the way tree bark swells and shrinks around the weeping lopped bough. *Proud flesh.* Throbbing like he was still striding along, beside all those marching boots massed down the road certain of their purpose, prepared to walk anywhere, holding their invisible banners proudly aloft.

The heat swam up his leg thick as syrup, staining the skin on his calf with infection, notching up his temperature again until he was starting to see things in his peripheral vision; figures and creatures that shifted jumpily out of sight, bushes that glowed with the aura of revelation.

He'd seen it, though. Looked into its eyes. He had it in the camera. Bigger than Rock Island Bend, more momentous. He squeezed his arms around himself with exhilaration. The shot of the century, without doubt.

And here was God's little extra: he was no more than twenty kilometres from Narcissus Bay and then, ludicrously, it was just a leisurely ferry ride to a sealed car park at the end full of air-conditioned buses.

His memory rocked, skewed a little in the ticking heat of his head. He'd got off that boat and stepped onto the jetty and the police were waiting but other people there too, ready to applaud him, and it was, he knew, a far, far better thing he did that day than he had ever done. It would be like that again, and this time all the evidence he needed was in the camera; proof that he'd been to some deep, deep place of hardship for the good of mankind. Humankind. Into the divvy van and on to the lock-up.

Not this time. No. He'd get off the ferry and there'd be hot coffee, and a phone. A gold phone at the kiosk, or someone's mobile, and the connection would smoothly click into place and set it all square again, tip it back on its wheels. And he could be there, composing himself to utter those magic words, smoothing down his matted hair with his hand as he explained what he had. Why he'd done what he'd done.

'You know what bothers me?' said Ian Millard, 'just the one thing?' He was talking to Paul Colegate on the phone, doodling on the corner of the report.

'What's that?'

'This guy you've been talking to, Russell Cameron. Says that the father had a bad blister, had walked on it for almost the whole track. Wouldn't you think, if that was you, that you'd be heading for Narcissus from Windy Ridge as fast as you could, with no side-trips? Just the easy flat three hours?'

'You would think that, yes.'

'But not only does this guy do the extra unnecessary kilometres to Pine Valley Hut, then he slogs another two hours up into the Labyrinth. So he goes — what? — four or five hours of hard walking out of his way, into some of the most impenetrable country in the park.'

'And back out again, in theory, so add another five hours.'

'With a blister, some kind of infection. And now — surprise surprise — they've vanished.'

'Yeah.'

'And now the mother's telling us the guy's got an axe to grind.'

He heard Paul suck in his breath.

'Mate,' he said softly, 'not the best choice of words.'

The phone tugged Sandy up to panic, breaking the surface of consciousness gasping for air, brain fumbling for reconnection.

Her girl was still out there, and the best-case scenario, the *best*, was that she was uncomfortable, cold and tired. Imagine if it were her now, borrowing some ranger's mobile, breathless with relief.

Sandy's mobile ringtone was high and bell-like, the one that most resembled a real phone. Jump and pick up that phone. Just collect your thoughts and remember where it is, and put your hand on it. Bright, insistent ring. Never lasted for long enough, never gave you enough time to remember where you'd left it, but surely this was it in her pocket, ready and waiting. Getting her fingers round it, desperately imagining Sophie somewhere warm, some park ranger's jeep, or office, listening to that ring, waiting for her to pick up. *Mum*, she'd say. *Stop worrying. It's all good.*

'What on earth is going on with your landline?' said Janet's voice with irritated relief as soon as Sandy answered. 'Your phone's been engaged four times this afternoon when I've tried to call. You really should be leaving the line open, Sandy; you could get news at any moment, you've got to be ready to jump if you need to.'

'Mum.' The disappointment was something palpable, something she could taste. She cupped the mobile against her ear and slid into the desk chair, weak with need for the sound of her daughter's voice, which was evaporating now, dreamlike.

'What's the news, darling? What's happening?'

'I haven't heard anything. I'm just waiting. They're going to mount a search with a helicopter, down there at the park.'

'Oh my God, you'll be costing the taxpayers a fortune.'

Sandy's free hand closed on the mouse, clicked on the dial-up internet icon. She'd been checking the weather website, on and off, all day.

'They must think it's serious, then?'

'It's what they do when someone's lost.' She watched the computer think about connecting her, the way it always did. Sophie had begged and begged her to get broadband. She'd resisted as though it was something to be proud of, like a social virtue. Pointless bloody nonsense.

'Really? Even if it's just a couple of days?'

She moved the cursor, clicked on the Google icon. Her mother's voice sounded wary with doubt.

'Can't they just send a search party of rangers down the track, or something? Or use their mobile phones and tell people where they are?'

'Hang on, hang on. There's no phone reception down there, and there's been a storm, the ranger says, which has stranded lots of walkers, but no, they're not there just sitting in a hut somewhere, Mum; they're missing.'

'When were you meant to meet them?'

'Yesterday,' she said, and couldn't believe it as she said it, couldn't take in that only a day had passed. There was a short incredulous silence, then she heard Janet sigh. Such a familiar sound, that exhalation, that genteel annoyance.

'*Yester*day? My God, you sounded so frantic on your phone message, I assumed ...'

'I am frantic, Mum. I'm totally beside myself. How did you think I'd be? They were meant to finish the walk by Monday morning and catch the flight from Launceston on Tuesday.'

'Well, to be perfectly honest, if you thought it was that serious I imagined you'd have flown down there by now.'

'To Tasmania? Where would I fly to? Why would that make things any different? The police say the best thing to do is just sit tight ...'

'You're not telling me you've gotten the police involved?' Her mother's voice went up a notch now, exasperated and horrified at the same time.

'Of course I have. The police co-ordinate the search and rescue down there. I thought it would be Parks and Wildlife, but it's not.'

She typed with one finger into the search engine: *rescue remedy.* How automatic it was now, this deferring of attention to her mother, this placating and relinquishing. Today she hardly had the energy to care. She hit 'Search'.

'Did the police tell you you'd been very foolish, letting her go off with a complete stranger?'

Ah yes, Janet's world, where she imagined everyone in authority behaved just like her. Where she believed implacably that she was, in fact, the sole true authority.

'Mum. He's her father. There's nothing I can do to change that. Or you, for that matter.'

Here was the website. She scrolled down for a list of ingredients. *Five flower essences*, she read. She felt deadened with lassitude now, too drained to rise to Janet's bait or even to try justifying herself. It was like trying to cry more when you'd already cried yourself out.

'Sandy, what were you thinking? What on earth were you thinking?' It sounded as though her mother was weeping now, furious and impotent.

Here were the flowers, little botanical drawings and what each was for, each essence as outlined by Doctor Bach.

'Mum, can you come up and stay with me? I'm going mad here in the house by myself. And I know you're upset. But please, there's nothing we can do but wait. So can you?'

She'd never heard herself making such a bald and blatant request. And to Janet, of all people. Her mother had never known how to comfort her or her sister, never been someone you could confide in or hope for a sympathetic ear from. She was too eager to make sure you'd learnt the lesson she'd warned you about first.

Sandy had had counselling for quite a few years and knew how it stood now, had reconciled herself to it. The withholding mother. It wasn't as if it was rare or anything. It was a generational thing. You had to accept it and learn to break the cycle, become the warm parent yourself, give the love you were never given. But this was Sophie. This would crash through those traces, surely. Janet would come up to stay, she thought, and they would share this pain together, it would pull them closer. They would confide. And that was what the workshop had been for, she suddenly saw with a start of possibility. An exercise in opening her up and making her doubt. Being made to open up and doubt; that was good, that was part of it. Even a beautiful karmic plan, to heal those past unresolved rifts and buried, simmering, unspoken grudges. She'd look back and see it then — a pattern that made sense. The Universe answering.

And as she waited, certain of this, she heard the faint, familiar sound of her mother's sigh again. Then the rustle of paper. Listening, she knew exactly what she was hearing. A page of her mother's diary being turned. Her mother was standing there scanning her desk diary, annoyed that her schedule might be disrupted.

For trauma and numbness, she read next to the first flower. Then: *For inattentiveness.* And on down the list. *For panic or terror. For irritability and impatience. To prevent anger.*

As if flowers, she thought wonderingly, could hold so much power over human emotions, as if they contained the essence of all our frailties. As if we could be *rescued.*

'Sandy? Hello?' She tuned in again to Janet, heard the exasperation dampened down to appeasement, a kind of courteous distance. 'I couldn't come till Saturday, darling, I really couldn't, and I'm sure it will have all blown over by then. I just can't get away; this really couldn't have come at a worse time.'

She blinked, taking in the words. A memory rose clear and unbidden in her mind of the time she'd been to a chiropractor, that time she'd hurt her neck painting the ceiling. He hadn't even touched her neck. He'd put the heel of one hand into her lower back and confidently pressed the fingertips and thumb of the other at some point between her shoulderblades. Sandy had felt a strange glutinous shifting ascend up her spine; not a cracking or jarring, but a realignment. She'd heard cartilage pop, distantly, inside her ears.

Sitting there now, cradling her mobile and staring blindly at the screen, she felt it again, the sensation of something clicking into joint. She let her shoulders drop, remembering how it had felt. The spreading dissolving warmth, the feel of something loosening.

'I understand completely, Mum,' she said evenly. 'No need to come. I'll let you know as soon as I hear anything.'

The word 'mum' felt awkward in her mouth, like an unwanted spoonful of something. A counterfeit word. She thought of herself lying on the examination table that day, absorbing the idea of all the hidden dislocations the body could secretly carry. Astonished, that after an anticipated build-up of such dread, it could turn out to hurt so little.

He had the camera protected in a tight nest of clothing, inside its case and cushioned with socks, zipped inside the camera bag, safe inside the daypack.

He had to keep resisting the urge to cover it with his body.

She eyed him, expressionless.

'Why don't you show me how to adjust it,' she said finally, 'so that once the sky starts to clear we could set it up so that the flash keeps going off, and point it upwards, so that anyone searching for us in a plane or something will see it.'

He blinked, trying to clear his head to take in what she was saying, then shook it decisively. His arm stretched over the pack protectively. He imagined the Olympus fumbled out of her hand as she stepped over a fissure in rock, her grabbing for it, the lens snapping off, the hinge breaking and the back flying open. Everything exposed and ruined. He couldn't afford to risk it. Not now.

In his brief, rational moments of lucidity he knew he should unwind the roll of film from the camera itself and store it somewhere, inside a plastic container, wedged safe into a side pocket, but he couldn't stand to touch it. He couldn't even trust himself now, a risk like that. Anyway he had to think about the value of the rest of the roll as a documentary record of this event — proof of sequence, the shots after the thylacine, the terrain they were in, evidence of them both here, setting up this camp, Sophie in them, alive and well ...

Evidence, yes, in black and white, that his intentions had been purely honourable.

'I'm not sure the flash would have the power, during the day,' he said, thinking on his feet, his tongue too thick in his mouth. 'Night would be better, but I bet they don't search from the air at night. You know what we'd be better off doing? Waiting till this fog clears then climbing up the nearest peak and seeing if there's mobile reception. I should have thought of that straight away.'

'The battery's nearly dead,' she answered, her voice expressionless.

'How can the battery be nearly dead? You haven't been able to use it since we started on the walk. The ranger told us there was no reception. Surely you haven't had it switched on.'

She muttered something.

'What?'

'Intermittent. He said reception was intermittent and unreliable. So I've been checking now and then. A few times a day, just to see. Sometimes you can send texts even if you can't actually talk, if you get into range. Anyway, it's nearly flat.'

They sat in silence for a few minutes, sucking dry instant noodles.

'We should have got one of those beacons,' Sophie said. 'For a satellite to locate us.'

'They cost hundreds of dollars.'

'You could hire them. From the Parks Service. I saw them — they only cost $30 for a week. EPIRBs.'

'I know what they are. Emergency Personal ...' He hesitated. '... Ah ... International ... Ranger Beacons.'

'I don't think that's right.'

'I think you'll find that's what it is.' God, his father's savage know-all tone.

'I don't think so. I think it's something else.' She reached over to her pack and dug in the side pocket, pulled out a glossy brochure. He spluttered with impatience.

'What does it matter exactly what it is? I mean ...'

'Electronic Position Indicating Radio Beacon,' she read.

He reached over, snatched it. 'Let me see that.'

He glanced at the brochure, rolled his eyes and thrust it back to her.

'Must be nice knowing everything,' he muttered.

She crunched noodles, scowling. 'You can't just make shit up,' she said. 'That's what landed us in this. You. Thinking you knew everything.'

'Didn't I say there was no reason to be really worried? A few hundred walkers a week, turning down the track there and wandering here in the ranges, searching for a secluded spot? Someone's going to stumble across our campsite any minute. We can walk out with them.'

She shook her head scornfully. 'You're doing it again,' she said. 'Talking yourself into the same bullshit story. Give me the camera, and we'll try the flash idea.'

'You're not touching that camera,' he heard himself bark. 'It's staying right where it is. That's worth a million bucks, what's in there. Nobody's going anywhere near it.' He was stretched thin, he could hear it. Worked and worked like cheap metal, pushed beyond endurance, about to snap. But she didn't back down. She just looked at him, her lip curling.

'And you think you're going to walk out of here? Look at yourself. I mean it. You're weak as piss.'

He laughed hollowly, mopping at the sweat where his hair had stuck to his head.

'You know what, I think I liked it better when you had all those questions,' he said.

'Did you?' Her mouth turned up, crooked and sour, at the corner. 'So why didn't you answer any of them, then?'

'Ms Reynolds?'

She gripped the door handle. The young cop again. As the first shivering flush coursed through her she understood, completely and suddenly, how people could suddenly piss themselves with fear. It was like snapping on a current.

Oh please, please, please, no, please ...

'Don't worry, I'm not ...'

He wasn't experienced at this either she could tell, this shocking job of being the policeman on the doorstep watching people's lives end, the belief in anything extinguishing itself in their eyes at your words and it would be like a spell, where you'd speak the words and then watch them suddenly age away in front of you, decades of life draining from them, hanging onto the door like this and turning eighty then ninety then a hundred ...

'We've heard from the ranger, some news from some other walkers who've come out of the area,' he said. 'We haven't found them yet, but they did come across some signs that they'd been there in the last few days, so that's a good ... Do you need to sit down, Ms Reynolds?'

'Sandy.' Marionette voice, jaw opening on a hinge; a marionette hand jerking up to make him continue.

'They've struck a bit of bad weather down there so the ranger's been waiting to take out a search party, but now they've found this they'll be able to focus the search, so that's a very positive thing ...'

'What? Found what?'

She imagined a dead fire, flattened grass where a tent had been, a dropped glove, a splash of blood. The floor pitched like a boat and she clung to the door handle.

'It's a bit strange, so I was wondering if you could throw some light ... '

'What? For godsakes, what?'

'Well, they found some hair. You told us, didn't you, that Sophie had dyed black hair? And your ex-husband's is a dark brown?'

She felt the dragging current again, drenching over her face and neck and down to heave her stomach sideways; a cramping blow down into the pelvis, the dentist's probing torture instrument touching a nerve end: *If you harm one hair on her head, believe me, you will pay, you will pay, you will pay ...*

Hair. She'd spoken the word aloud, because he nodded bemusedly, raising his eyebrows.

'A pile of hair. Cut off and scattered around some rocks. Now' — he was raising his hand calmly to her, warding off her horror with a gesture — 'I don't think you should be unduly worried Ms Reynolds, because there might be a perfectly logical explanation for this ...'

'Oh Jesus. Oh my *God*.'

'Like, I don't know, their hair might have become tangled up or started to annoy them, caught up under their backpacks, or something quite rational, I mean ... '

'Oh God, God, God,' she chanted, her voice cracking into dry sobs. Her hands were on her face now, she realised, fingers digging into her eye sockets. 'What has he done to her?'

'We can't ascertain that yet until we hear more from the Search and Rescue team, obviously, but this is good news for them because they can direct their search into this area. They have a lot of experience, those guys. They know what they're doing.'

'What area are you talking about?'

He checked his notebook. 'It's called the Labyrinth.'

'How far off the track?' she said, not bothering to correct his pronunciation.

'Well, it can't be more than two days worth of walking, can it? No matter how fit they are. But it's a big area. Easy to get lost in, apparently. The landscape all looks much the same so people don't realise they've become disoriented. That's what the ranger tells me, anyway.' He glanced up at her. 'You've spoken with the park rangers already, right?'

'Yeah, I did, I rang them first. When Sophie and Rich didn't show at the airport. They said there's hardly any mobile phone reception anywhere around Cradle Mountain.'

'Yeah. You need all that satellite-navigation gear, now, if you're walking. But I can't imagine they'll be walking too far. Much more likely they'll be holed up somewhere, staying out of the weather, doing their best to stay visible.'

She gave him a look. 'Don't you get it? He doesn't want to be found. He's hiding. Cutting her hair off — Jesus Christ, does he have to spell it out to you? He's done it on purpose. It's some kind of threat or warning.'

'I did ask you this the other day, Ms Reynolds. If you're serious in these allegations, there'll be charges to be made once they're found. Obviously your daughter's testimony is going to be the one which really clears up what's happened. We'll alert the rescue teams to all this. But you have to rest assured we're doing everything we can. It's a complicated operation and for the moment we have to assume they've just innocently become lost.'

'What if I press charges now?'

He raised his eyebrows again, gave a dry humourless laugh. 'They're flat out doing their best — that won't make them look any harder.'

'If he's cut off her hair,' she said, her voice shaking, 'that means he has a knife.'

'Ms Reynolds,' said the policeman flatly, 'he'd be a fool to go bushwalking without a knife.'

'This is my daughter we're talking about,' she said, her voice tight. 'That's what you don't seem to understand. She's out there with him.'

'Yeah,' said the policeman reasonably, 'but think about it: if he was going to abduct her, why do it like this and make things so bloody hard on himself? I might be speaking out of turn here, but why not head straight to Queensland and hide out in a caravan park somewhere? He didn't come and take her by force, after all, so what would it be aggravated by? I mean, you agreed to this, didn't you, at the time?'

She swallowed. Powdered glass. Sandpaper. Four drops to cure inattentiveness.

'I did,' she said. 'Like a fool.'

She could smell the laundry powder in his clean-pressed blue shirt as he put his hat back on. Someone's ironed that, she thought dully, with Fabulon.

'You've got my details, anyway, if you have any questions at this point?'

She wondered at this new formality, his just-acquired distance. No coming in for a cup of tea this time.

'Do you think I should fly down there? To Tasmania?' she blurted as he was turning on his heel. He paused at the step.

'I think you should stay here and try not to worry unduly,' he replied. 'Don't try to read too much into things at this stage.'

'Easy for you to say. You don't know him.'

He didn't answer. Just turned around again and left her here to cope with everything on her own, the way blokes always did when things got too hard for them. Her women friends, naturally, had formed a hurried roster between themselves to come and wait with her and support her, but nobody would be here till eleven today. She sat on the back porch again, stunned at how totally without purpose she felt. Nothing whatever to do. No reason for anything.

It was one thing to ask questions of the universe, she thought; it was something else to listen to what the universe had to say in reply. Nothing. A disconnected line, a blank silence.

She sat staring at the couch grass and wondering if she could already see it yellowing, that irreversible, invisible damage done.

Twenty-Two

They sat in the tent, surrounded, still, by vaporous white. She had all her layers on now — both Libby's thermal tops, her leggings under her spare tracksuit pants, two pairs of socks.

'Got to get my head straight,' Rich said for about the twentieth time. 'Got to get some perspective on what this is going to mean. It's going to hit the news like a bombshell.'

Lying there holding his camera bag to his chest, wrapped in his sleeping bag, staring off into space. Like a dead pharaoh, clutching his bloody treasure.

She could see a muscle jumping in his jaw, creasing at the corner of his mouth. It had been like this all morning — sometimes he made sense, sometimes she didn't have a clue what he was talking about. He'd blink too much and start to mumble away like he was having an argument. Then there'd be moments like this, when he became agitated thinking about his photos again — much more agitated than he'd been when he'd first got them lost. Which showed what he really cared about. He looked over at her.

'They'll want to interview you too,' he said. 'Are you ready to be a celebrity?'

She wondered if she could sit outside. Put on her hat and jacket, maybe, just sit nearby where she could see the tent. She'd told him over and over it was a dog.

'They have to find us first,' she said finally, when she realised his sly glassy-eyed grin meant he was waiting for her to answer.

'Imagine what it's going to do to this place! Tasmanian Tiger still alive! Boy, if they think they're inundated with tourists now, imagine how it's going to be when they find out it's still here. There's going to be ten thousand Russells swarming over the place! Danish tour groups scouring the hills!'

That cracked smile again.

'That's the thing about nature, isn't it, Sophie? It always turns round to surprise us. Keeping its deepest secrets from us, nurtured here in the wilderness.'

He was planning his media interview, she could tell. Rehearsing his alibi. She had to stay on her guard, and not believe a word he told her.

'Funny how you're so gung-ho to get out of this and be famous now but you didn't give a shit when it was just me.'

'Not true. We got disoriented in that storm. Who on earth's going to think otherwise?'

He didn't care about anything but himself. Liar. She thought of Sandy's voice at the party when she'd boasted about Rich. *Oh, Soph. Listen* ... The pity in it. Maybe not fake pity, after all.

'Mum will. She'll ... she'll press charges.' Hating the falter in her voice, giving her away.

'What — you can be charged with accidentally getting lost now, can you? Who do you think's going to listen to Sandy's crackpot theories? It'll be her word against mine.' God, the arrogance in his voice.

'No,' she said. 'Your word against *mine*.'

Paying out on him, and why shouldn't she? He deserved it. There was a silence, and she saw his fingers shift suddenly, grip the camera case.

'You don't mean that.'

'Yeah. I do. That's what it bloody looks like to me.'

'You can see I've just about killed myself trying to get us out of here. Anyone could. Haven't I?' He raised himself on an elbow, glared at her. 'Haven't I? Sophie?'

There was nowhere to go.

'Yes,' she said.

'You're pissed off,' he said eventually, 'that you wanted everyone to think I was this malicious bastard, dragging you off into the wilderness, and now all they're going to be thinking about is that I'm the one lucky photographer who got to see a real, living, breathing myth, who proved it's still there. Don't you get it, yet? That photo's going to make *history*. Nobody's going to care about anything else. It's going to change everything.'

Sophie thought of the photos in the envelope. A polar man, she thought. A cold man looking away from you, in a white, empty world. Yes.

'Listen to you,' she said flatly. 'Mr Weaver, bagging his tiger.'

'Who?'

'Forget it.'

Sandy called Search and Rescue again.

'Yes, Ms Reynolds. Hello.'

'I need to know what's happening.' She was pacing up and down the room as she spoke, tracking back and forth in a room cleaned and tidied by all her friends, fresh oil in the burner and a huge bunch of flowers on the table.

'Well, at the moment we couldn't send in the helicopter no matter what the circumstances — it's a total white-out over the area at present. There's so little visibility it would be useless. And looking at the state of things on the map it would be too dangerous to send in a ground search crew either. They'd be lost themselves, probably, within minutes. The ranger knows that region like the back of his hand but he's not prepared to risk it with anyone else. It's not called the Labyrinth for nothing.'

So reasonable and calm, that voice. Weighing up everything rationally.

'The police told me about the hair,' she said.

'Yeah, that's odd, but it means they were definitely there. So it's good in a way. We have to sit tight now though, Ms Reynolds, wait for this weather to lift then go in the first chance we get.'

Sandy walked back down the room again. It all looked so dull and used-up — the old lounge suite with the batik throws, the rice-paper lamps. Exhausted. She stopped and blew out the candle under the oil burner.

'I'm afraid there's really nothing we can do now except wait it out,' the guy said.

She thought of the meditation session at the retreat, where the woman running it had said *let us sit now and simply be attentive to everything we cannot change so that we learn to sit with powerlessness* and she had nodded impatiently to herself, waiting for the little Tibetan gong that meant they could all stand and stretch and smile smugly at each other before breaking for lunch.

An intervention order. That's what Sandy would do, Rich thought, feeling a tremor jerking in his face. Keep Sophie away. Charge him with negligence, at least, or breach of trust, or something.

But those pictures would vindicate him. Everything else would be forgotten in a flurry of amazement and publicity. He'd insist on being in the darkroom himself, whatever happened. The need in him, to see those stripes form slowly in the developer bath and look around triumphantly at the astonished faces in the red light, pressed on a nerve somewhere. Need that was like a cavity in a tooth, probed with his tongue over and over, unbearable.

He'd get up tomorrow, when this fog lifted, and he'd build a huge fire somehow, or climb the nearest mountain and get his bearings again. He wanted to walk out, limping but holding the camera aloft, holding Sophie's hand. Didn't want to sit like a useless urban loser and be rescued. He wished he'd twisted his ankle now, or sprained it. Something more like a real injury — broken collarbone or wrist. Head wound. Not a bloody *blister*, for godsakes, the foolish injury of the greenhorn, the woman, the dilettante.

It didn't matter, though. The photos were going to sweep all that away in any case. Front-page news. You only got one moment really, he thought, and it would come at you just like it had for him, out of your darkest hour, just when you'd almost given up. Your test.

He was so thirsty. Getting warmer all the time. Just rest here,
wait till night fell, then get through the night, and it would be
morning. If he kept his eyes closed he could be here and not here
at the same time, ride it out that way.

'They'll try to capture it now, won't they?' Sophie's voice.

'Probably. They'll want to microchip it, track its movements,
that kind of thing. We don't even know how many there are.
There's so much science still has to find out.'

'They'd never just leave it alone, would they?'

'What would that achieve?'

A long pause. 'What would it *achieve*?' He heard the measured
tone in her voice that let him know he'd reached a new low in
her estimation. She said it louder, full of smothered rage. 'What
would it *achieve*, did you say?'

'Well, yeah. I mean ...' She let him trail off, she let him feel the
full fumbling, incapacitated blankness in his head. Then she sat
up and pulled off the sleeping bag.

'I don't care if it's freezing out there, I'm going outside. I'd
rather get frostbite than listen to this.'

Jesus, the dark recess of exposed nerve in the cold. The
thought of the decay in there, the unspeakable craving to have it
cauterised, and gone.

The house seemed stuffed with things, suddenly. Crammed with
them. Jugs and cushions and old magazines and worn throw rugs,
candles and vinyl records and tea canisters and lamps. Sandy
walked around looking at it, feeling listless and unsettled. She
wandered from point to point, brushing her hand along things
that used to give her comfort; all these objects imbued with her
stories and memories.

A memory rose unbidden of the nuns at her school, who'd all
been old women by the time Sandy was a teenager, old relics in
their habits who'd walked around the chapel reciting the rosary,
stopping and kneeling at the Stations of the Cross. Fingering
their beads and murmuring through the litany of prayers, she
remembered, a repetitive chant you could lose yourself in. And

that big basalt slab set into the floor at the chapel's entrance where years and years of feet had turned and shuffled; a step worn slightly concave, and burnished with use, testament to years of the pious footsteps of the faithful and the reluctant, dragging steps of generations of bored schoolgirls. Sandy walked slowly around the living room, her hand touching everything she'd collected. Remembering that step, worn smooth and polished and treacherous.

She'd always liked to think of herself as a collector. A great bargain hunter at op shops. A keen-eyed clearing sale afficionado. That's where most of this stuff had come from anyway. She never bought anything new. Now she thought of the crowd following the auctioneer along at clearing sales, along the rows and rows of unwanted stuff up for bids. Sundries, that's what she had always looked for. *Item 46: box of miscellaneous sundries.* Sometimes the sundries were poignant: bundles of old postcards and carefully annotated photo albums — these especially plucked at Sandy's heart — half-finished knitting projects, collections of ceramic animals, someone else's life up for grabs. And sometimes the box contained things so worthless they failed to attract a single bid, and the auctioneer would cast his eye over the blank, unmoving sea of bidders, and he'd call, with a sort of ruthless cheerfulness: *Put it aside.*

That's it, she thought. It was other people's cast-offs, things already worn out, the virtuous feeling of taking something unwanted and fashioning a home out of it. She'd done it too. She'd pulled it all together, scraped by on nothing.

But in the end this was all it was, just this grab bag of accumulated sundries. Put it aside. Get a box, and clear it away. Put your hand out, without even thinking, and sweep it clear.

When she crawled back into the tent he was glowing with heat again. 'Do you want to get up and walk around for a while?' she said. 'It's really stuffy in here. And it stinks.' No point mincing words.

'Can't really walk,' he said. Much worse. Shrunken, somehow.

'Well, have some water.' She gave him her water bottle. She'd
fill them both up again later, when the fog lifted and she could see
all the way to the little lake.

'A *strut*,' he said out of nowhere, and laughed. A chugging
sound, like sobs.

'What?'

'That's what we used to call a walk in the bush, during the
campaign.'

'The Blockade.'

'Yeah. We used to go on these struts, checking out the HEC
transect lines, imagining we'd find something massively important.
Spying, documenting it all. Hoping they'd find us, so we'd get an
adrenaline hit hiding in the bush. Strutting. It's funny, isn't it?
Going for a *strut*. A quick strut around the moral high ground.'
He laughed again, his eyes glazed and dark with something she
couldn't see. Sweat was dripping off his neck.

'What day is it again?' he said.

'Thursday.'

'Right. And what's the time?' he said after a while.

'Four o'clock.' She checked the clock on her mobile.

'Really? Be dark again soon.'

'Yeah.'

'I'm not good here, Sophie. I'm struggling.'

She tucked her knees closer to her chest. She didn't want him
to touch her, couldn't deal with him getting all clingy and pathetic
now. So useless and needy and diminished, eroding her resolve. 'I
think you should have one of my electrolyte drinks.'

'That's your secret formula, is it?' He was raving, damp with
sweat.

'Yeah. I think you should have one.'

'Sophie' — he was reaching for his pack now, fishing for the
tupperware container he'd brought his food in and pulling the last
sachet out — 'I've got one more Creamy Fettuccine.'

'Yes.'

He reached for her hand, and put the packet in it. Closed her
fingers round it.

She could feel it, the ocean of unsayable things between them.

'I'll do you a deal,' he said.

Too much pain to sleep, the skin around the wound violet now. Like something ready for a graft. She'd given him a Panadol and he was cooler and clearer and he forced his thoughts into order.

She was fifteen, for crying out loud. She was furious now, paranoid and tired, but she'd come around, once the story broke and some women's magazine was ringing her asking her for an exclusive. She'd get some perspective then, and regret the way she'd misjudged him. That was all he wanted, to be granted a chance like that, and OK you can't just win someone's respect, you have to earn it, *yada yada*. He didn't expect her to hero-worship him or anything, but surely she could see how totally different things were now.

'Are you still awake, Sophie?'

'Of course I am.'

'Hear that wind? That probably means the fog will start lifting tomorrow and someone will come looking for us.'

'Yeah. I know.'

'What's bothering you, then?'

He heard her exhale slowly. A tired sigh.

'What do you reckon? Once someone finds us, and you tell them your fabulous news, the hunt's going to be on, isn't it? You were right — this whole place will be under siege.'

'You can't blame people for wanting to come to beautiful spots.'

'I wish I'd never come. We shouldn't even be here; nobody should.'

'That's a hopelessly idealised attitude, I'm sorry to say.' He couldn't marshal an argument, couldn't pick up his scattered thoughts.

'Whatever wild places are left on the planet, we should just lock them up and throw away the key, keep people out of them.

We wreck everything we touch.'

'Mmm, I used to think like that ...'

'No, you didn't. Just don't even ...'

'Look, you can't change reality. You have to work with it, not against it.'

'You told me,' she said venomously, 'you told me it was worth saving, and you put yourself on the line to keep it untouched.'

'Look.' He sighed, rubbed at his mouth. 'Say people see those photos ...'

'I'm telling you. It was a dog.'

'It wasn't a dog. You'll see what it was when I develop that film. See how that's going to be a good thing, a fantastic thing, for the wilderness? Once the world realises that the tiger is still out there, of course people are going to want to come here. There'll be scientists and documentary-makers and photographers and a whole lot of ecologists and conservationists, they're all going to make their way here and explore this habitat and learn about it.'

'That's right,' she said. 'It won't be ten thousand guys like Russell. It'll be ten thousand guys like you.'

She was lost to him now, he could see that. Hear it in her voice. He'd phone her and she'd hang up. Return his letters unopened, vanish out of his life, leave him with this new intolerable blank emptiness. He'd almost managed it, but she'd slipped from him.

'This could actually be a great thing for the thylacine,' he said after a while, cautiously. 'Imagine the new respect it's going to create for the species, surviving all this time against the odds. It'll be such a perfect symbol of how threatened the wilderness is, and see, we can use that — make all those forests World Heritage areas, exert global pressure to stop logging here. Teach people how to be tourists in a whole new enlightened way. A sustainable way.'

His throat was parched, and he swallowed into the silence.

He heard her laugh softly, an exhalation in the darkness. He could have understood contempt in that laugh, or unforgiving recrimination, but not what he heard, not wise and terrible sadness.

'Soar with the vultures, Rich,' she said.

'Ian? It's Mal. It's clearing, by the looks of it.'

'So we're rolling?'

'Just gotta clear the paperwork and call the pilots in. I'm phoning Western District S and R now.'

'See you then.' Ian hung up and thought: due to walk out on Monday, a couple of days' extra food maybe, and today's Friday. The Swiss guy had been gone for four days, but that was in the snow and without his gear. Ian had thought for a long time about the way that pack had been placed carefully against the rock. As though it had been abandoned. He'd been twenty-five, that boy. Just finished university, letter to his girlfriend in his diary. Travelling alone. Ian had been in the group that had found him, trekking up on foot to the summit and circling back down again. Not the time to think about that now.

Ian kissed his wife, still in bed.

'Was that work?'

'Yep.'

'You're going out there?'

'Yep. It's on. I'll call you later.'

He tossed yesterday's unread paper into the recycling as he went out to the carport. His guttering was choked with early autumn leaves. The dawn cloud swirled around Mount Wellington like a wedding dress.

Twenty-Three

Sophie stood on top of the outcrop at last, scrambling up the last incline and panting as she wrapped the green garbage bag more tightly around her waist.

The wind caught it and whipped it around. It was keeping her surprisingly dry, she thought, and even a bit warmer, like a perfectly functional piece of clothing with the holes for her head and arms, but God, imagine wearing it anywhere but out here.

She'd woken at dawn and seen the light outside the tent, realised the fog had lifted, and climbed the nearest peak. Now she paused, catching her breath as she felt the heat of the climb tingle in her cheeks against the sting of cold here at the summit. She gulped air so cold it ached in her throat and lungs, concentrating on the mobile phone she held at arm's length. The flashing low-battery symbol pulsed on the tiny screen as she turned slowly on a full axis, willing a bar of reception to register.

She faced all cardinal points, carefully raising the phone in the air before her like a dowsing rod. Wind blustered in her ears. She blinked away cold tears as she turned gradually and pointed the phone to each direction on the horizon. There had to be something.

But the screen was uselessly blank, filmed only with beading mist, and as she rubbed it dry on her sleeve the flashing orange battery image faded completely. OK. OK then. So that was that.

Sophie raised her face into the headwind, feeling as bleak and empty as that dead, grey screen. She'd never been out of range in her life. It was like being on a distant abandoned planet. Far away on a home star, a giant comforting network of a billion reassuring conversations murmured in the dark, forgetting all about her. Passing her over.

She slipped the dead phone into her pocket under the garbage bag, and rubbed her other hand across her eyes, her vision blurred with focusing on the phone, unable to adjust to the stretching distances all around her. Her feet kept shuffling her in a sleepwalking small circle, 360 degrees around.

She was a speck, she saw again. Impossible, out here, not to be aware of that; just a tiny wobbling figure surrounded by the rumpled, jagged vistas in all directions; the mountain contours in the distance softened like some massive bolt of rough fabric. Closer, they sharpened into shadowed focus, revealing flinty plunges and ice-split rocks and tough vegetation that crept across the scattered subsoils, and her in the middle of it up here above the tree line, a soft-bodied scrap of warmth, cradling herself inside a plastic bag.

If she could just drag some dry wood up here somehow, find a sheltered spot, pray that the wind dropped, she could light a fire. Send up a column of smoke like in the movies and someone would come and rescue them. Rich was down there, at their camp. She'd spoken to him, told him she was walking up to the summit to see if she could get reception before her phone battery finally went dead, and he'd just nodded vacantly, given a little twirling wave as if he couldn't care less.

He'd lie there and starve to death clutching that camera to his chest, and when searchers finally found him months or years into the future they would develop that film and find it, the animal they'd both seen. There would be a TV special with those photos shown over and over, and this place, so unmarked by humans, would be overrun. Besieged. With rubberneckers and eco-tourists and tiger hunters. People wanting to glimpse it, people wanting to microchip it, people wanting to commune with it and everybody wanting to be the one and only.

A big dog, she thought for the thousandth time. Brindle, like that Staffordshire bull-terrier a friend at school had, like those Great Danes crossed with mastiffs people bred. Someone's hunting dog escaped and gone feral, that was all it was, wasted with hunger and its poor knuckled spine curving, its ribs pushing through the fur. That's what had made the shadows like stripes in Rich's flash.

But people looked at something like that, and saw what they wanted to, or needed to. She could almost understand it, the way you wanted something so much it warped what you saw, distorting and blurring what was there. Just look at the image she'd held in her mind of her father for all those years. Two old, discoloured snapshots, just a momentary arrangement of light and shadow, nothing to do with Rich himself. Something to pore over and fantasise about. People would come here with a craving that took them over, an irrational belief that they were seeing one thing when another thing was staring them in the face, and yes, if she were honest, she could understand that too. They'd turn the place upside-down, blindly pulling it apart, corner to corner. And what if. What if.

She heard the chipping scatter of pebbles to her left and jerked her head to see a black glossy shape bob behind an outcrop. The crow bounced to the rocky point with an ungainly flap, tightened its claws and looked at her.

'Hello you,' she said. It found a better grip against the pour of wind and lowered its head to whet its beak energetically against the stone, turning into the slipstream.

She thought of the dark gleaming rocks pictured in her mother's gemstone book. Anthracite. Obsidian. She moved closer, a patch of spongy vegetation cushioning her steps for a few metres before the soles of her boots hit rock again. The crow observed her shrewdly, its head and body a wedge of perfect streamlined design, its eye bright with some private joke.

Sophie remembered a biology project from school, the breakthrough discovery a few years back of the Wollemi pines scientists had thought were extinct. The way they'd gone to such lengths to keep the location a secret, to barricade it against a barrage of the curious. There was no way they could hide this location though. She tried to imagine this whole summit fenced off, lined with gravel walkways.

Or concrete paths, probably. The whole of the park ending up like the orientation centre. Thousands of tourists getting out of tour buses with faces like the ones who came on daytrips to Ayresville, demanding hot chips and public toilets and promised mysteries, demanding a bang for their buck. They'd want an interpretive centre and a kiosk and a night-time full-moon Tiger Vigil tour, and of course they'd want the real thing. In a cage, like that one in the museum, just an eco-cage this time. Blinded by a strobe of digital flashes as it turned its black bottomless eyes towards them. The world was so horrible, and so messed up, you couldn't stand it.

Sophie peered over the rocky outcrop where the crow had disappeared and stretched out her hand to clamber closer, the other hand going absently to her face to wipe her streaming nose, when suddenly her boot lost traction. Rock edge jutting into space, a grunt of pain as her hip hit stone, a second of scrambling, tilting disbelief, and she fell.

Rich's head was full of stars. He felt pummelled by clenched and knuckled hands, twisting around him, refusing to disentangle and let him drop. Sophie was gone again. Couldn't stand even being near him now. He got up, steadying himself against the boulders. His head was a balloon, floating metres above his body, bobbing above his shoulders as he tottered over the stones and hoisted himself painfully across tussocks in the early light. Both boots off now, his limp giving him a rolling gait. A barefoot man wandering on the spongy pastures of the new, uninhabited earth. Far below, the soles of his feet registered the textures of the ground beneath him, the prickly moist give of grasses, the hard, stippled bones of rock underneath. One foot fine, the other hardly his; hot and puffy, so tightly swollen with pus he could feel it quiver with each step. The weakly lit world was monochromatic, fabulously detailed and every molecule of it in minute focus like an acid trip, pressing in upon his burning consciousness as startling and ephemeral as a single snowflake. As he limped forward the landscape swam in and out of his vision like something through a viewfinder and he admired the metallic sheen of a tarn, true deep blacks he could make out in the shadows before him, the myriad greys. See, this was why he used film, with its perfect possibilities for those tender highlights instead of the loss of dynamic range you got with digital. He could have stood and looked at this framed black-and-white textured world all day, thinking about agitating the film in the developing tank, timing it, then holding up a slippery strip of negatives and seeing the images there, ready for him. The calm, inexpressible comfort of sliding exposed paper into the fixing bath and tilting it back and forth, rinsing away the unused silver halide, that moment he loved.

He realised he was standing at the bank of the tarn. He'd walked here to get to the water, driven by the thought of lowering his foot into the clean coldness of it. He sat down awkwardly, pulling his jeans and thermals above his knees. The extent of the infection, the huge pulpy rawness of his heel, made him blink, certain for a second he could see the bone beneath the flesh, just white then black again, positive then negative, a flash from bone to blood. Then he lowered the foot into the freezing water and his breath stuttered into his chest with the sensation; not really pain, beyond pain now, more a memory of numbness. A novocaine shot in a dream.

He looked down at the foot floating under the water, a few bubbles on the ghostly skin. His skin. He'd walked a very long way on these feet. He'd always liked seeing the journey as a road, a lifelong trip to the somewhere up ahead it was always going to be worth getting to, if he could just outpace life and stride into that perfect place. But it wasn't a road. There was no trail.

He looked at the back of his hands, laced them together. When you looked honestly at a photo you saw its flaws, you needed to manipulate it to make it as perfect as your vision had been. Parts that needed more detail — you had to burn them in. Dodging, it was called. Just you, standing alone there in a darkroom with that single light pouring down, light that had the power to turn everything to black, trying to cup your hands and fingers as the timer whirred, trying to make light fall on the burning-in spot. So easy to ruin it, and turn all that hard-won detail to blackness.

He'd travelled, yes, but so rarely on actual roads. His feet, instead, had taken him hurriedly out of rooms, backing out making excuses and calling goodbyes, then into airports, in and out of train stations, looking for the minibus outside to carry him to the hostel, anxious to sling his backpack in someone's boot rather than heft it himself. Then looking for a way to write up the journey so that it seemed he walked every step like a pilgrim, like some mystic. Dodging. Carrying with him all his negligent, slipshod leave-takings, all of them hidden in a light-sensitive box over his shoulder, ready to be developed and scrutinised in secret later.

He gazed at the bubbles forming on his submerged skin, felt the exquisite relief of the cold water on his wounded flesh. And if he could just climb that range there he'd see vista after vista to vanishing point, and the rainwater that had poured onto them during the storm would now be trickling into rivers and tributaries and creeks, downhill all the way, across some imaginary borderline from here into the Franklin–Gordon Wild Rivers National Park to the south, churning into those empty, forbidding places, right down to the deep, protected-forever Franklin, where he'd plunged his foot in another time, another place. And onwards down to the sea.

Here he was, finally, back in one of the last of the earth's immaculate and undespoiled places, desperate for just a shadow of that certainty he'd felt back then, and he was barefoot, crippled, outgunned. *Instant karma's gonna get you*, he thought dully, the line ribboning through his mind, dredging blue round glasses and poor John dead at forty.

He sat there, retrieving thought after thought like detritus on a beach as his brain frothed shallowly with fever, his head swayed there on its invisible string, light as air.

He feared for himself. Feared standing up, and turning, and not seeing the way back to their camp. All these tarns and boulders and dead ghost gums staring back, implacable. And that vast sky, washed depthless, the lakes below mirroring the endless vault of clearing air, the white mist drawing backwards like a caul — all of it filled him with terror.

It was like discovering a world beneath the other world, holding you carelessly in its inconceivable fist. A world which showed you the underneath of everything with such supreme indifference that it squeezed the breath out of you. Where a wind or tide would turn, and disorientation and urgency would come pouring back into you like the heaviest weight you could endure.

Over the edge. Rock freezing, slippery as glass with algae and moss. Her fingers clutching nothing, her knee folding and hitting the sloping rock. The garbage bag crackling as she rolled, wrenching itself up under her armpits. She was dimly aware of the crow flapping into the air above her with an alarmed caw. No freefall, no clear air. She was scrabbling, her spine and elbows scraping the boulders going down, the rock nipping at her with flinty, jagged teeth.

In four snapping seconds she'd gone from glancing carelessly at the view to pitching over the edge of a freezing, windswept mountain, and now she was going to just disappear, and nothing in this place could care less or even notice. It would dust her with snow like icing sugar, leave her blue-lipped and stiff, jammed down a crevice somewhere.

She heard a sound she hardly recognised escaping from her. It wasn't a cry of fear, but a long open-mouthed yell of frustration, of fury. She was going to die here and she had never even learned to surf or had sex with a boy, she'd hardly started her life and yet the world was going to allow this; here was where it was going to end, bundled dead in a plastic bag like rubbish.

Then her head snapped back and her teeth jabbed sharply into her lip, drawing rusty blood. Her knees and arms struck a sharp, whipping tangle of branches. She grabbed blindly at them, conscious of how spindly they seemed, how silent things were now. And how loud her breathing was, she noticed with an odd detachment, how single-minded, the desire to haul that oxygen in and out of her lungs, to claw inelegantly at every precarious twig. *Holding on for dear life*, people said; lives they held dear, lives that were costly. She'd crash through in a second. She would be like a body in that show where forensic investigators reconstructed the accident scene, showing where she'd slipped and plunged to her death; the snapped twigs, the sheared-off moss. She'd seen a frozen body on *CSI*, purple-faced and staring, lying on the slab while the investigators joked to the morgue guy, the old one …

But still, she hung there, suspended by a mass of branches, of wiry, entangling limbs. She opened her eyes and saw she wasn't clinging onto the edge of a cliff.

No sheer precipice. No cinematic heart-stopper. Nothing as dramatic as that. She was bruised and shaken but there were two ways she could be saved, either by sliding down to sit on the ledge or simply dropping to the wide shelf of ground which lay, with an anticlimax that was almost insulting, less than three metres below.

She took a deep shaking breath. Waited to cry in earnest, to be engulfed by the aftermath wave of shock. But instead she clung there, dazed and blinking at what lay below her. The colour was wrong, the register turned up to the wrong saturation, at the opposite end of the spectrum from the grey-greens of lichen and bog and cushiongrass, and it took her a while to work out what it was.

The BCG effect, she thought finally, twisting her boots free of a branch cleft and getting a good handhold to swing herself down into it, the thicket bending and springing to accommodate her, to deliver her, slithering, to the ground. She dropped gingerly into that deep unlikely carpet of orange and russet and yellow leaves.

Deciduous beech. Fagus.

Rich staggered back to the beacon, the safe haven, of the green tent. He collapsed onto his sleeping mat, groggy and dazed.

She was right — he was weak as piss. Weak as a kitten. Weak as water. All these years priding himself on staying unencumbered and now he had shed it all and was just this, his own pared-down and insubstantial self.

Still doubled over, though. Staggering under the weight of all the clanking paraphernalia and accessories of this guy on his back, kicking him on. No need to look behind at that face.

His brain swam in lush heat, tracking down corridors and trying the handles of doors. Searching for something forgivable. But instead he opens the door of the room at the nursing home. Not this. Christ.

His mother in the single bed. She turns to him as he comes into the room, seeing her dressed in some nondescript synthetic dress and cardigan like all of them, clothes she would have absolutely hated, and he's certain that she knows who he is, despite what his father kept telling him.

'It's Rich, Mum,' he says, just to be on the safe side, his smile feeling held open with fishhooks.

'I can see it's you,' she says distractedly, patting the small quilt she holds on her lap — a crocheted afghan, something they'd clearly fished out of the communal box.

'Close your eyes now,' she says, startling him, then he sees she's not talking to him, but a doll she holds wrapped in the quilt.

It doesn't help that its cheap nylon hair stands up in a quiff like a fright wig, or that one eye stays wide open while the other is half-closed. Like someone with Bell's Palsy, he thinks, his heart jumping with horror at the sight. No, that's not it. And not a horror movie. Something else. One eye open and the other half-closed. A memory stirs in him.

'Close your eyes,' she says again tenderly, pressing down on the black glued eyelashes with gentle fingers. The plastic eye, the good one, springs open again to stare balefully up at the ceiling.

'She can't sleep,' his mother confides ruefully to him, and he feels a thrill of fear ripple down his arms. He holds on to the tubular bedrail, the smile aching on his face.

'Will you do something for me?' she goes on hoarsely, patting the quilt.

'Of course.' He's going to add 'anything' but is so afraid she's going to ask him to take her home. To save her. He imagines his father's uncomprehending face, slowly growing slack with utter disgust, gazing at him from the recliner rocker as he enters the lounge room with his mother and her suitcase. *They said I could bring her home*, he imagines himself saying, *like she's been asking for every day since we stuck her there*. And he sees, clearly, the three of them, propped there in the room unable to move, both his father and himself as vacant and hesitant and stupefied as his mother, unable to act, their instincts deadened by the long medication of denial.

He feels the cold steel of the bedrail, smooth and beige and glossy. His moment missed again, the quick suppressed bloom of shame.

'Will you give my baby a bath?' says his mother. He feels it flicker in him.

'Of course,' he says.

'You'll need my special soap. The Yardley. It's in my drawer there.'

He opens the drawer next to her bed and feels a stinging pressure in his throat at every humble, abject thing hidden there inside it. At the back, the brown purse he remembers from years ago.

'There's no money in there,' she says without looking up, her eyes on the wrapped doll.

'I'm not looking for money, Mum. I'm looking for your soap.'

But his hand reaches in and picks up the purse. He thinks of all the times he slid his fingers inside its side pockets years ago, hunting for fifty-cent pieces, gathering coins from the pockets of her coat and down the back of chairs, him and his sister taking the money to buy Coke and hot chips at the takeaway, and eating them without speaking to each other down at the football oval as his father stayed at work for as long as he could and his mother lay watching television, a bottle on the floor beside her, with one eye open and one eye half-closed.

He feels inside the pocket now. A wrapped half-page, carefully clipped, is hoarded in there, with something inside it. He hesitates, but it's as if his mother has forgotten he's there. He unfolds the limp, soft paper and scans it. Some Sunday supplement or magazine page from years ago. *What's hot are these funky pieces made from restrung beads by Ayresville resident Sandy Reynolds*, he reads. *Chunky and colourful, they're bound to turn heads with Sandy's inspired take on recycling.*

Two small stiff squares lie against the page, and he turns them over. A photo of Sophie at two, the emulsion faded, all blue and green tones now; and the school photo he'd sent his mother in a card that time, Sophie at eight, her sweet gappy smile looking out at him trustingly, levelly. His beautiful abandoned girl.

'Wash her hair, won't you?' his mother says, her fingers still stroking, rearranging the wrap around the doll she cradles. 'You have to support her head. You'd know that, though, if you're a nurse.'

Where has this tightening come from, this awful constriction up inside his jaw and behind his eyes?

'I'm Rich, Mum,' he says, and the words seem dry as sawdust. She raises her eyes and meets his, leaving him in no doubt.

'I know who you are,' she says, and lifts the doll into his arms.

She walked down the mountain, residual adrenaline still sending a shake through her; exultant trembling in her knees and thighs and a fluid lightness in each step. The knotted garbage bag, full of leaves now, bouncing against her calves weighing nothing, the blood from her cut lip salty and mineral on her tongue. *When I had you*, she remembered her mother saying to her once, *they put you on my chest and you started to crawl upwards, I couldn't believe the strength in you. Just born, and your arms and legs so full of power, like you'd been designed just for this.*

She was striding now with a bird's hollow-boned energy, light-headed and impatient, effortlessly closing the gap.

They had to take you so I could have some stitches, Sandy had said, *and my arms ached for you. They ached.*

Rich looked really sick now, feverishly clammy, rapid-eye movement behind his lids. She crouched at the tent fly, studying him. He had a few days' stubble and it was silvery grey, which explained why he didn't have a beard. And he smelled bad. Not just sweaty and dirty. Something else.

'Rich,' she said, 'I'm going to crush up a couple of panadol for you.'

She went to her pack and felt down inside, past her book and the tangle of her MP3 player cable, the rolled-up dirty clothes she'd put back on again later. Methodically, she went through each zippered side pocket looking for the foil of tablets, and maybe she should make him take it with another electrolyte drink too — she still had two packets left. Put some more Betadine on that ankle.

Her fingers found an internal Velcro flap in the lining and tore it open, and she touched a stack of something like thick pages, and pulled it out.

She looked blankly at what lay in her hand as she crouched there. Five sachets wrapped together with an elastic band — dehydrated potato, dried peas and corn mix, and three others, thicker foil packets, stamped *Hiker's Pantry Gourmet Trail Food*. She sat back on her heels, mystified. Hiker's Pantry? She hadn't packed these. She'd never seen them before in her life. But *Vegetarian Mushroom Risotto* — who else but her mother, she thought, her lip quivering, would choose vegetarian? She would have had to order it especially, probably, from the guy in the health-food shop in Ayresville. She would have slipped them in here, and hugged the secret to herself, like the way she believed in random acts of kindness, like her foolish, harmless faith in miracles.

She glanced up to tell Rich, and was shocked to see his shuttered face wet with tears.

'Rich,' she said. 'Wake up. I'm going to get you those panadol, OK?'

He looked like some old vagrant lying there, she thought, repelled by his grey stubble and creased, bleary face, the unkempt hair on end.

He opened his eyes and blinked at her, but she didn't think he was really seeing her.

'Both photos,' she heard him say, his voice cracking. 'Both of them, all that time.'

Her heart hardened a little then. Sure he was weak and sick and probably a bit delirious, but you'd think he could stop obsessing about those bloody pictures in his camera just for a few minutes.

'They're safe in your pack,' she muttered, turning away. He reached out a haphazard hand and patted his pack, nodding. She told herself she'd get him the panadol in a second, once she worked out how much fresh water she'd need to rehydrate the risotto. She read the instructions, swallowing saliva, almost grinning at herself: 150 grams of dried rice, dehydrated mushrooms and powdered flavouring, pretty much, she thought, and look at her; here she was, starving for it. Absolutely starving.

Someone was touching his shoulder. That police officer, doing everything by the book, just stepping up to each of them in turn, grasping their shoulders. 'You're arrested,' he'd said, looking Rich gravely in the eye. 'OK. Good,' he remembered answering.

This hand now. Smaller. Giving him a quick shake, so that he opened his eyes and it was his daughter. He'd done all wrong by her. Bringing her out here, revealing himself as the mediocre shit that he was.

'Sit up and eat,' she was saying to him. 'Mushroom risotto.'

He squinted at her in the dim light of the tent. She was unrecognisable now as the girl he'd been dazzled by at the airport, all anarchic vampire black and ugly sweeps of eyeliner. This Sophie had short stringy hair tucked hastily behind her ears, and her eyes, without their flamboyant camouflage, no longer shocked you with the artifice of glittering, defiant challenge. They were ordinary eyes now; plain and appraising and exposed, along with the chapped lips and reddened nose, in a face made sallow by the beige poloneck she was wearing. He still flinched beneath her gaze, though, as he took the plate from her. She was suffused with something. An iron will made incandescent, something he could see around her like an edge of light, as if she were drawing strength from his own debility, breathing in his stale, used air and breathing out cool blue oxygen. It took all his concentration to get the spoon loaded and wavering between his lips.

'You been saving this?' he said finally after he'd swallowed a mouthful. He had to enunciate carefully. He wasn't sure what might come flying out of his mouth.

'It's from Mum,' she said. 'Not me.'

Yes, he thought, swallowing. Here thanks to him, fed and alive thanks to her.

His skin throbbed tightly, as though he was encased in a carapace. Some scuttling bloody bottom feeder, invertebrate and unevolved. Every joint aching and seized. *You're arrested*. He was. It was true. Detained, blocked, undeveloped, arrested. The hand on the shoulder, sombrely delivering him the bad news like a final, honest verdict.

He ate carefully, food someone else had provided for him, someone else had cooked for him, while he lay there, a prostrate and useless liability. Hunger made him humble. Something his father used to say, jubilant at making his son admit he was wrong. *Time to eat crow*, he would say, pointing an unerring finger. *Time to eat crow.*

Twenty-Four

Ian hadn't been the first to sight the walker, back there on Mount Ossa. One of the SES volunteers had shouted to him, cupping his hands around his mouth from the other side of an outcrop of boulders, striated and fissured like icebergs made of stone. The snow had started to melt on the ground then, but there were still fingers of it, long and perfect, crisscrossing the rock. He'd known, as soon as he heard the tone of the call, the defeat in it. He'd scrambled up and across the saddle, seen the boy sitting against the rock wall, tucked so poignantly into the shelter of a crevice, useless high-tech boots out straight, his head fallen onto his chest. Like he'd just dozed off, in the face of all that rugged grandeur, just closed his eyes against the overwhelming enormity of the view and fallen calmly asleep. Part of Ian's brain registered that, to remember to tell the boy's mother, how calm he looked. Then without thinking he put his palm on that dark curly head, seeing the fleece beanie clasped loosely in the hand fallen in the lap, and crouched down. All spark gone now, all of it extinguished. Just that hat in hand, like a last gesture of salute, or deference, or respect. Head bowed in submission. Ian paused in the huge thawing stillness on the mountain, then got up, heart heavy as a lead sinker.

He'd glanced back up to the summit, gauging it. The boy had been just four hundred metres from his pack.

'You right, Ian?' Tim was holding out a helmet to him.

'Good as gold.'

'Want to check the headset mics?'

'Sure. Fire away.'

He put his on and flipped the switch, waited. Tim's voice, close and calm in his ear.

'Can you hear me?'

He gave the thumbs-up. 'Loud and clear.'

'It was minus seven that night, mate. Nothing like this, and nothing anybody could have done. They're alright. You wait and see.'

Vitreous light, cold thin air, pure and empty. Rich had got up and staggered outside, lay now with his head resting on his jacket. Thoughts unspooling into slackness, his breathing slowing, Rich could see ground developing slowly in front of him, stunted, snowline bushes and tufts of grass. The same ground he'd raked his eyes over, searching for signs of wear, for a human track or sign. Wait though — not here. Staring in the safelight's redness at the sharp dark details appearing in the wash, his memory tipping that tray back and forth.

Not Tasmania, that other hillside, in Langmusi.

The name dropping dense and compact, like a stone in a pond.

Langmusi. Yes.

The other tourists gone; the red-robed monks gone too. Just him, watching the vultures with their bald heads scarlet and shining with gore, their weird hunchbacked movements. Dizzy as he stood there, his feet treading uneasily beneath him taking him closer for a better shot. Watching the birds swallow and duck their necks to glare back at him. Then he'd looked down at his feet. Rich blinked now, remembering it, swallowing the same metallic saliva.

At his feet, shredded scraps of cloth, black clumps of hair stuck to dessicated strips of scalp. He was standing on them — the picked-over pieces of forgotten people trampled like litter amongst the tussocks of grass and exposed rock.

That would be him. Two red holes in his face — ragged sockets — where the ravens had been. Those crows. That's if they found him, of course; otherwise he'd be blackened and shrivelled like fucking Peat Man.

He closed his eyes against the acidic, dazzling light. Light like lemon juice, like fixative. You need a fast exposure for it, or you'd bleed out all your details: people's faces death-masks of pure white, hard black holes for eye sockets because of the shadows.

That's how the tiger was going to look in his photos, a silhouetted blur against grainy rushing dark, a nebula of bone-white light. He'd fought against how savage that light was every time he'd ever taken a shot in outback Australia in daylight. Light that sucks the moisture out of you, turns you into dried-out compost. That's all you are. Just hair and teeth and scraps of leathery skin trodden under.

Then his face is in the shade and squinting with confusion he can make out a figure hovering above him, a boot rasping on the rock next to his head.

Something brushing him like feathers.

Sophie.

There's nothing he could do now that would humiliate him any further, so he'll tell her. Tell her sorry, ask her to forgive him. He licks his lips. A croak comes out. A caw.

'I don't want to die,' is what he hears himself say. Jesus, is there no end to his cowardice?

She pushes something into his mouth, onto his tongue. It's a coin. It's a stone. He moves his tongue and it slides against the roof of his mouth, melting.

'You're not going to die,' she says.

Feels the thick buttery slip of it, hears *I'm a sucker for chocolate, actually, but only the really good, pure, dark organic stuff,* that rich bittersweet melt of it granular and smooth at the same time liquefying in his mouth, filling it, impossibly, with chocolate, dense as compacted earth dissolving into sweet smoothness, and he blinks, certain he's hallucinating the taste, confusing it with water she's giving him, the cold lichen-flavoured rock-filtered water of the landscape they're in now, the freezing nerve-exposed hurt of it to your teeth. He gasps again. It must be said.

'You. I mean you. I don't want you to die.'

There's a pitiless, efficient beak burying itself in his throat and pulling something free, some bloody and vital internal organ he can't breathe without. An awful animal smell of oily feathers is threatening to gag him and that's the price it will be for saying it, for committing it to the air.

'Not going to happen,' her voice says.

He sees her break off another corner and feed it to him, peeling off the gold paper.

'I was saving it,' he hears her say, and the thought of her sheltering such an innocent and hopeful secret — paying attention to his pronouncement in the shop in Hobart, in that other universe, wanting to buy him a gift, the stranger who'd given her nothing, ever, the thought of her believing there would be a time to present it to him — all this melts into him as exquisitely as the fragments of chocolate.

Nothing left to humiliate. He wonders why, of everything, her tenderness is the very worst thing, and he unclenches his aching teeth, his mouth crammed with sweetness, and cries like a baby.

Sandy smoothed her hand over Sophie's bed. She didn't want to change those sheets. She could bury her head in that pillow and, faintly, smell her daughter still, and she was hanging on to that. The mobile phone was heavy in the breast pocket of her shirt, and part of her was attuned, constantly, for its ring; she could feel a whole dimension of her attention focused there. Nobody else would call. Not any of her friends — she'd told them to leave her alone today.

'I need a break,' she'd said yesterday, lamely, and Margot had said, 'Sandy, when this is sorted out, don't worry, I'm going to organise for all of us to go down to my sister's beach house.' She'd looked at them, all gazing at her like a Greek chorus, ready to narrate her life, and heard herself say from a calm distance of disbelief, 'No, I mean a break from you.'

And there was no Janet, either, clicking through the house making her feel inadequate, no insistent voice drowning out her own. Janet seemed to have left the building. Sandy kept catching herself stunned at how quiet the house was, or how long since it had seemed this still.

Still with emptiness. With nothing but her in it. It wasn't to be endured, the thought of the life gone out of this house, this bed made and tucked like a shrine, the day's useless light shifting across an unused room.

Unthinkable, but she had to countenance it, sooner or later, the possibility. Had to steel herself and touch it quickly, like a red-hot stove, press down on it like a spinning metal lathe and let it wound her, feel the unbearable hidden bite of it. You're meant to get something, she thought savagely, for pain like this. Some kind of homeopathic insight which inures you to horror of it; something that hardens you, immunises you.

Or the enlightenment everyone talked about descending on you like a thunderbolt, letting you feel the oneness in all things etcetera. You're meant to get something back.

She stood in the doorway of Sophie's room gazing in, that raw and newly attentive part of her brain registering something discordant. She let her eyes travel slowly over the room, noting its details. And why not? She had the time. She had the whole day.

Everything seemed so ... picked out, so crammed with minutiae: the pinboard of photos and quotations sharply in relief now, against the white particle board, the thin, precise shadow each piece of paper threw as it curled away. Sophie's desk with its novels stacked against the wall, authors Sandy had never heard of. A row of Easter eggs, untouched in their lurid foil — why hadn't she noticed Sophie had never eaten those eggs? What had been *wrong* with her? — the quilt Sophie had bought for herself last year. She remembered criticising that quilt, impatient and damning. Sighing gustily in this same doorway. 'Do you think you could buy just one thing for yourself sometime that isn't black?' she'd said. 'Honestly, anyone would think you were in *mourning* your whole life.'

She gripped her hands together remembering that now, the wringing ache in her chest unbearable, emptied of tears. The only sound her own breathing, doggedly in and out, her eyes vacant as she stood wondering what was keeping her there, her attention snagged on something under the surface. Eyes settling, finally, back on the quilt.

It wasn't black, she saw now, it was a deep, rich purple, dark as the skin of a plum.

That was what was different. Everything in the room was lit up, the gloom cut through with light that illuminated every floating dust mote.

Her dawning realisation, when it came to her, didn't hit with some transcendent epiphany, the way she'd always secretly hoped.

She just saw what was there: bright mid-morning sunlight coming through her daughter's bedroom window now that the tree outside, with its canopy of heavy foliage, was gone. That's all it was.

When he sat up again he saw she'd been collecting wood, and was busy shaving flakes of wood from a branch she'd pulled from the gnarled and stunted trees. Pencil pines, by the looks of them.

Too wet and green to burn, too big. He watched with the pinpoint detachment his fever gave him, hardly caring. She'd waste their last few damp matches trying to light that sappy bark, and he'd lie here watching her, and that fog would come down again and they'd freeze to death inside that one damp sleeping bag, which might be better than starving. Hypothermia, the easy death. The dulled, grateful sleep.

Then she slid her hand into the front pocket of her pack and took out a brochure, the useless one he'd picked up instead of paying for a map at the information office. She screwed it up carefully and made a little pyramid of it and the green pine chips. Opened the pocket knife and sawed off a lock of her hair like it meant nothing to her and sprinkled that on too. Spent, he watched her like she was a movie, like he was viewing a stray bit of footage he lacked the energy to edit anymore.

Not going to work. Nothing there going to combust. He'd just watch this and then he could sleep.

She put her hand down the side of her pack again and felt around. She caught his eye but her expression moved over him as if he was a bush or a rock, something inanimate she barely registered. She pulled out four or five little curled pieces of something and pushed two into the bottom of the pile, took a match.

Never, he thought, feeling his own treasonous body, despite everything, aching for a possibility still. There was a fizzing crackle and he saw a flame, a steady flame. It caught. The brochure went up fast, the dyes in it flaring blue and green and then the page quickly curling to ash as he stared mesmerised, watching the flame disappear. Gone. Over. Then Sophie bending her head calmly and breathing life into it somehow, the curled little chips crackling and popping like oil, the woodchips snapping now as it began to burn. He waited, incredulity leeching into his dullness, until she'd nursed the fire into something that would keep going, until he smelled the pine resin in the smoke and knew it wouldn't go out. She would keep feeding it with wood until it warmed them and made a plume of smoke someone in a plane overhead would see, and this was what she had been waiting for, he could see that now — a clear sky finally, and his relief was so humiliating that he slumped down again and let his face press against the ground, smelling rot and water, ice-melt and earth.

'OK,' he said at last, like a man trumped fair and square. 'OK.' His mouth hard against the dirt beneath him so that he heard his own muffled voice, the ground soaking it up, listening and expectant and waiting for him to yield.

He turned his head, then, to face her. 'What was it?'

She glanced up at him, eyes hooded with exhaustion. A tired parent.

'Orange peel. Dried over the stove. Back at the Windy Ridge Hut.'

He nodded, waved his hand vaguely to her in a defeated, sweeping salute.

'Where did you learn that?' he said, and she raised her eyebrows as if the question surprised her.

'Russell showed me,' she said. A log fell from the fire and she pushed it back, holding her power so lightly and easily, so thoughtlessly, that even that gesture took his breath away, it was so full of grace.

What Ian Millard saw as the chopper banked across the striated dolorite surfaces of the Du Cane Range was the ridge of mountain like a knuckled pair of fists before they dipped into the rocky cradle of the Labyrinth. Mammoth glacial boulders lay stacked and strewn as though someone had tipped a boxful looking for something. He'd been up here several times, then last year, after they'd found the body and after he'd said no thanks to the counselling, he'd made himself come back with a couple of colleagues one long weekend. It had been middle of summer and they'd still frozen their arses off in a surprise snap hailstorm, and they'd kept this part for a day walk and headed back to the coal fire in the hut at night. Plenty of water, lots of overhanging outcrops and shelter if you were using your head and got in somewhere down out of the wind.

The helicopter cast a shadow that stretched an elongated distortion of itself into the fissures and tussocks of cushion plants, the spreading fingers of coniferous heath. It was early enough to see the surface of the shaded rocks and vegetation dusted with dawn frost, which would melt by mid-morning. One time he'd been up here when the ground had melted and thawed over and over and it shone like caramelised sugar, a dazzle too bright to see when the sun bounced off it and into your eyes. Even now, the moisture on the rock surfaces across the range made the contrasting colours of the lichen patches shine against the smoothness; the exposed rocks dark as giant Christmas puddings studded with fruit and mixed peel, the deep corners and crevices frosted with sugary white. Good visibility today. He was letting himself hope. They had water, they had all their gear as far as anyone knew, it was only day four and there was no reason to think — if they hadn't fallen or lost their clothing and sleeping bags — that they wouldn't be alive.

'See that?' said the pilot through the headset.

'What?'

'I thought I saw some smoke. Just a haze of it. Pity the wind won't drop.'

'Go there anyway.'

They were over Hyperion now, banking across the flash of Lake Helios and up above the tree line, the scoparia massing here and there against the rolling alpine pasture and heath. Ian watched shadow and rock and grey-green vegetation and their own gliding shadow. In and out of the dips, stretching and shrinking.

Then, suddenly, a colour that didn't fit. Three orderly lines of orange and red. He blinked a couple of times. Stark against the muddy khaki on a high flat expanse of grass, it looked like scarification, like a fresh series of scratches in skin, pinpoints of bright blood welling up.

Three lines in a row — that had to be them. He signalled to the pilot to go down, grabbing his binoculars. It was heaped fagus leaves. That would be the girl, he suddenly knew instinctively. So she was mobile, at least. Still thinking. OK. He told the pilot to find a place to put down safely, and reached to flip on the radio switch. Now to see, he thought. To try to read the situation. Just take it slowly.

Back in the tent, he was dreaming of a time he'd blown a tyre on the van, the *whomp, whomp, whomp* juddering that filled the cabin as he'd slewed and braked, eyeing the gravel desperate for a wide place to fishtail to a stop. The tyre kicked and shredded itself to pieces and he was suddenly on the rim. He plunged his foot onto a phantom brake pedal and pain drove a nail deep into his foot, one confident heedless whack with a hammer. Then as he writhed the zip shot up and Sophie's head appeared through the fly.

'They're here,' she said.

'What?'

'Hear that?' She motioned for him to hand her his folded jacket. 'I'm going to make sure they've seen us.'

'Who?'

'The police, the rangers, whoever it is,' she said impatiently. 'Pass us your jacket — it's orange.'

He pulled it, rustling, from the daypack. Feeling the camera bag secure inside its wrapped nest of t-shirts, incubating there precious and fragile as an egg.

'Sophie ...' he began, his voice a croak still. A helpless hoarse whisper. A loser voice, wheedling and weak.

'You wait here,' was all she said.

Now here was the girl, thank God, alive and standing, looking thin as a whippet but OK, waving an orange jacket at them. Ian could see her bright windburned cheeks and nose, stark against the paleness of her face as she tilted it up towards them as morning sun bounced and dazzled off the windscreen.

'I've sighted the girl,' Ian said through his headset mic. Hard not to let the exultation show in his voice. 'She's waving and looks fine. So could you notify her mother immediately on that direct mobile number. We're just putting down now to assess the situation.'

He could be gone, though, the father. Could be down a hole, off a cliff, a twisted crumple of broken bones in a crevasse. Could have done it deliberately. The helicopter landed and Ian felt the solidity of smooth rock beneath his boots as he alighted, felt the suck of the updraft and motioned to the girl to stay where she was.

She nodded as the whipped-up air thrashed her hair around her face and tossed thousands of tiny red and orange leaves into the air.

'Where's your father?' Ian yelled straight away. She pointed into a rocky overhang, somewhere they would have probably never seen from the air. Stunted trees bent away from it, and Ian saw the unnatural green of the tent, and smoke from a fire they'd started, gusting and thinning in the breeze. On a still day, he thought, they would have seen that first. She'd done everything right.

'Are you alright?' he yelled into the din of the rotors. She nodded firmly. He pointed to the tent with his eyebrows raised enquiringly, and she nodded again.

'Both of us,' he heard. Her next words were inaudible until he jogged closer. Her hands had dropped now, wrapping themselves around and around the crumpled orange jacket, and her black hair hung in rats' tails from beneath her hat. Tears, he saw, were streaming down her reddened face.

'Tell my mother,' he heard. Her mouth squared into a child's exhausted sob. 'Tell my mum I'm alright.'

Ian Millard, who had two girls of his own at home, knew to open his arms before he climbed back into the cabin to confirm by radio. They stood there, the two of them, the rushing pulse of air from the rotors beating on them over and over, like a heart pushing blood through veins.

The second chopper landed on a nearby stretch of flat exposed rock, and Ian was glad to see it. Two separate helicopters back, was his gut instinct. Two separate statements.

She was still a minor, and she wasn't saying too much, but Ian didn't think the girl was in shock. He thought she was fine, wrapped in her silvery blanket just staring out, as the rotors slowly revolved above, at the other search crew taking down the tent and talking to the father, not exactly getting a statement, not yet, but just sounding things out. Tim could put out the fire, follow with the father and whatever gear they'd been carrying.

'You realise we'll have a few questions for you?' he said at one stage to the girl, and she gave a single brief nod. He poured her a hot drink out of his thermos and she sipped at it slowly, meditatively, lowering her face into the steam as if she were sitting in a café waiting for someone. Just watching her father.

Estranged, Ian had explained to Tim over the headset earlier. One of those awkward situations, so watch your step. But as he waited, the guy looked up at the helicopter, catching the girl's eye as the crew kept talking to him, and he moved away from them a bit, onto a flat patch of rock in his bare feet, limping and shaking off the restraining arm that tried to stop him. For all Ian knew, they were already reading him his rights, but he ignored them, pointedly.

Then he took his camera out of its case. It was unbelievable, what some of these people did. Wanting a souvenir shot of the helicopter, or something.

'Check out this guy,' muttered Ian to the pilot. He felt the girl beside him lean forward, her body going absolutely still.

And the guy opened the camera up and his fingers went in to the back of it — one of those old non-digital SLR cameras — and he pulled out a spool of film, an arm's length of it, snapping and glinting transparently in the light and buffeting breeze. Then he grabbed another metre and pulled that too, arm high, rigid and outstretched like a magician pulling an impossible length of ribbon out of his sleeve. All of it, then he popped the canister and held that up to show it was finished.

'What's he up to?' grunted the pilot, shaking his head and turning back to the instrument panel. The man stood there holding the camera in one hand and the twisting length of film aloft in the other for a long moment, his dark-shadowed eyes never leaving the girl, and then the spell was broken and Tim tapped the guy on the arm, shouting something, and he turned away.

'Let's go, eh?' said Ian to the pilot. He felt ridiculously happy. He hoped they wouldn't leave that film lying there, littering the place.

The girl sat back in her seat, her face smoothly still. Both hands wrapped tight around the thermos cup, as if she feared she'd spill it. Ian motioned for her to fasten her seat belt and then stayed twisted slightly in his own seat, leaning back towards her to give her the chance to say something, to let him in on what was going on.

Still, he wouldn't push it. It was none of his business, what went on in families.

Twenty-Five

Sophie was working the comb down, methodically. Her mother sat on a chair in the garden, her chin tucked to her chest.

'I've had it long for so many years,' Sophie heard her say.

'I know. You're sure?'

'Oh, yeah.'

'You wouldn't rather go to a hairdresser's?'

'Of course not. You'll do a much better job than them.'

She ran the comb through dreamily, watching the hair drop henna-red and thin between Sandy's shoulder-blades. How pale the back of her neck looked, so intimate and soft against the teeth of the comb. And oh, that stripe of darker colour at the roots, the grey and plain brown coming in against the red. Such valiant effort, Sophie thought, wonderingly, to hold out against time. She wanted to put her hand against the strong cords of her mother's bowed neck, feel those vulnerable, tender vertebrae.

'Do you remember,' she said instead, 'when you broke the lawnmower running over those forks out here?'

'Spoons,' said her mother's voice indistinctly. 'I forgot I'd buried them there.'

'But why on earth?'

Her mother's hand came up and scratched vaguely at a loose lock of hair, tugged it back behind her ear, gazed at her two upturned palms as if for the first time.

'I'd had an argument with the neighbour who used to live

there,' she said finally. 'Someone told me to push a row of spoons into the ground to reflect back his bad energy. It's a feng shui thing.'

Sophie lifted the comb to the parting on her mother's crown and pulled it down again meditatively. She thought she felt her mother shiver with pleasure, then realised she was laughing.

'The grass grew,' she heard, 'and I forgot they were there.'

Shaking with mirth now, helpless with it.

'Tell me honestly,' Sophie said, grinning, tugging through a knot, feeling the dryness of the split, sun-bleached ends. 'Did you really expect it to work?'

'Well, he moved away, didn't he?'

Her mother tilted her head back now, still laughing, closing her eyes in the sun, and Sophie saw the deep maze of lines at the corners, the legacy of all these years of doing just that, thousands of times, the way they fell into their delicate, accustomed tracks.

'I'm laughing now,' Sandy said, 'but believe me, I was crying then.'

Sophie put her hand on her mother's head, and pushed softly until it was bowed again. Then she said, 'I'm going down to see Rich on the long weekend.'

She felt the stillness settle as Sandy breathed in sharply then exhaled, a faint sound of acknowledgement.

'OK.'

'I'm going with him to see his mum.' A long silence.

'Right.'

The pale skin of her mother's neck, the three empty holes in each earlobe, the hands resting on her knees — Sophie looked at it all in this still moment with a kind of avid intensity, as if committing it to memory. Then she gathered up hair into her fist and piled it gently in a twist on top of Sandy's head. When she released her hand, it fell back like a skein of wool.

'Good,' she heard Sandy say finally. 'That's good.'

Her heart lurched. She could smell the cool, turned earth beside them, where the half-full wheelbarrow sat abandoned. She chewed her lip.

'Another thing.'

'Oh God, fire away then.'

'I want to go back. Do volunteer work with the rangers in the summer holidays. I need your signed permission.'

She could feel, under her hand, her mother's slow, almost imperceptible nods as she absorbed this. The silence lengthened like shadows and she heard Sandy swallow, heard her breathing. She opened the scissors and aligned a cool metal blade against the delicate skin at the nape of her mother's neck. As she brought them closed a neat length of shorn hair slithered to the ground.

'You're going to love this,' she said. 'Trust me.'

Her mother raised a hand to her concealed face, fingertips against the slope of cheekbone, her head obediently still at the sound of the scissors.

'You OK?' Sophie said lightly, snipping.

'Something in my eye,' said Sandy.

The light was too perfect to waste.

'Leave that,' she said to Sophie, impulsively putting down the trowel. 'We'll put them in after the sun's gone down. That's better for them anyway.'

Sophie paused and glanced over at her, eyebrows raised enquiringly, still holding a punnet of basil seedlings in her hand.

'I'm going to go inside and get the camera,' Sandy said, 'and take our photo. Then in summer when we're eating tons of pesto and fresh tomatoes, we'll look at it and congratulate ourselves.'

She stood up and hurried inside. Where was that camera? She had to get back out there before that stretching, golden sunlight sank down behind the horizon and it was over. She caught a glimpse of herself in the mirror as she saw the camera on the mantelpiece, and was startled afresh. It would take some getting used to, this new hair.

'OK, get ready,' she called as she pushed the screen door open again. 'I'm going to get one just of you then I'm going to put the self-timer on so we can both be in it.'

She looked through the viewfinder at Sophie standing, arms

folded and waiting. That resigned smile on her face, that laconic raised eyebrow as she pretended to be putting up with this with stoic forbearance.

She was terrifying, Sandy thought. Just look at the length of her shadow. She saw the sun tipping behind her, about to melt and fade, and her daughter's silhouette fuzzy with it, a bleeding, swimming edge of gold.

'Wait,' she called, squinting. Where on earth had she left her glasses? She'd had them earlier, she was sure, reading the planting instructions ...

'They're on your head, Mum.'

'Ah yes.'

Grinning as she lined her up in the viewfinder now. She'd be blurred, Sandy knew. Moving, shifting self-consciously. Impossible to capture. She pressed the button anyway.

Another sixty seconds of this golden, forgiving light, if she was lucky. She adjusted the camera's timer to automatic and set it down on the stump, bent a couple of sprays of shooting blue gum regrowth out of the way of the lens. This was it, now. You pressed that button and then you ran to get into position; this was your one small ration of time, ready or not.

'Come on, Mum,' Sophie called. God, she was so composed!

Sandy pressed the button, and ran.

Acknowledgements

Thanks to Cathie Plowman, John Hale, Martin Elliot and Bill Forsythe for generously sharing their time, knowledge and memories. Thanks too to Kathryn Lomer, John Holton, Joda Plex, Alikki Vernon, Nam Le, Craig Cormick and Fleur Rendell for the right conversations at the right time.

I'm grateful to Joe Bugden and the Tasmanian Writers' Centre, which provided time and space for writing and research in 2007; Kathryn Medlock of the Tasmanian Museum and Art Gallery; and Sarah Castleton, whose early encouraging email about this book has stayed pinned to my noticeboard for the duration.

My biggest thanks go to my editor, Aviva Tuffield at Scribe, whose dedication and attention to detail have made me realise how important it is, when you're driving at night, to have someone in the passenger seat, ready to hand you a coffee, change the radio station, or just pull out a map. Thanks.

A GROVE PRESS READING GROUP GUIDE
BY LINDSEY TATE

THE WORLD BENEATH

CATE KENNEDY

ABOUT THIS GUIDE

We hope that these discussion questions will enhance your
reading group's exploration of Cate Kennedy's *The World Beneath*.
They are meant to stimulate discussion, offer new viewpoints,
and enrich your enjoyment of the book.

More reading group guides and additional information,
including summaries, author tours, and author sites for other
fine Grove Press titles, may be found on our Web site,
www.groveatlantic.com.

QUESTIONS FOR DISCUSSION

1. Set against a beautifully realized Australian backdrop, Cate Kennedy's debut novel examines contemporary family life. Start your discussion of *The World Beneath* by considering how familiar you found her depiction. With a change of locale, could she have been presenting modern America?

2. Would it be fair to say that Kennedy skewers modern society, or does she present a more subtle, more hopeful narrative of the modern human condition? In her view, where have we gone wrong, and where might our salvation lie?

3. How representative are Sandy, Rich, and Sophie? Were you able to view them as archetypes or, at least, were you able to recognize them as typical?

4. The theme of delusion—and self-delusion—runs throughout the novel. Find instances in which the main characters allow themselves the luxury of skirting the truth, or when they see only what they want to—or need to—believe. Why do they do this? Does it help or hinder them in the long run?

5. Continuing your discussion, talk about the symbol of the Tasmanian tiger. If Rich needs to see a tiger, why does Sophie need to see a dog?

6. Talk about Sandy and her inability to take control of her own life. Why is she so willing to hand herself over to the "care" of her teenage daughter? Why is it so hard for her to live spontaneously, without forever thinking about the potential reactions of others to her every action? Why has her life become so contrary to everything she believes in?

7. On the verge of her fifteenth birthday, Sophie is presented as a typical teenager, glued to her iPod and cell phone, disdainful

of her mother, with dyed black hair and heavy eye makeup. But how typical is she really? Who is she beneath her teenage "costumery"?

8. Rich enters the novel seeking a paternal relationship with the daughter he abandoned fourteen years earlier. Why do you think he has waited so long to try to reenter her life? What are his reasons for doing so now? How honest is he in his representation of himself? What image is he hoping to portray? Why?

9. Sophie has waited a long time to have a father in her life and has certain expectations of Rich. Are these expectations realistic or is she setting herself up for failure? On their first encounter she sees him as someone who "would know Sandy as well as she did; he of all people would understand . . . what it was like having to live with her. He was an ally" (p. 90). When do Sophie's positive feelings for Rich become mixed, and then negative? How does he fail her most?

10. Full of secrets—including an eating disorder—and hiding behind heavy makeup, Sophie does not show her true self to the world—just like most of the other characters. For all her attempts at artifice, however, it could be said that Sophie's is the most honest voice in the novel. How far would you agree with this statement? Why, or why not?

11. The novel is carefully structured to move between the viewpoints of each of the three main characters. What is the effect of such a technique? Did you find you were able to more fully understand the characters and their feelings, or were their true selves obscured by varying viewpoints? Were you overly conscious of technique when reading or did the different characters' narratives pull you right into the novel's action?

12. Both Sandy and Rich constantly look back to the defining moment of their lives: their involvement in the campaign against

the Franklin Dam in Tasmania. What does this episode of their lives mean to them? Is it symbolic in the same way to each of them? Why do they seem unable to move beyond it?

13. How far do you agree with Sophie's take on her parents' role in the Franklin River Blockade? "Sitting back admiring yourselves for turning up to be part of one big thing twenty-five years ago, doing nothing since. Nothing" (p. 257). How fair is she?

14. Consider Rich's love of the photographer Henri Cartier-Bresson and the "defining moment" in his work. "The defining moment spoke for itself, it didn't need any Photoshop trickery later . . . it separated the purists from the pretenders" (p. 48). Does Rich have higher standards for his photography than he does for his own life? Discuss.

15. Mother-daughter relationships form an important part of the narrative with Sandy at the center as both daughter and mother. What influence has Sandy's mother, Janet, had on her life? Why does she still hold such sway in her adult daughter's life? How is Sandy's parenting of Sophie affected by Janet? Do you think Sandy sees herself as a capable parent and is pleased with Sophie's outcome? Over the course of the novel, these relationships undergo a change. Discuss these changes and talk about why you think they take place. What do you see in the future for Sandy and Janet, for Sandy and Sophie?

16. Rich, too, faces a change in his relationship with his mother—a reconciliation. Why exactly do you think this was brought about?

17. Find examples of humor in the novel, and discuss their importance.

18. Discuss the parallels between Sandy's spiritual retreat at the Mandala Holistic Wellness Centre and Rich's wilderness trek into Tasmania. What are they both hoping to achieve from their

experiences? When Rich and Sophie are lost in the wilderness he thinks, "He would be alright if he could just rise above it, float up there . . . and get some perspective" (p. 286)—then he could find the way out. How is this a metaphor for his life in general, indeed the lives of many of the novel's characters?

19. What do hikers Russell and Libby represent? Why does Rich dislike them so much, yet Sophie is drawn to them?

20. Rich has the opportunity to build a new relationship with Sophie during their Tasmanian adventure but fails to seize it. Why do you think this is? Why is it so hard for him to respond to Sophie's question, "Did you love me when I was born?" (p. 212). In looking at other relationships and friendships in the novel, is anyone experiencing anything real or genuine? What are some of the barriers to true relationships that people erect, often without meaning to do so?

21. At one point Rich sneers at tourists "pointing their hand-held digital recorders at everything, every second, and racing to upload it onto their Facebook pages" (p. 49). Discuss his disapproval of things digital, then broaden your conversation to consider how technology in general is portrayed in the novel. Think about Sophie longing to text on her cell phone with her iPod glued into her ears and the way people connect—or disconnect—through such devices.

22. One could say that the Tasmanian landscape, vividly wrought with beautifully detailed prose, is a character in the novel. What effect does the vast, wild place have on Rich and Sophie? What about the other tourists walking the trail? Consider the quote from the beginning of the book: "In every walk with nature one receives far more than he seeks" (John Muir).

23. Once Rich and Sophie are officially lost in the wilderness they begin to undergo changes. Are they ever truly able to cast off

their masks and disguises and present themselves to each other truthfully?

24. How is Sandy finally able to find herself again? What is it about the sudden onset of her friends, "shining-eyed and avidly motivated" (p. 287), that allows her to break free of the life she's been leading?

25. Despite their many weaknesses and shortcomings, Kennedy presents her characters with warm sympathy. She seems to genuinely like them and wants things to work out for them in the end. How did you feel about them? Were you able to empathize?

26. "It was like discovering a world beneath the other world, holding you carelessly in its inconceivable fist. A world which showed you the underneath of everything with such supreme indifference that it squeezed the breath out of you" (p. 319). Discuss the importance of this statement, its relevance to Rich's situation, and to the novel as a whole.

Suggestions for Further Reading:

Arlington Park by Rachel Cusk; *This Book Will Save Your Life* by A. M. Homes; *The Good Parents* by Joan London; *Light on Snow* by Anita Shreve; *Family History* by Dani Shapiro; *The Slap* by Christos Tsiolkas; *The Hiding Place* by Trezza Azzopardi; *Goldengrove* by Francine Prose